THE
PROVIDENCE
RIDER

THE PROVIDENCE RIDER

ROBERT McCAMMON

SUBTERRANEAN PRESS 2012

First Edition

Limited Edition ISBN
978-1-59606-465-2

Trade Edition ISBN
978-1-59606-466-9

Subterranean Press
PO Box 190106
Burton, MI 48519

www.subterraneanpress.com

⌘

To kc dyer.

Thanks for the help, the encouragement,
and for showing me the silver swan.

⌘

ONE

THE GRAY KINGDOM

ONE

T HE crab that scuttled amid rocks in the liquid dark knew nothing beyond its shell. Born from what? Struggling toward where? It knew not. It tasted the cold currents, and within them the essence of flesh to be consumed, and so it changed its course to the direction of that call and labored slowly through the muck toward its prey.

Over more rocks again, into crevices and cracks, sliding down and clambering up in its sideways gait, its claws thrusting here and there as was the nature of the crustacean. On its passage over an oyster bed the crab's presence sent a tremor across the field of plate-sized shells, as if in their moist senseless dreaming the mollusks felt the shadow of nightmare where no shadow could be. The crab went on, and whatever small panic had roused the oysters beyond their state of somnolence died in an instant, and life between the shells continued as before.

Whither it travelled, the crab stirred whorls of mud beneath its claws. The hard-backed and determined dweller did not know the full moon painted silver light upon the surface of New York's harbor, or that the month was February and the year 1703, or that lamps glowed in the windows of the sturdy houses and well-seasoned taverns of Manhattan on a Saturday night, or that a cold wind from the northwest ruffled its roof. It knew only that it smelled something good to eat in this nightblack and muddy morass spread out before it, and so it went on hungrily and one might say clumsily, without forethought or plan.

Therefore when the mud beneath it opened up and tentacles sprouted forth and what appeared to be mud shuddered with voracious delight, who was to blame but itself? When the tentacles wrapped around the crab and flipped it over and the beak of the octopus began to gnaw into the underbelly, what thought flashed like a scent of dead herring through the crustacean's nerves? For truly the crab struggled to escape, but of chance for this there was none. In bits and pieces the crab began to come apart, to lose itself to biting beak and impartial sea, and as the smaller fish darted in to seize these little floating shreds of meat the octopus pulled its prey closer like a jealous lover and squeezed itself down into a hole where two rocks kissed. Thus very soon the last of the crab was down in an even darker place than before, and so farewell to the solitary traveller.

Having completed its meal, the octopus sat in its hole. It was old and slow, and in its own way it seethed and fumed against the indignities that time had laid upon it. But it had been lucky, to feast so well. Very soon, though, the feelings of hunger began gripping its innards again. So it pulled itself from its crusty den tentacle by tentacle and ventured forth upon the battlefield once more, and drifting hither and yon like a speckled cloud it searched for a nice plain of mud and weeds to sink itself into. There it would wait for the next hapless denizen of the deep to cross its path, and woe to the crabs and small fish of the night.

The octopus, dedicated to its own progress and appetite, floated past a cluster of rocks upon which was jammed the rusted remains of an anchor torn from a Dutch ship in a storm many years before. The creature whose home and refuge these rocks and anchor had become immediately woke from its stupor and, sensing the presence of food in a tingle of its inner ear, thrust its tail from side to side and propelled itself outward. Thus the grouper's mouth seized the bulbous head of its prey. As the alarm of black ink jetted

forth—far too late—the octopus was pulled into the grouper's maw and crushed by the heavy tooth plates within. The flailing tentacles were ingested in a gulp. It was such a clean dinner that not a shred was left for the little beggars. The grouper swam in a kind of victorious trance, its belly grazing the bottom and its tail sluggishly moving water.

Presently a new smell of food beckoned the grouper, which changed course like a barnacle-blotched frigate. Searching high and low, it came upon an oily piece of meat suspended in the water, there for the taking.

It took.

When the mighty maw closed over the meat, there was a sudden jerk upon the line that rose up forty feet to the surface. The fishhook set. The grouper, mildly annoyed, pulled back and intended to return to its den, yet was stopped at this attempt by an admirable resistance from the upper regions beyond which the grouper had no knowledge. Hook, line and grouper began a test of wills, and if anything the grouper was strong and stubborn. Still, the grouper was pulled toward the surface little by little over the following few minutes, and try as it might the fish could not shake the hard spiny thorn that set tight in its throat. On its way up from depths to heights its eyes caught sight of strange shapes in the world beyond. A round light shone down in a most beautiful silver glow that nearly transfixed the grouper. The fish shivered in its attempt to escape this nuisance of being pulled where it did not wish to go, and its gills swelled with the flush of anger.

In another few seconds it would be up through the surface. It would be in the clutches of another realm, for better or for worse. It would know, in its own way, a secret. And yet it resisted this knowing, and it thrashed and thrashed yet the line still pulled and it yet rose upward. The surface was about to be broken, and the grouper's eyes would see a world foreign and alien and wholly fantastic in its being, just before it perished.

But before that could happen the blue shark that had been observing this situation and circling the picture darted in and tore most of the lower portion of the grouper away in its teeth, so that only the grouper's head emerged on the end of the line. The fisherman in his little rowboat, who had been reeling in his catch for the better part of six minutes, saw the grouper's dripping head and the white wake of the shark's fin. He threw his rod down in an expression of rage and in his raspy wind-weathered voice gave a shout likely to roll across the waters and waken the sleepers in the graveyard of Trinity church.

"For sakes of Almighty Jazus!" hollered old wild-haired Hooper Gillespie. "T'ain't fair, you hard-hearted robber! You wicked piece a' God's spite! T'ain't *fair!*"

But fair or not, that was life both above and below the surface.

After a few more choice morsels of twisted lingo had been flung at the since-departed shark, Hooper Gillespie gave a heavy sigh and pulled his tattered coat tighter about himself. His thick white hair stood out from his head in bursts of cowlicks and circular whorls, an untameable field that had once broken his mother's best brush. But his mother was dead now, long dead, and never would anyone know that he kept a small ink drawing of her face in a pewter frame in his cabin, done from memory. It was perhaps the only thing he valued in life, besides his fishing rod.

He reeled in the mangled head. He removed the hook. Just before he threw the mess over the side, he caught the gleam of the moon in the sightless eyes and wondered what fish knew of the world of men. But it was a passing thought, like a shadow without substance. He turned in his boat to regard the bucket of the night's catch, three small mackerel and a nice-sized striper. The wind was getting colder. His arms were tired from his recent efforts. It was time to head for shore.

The sound of fiddle music drifted to him across the bay. It was joyous and lively, and it made a hot surge of fresh anger rise up within old Hooper. "Good for *you!*" he growled in the direction of people and dances and candlelight and life in general. "Yessir, go on about y'selves and see what I care!" He stored his rod away and began rowing toward the dark shape of Oyster Island. "I *don't* care!" he said toward the world. "I'm my own self, is what I am! Thinkin' they can get away with it, and me down in a puddle. No sir, that ain't the half of it!"

He realized as he rowed that he'd begun talking to himself quite a lot lately. "Never no mind to that!" he said. "Done is done and is is *is!*" He paused to spit bitter phlegm over the side. "So *there!*" he said.

Back in the summer, Hooper had been running the ferry between Manhattan and Breuckelen. But the river ruffians, the 'bullywhelp boys' in his opinion, who kept waylaying the ferry and robbing its passengers had put paid to that effort, at least for Hooper. He had no wish to be the bearer of a cut throat. In fact he'd complained about the situation at Governor Lord Cornbury's first meeting with the citizens at City Hall and insisted that High Constable Gardner Lillehorne should be doing something to clean up the river trash.

"And look where that got me!" he hollered to the stars. "A-rowin' out here in the cold like to catch a death and what's it all the better for?"

The truth was, in November Lillehorne had found the robbers' hidden cove and broken up that merry little band of nasties, and yet the job of ferry master had gone to a younger man. The closing of many doors in Hooper's face had made him think complaining about the high constable in front of the gown-wearing Cornbury— the queen's cousin and, it was fair to say, a little queenly himself— was not something a sane man ought to do.

"But I ain't crazy!" Hooper muttered as he rowed. "I am as fit in the head as a new nail!"

Circumstance found him now nearing Oyster Island's rocky beach. Circumstance and, of course, the cold hard fact that no one else wanted this task. The island was mostly a tangle of woods and boulders, but for the small log cabin built to house the watchman. That was Hooper's job, and had been for three weeks. Watchman, climbing the watch tower on the southern end of the island and mostly watching the tide roll in and out, but also alert to masts on the horizon. If his spyglass picked out an armada of ships flying Dutch flags, he knew it would be Holland's oak-walled men of war coming to take back New York, and he was to scurry down to where the cannon faced the harbor and fire off a warning blast before the invaders made landfall.

"Hell if I know 'bout firin' a damned cannon," Hooper said quietly as he thought about it, his oars moving water. Then he heard the drift of fiddle music again, and he turned his face toward the lamplights of the town and hollered, "I ought to blast ye all, right out a' your dancin' shoes! Go on with ya!"

But, as always, no one bothered to answer.

Something caught his squinty eye.

He saw a red light flash.

It was up in the darkness, up maybe a half-mile or so from the town proper. Up at the edge of the woods that still held the criss-crossing of Indian trails. It was a red light, blinking on and off. On and off. On and off.

"That there's a signal lamp, I'm be thinkin'," Hooper told himself. It was likely a flame behind red glass, and somebody's hand or hat moving down to obscure the glow. "Now that's the question," Hooper said. Then he realized he hadn't asked the question yet, so he did: "Who's it signallin' to?"

He looked out to sea, out beyond the rough rocks and wild forest of Oyster Island.

Far out there. Out in the dark.

A red lamp blinked on and off. On and off. On and off and... gone.

He turned his head again toward Manhattan and the dark edge of the untamed woods. That red signal lamp had also been extinguished.

It came to Hooper Gillespie that whatever the message was, it had been delivered.

The bottom of his rowboat scraped oyster shells and stones. His heart had jumped and stuttered and was now beating wildly, for one thought had invaded his unbrushed noggin.

For Hooper, thoughts were to be spoken as loudly as possible. "No they *ain't*!" he shouted. "Comin' over sea swell and mercy knows to bleed us to pieces, no they ain't!" He leaped from the boat, stubbed his right boot on a rock and went for a face-first splash. Then, spitting and cursing in a language not fully English nor fully understood by any other human being but his own self, Hooper struggled up and ran through the little wavelets that washed upon the gritty earth. He ran past the cannon along a trail that led to the watch tower, and at the base of the tower he paused to flame a torch from the tinderbox there. With torch alight, he climbed the rickety wooden steps to the top. On the upper platform he leaned forward as far as he dared against a worm-eaten railing with the torch held high. "Liberty's blessin' ain't to be took!" he shouted toward the unknown and unseen ship that sat out there in the dark. Of course the torch showed him nothing, but at least the Dutchmen would know they'd been seen. "Come on in here, ya blue-hinded rascals!" he hollered. "Let's see the shine a' your greedy eyeballs!"

His voice pierced the night but the night swallowed it up and gave nothing back.

The red lamp at sea was gone, and did not return. Hooper looked toward Manhattan's woods. That lamp, also, was a goner. Whatever had been said, it was not to be repeated. Hooper chewed his bottom lip and waved the torch about, throwing sparks. "Seen ya good, ya traitorous bag a' crooked bones!" he yelled. He didn't expect to be heard at this distance, but it felt good to unload. Then the idea of *loading* came to him. If what he thought was about to happen, and all the Dutchmen in their ships were about to sail right into the harbor with cannons and cutlasses ready to crash and carve, then he had to do his duty and warn the citizens. He scurried down the tower's steps again, torch gripped in hand, and near the bottom almost tripped and put paid to not only his heroic plan but to the way his head sat atop his neck.

Hooper stopped at his cabin to hurriedly open a wooden box for a small bag of gunpowder—about two thimbles full, enough to make a sizeable noise—and a six-inch piece of fuse. He took a knife to slit the bag. Then he went on to the cannon and, hands shaking, placed the torch in a metal holder put there specifically for the purpose. Muttering and fretting to himself about the future of New York if the Dutch got hold of it and threw every British citizen man woman and child into the brigs of their boats, Hooper put the fuse into the cannon's vent hole. How much had he been told to leave showing to carry the fire? he asked himself. He couldn't remember. He just had the memory of a mouth moving in a pallid face under a tricorn hat, and himself thinking about getting some fishing done while he was out here.

There was no ball to be loaded; this was for noise only. Hooper looked back over his shoulder at the nocturnal sea. Did he sense the motion of a hundred ships closing upon the bay? Did he hear the flap of flags and rattle of chains as guns were readied? But there were no lights visible, not a single one. Oh, those Dutchmen! Hooper thought. They were devils of the dark!

He turned to his task once more with frantic purpose. He had to pee but had no time, so let it run in his breeches. It was the least a hero could do. He knifed open the bag of gunpowder, poured the powder into the cannon's barrel and then remembered to use the ramrod like the moving mouth under the tricorn had told him. He packed the powder with a hard shove and then stood for a moment trying to recall if he was supposed to flame a match to fire the fuse or use the torch. He pushed the fuse down good and short so the wind couldn't whip it out. One more backward glance to make sure the Dutch armada wasn't gliding past Oyster Island, and then Hooper put the torch's flame to the cannon's fuse.

It sparked, hissed, and the fire began to travel. Hooper stepped back a few paces, as he'd been told. The fuse burned down. When it disappeared into the vent hole there was a sizzling sound like bacon in a frypan, followed by a weak little *pop* and a puff of smoke that floated away as delicately as a lady's lace handkerchief.

"Well, that ain't *right*!" Hooper moaned. "Jazus save me, I've pulled a boner!"

He peered into the vent hole. There was no spark visible. Either the fuse had gone out or the powder was bad. He went to the cannon's business end and put his face to the muzzle. He could smell a smouldering, but where was the flame? "Damn me!" he hollered, as the thought of his heroism at this time of New York's need turned to ashes around his soggy boots.

A scant three seconds after Hooper pulled his face away from the cannon, there was a gout of fire from the vent hole and the gun went off.

The blast of smoke itself almost knocked him crazy. The noise slapped his ears deaf. He staggered back, gasping like a hooked grouper, and fell on his butt. Dazed, he saw blue fire and sparks whirling up from the cannon toward heaven, and then he saw something else that nearly made every sprout of wild hair jump from his head.

Something exploded across the bay in town. A building, looked to be down toward Dock Street. Hooper couldn't hear the noise, but he saw the red fire leap up. Whatever it was, it was burning hot with a white center. Pieces of roof came down. Parts of the building were still flying upward like fiery bats.

"Oh no," Hooper whispered, though he couldn't hear it. "Oh no, oh no!" His first thought was that he'd forgotten and put a ball in the cannon and blown something up himself, but then he remembered there was no ball in the cannon, and how in the name of bleedin' Jazus could somebody forget about *that*?

No, it had to be the Dutch. They had just fired on New York, and the war had begun.

He scrambled up. It was time to vacate these premises. Still there was no sign of the warships, no battle lamps or cannon flame. He didn't care. He ran to his rowboat, which was still up on the rocks. As he pushed it off and got in he realized something else very strange.

The three small mackerel and the nice-sized striper in the bucket?

They were gone.

It was the ghost, Hooper thought. The phantom that walked out here. It was why he'd been given this job, because nobody else wanted it. The last watchman had left the island the night his overcoat had been stolen from a post next to the outhouse. Whoever had the watchman's job, they weren't alone. Hooper had never seen evidence of the phantom before, but here it was.

"Christian of ye to leave the damn bucket!" he shouted toward any listening ears, though his own were still fried and sizzling.

He was quits with this Godforsaken place. He took the oars and put his wiry muscles to the labor, and with hammering heart and fearful soul and wild smoke-scorched hair old Hooper Gillespie rowed for Manhattan, with red flames before him and the dark sea at his back.

Two

As a crab scuttled amid rocks in the liquid dark, so Matthew Corbett danced across the plank floor of Sally Almond's tavern by golden candlelight. Perhaps he was not as ungainly as the crab, and perhaps he did comport a certain amount of grace and style, yet there was definitely room for improvement in his technique. In its largest room the tavern's tables and chairs had been pushed back and space arranged for a right fair gathering. A fire crackled in the brick hearth to warm the air, though the heat of energy filled the place. Two fiddlers played, a squeezeboxer squeezed, and a drummer rattled his bones at a merry pace. The stately gray-haired figure of Sally Almond herself had joined the festivity, clapping her hands to the bounding beat.

Round and round went the swirl of dancers, among them the blacksmithing apprentice and Matthew's friend John Five and his bride Constance, the potter Hiram Stokely and his wife Patience, the Munthunk brothers Darwin and Davy and their corpulent but surprisingly light-footed Mother Munthunk, Dr. Artemis Vanderbrocken who at seventy-six was content to mostly sip the spiced punch and enjoy the music, Felix Sudbury the owner of the Trot Then Gallop tavern, the printmaster Marmaduke Grigsby, Madam Kenneday the baker, another of Matthew's good friends Effrem Owles the tailor's son, and Jonathan Paradine the undertaker who was thin and pale and seemed to slink from place to place on the floor rather than actually dance. His ladyfriend, a newly-arrived widow by the name of Dorcas Rochester, was equally thin and pale and slinked just the same as her beau, so the couple seemed to all to be well-matched.

Matthew Corbett had been in some demanding predicaments in his twenty-three years on earth. He had weathered the attack of a bear whose claw had left a crescent scar from just above the right eyebrow into the hairline. He had outrun a triad of hawks determined to remove his eyeballs in the most ungracious fashion. And he had literally managed to keep his face situated on his skull in a millhouse fight with the brutal killer Tyranthus Slaughter, among many other moments of dramatic danger. But at *this* moment, in the golden candlelight of Sally Almond's tavern with the music playing and the dancers stepping through their paces, Matthew thought his own feet were perhaps the most dangerous enemies he'd yet faced, for the crossover mirror reels were treacherous in their complexity and the elaborately bewigged dance master Gilliam Vincent— who also served as the prissy proprietor of the Dock House Inn— wielded a leather glove on the end of a hickory stick to slap the heads of imperfect offenders.

And, as Matthew made a slight stumble, here came the stick and glove. *Smack* upon the back of his skull. When Matthew turned his head to give Gilliam Vincent a glowering stare, the dance master had lightly moved away and so was Matthew moving away as well, caught up in the procession. Yet Mr. Vincent bore a smirk beneath his bony snoot that said he enjoyed the correcting perhaps a bit more than he ought to.

"Pay no mind to him!" said Berry Grigsby as she came up alongside Matthew on their right-shoulder pass. "You're doing fine!"

"A relative term," he answered.

"Better than fine," she corrected as she moved past. *"Wonderful."*

Now that, he thought as he continued along the path this particular reel required, was skinning the onion and calling it a potato.

Then he turned to find himself face-to-face with the two-hundred-and-forty pound shock of woman called Mother Munthunk, and she gave him a black-toothed grin under her hatchet nose and a whiff of breath a goat could not suffer.

What a joy this evening was, Matthew thought when his eyes had ceased their watering. He regretted accepting this invitation from Berry, though he had twice before declined her note. *Matthew,* she'd said at his door last week, *I'm only going to ask you once more, and if you say no I'll never—never—ask again.*

And what could he do then but accept? Not only was Berry breaking what seemed like the law of God by inviting a male to a social gathering, but also implicit in the tone of her request and the low fire in her dark blue eyes was the suggestion that not only would she never ask him again, she would never *speak* to him again. Which would be a problem for him, since he lived in a converted dairy-house just behind the Grigsbys' abode and he took supper there on occasion with Berry and her moon-faced and usually ink-stained grandfather Marmaduke. So in respect with keeping the peace and the more selfish ambition of keeping his place at a very hospitable supper table, what else could he do but accept?

"Half reels of three!" Gilliam Vincent announced, with an expression that verged on a sneer. "Then we shall turn to the left, give both hands, make a complete clockwise circle and assume our places for the Mad Robin!"

This was *supposed* to be enjoyable, Matthew thought grimly. Berry had taught him the positions and steps last week, but with the fiddling and the drumming and Gilliam Vincent's stick poised to strike a blow for artful perfection it was torment for a young problem-solver who would much rather be studying the pieces on a chessboard or, for that matter, be out on a task somewhere for his employer, the London-based Herrald Agency.

Onward! he told himself. His feet were more or less where they needed to be. He mused upon cocking a fist at Gilliam Vincent if that stick came near his skull again, but he had had enough of violence lately to last him a lifetime.

He still had nightmares of Mister Slaughter. In some of them, he was being chased across a black bog by the killer, his feet and legs were sinking into the muck, he couldn't get himself free to move fast enough, and when he looked back through the red-tinged nightmare gloom he saw the approaching figure and the glint of a knife gripped in the right hand. And then from the opposite side another figure was coming toward him: a leonine woman with an axe in one hand and under her other arm a burlap bag marked in crimson paint *Mrs. Sutch's Sausages, Sutch A Pleasure*.

"Places for the Mad Robin!" Gilliam Vincent called out. "Find your places!" *You idiot children*, he might have added.

Matthew moved, but he sometimes felt dazed and unsure of his direction. Sometimes he felt as if he belonged to another world that the people in this room knew nothing about. Sometimes he felt that even though both Mister Slaughter and Mrs. Sutch were dead, part of them kept clawing at him deep inside as if he were the entrance to their crypt and they desperately wished to open him up so they might rejoin the living. For in a way he was their brother now.

He was a killer.

Of course Tyranthus Slaughter had died due to the combined efforts of Matthew, the vengeful boy Tom Bond and the Iroquois tracker Walker In Two Worlds, but Matthew had cleaved an important portion of Lyra Sutch's head from her shoulders with an axe, and he would never forget the expression of hatred on her bloodied face and the way the scarlet rivers had flowed. That hideous cellar was a memory bad enough to drive any man to madness. Since it had happened Matthew could never again sleep in the dark. A candle—or better, two—had to be burning all through the night beside his bed.

"Step lively!" commanded Vincent. The curls of his wig were as big as cotton balls. "Corbett, wake up!"

He was awake, yet was he? When he got this horrible business on his mind reality became fogged, like a dirty glass. He recalled speaking to Sally Almond about how the great fans of Mrs. Sutch's sausages were reacting now that there were be no more of the spicy things laid out on the dark red—Indian blood, they were called— platters Hiram Stokely supplied to Madam Almond. *Most are faring well*, the lady had told him. *But a few who seemed to crave those sausages beyond all reason tell me they sweat at night and do not sleep very soundly.*

"They'll get themselves in order," Matthew had answered, but he was thinking he should get the names of those particular sausage-lovers so he might studiously avoid them in the streets and alleyways of New York.

A pity that Mrs. Sutch left the country so suddenly, said Sally Almond.

"Yes, and most likely it was a one-way destination," Matthew had replied, leaving Madam Almond to frown with puzzlement for a few seconds before she gave a shrug of finality and returned to her kitchen.

"Step! Step! Step! *Pause!*" shouted the bewigged tyrant, who was doing his best to make a pleasant pasttime into an onerous odyssey.

Matthew Corbett wore tonight a plain dark blue suit with a white shirt and white stockings, his shoes buffed to a polite shine. He was no longer interested in presenting himself as a cock-of-the-walk, as had been the case back in the flush of autumn. He was absolutely fine with his current position in life, which was as a problem-solver tasked to do many various things for the Herrald Agency, some as mundane as carrying land deed papers to a particular personage and others as interesting as had been the incident of the Four Lamplighters just this past December. Problems such as Lord Mortimer, the wealthy man who'd hired Matthew to help him cheat death, and the tricky— yet sadly comic—situation faced by Lady Pink Manjoy had helped Matthew put some distance between himself and the Slaughter tribulation, yet he still felt he had many miles to go.

He moved within the flow of dancers yet felt himself drifting apart. Even when Berry passed him once more and gave him a lingering appraisal, he saw only the fact that he had taken a human life. And perhaps it had been his life or the wretched life of Mrs. Sutch in the balance, but still...he remembered asking his friend Walker In Two Worlds the question *How are you insane?*

And the Indian's answer, which seemed more appropriate now to Matthew's state of mind: *I know too much.*

Matthew was tall and slim, yet with the toughness of a river reed about him. Surely, he knew by now the virtues of bending with the flow of events. He had a lean, long-jawed face and a thatch of fine black hair that was now brushed and tamed for the civilities of the evening. His pale candlelit countenance attested to his interest in books and nighttime games of chess at the Trot Then Gallop. His cool gray eyes with their hints of twilight blue were on this night thoughtful upon matters more of flesh-and-blood than music and dance. Yet he was here, in a way, on a mission.

When he and his problem-solving associate Hudson Greathouse had been assaulted by Tyranthus Slaughter and had wound up at the bottom of a well in the ruins of a Dutch fort, Matthew in his efforts to escape death and save his friend's life had been fortified by the image of the lovely, intelligent, artistic and quite willful young woman who had just passed by his right shoulder. In fact, he had fixed upon her as he had attempted time and again a precarious spider-like climb to the top of the well, which had seemed at the moment as far away as Philadelphia. During that struggle to survive he had made the vow to invite her to a dance if indeed he lived through the episode. And he had vowed to dance the floor to woodshavings in appreciation of a life returned to him. Mayhaps it had been Berry doing the inviting, and the dancing was more regimented than he would have liked, but nevertheless he felt he was alive because of her, and so he was here— dancing with her, every few turns of the reel—and he was in his own way ecstatic to still be a citizen of this earth.

So when Berry passed next to him the following round—she of the curly coppery-red tresses, blue-eyed and fresh-faced and all of nineteen years old with a scattering of freckles across her nose and a gap between her front teeth that Matthew found not only endearing but exciting—he raised his face to her and smiled, and she smiled back at him, and he thought she looked radiant in her sea-green gown adorned with purple ribbons on the front, and per- haps an errant thought of what her lips would taste like when they were kissed crept in and surprised him, and caused him to lose the pace, for he stumbled against Effrem Owles and suddenly Gilliam Vincent was there glowering his disapproval and the stick was com- ing down to swat Matthew's noggin with the leather glove.

But before the glove could smack home, the length of hard hickory met with resistance in the form of a gnarled black walking- stick that got in its way. There was a little *crack* of wood against wood, more like the horns of two rams clashing.

"Mr. Vincent?" Hudson Greathouse had stepped forth from the throng of perhaps twenty or so onlookers to this slow death called a 'dance.' He spoke quietly, so that only Matthew and the dancemas- ter could hear. "Have you ever had a glove up your ass?"

Vincent sputtered. His cheeks reddened. Maybe the answer was *yes*. It was hard to tell.

In any case, the hickory stick went down.

"Time, everyone!" Vincent announced. "Time, please!" And then, to no one in particular, "I'm going out to get some *air*!"

"Don't rush back on our accounts," Greathouse said as Vincent departed with a wobble in his wig.

The little commotion caused a hiccup in the music and, the pacing lost, the company of reelers banged and bumped into each other like a caravan of carriages that had thrown their wheels. Instead of the kind of indignation that Vincent might have shown at this lack of dancely decorum, the collisions brought forth laughter both brassy and silvery and thus revealed was the true metal of friendship among the Mad Robins of New York.

The musicians decided to rest their fiddles, drums and squeezebox. The dancers dispersed to get their share of apple cider and sugar cakes from the table in the other room. Berry came up alongside Greathouse and Matthew and said with appreciable generosity to the young man, "You're doing very well. Better than you did at the house."

"Thank you. My feet don't believe you, but thank you anyway."

She gave a quick glance at Greathouse and then focused her attention again on her object. "Cider?" she asked.

"In a minute." Matthew was aware he was not the most genial of company this night; perhaps it was the fact that he'd just seen the Mallorys—the devilishly-handsome, gentlemanly Doctor Jason and his beautiful black-haired wife Rebecca—standing across the room pretending to be talking but actually keeping their eyes on him. Those two had been haunting him seemingly wherever he went ever since he'd returned from the Slaughter incident.

We have a mutual acquaintance, Rebecca Mallory had said to Matthew one day on a quiet waterfront street while her husband silently stood watch. *We believe he'd like to meet you.*

When you're ready, the woman had said, *in a week or two, we'd like you to come visit us. Will you do that?*

And what if I don't? Matthew had asked, because he knew full well to what acquaintance Rebecca Mallory must be referring.

Oh, let's don't be unfriendly, Matthew. In a week or two. We'll set a table, and we'll be expecting you.

"*I'll* certainly be glad to have cider with you, Berry!" said Effrem Owles, pushing past Matthew in his eagerness to inhale the girl's essence. His eyes were large and round behind his spectacles. The tailor's son was dressed simply but elegantly in a black suit, white shirt and white stockings. His teeth gleamed at the center of his giddy smile. Though Effrem was only twenty years old, premature gray streaked his brown hair. He was tall and thin. Gangly would be the proper word. An excellent chess player, but the only game he was playing tonight had to do with Cupid. Tonight he was obviously hanging onto the hope that Berry would grace him with the opportunity to watch her drink cider and eat sugar cakes. Effrem was in love. No, more than love, Matthew thought. Effrem was obsessed with Berry. He talked about her incessantly and wanted to know everything of her comings and goings, and did Matthew ever put in a good word for him and say how much money an able tailor could command and all such nonsense. Between Effrem and the town's eccentric but highly-efficent coroner Ashton McCaggers, Berry had her choice of ardent pursuers.

"Well..." Berry made it sound like not only a deep subject but also one that greatly perplexed her. "Matthew, I thought—"

"Go ahead," Matthew told her, if only because he feared getting saliva on his sleeve from Effrem's tongue. "I'll be there in a few minutes."

"Grand!" said Effrem as he positioned himself beside Berry for the stroll into the other room. She went along, because she did like Effrem. Not in that way he wished to be liked, but because Matthew counted him a good friend and she saw in Effrem the loyalty of friendship she considered among the highest blessings in the world.

In the departure of Berry and Effrem, Hudson Greathouse leaned lightly on his stick, cocked his head to one side and gave Matthew a grin that was also half-cocked. "Brighten your candle," he advised. "What's wrong with you?"

Matthew shrugged. "I suppose I'm not in a festive mood."

"Well, *get* in one. My God, boy! *I'm* the one who can't dance anymore! And I'll tell you, I could shake my shillelagh in my younger days. So use it while you have it!"

Matthew stared at the floor between them. Sometimes it was hard for him to look Hudson in the face. Because of greed and a bad decision, Matthew had allowed Slaughter to get the drop on them. Greathouse got along fine on his walking-stick, for sure, and sometimes he could get along just fine without it if he was feeling more like a stallion than a gelding, but being stabbed four times in the back and then three-quarters drowned had a way of aging a man, of slowing him down, of thrusting the bitter truth of mortality in his face. Greathouse of course had always been a man of action, and thus knew the pitfalls of putting himself in harm's way, but Matthew still blamed his mendacity for the darkness that sometimes passed across Greathouse's face like a shadow, and made the man's deep-set black eyes seem yet more ebony and the lines around them more numerous. To be certain, a diminished Hudson Greathouse was still a force to be reckoned with, if anyone dared try. Not many would. He had a ruggedly handsome, craggy face and wore his thick iron-gray hair in a queue tied with a black ribbon. He stood three inches over six feet, broad of shoulders and chest and also broad of expression; he knew how to conquer a room, and at age forty-eight—having turned so on the eighth of January—he possessed the canny experience of a survivor. And well to be so, for the wounds and the stick had neither made him put quit to his work with the Herrald Agency nor made him any less desirable to any number of New York females. His tastes were simple, as attested to by his gray suit, white shirt and white stockings above unpolished black boots that knew how to kick a tail or two, if need be. Matthew mused that Mr. Vincent should consider himself lucky to have gotten out of the room with just an insult, because since Matthew had saved his life Greathouse was the finest of friends and the fiercest of protectors.

Yet, still, there was the nit to be picked.

"Are you that much of an idiot?" Greathouse asked.

"Pardon?"

"Don't play dumb. I'm talking about the girl."

"The girl," Matthew repeated, dumbly. He glanced to see if he was still the center of attention from Doctor Jason and the beautiful Rebecca, but the Mallorys had moved to a different position and were conversing with the ruddy-faced sugar merchant Solomon Tully, he of the Swiss-geared false choppers.

"The *girl*," said Greathouse with some force behind it. "Can't you tell she's got it set for you?"

"What's set for me?"

"*It!*" Greathouse's scowl was a frightening thing. "Now I *know* you've been working too much! I've told you, haven't I? Make time for *life.*"

"My work is my life."

"Hm," said the great one. "I can see that carved on your gravestone. Honestly, Matthew! You're *young*! Don't you realize how young you are?"

"I haven't thought." Ah, yes! There was the quick glance from Rebecca Mallory again. Whatever she was thinking, Matthew knew he was never far from it. Of course, owing to events revealed to Matthew after the deaths of Slaughter and Sutch, it was clear to him that the Mallorys were somehow involved with the personage who seemed to be becoming a dark star on the horizon of Matthew's world. That personage being Professor Fell, emperor of crime both in Europe, England and now desirous of a place of control in the New World, the better to spread his clutching tentacles like his symbol the octopus.

We have a mutual acquaintance, Rebecca Mallory had said.

Matthew had no doubt the Mallorys knew Professor Fell much better than he. All he knew of the man was that he had a slew of nefarious plans—some of which Matthew had already upset—and that at one time Professor Fell had laid a 'blood card' down upon the young problem-solver's life: a bloody fingerprint on a white card that meant Matthew was marked for certain death. Whether that threat still held true or not, he didn't know. Perhaps he should stroll across the room and ask the Mallorys?

"You're wandering off from what I'm saying." Greathouse shifted his position so that he stood between Matthew and the handsome couple who hid their secrets. Matthew had said nothing of any of this to his friend; there was no need, as yet, to pull him into this intrigue. Particularly now that the great one was somewhat less great and much more human in his vulnerable flesh. "And if you're thinking what I think you're thinking, *stop* thinking it."

Matthew looked Greathouse in the eyes. "What might that be?"

"You know. That you still carry a burden, and you blame yourself and all that. It happened, it's done and it's over. I told you before, I might have done the same thing in your shoes. Hell," he growled,

"I'm *sure* I would've. I'm all right, believe me. Now let that go and come back to life. I don't mean just halfway. I mean *all* the way. Hear me?"

Matthew did. Greathouse was right; it was time to let those things of the past go, because they were corrupting both his present and future. Maybe it would still be awhile before he could come back all the way, but he forced himself to say, "Yes."

"Good boy. Good *man*, I mean." Greathouse leaned in a little closer. His eyes caught candlelight and glinted with devilish humor. "Listen," he said quietly, "that girl favors you. You know she does. She's a mighty comely girl, and she could make a man excitable if you know what I mean. And I'll tell you, she hides more than she shows in that area."

"What area?" In spite of himself, Matthew felt a smile pushing at the corners of his mouth.

"*Love.*" It had been nearly a whisper. "You know what they say: Gap between the teeth, hot between the sheets."

"Oh, they say that, do they?"

"Yes. *Definitely* yes."

"Hudson? *There* you are!" The person who'd just spoken was a woman, and she came forward with a rustle of lemon-colored skirts and an expression of bemusement. She was tall and willowy and had a lush garden of blonde hair that in defiance of the proper ladylike fashion fell unconfined about her bare shoulders, which of itself spoke volumes of both her nature and the future of modern women. Upon seeing a small heart-shaped birthmark in the hollow of her throat Matthew thought they would have seized on this rather brazen female as a witch in the since-departed town of Fount Royal. He doubted she would've gone nicely to the gaol. She got up alongside Greathouse and actually put her arm around his shoulders. Then she stared at Matthew with her warm and inviting brown eyes and said, "This is the young man." No question, just statement.

"Matthew Corbett, meet the widow Donovan," said Greathouse.

She offered an ungloved hand. "Abby Donovan," she told him. "I arrived last week from London. Hudson has been so helpful."

"He's a helpful sort," Matthew said. His hand would remember the woman's remarkably firm squeeze.

"Yes, but he does get away from you. Particularly when he says for you to get cider and that he'll return in a moment. I don't think 'a moment' is the same for Hudson as it is for other men." All this was said with the slyest hint of a smile and the brown eyes fixed on the man of the moment.

"Never was," he admitted. "Never will be."

"I admit, he's one of a kind," said Matthew.

"Don't I know it!" answered the lady, who when her smile broadened into nearly a laugh displayed a gap between her front teeth that made Berry's appear a crevice compared to a canyon. It shocked Matthew that his first thought was wondering what might fit in there, and then he got redfaced and had to swab his temples with his handkerchief.

"It *is* warm, this close to the fire," observed the widow Donovan, who Matthew figured might have burned her dearly departed to cinders under the sheets. But anyway, it was up to Greathouse now to brave the flames, for the woman stood close against him and stared desirously at the side of his face, so much so that Matthew wondered how a week might pass so intensely heated for some and yet so frozen with blue ice for others.

"Excuse us," Greathouse said at length. He shifted his balance, perhaps because he had to reposition his stick. "We'll be going now."

"Don't let me stop you," Matthew said.

"Oh," said the woman with a lift of her blonde brows, "when Hudson gets going, there's no stopping him."

One week! Matthew thought. And here he was, brooding over the great one's disabilities! Perhaps it was true, Greathouse could no longer dance. Standing up, that is. But otherwise...

"Goodnight," said Greathouse, and he and his new kitten—cat, really, for she was likely in her late thirties but very well assembled for her age—went out of the room as close-stepped as two people could be who were not in a military parade. Then Matthew got upon his mind the matter of salutes of a certain kind, and so he was redfaced again when a female voice beside him quietly said, "Matthew?" and he turned to set eyes upon a person whose presence he would not have predicted from now until the impossibly distant twenty-first century.

THREE

T HE girl had her hands clenched before her, either revealing she was nervous or that she'd taken a posture of supplication. "Hello, Matthew," she said, with a trembly smile. "I did what you said. I come here to find that Number Seven Stone Street." She swallowed hard. Her blue gaze, which he recalled to be nearly crackling with energy, now seemed timid and fearful, as if she was sure he must have forgotten. "Don't you remember? I'm—"

"Opal Delilah Blackerby," Matthew said. Of course he remembered. She was one of the girls on the staff at Paradise, the 'velvet prison'—as she'd called it—for the elderly operated by Lyra Sutch in her incarnation of Gemini Lovejoy. If it were not for Opal, the black heart of Lyra Sutch's operation would not have been revealed, and Tyranthus Slaughter would now not be in his grave. So, Matthew thought, all praise to this brave young girl who'd really risked her life to help him.

He reached out and took her hands, at the same time offering her his warmest smile. "How long have you been here? In New York, I mean."

"Just one day," she answered. "Well, not a *whole* day yet. I got here this mornin'. I know you told me 'bout comin' to that Number Seven placey, but I was kinda fretful of just showin' up there. So I been askin' around 'bout whose place that is and all, and a fella told me your name. Then I seen the broadsheet 'bout this dance, and I thought maybe..." She shrugged, hopeless in her explanation of why she was here.

"I understand." Matthew remembered she was the girl who'd longed for warmth in Paradise, and perhaps a dance was the place she could find it on a cold winter's night in New York. As thanks for her help, he had given her a gold ring with a small red stone that may or may not have been a ruby; whatever it was, it had been part of Slaughter's hidden treasure that had led Matthew and Greathouse nearly to their deaths.

"It's so good to see you," Matthew said, and he meant it. He took quick stock of her and saw that she'd decided to alter her appearance somewhat, by removing the small metal rings that had ornamented her lower lip and right nostril. She was a small girl, slim and wiry, and when Matthew had met her she'd been nearly quivering out of her shoes with what might be termed indecent energy. Now her jet-black hair had been brushed back and was decorated with a modest tortoise-shell comb. Her blue eyes, so eager to get Matthew behind Paradise's church for a tryst in the woods, were diminished by lingering doubt that, he surmised, she had no place either here or at Number Seven Stone Street. She wore a gray dress with a white collar, not very different from her uniform at Paradise, which made Matthew wonder if she'd made use of the gold ring and red stone.

He was about to ask her that question when Hell broke loose.

Or, at least, a small portion of Hell confined to the other room, for in the next instant there was a tremendous crash, the sound of breaking glass, and a chorus of startled cries both male and female. Matthew's first thought was that the floor had given way, or that a cannonball had smashed through the ceiling.

He rushed past Opal to see what had happened, and she followed right at his heels.

The floor was still firm and no cannonball had come sizzling from the night, yet certainly disaster had struck. The table that had been holding the fine glass bowl of cider, the clay cups and the

Indian-blood platters of sugar cakes had, plain and simply, pitched over like a horse with a broken leg. Apple cider spread in a small flood across the planks. The sugar cakes were being crushed under the feet of dames and dandies alike. Glass and broken crockery was everywhere and it was truly a mess.

"I swear!" came the agonized voice of Effrem Owles. "I hardly leaned on the table! Hardly at all!"

And Matthew saw Berry standing there beside him, blushing to the roots of her hair, her eyes darkened by the events of the moment. He knew what she was thinking: her bad luck, which had knocked the stuffing out of so many of her suitors and otherwise complicated her life in a series of misfortunes, had reached out and—like Mr. Vincent's glove—given poor innocent Effrem a smack on the noggin. And what a smack! For someone who was for the most part very shy and wished to be anywhere but at the center of attention, this was truly Effrem's nightmare. And him trying to impress Berry so much! It hurt Matthew's heart to even think of it, much less witness it.

"It's all right! We'll get it cleaned up!" said Sally Almond, who was already summoning a serving girl to bring a towel.

But Matthew saw the tears of shame jump behind Effrem's glasses. He started to go forward and put a hand of comfort on his friend's shoulder but he was nearly shouldered aside by Opal Delilah Blackerby, who waded into the cider, knelt down to the floor and started gathering up pieces of broken glass into the apron of her dress.

"Opal!" Matthew said, pushing his way to her. "What are you *doing?*"

She looked up at him, and then at Sally Almond who was also staring dumbfounded at her. Opal stood up, clutching glass fragments in her dress. She had a hazy expression in her eyes, as if for a moment she'd forgotten where she was. "Oh!" she said to Matthew. "I'm sorry! I just...I mean to say...I'm so used to cleanin' up messes...I just...that's what I do, y'*see?*"

"You're a *guest* here," said Sally. "Not a servant."

"Yes'm." Opal frowned, perplexed. "I'm sorry, but...I don't think I know how to be a guest." She was still holding the front of her dress with the pieces of glass in it, and as the regular serving-girl came to sop up the spilled cider with a bundle of towels Opal reached out to take one of the cloths and, startled, the girl pulled away.

"Opal!" Matthew said, grasping her elbow. "You're not expected to clean up anyone's mess. Come on now, let's get out of the way."

"But...Matthew," she said. "That's what I *do*. That's what I was doin' just yesterday, at a tavern on the pike. I mean...that's all I've *ever* done. *Oh*," she said, and she looked at the fingers of her right hand. They were leaking blood. "I suppose I've cut myself a little bit."

Matthew was quick to pull out his handkerchief.

But he was not quick enough.

"Here, miss! Let me see!"

And Matthew witnessed something he had no idea would ever take place. When the blue eyes of Opal Delilah Blackerby and the brown eyes of Effrem Owles met, you could almost hear a distinct *pop*, as if a pinecone had burst in the overheated hearth. Matthew was certain Effrem was only being his gentlemanly self, and perhaps thinking he was to blame for this girl cutting herself, but in that instant there was something more. In that instant there was an exchange of something, maybe a recognition, something...a powerful instant, and Matthew saw the girl who knew only how to clean up messes and had been searching so long for a little bit of warmth flutter her eyelashes, and the shy young tailor's son who liked to play chess and wished desperately to mean something to someone's heart reddened a little on the cheeks and had to look away from her, but she had offered her hand and he took it, and as he pressed his own handkerchief against the injury he brought his eyes back upon hers and Matthew saw him smile—just a small, shy smile—and Effrem said, "We'll get this fixed."

"Ain't nothin'," Opal replied, but she didn't pull her hand away.

Matthew glanced at Berry, who also had taken note of this exchange. She nodded almost imperceptibly, as if to say, *Yes, but it may yet be something after all.*

And in that instant Matthew felt the world tremble.

Or, to be more precise, it was the floor that trembled. He was not the only one who felt it, for conversations halted and Berry blinked in surprise because she'd also felt it. In its aftermath the floor's planks growled like old brown lions stirred from sleep. Then the front door crashed open and from the bundle of his black coat and beneath the tilt of his yellowed wig the white face of Gilliam Vincent painfully shouted, "The Dock House Inn has blown up!"

Decorum was lost and dancing forgotten in the rush upon Nassau Street. Matthew was out the door amid the throng, finding himself behind John Five and John's bride Constance. Berry bumped into Matthew's side as they all looked toward the dockfront at smokeclouds and bursts of flame roiling up into the night.

"Oh my Jesus!" Gilliam Vincent cried out. He began to run southward along Nassau Street toward the point of conflagration perhaps nine blocks distant. Matthew saw Vincent's wig fall off, exposing a pallid scalp where a few sprigs of gray hair stood upright like shocked soldiers on a barren battlefield. For all his vanity, Vincent cared not for the wig so much as he cared for the fate of his beloved Dock House Inn, where he was the narrow-eyed and supremely arrogant king of his domain, and so he put wings to his heels and was off hollering "Fire! Fire! Fire!" all the way.

Cries of alarm were quickly echoing across the town. From Manhattan's previous experience, flame was a disastrous enemy. Matthew surmised that if indeed it was the Dock House Inn that had somehow 'blown up,' as Vincent had put it, there might not be very much left of the guests who'd been sleeping there. The fire shot yellow and orange tendrils a hundred feet into the air. If clouds had not already slid in to mask the moon, the dark plumes rising from New York would have blackened Selene's lunar face. "Come on, men!" someone shouted, a call to fetch buckets and get to the wells that stood here and there on the cobbled streets. Some went back into Sally Almond's tavern to get their coats, scarves, gloves, caps, tricorn hats before they started off. Matthew took his black fearnaught from a hook on the wall, donned his gray gloves and woolen cap and with a quick glance at Berry that said *I think dancing must wait* he was away among the men fast striding or outright running for the scene of fiery destruction.

The houses were emptying their people onto the streets. Many folk wore their flannel robes and were bare-legged against the cold. Lanterns swung back and forth, a midwinter congregation of summer's fireflies. Night watchmen scurried around rather helplessly, showing their green lamps of authority for whatever they were worth. At the corner of Broad and Princes Streets Matthew nearly collided with elderly Benedict Hamrick, an ex-soldier of the realm with a white beard that hung to his spit-polished belt-buckle. Hamrick marched around blowing into an ear-piercing tin whistle and shouting incomprehensible orders to anyone who would listen, which meant he had utterly no troops to command in his fantasy of the Coldstream Guards.

For all its everyday chaos, nattering of merchants, horse manure in the streets and slaves in the attics, New York at a moment of crisis became a purposeful juggernaut. Much as ants will boil over from a heel-kicked nest and begin feverish defenses, so were the Manhattanites. Buckets materialized from houses and barns. A horse wagon hauling buckets came clattering down Broad Street. Teams of men gathered, took hold of buckets and set off at a run to station themselves at wells. Somehow, the chains of the bucket brigades solidified within minutes of Gilliam Vincent's first cry. Water began moving, faster and faster along the line. Then the line split into two and three and thus multiple dowsings of water were thrown upon the fire, which turned out not to be consuming the Dock House Inn but to be eating a Dock Street warehouse where nautical ropes were made and stored.

And it was surely a hot fire. A fire with a white center, and a power to scorch the eyebrows and puff the faces of those at its edge. Even Matthew, working with the other feverish ants a block north of the scene, could feel the waves of heat rolling past him in dusty swells. The labor continued on, the buckets moving as fast as muscle would allow, but very soon it was apparent that the warehouse was a goner, and all liquid must be used to wet the surrounding structures thus to prevent a disaster of the worst kind. At one point old Hooper Gillespie appeared, ranting about an attack by the Dutch, but no one paid him any attention and so he slinked away scowling and spitting toward the harbor.

Hollers and shouts went up when the last wall of the warehouse collapsed. The sparks that flew up were stomped under boots when they landed. More water was thrown upon the soggy, steaming wood walls of the buildings to left and right, and finally as the hours passed and the muscles weakened, the southernmost portion of the town was saved but the rope merchant Johannis Feeg wept bitter tears over his pile of smouldering ashes.

The work was at last finished. The tavern owners brought out kegs of ale and opened them in the street; one never knew when one might need a bucket brigade, and it was safer to be on the good side of the citizenry rather than pinch ale pennies at a time like this. Matthew scooped up a drink in a wooden cup he'd been given, and along with other bedraggled fire fighters he walked toward the smoking remains.

There was very little left but smoke. Matthew saw other men walking through the ashes, kicking embers between the eyes and then crushing them for good measure. The smell of acrid smoke, dust and heat was like coarse flannel in the lungs. Men who had been closest to the fire staggered around blackened and nearly cooked, and they nodded wearily as others put cups of ale into their hands.

"Now *this* was a merry moment, wasn't it?"

Matthew turned to see who'd spoken, but he'd already recognized the voice of Gardner Lillehorne, which tonight was the hum of a wasp seeking a place to sting.

The spindly-framed high constable was in less than his usual perfection, for ashes marred his overcoat of bright holly green, trimmed at the collar and cuffs with bands of scarlet. Alas, the cuffs were filthy and his white shirt the color of dirty teeth. His holly green tricorn was dark with ash and its small red feather burned to a wisp. Ashes streaked his long, pallid face with its narrow black eyes, small and pointed nose, precisely-trimmed black-goatee and black mustache. Even the silver lion's head that topped his ebony cane seemed to be scorched and dirty. Lillehorne's eyes left Matthew's and scanned the wandering crowd. "A merry moment," he repeated. "For Mr. Feeg's competitors, that is."

Matthew felt someone coming up behind him. He turned his head and saw Berry, her hair wild in the smoky breeze and ashes on her freckled cheeks. She was bundled in a brown coat. She stopped when he saw her, as if understanding a statement not to get too close.

At nearly the same time, Matthew noted the presence of the nasty little watchman and general troublemaker Dippen Nack coming up like a small creeping predator beside the high constable, who seemed to be his idol in all things either arrogant or assinine. Matthew considered the barrel-chested, red-faced Nack a brutal bully and, worse, a coward who used his black billyclub to wallop only those who could not return the blow.

"What's the tale?" Lillehorne asked Nack, indicating that the high constable had recently sent his devilish devotee out on a misson.

"Number a' people heard it, sir," Nack answered, in the manner of slump-shouldered subjugation, be it ever so false. "Yessir! A cannon blast is what they all said it was!" And he added, just to polish the worm-holed apple: "*Sir!*"

"A cannon blast?" Instantly Matthew's curiosity had spun toward this information like an arrow on a weather vane. "From where?"

"I don't have that information yet, thank you for asking." Lillehorne's nostrils wrinkled, and he gently patted them with a green handkerchief. Over the reek of smoke Matthew caught the reek of a too-sweet perfume water.

"Some folk say they thought it come from out thataway." Nack motioned with his club toward the south. "Then this thing blew up."

"'Blew up'?" Matthew asked. Nearly the same choice of words that Gilliam Vincent had made. "Why do you put it that way?"

"Just *look* at it," Nack answered, the anger never far from his curdled surface. "Ain't no regular fire! Pieces layin' all up and down the street!" He gave a mocking grin for Lillehorne's benefit. "I thought you was supposed to be such a *brain!*"

Matthew kept his attention directed to Lillehorne, even though the gypsies had arrived at the scene and stood nearby scratching their squalling fiddles while their dark-haired girls danced for coins amid the ale-drinkers. "You're saying a cannonball did this?"

"I am saying that a cannon was *heard* to be fired. Corbett, restrain your interest. I've already sent some men to watch the harbor, if indeed it was the signal from Oyster Island. The town is not paying for your abilities tonight. *Keep that noise down!*" Lillehorne shouted at the gypsy fiddlers, but the volume altered not an ear-spike.

Matthew gazed out over the ashen plain. There were cannons on the walls at what had been Fort William Henry, now called Fort Anne, at New York's southernmost point; they were manned day and night and aimed at the sea. The single cannon on Oyster Island was used as an early signal of invasion by the Dutch fleet, even though commerce and profits had made steady companions of London and Amsterdam. No one ever truly expected a Dutch armada to try to retake their once-possession, but...why had the cannon fired?

"I have no earthly idea," said Lillehorne, and only then did Matthew realize he'd asked the question aloud. "But I'll get to the bottom of this without your so-called *professional* assistance, sir."

Matthew then saw another element of interest in this cold night's play. Off beyond Lillehorne, lit by the lamps they carried, were the handsome Doctor Jason Mallory and the beautiful Rebecca. They were talking quietly and surveying the ruins, but did both of them now glance in his direction? Did they speak again, and then glance again before they turned their backs and moved away?

A whistle blew, loud enough to be heard over the caterwauling of gypsy fiddles.

Then blew once more, stronger, with a demanding note. And a third time, equally demanding.

"What the *devil?*" Lillehorne's gaze was searching for the annoying source, as well as did Matthew, Nack and Berry. A group of onlookers was coming around, intrigued by the noise. Matthew saw Marmaduke Grigsby, the old inkslinger and editor of the *Earwig* broadsheet, step up beside his granddaughter, his eyes large and questioning behind his spectacles in the moon-round face. The whistle continued to blow, stridently now.

"Over *there*, sir!" It was Nack who pointed toward the other side of Dock Street and just east of the destroyed warehouse.

Matthew saw Benedict Hamrick standing next to a wall of brown bricks, which was part of a storehouse for tarbarrels, anchors, chains and other nautical goods. Hamrick's beard and crusty coat blew in the rising wind. He was manning his whistle as if commanding an attack of grenadiers. And furthermore, he was pointing to something written on the bricks.

At once Matthew was following Lillehorne toward the whistle-blower, with Nack almost stepping on his heels. "Matthew!" Berry called out, but he didn't stop though he thought that, oddly, she was telling him not to go.

A group of people congregated around Hamrick, who abruptly ceased his tin-whistling and pointed with a thin, gnarled finger at the two words written about head-high on the wall. The white paint had trickled down, making the words look like crawling spiders.

The first word was *Matthew*.

The second was *Corbett*.

Matthew felt his heart stutter as Hamrick's hand moved, and the finger pointed at him.

Lillehorne took a lantern from the nearest citizen and lifted it to shine a direct light upon Matthew's face. He stepped forward, his eyes further narrowed, as if to examine something he'd never seen before.

Matthew could do nothing, nor could he speak.

"Yes," said the high constable. He nodded. "You can be sure I'll get to the bottom of this."

FOUR

"I WOULD sincerely love to hear an explanation," said the man in the lilac-colored gown with blue lace trimming the neckline. To the silence that followed, his painted lips smiled faintly. Under his elaborately-curled and coiffed wig, his blue-shaded eyes ticked from person to person in the room. "Please," he said, with a lift of his white silk gloves, "everyone should not speak at *once*."

Gardner Lillehorne cleared his throat, perhaps a bit too explosively. He held his pumpkin-colored tricorn in his hands, that color being his hue of the day. "Lord Cornbury," he said, "the facts are as I've told." Matthew thought he sounded a bit nervous, and in truth when one looked into the face of Edward Hyde, Lord Cornbury, Governor of the colony of New York and cousin to Queen Anne herself, one did feel one's breakfast tumble in the gut.

"Told," said the well-dressed man behind his desk, "but not made *sense* of." The white silk fingers steepled together. The horsey face might have broken any mirror in town. "That mumble-mouthed fool made no sense, either. What's all this about red lamps and a Dutch invasion and fish being stolen from a boat?"

Hooper Gillespie had just given his statement a few moments ago, before his nervous agitation had caused him to stagger and fall upon the floor. He'd had to be taken out of Lord Cornbury's office on a canvas stretcher. And his statement? That too seemed to Matthew to be in need of a stretcher, or perhaps it was already stretched.

The fourth man in the room pursed his lips and let out a sound like a wet fart.

"You wish to speak, Mr. Greathouse?" the governor asked.

"I wish to *complain*," the great one answered. He wasn't leaning on his stick this morning; it was crossed over his right shoulder. Matthew had noted the dark hollows beneath his tarpit eyes. It appeared to him that Hudson had fought his own fire last night, after being roused out of Abby Donovan's cottage by the conflagration and noise, and the more intimate flames had fairly scorched him. "As a character witness for Matthew, I—"

"Why exactly are you *here*, sir?" came the interruption, which Matthew knew dared violence, even against a lord in a dress.

"I'm *here*," came back the response, which was dangerously close to a sneer, "because I was in our office when the high-and-mighty constable barged in there and all but arrested my associate. Then dragged him over here for what he called a 'hearing.' Well, I came along of my own free will."

"Couldn't stop him, I fear," said Lillehorne.

"Couldn't *be* stopped," said Greathouse, his grim gaze directed to the gowned governor. "I don't know what happened last night and neither does Matthew. Yes, his name was painted on a wall across from the fire. But he had nothing to do with that! With any of it! How could he, when he was at Sally Almond's tavern *dancing* when that building…blew up, or whatever happened to it."

"There was a *dance* last night?" Lord Cornbury asked Lillehorne, with a plaintive note in his voice. "My wife and I love to dance."

"The common folk's dance, my lord. Not to your liking, I'm sure."

Matthew had to sigh at this exchange. True, he'd been brought here by Lillehorne from the Herrald Agency's office at Number Seven Stone Street about thirty minutes ago. To avoid having to look at this scene of foolishness, he gazed out the window to his right, which gave a view of the town along the Broad Way. A light snow had begun falling before dawn, and now in the gray glow of nine o'clock the roofs were white. A few wagons trundled up and down the Broad Way. Citizens wrapped up in their coats were going about their business. The steeple of Trinity Church was outlined in white, and white robes covered the sleepers in Trinity's graveyard. At Wall Street, City Hall was getting a white frosting upon its yellow-cake paint, and Matthew wondered if up in his attic wonderworld of skeletons and grotesqueries the eccentric coroner Ashton McCaggers was firing his pistol at one of his dress dummies in order to measure the bullet hole.

"Why do you two always seem to be..." Cornbury paused, tapping his chin with a finger in order to urge the proper word loose. "*Afflicted?* With *trouble*," he quickly added, seeing the storm brewing in Greathouse's face. "I mean to say, why are you always followed by trouble?"

"It's our business," Greathouse answered. "Just as yours is sitting here trying to blame Matthew Corbett for something he had no part in."

"Mind your mouth, please!" Lillehorne warned, though it came out more as a shaky request.

"I'm not blaming anyone, sir." When he needed to, Cornbury could display ample composure. His bosom seemed somewhat ample today as well, but Matthew chose not to linger a gaze or thought on that subject very long. "I'm simply trying to understand *why* his name was there. As in: *who* painted it upon the bricks? And also: for what reason? You must admit, this is a very peculiar situation. First that...that Gillespie person nearly faints dead away telling me he has seen a red signal lamp drawing a Dutch armada in to the attack, that he'd...how did he put it?... 'pulled a boner' on his cannon, and that the phantom of Oyster Island stole his codfish."

"Three mackerel and a striper," Greathouse corrected.

"All right, whatever they were. Then this warehouse burns to the ground and the young man's name is there on the opposite wall. And I will tell you, sir, that Johannis Feeg was first in my office this morning, with his lawyer, and the talk of monetary restitution reached a rather high volume."

"Monetary restitution?" Greathouse's scowl was a fearsome sight. "From whom? Matthew? Feeg and his lawhound will have to bore a hole through my body to get past me!"

"Let me hear," said Cornbury in a quiet voice, "the silent one speak. Mr. Corbett, do you have anything to say?"

Matthew was still staring out the window, watching the snowflakes fall. He wished he were a thousand miles away from this ridiculous room. Again, since becoming a killer everything seemed so small and unimportant. Ludicrous, really. He mused on the fact that Professor Fell had not only controlled Lyra Sutch and Tyranthus Slaughter, but now also had a hand in his own destiny. Matthew was not who he had been, and he wondered if he would ever find his way back.

"Mr. Corbett?" Cornbury urged.

"Yes?" Then Matthew realized what was being asked of him. His mental wheels were clogged today. Three hours of fitful sleep would muddy up the best brain. He rubbed his forehead, where the crescent scar of a bear's claw would forever remind him of the price of being someone's champion. "Oh. All right," he said hazily. "I was dancing at Sally Almond's. No," he corrected, "I was standing at the table that had gone over. Everything spilled. Effrem was there. The girl. Opal. And she cut one of her fingers on the glass."

There was a short pause.

"Oh dear," said the governor to Lillehorne. "Is he related to that Gillespie creature?"

By an effort of will and concentration, Matthew righted his foundering ship. "I had nothing to do with that fire," he said, with some heat behind it. "Yes, my name was painted on the wall. By someone." Or more than one, he thought. But the Mallorys had been at the dance when the warehouse had gone up. How could they have been responsible, and what would be the point? "Someone wished to...implicate me, I suppose? Or something else? Because I had dozens of witnesses and, besides, why would I be fool enough to sign my name to a warehouse-burning? Why would I want to set fire to a storehouse of ropes?" He waited for a reply. When there was none, he shot the question at them again: *"Why?"*

"Listen to him," said Greathouse, the loyal friend.

The moment hung.

With a rustle of stiffened muslin, Lord Cornbury rose to his high-heeled feet. He went to the window and aimed his shadowed stare at the dance of white flakes that swooped and swirled from the gray ceiling of clouds.

After a measure of reflection, the governor said in a low voice not suiting his suit, "Damn this. I understand none of it."

Welcome to my world, Matthew thought.

After a spell of what seemed like deliberation but may have only been hapless and aimless thought of what color sash went with what color gown, Lord Cornbury turned toward the high constable. "Can you handle this, Lillehorne?"

For once, the high constable sought his rightful level of truth. "I'm not certain, sir."

"Hm," came the reply; a decision had been made. The rather unsettling gaze ticked between Matthew and Greathouse. "You two are the problem-solvers. Solve the problem."

"We'd like to do that," Greathouse replied without hestitation, "but our business requires a fee."

"Your usual fee, then. Nothing too exorbitant for the town's coffers, I trust." A gloved finger was lifted. "Now both of you listen to me before I dismiss you. If I discover that you have worked this situation in order to wrench money from my pockets, I shall have your stones boiled in oil before they're cut off with a dull knife. Do you understand me?"

Greathouse shrugged, his way of saying he did. Matthew was still wondering where Cornbury's pockets were.

"Get out," said the Lord Governor, to all three of them.

"Good fortune to you gentlemen," said Lillehorne as he stood at the top of the stairs and the two problem-solvers descended. He tapped the silver lion's head against the palm of his hand. "I shall be watching you to make sure all is right in your investigation."

"You should be watching the Princess," Greathouse answered, speaking of Lillehorne's rather shrewish wife. "I have it on good authority that she is still on intimate terms with Dr. Mallory, and not for medical reasons this time." He gave a brief catlike smile to Lillehorne's stone face, his statement referring to a case in October wherein Maude Lillehorne was secretly visiting the handsome Dr. Jason for a 'women's health' cure that involved an unhealthy dose of coca leaves.

Outside, with their coats wrapped around them against the cold and whirling snowflakes, they walked away from the governor's mansion toward the Broad Way.

"Is she really?" Matthew asked, his gray woolen cap pulled down over his ears. "Maude Lillehorne," he reminded Greathouse. "Involved with the doctor?"

Greathouse frowned, the brim of his black tricorn catching snow. "What do *you* think? If you were Jason Mallory, would you give the Princess one look? Especially if you had that wife of his to warm your cockle every night?"

"I suppose not."

"I *know* not. I just said that to give Lillehorne something to think about. Stretch his mind a little. He needs it."

Speaking of warming a cockle, Matthew thought, how goes the merry widow? But he decided there was valor in silence. Plus, on his mind he had this warehouse blaze and levity was not welcome there today.

"Walk with me a ways," said Greathouse, though they already were. Matthew knew this was the great one's method of saying there were serious things to be contemplated and talked about, and so they would walk a crooked route through the town's streets in search of a straighter path.

Though the snow flew and flitted and did its work of whitening the bricks, stones, timbers and dirt, Matthew thought that today New York seemed to be gray upon gray. A gray fog seemed to lie close to the earth, with gray clouds above and gray buildings between. Windows blurred the candles behind them. From the multitude of chimneys rose the morning smoke, drifting with the wind toward the winter-sheared woodland across the river in New Jersey. Wagons on the streets moved back and forth in near silence, their horses snorting steam and their drivers hunched forward, shapeless in heavy coats and weather-beaten hats. The boots Matthew and Greathouse wore crunched snow. The great one's stick probed ahead for treacherous footing.

They turned to the right along Beaver Street, Matthew following his friend's lead, and headed toward the East River. A bright red parasol coming in their direction startled the eye and for an instant Matthew thought it had to be Berry underneath it, but then came clear the tall and handsome figure of Polly Blossom, the owner of the rose-colored house of ladies of the evening on Petticoat Lane. Actually, truth to be told, also ladies of the morning and the afternoon.

"Hello, Matthew," said Polly, with a polite smile and a nod. Matthew had done a favor for her in the summer, regarding a member of her flock, and thus had what she called a 'season's pass' to her establishment, though he had not yet ventured so deeply into that territory. Then, for Hudson, her smile became a little wicked and her eyelashes fluttered. "Good morning to *you*," she said, and as she passed she gave him a little hip-bump that made Matthew think he ought to get himself a walking stick and pretend to be in need of tea and sympathy.

"Don't say it," said Greathouse as they walked on, and so Matthew did not. But it occurred to him that some afternoons when the great one was supposed to be uncovering an investigation he must instead be investigating an uncovering.

They found themselves walking in the snow along Queen Street, heading southward toward Dock Street and the Great Dock where the masted ships rested, groaning softly in their cradles of ropes. Yet even in this wintry weather the work of a maritime colony continued, for several new vessels that had recently arrived were still being unloaded by the dock crews and several scheduled to leave on the next favorable tide were being loaded. There was, as always every day of the year, much activity and shouting of orders. Someone had built a fire from broken pieces of lumber and a few men stood around it warming themselves until they were shouted back to work. Ropes that ended in iron hooks moved cargo from place to place. Wagons stood ready to accept the freight or give it up. And as always, the higglers and their fiddles and tambourines were present to urge coins from the seafaring music-lovers, yet today their music was gray and not a little sad, as befitting God's picture this morning of New York.

Matthew and Greathouse came to a place where could be seen through the masts and between the hulls the foggy outline of Oyster Island. Greathouse stopped, staring toward that unlovely isle, and Matthew also paused.

"Curious," said Greathouse.

"A general statement?" Matthew asked when no more was offered. "I'd say more than curious. I'd say my name written on a wall before a burning building is downright mysteri—"

"The phantom of Oyster Island," Greathouse interrupted. "You know the stories, yes?"

"What there are."

"And you of course have figured out that this phantom has only come to be noticed in the past two months. Cold weather set in. He needed a coat, and he needed food. Though he, I'm sure, is an able hunter and fisherman. But perhaps the game out there has become more wary, and the shoreline's fish have moved because of the cold? And now one would need a boat to catch fish from deeper water?"

Matthew didn't speak. He knew exactly who Greathouse was referring to; it had already crossed his mind. It had already, as a matter of fact, been ninety percent settled in his mind.

"He was a strong swimmer," said the great one. "Maybe no one else could get there from here, but Zed did. I have no doubt he's our phantom."

Again, Matthew held his silence. He too stared out toward the island, abandoned by its watchman. Zed owned the place now, if just for a short while. A freed slave in possession of part of a crown colony! It tickled the pink.

Back in the autumn, Matthew had watched as the massive, mute and scar-faced Zed had—upon realizing from Berry's language of artful drawings that he was free—run to the bitter end of one of these wharves and leaped with joyful abandon into the water. Zed had been at one time the slave to Ashton McCaggers, until Greathouse had paid for his freedom and secured the writ of manumission from Lord Cornbury. Greathouse's interest in Zed had not been entirely altruistic, for Greathouse had realized due to the tribal scarring that Zed was a member of the West African Ga tribe, some of the fiercest warriors on earth, and it had been the great one's desire to train Zed as a bodyguard for Matthew. But such was not to be, for the hulking warrior was obviously determined to get back to Africa or die by drowning. It seemed now, though, that Zed's journey had been interrupted for a time, as he sat out there in the wilderness of Oyster Island, most likely in some shelter he'd created for himself, and pondered how a huge, black-skinned, mute, scarred and absolutely fearsome son of the Dark Continent might follow the star that beckoned him home.

Even though Zed might not know much about the world, Matthew figured he knew he was very far distant from where he longed to be, and so Zed stole himself a coat and ate fish and, hunkering down in his shelter, waited for his own favorable tide.

That was Matthew's theory, at least, and though they'd never discussed it he was pleased that Greathouse had come to the same conclusion.

"Strange business, your name upon that wall," said Greathouse, at last coming around to the problem at hand. It wasn't the first time they'd discussed it, but now they were problem-solvers under warranty to the governor and, of course, the townspeople who would be paying their fee. "Let's walk," Greathouse suggested—more of a command, really—and again they were off under the bowsprits of the nested vessels.

After a few strides measured by Greathouse's stick, the question came: "Do you have any ideas?"

Yes I do, Matthew thought at once. *I have an idea a snake disguised as a doctor and his equally-reptilious wife have something to do with this, yet I have no proof and I have no sense of what their motive might be. Minus either of those, I am as far from solving this problem as Zed is from walking on the shore of Africa.*

Therefore he answered, "No, I don't."

"Someone," said Greathouse, "doesn't like you."

Yes, Matthew again thought, his jaw set and grim, his face whipped by a cold wind. *And that club seems to be getting larger by the day.*

They came upon a new ship that had evidently just arrived in the past hour or so, for the gangplank was lashed down and the crew was staggering off one after the other in search of their landlegs. A pair of empty wagons stood at the ready, but no cargo was being served to them. On the wagons were painted in red the slogan *The Tully Company*. Referring, as the problem-solvers knew, to Solomon Tully, the sugar merchant, he of the false choppers and a grand and glorious windbag to boot. Yet he was not such a bad sort when reciting his tales of visits to the Caribbean sugarcane plantations, for he could bring forth a heartening description of the tropical sun and the azure water and thus was welcome in any tavern on a winter's day. And there stood on the wharf the stout and ruddy-cheeked man himself, wearing a brown tricorn and over what was assuredly an expensive suit a beautifully-made tan-colored overcoat of the finest weave from the Owleses' tailor shop on Crown Street. Solomon Tully was very wealthy, very gregarious and usually very happy. This morn, however, he was sorely lacking that third attribute.

"Damn it, Jameson! Damn it all to Hell!" Tully was raging at an unfortunate, thin and ragged individual whose beard appeared to be formed from different colors of mold. "I pay you a fine sum for *this* sort of thing?"

"Sorry, sir...sorry, sir...sorry," the unfortunate Jameson replied, eyes downcast and demeanor wretched.

"Go on and get cleaned up, then! File a report in the office! Go on, before I change my mind and send you packing!" As Jameson trudged away, Tully looked toward Matthew and Greathouse. "Ho, there! You two! Wait a moment!"

Tully was on them before they could decide whether to stand still or pretend they hadn't heard. Tully's face was flaming with the last of his anger. "Damn this day!" he raged. "Do you know how much money I've lost this morning?" His false teeth with their Swiss-made gears might appear perfect, Matthew thought, but they made strange little metallic whining noises as Tully spoke. Matthew wondered if the springs were too tight, and if they broke would Tully's teeth fly from his head and snap through the air until they bit hold of something.

"How much?" Greathouse asked, against his better judgement.

"*Too* much, sir!" came the heated reply. Steam was wafting around Tully's head. Suddenly Tully leaned toward them in a con-spiratorial pose. "Listen," he said more quietly, with an expression of pleading, "you two are the problem-solvers—"

Who seem to be much in demand today, Matthew thought.

"—so do me the favor of thinking something over, will you?"

Greathouse cleared his throat, a warning rumble. "Mr. Tully, we do charge a fee for such efforts."

"All right, hang the damned fee! Whatever you feel is proper! Just hear me out, will you?" Tully looked as if he might stomp his feet on the dock timbers like a child deprived of a sweet. "I'm a man in distress, can't you see?"

"Very well," said Greathouse, the picture of calm solidity. "How can we help you?"

"You can tell me," Tully replied, either tears or snowflakes melting on his cheeks, "what kind of pirate it is that steals a cargo of sugar but leaves everything else untouched?"

"Pardon?"

"Pirate," Tully repeated. "Who steals sugar. *My* sugar. The third shipment in as many months. But left behind are items you'd think any brigand of the sea would throw into his bottomless pot of greed! Like the captain's silverware, or the pistols and ammunition, and anything else of value not nailed to the deck! No, this ocean wolf just takes my *sugar*! Barrels of it! And I'm not the only one affected by this either! It's happened to Micah Bergman in Philadelphia and the brothers Pallister in Charles Town! So think on this for me, gentlemen...why does a rat of the waves wish to steal my sugar between Barbados and New York? And *only* sugar?"

Greathouse had no answer but a shrug. Therefore Matthew stepped into the breech. "Possibly to resell it? Or to..." Now Matthew had to shrug. "Bake a huge birthday cake for the Pirate King?" As soon as he spoke it, he knew he had not done a very good thing.

Greathouse suffered a sudden fit of coughing and had to turn away, while Solomon Tully looked as if his most-trusted dog had just peed on his boots.

"Matthew, this is no laughing matter," said the sugar merchant, every word spaced out like cold earth between graves. "This is my *life*!" The force with which that word was spoken caused a sprong-ing noise from within Tully's mouth. "My God, I'm losing fistfuls of money! I have a family to support! I have obligations! Which, as I understand, you gentlemen do not share. But I'll tell you...something's very strange about this situation, and you can laugh all you please, Matthew, and *you* can cover up a laugh with a cough, Mr. Greathouse, but there's something wicked afoot with this constant stealing of sugar! I don't know where it's going, or why, and it troubles me no end! Haven't you two ever faced something you *had* to know, and it was just grinding your guts to find out?"

"Never," said Greathouse, which immediately collided with Matthew's "Often."

"A two-headed answer from a one-headed beast," was Tully's observation. "Well, I'm telling you, it's a problem to be solved. Now I don't expect you to ship yourselves to the sugar islands, but can't you put some thought to this and tell me the *why* of it? Also, what I might do to prevent this from happening next month?"

"It's a bit out of our realm," Greathouse offered. "But I'd suggest the crew taking those pistols and ammunition that are likely locked up in a chest and using them to blast the shit from between a pirate's ears. That ought to do the trick."

"Very good advice, sir," said Tully with a solemn expression and a curt nod. "And surely they would appreciate that advice from their watery graves, since the damned sea roaches have already made it clear that cannons win over pistols any day, even on the Sabbath." He touched the brim of his tricorn with a forefinger. "I'm going home now to have a drink of hot rum. And if one drink becomes two and two become three and on and on, I'll see you sometime next week." So saying, he turned himself about and began to trudge off toward his fine house on Golden Hill Street. In another moment he was a vague figure in the flurries, and a moment after that it was just flurries and no figure.

"I share the need for some hot rum," said Greathouse. "How about a stop at the Gallop?"

"Fine with me," Matthew answered. He might peg a game of chess there, to get his brain working as it should be.

"Good man," said Greathouse. And he added, as they started off side-by-side toward Crown Street: "You're buying."

FIVE

T what was figured to be nearly half-past one in
the morning of the twenty-third of February, four days after Hooper
Gillespie had hooked a grouper, a well-known building on the corner of Crown and Smith streets was ripped apart by an explosion.

Its power was fierce enough to blast the roof into flaming pieces
and crash them down again in the middle of the street. Shutters and
door blew out. The glass of the display window was later found imbed-
ded across the way in the wooden walls of the Red Barrel Inn, which
itself took a buckling that made the last drunks within think that
God's fist had come knocking for their sins. The building on the corner
of Crown Street did not so much burn as it ignited with a flash, like a
torch wrapped with rinds of hog's fat. The noise of the explosion threw
everyone out of their beds from Golden Hill to Wall Street, and even
the late-night entertainment at Polly Blossom's on Petticoat Lane was
interrupted by the echoing boom that chased itself across the town.

"What *now*!" shouted Gardner Lillehorne, sitting up in bed
beside his Princess, whose face was smeared with green cream known
to restore beauty to the ugliest woman in Paris.

"Damn what a noise!" shouted Hudson Greathouse, sitting up in bed beside a certain big-boned blonde widow who had long ago forgotten what the word *no* meant.

"Dear Lord, what was *that?*" asked Madam Cornbury, sitting up in bed beside the bulk of her husband, who was curled beneath the quilt with cork plugs in his ears for his own snoring sometimes woke him up.

And Matthew Corbett sat up in silence in his small but neatly-kept dairyhouse, and he lit a third candle to go along with the two that he kept burning at night to ward off the demons of Slaughter and Sutch. Emboldened by the light, he got out of bed and dressed himself and prepared for the worst, for he had the sure sensation that this blast had claimed something more vital than a warehouse full of ropes.

The flames burned with tremendous heat. The night was filled with sparks and smoke, and lit as orange as an August morn. The bucket brigades worked feverishly. They did their best, but then they had to turn their attention to the surrounding structures to keep the fire from travelling.

And so died the tailor shop run by Benjamin Owles and his son, Effrem.

In its last moments it coughed fire and gasped ash, and standing alongside Effrem in the crowd Matthew watched one black-scorched brick wall collapse and then another, until the rubble covered everything that had meant success in the lives of the Owles family.

"It's over," Matthew heard his friend say, in a very quiet voice. Matthew put his hand on Effrem's shoulder, but it was a small gesture for such a huge tragedy. Nearby, Benjamin Owles stared into the flaring embers; he had been stoic until now, but the end had come and so the tears began to trickle down his face.

A ripple suddenly passed through the gathered throng. Matthew felt it like the passage of a knife's blade down his spine. Someone shouted something, across Crown Street, but it was unintelligible. A murmur seemed to surround Matthew, like the whispering of a secret with himself at the center. "What is it?" he asked the silversmith Israel Brandier, standing to his right, but Brandier just stared at him through his horn-rimmed spectacles and said nothing. Beside Brandier, the laundress Jane Neville also aimed at him an expression of what could only be called uneasy doubt. Matthew had the sensation of being in a dream painted in shades of gray smoke and red embers. The figures around him were less human and more blurred. Someone spoke his name: "Corbett?" but he couldn't see who it was through the murk. Then a man in a purple suit and purple tricorn bearing a white feather came through the gathering and caught his arm, and Matthew recognized Gardner Lillehorne.

"Come with me," said the black-goateed high constable, who held a lantern in his other hand and clasped his lion's-head cane beneath his arm.

Matthew allowed himself to be guided. At his heels nipped Dippen Nack, who made smacking sounds as if feasting on the meat and bones of an earnest young man. "What's this about?" asked Hudson Greathouse, coming forth from the crowd. Lillehorne did not bother to answer. "Stop!" Greathouse commanded, but the high constable was in charge and he listened to no one.

Matthew was aware of others following him; he was creating a small wake, like a ship crossing the icy harbor. He caught sight of Berry and her grandfather, whose nose for news for the *Earwig* must be twitching aplenty. He saw Hudson, of course, close beside him and still mouthing questions at Lillehorne that were not going to be answered. He saw Effrem Owles, who moved like a smoke-stained sleepwalker. He saw the rotund and gray-bearded Felix Sudbury, owner of the Trot Then Gallop. He saw the constable Uriah Blount and the stable owner Tobias Winekoop. And there on his right, keeping pace with this strange procession, were the Mallorys: Doctor Jason and the beautiful Rebecca. They had linked their arms together, Matthew noted. They stared straight ahead, looking to all the world as if they were out on the most relaxed stroll of a midsummer eve. Yet the air was biting and cruel, and so too Matthew saw cruelty in their faces.

The high constable led Matthew to the nearest well, which stood about forty paces east on Crown Street. He released Matthew's arm, leaned forward under the wooden roof that shielded the well from the elements, and he shone his lantern upward.

"Mr. Problem-Solver?" said Lillehorne, in a voice tight enough to squeeze sap from a stone. "Would you care to solve this problem?"

Matthew got beside Lillehorne and, with an inward shudder of what might have been precognition, he looked up along the candlelight.

And there.

There.

Painted in white on the underside of the roof.

Matthew Corbett, for all to see.

"It wasn't noticed at first." Lillehorne's voice was not so tight now as it was simply matter-of-fact. "Not noticed until the fire was almost done. I think, Mr. Problem-Solver, that you most certainly *have* a problem."

"What the *hell* is this?" Hudson Greathouse had thrust himself under the roof to peer upward, and Matthew had to wonder if the man's guts didn't clench just a bit, being so close to what had almost killed him in October. Greathouse at once answered his own question. "This is a bagful of *shit*, is what it is!"

"I seen it first!" said a man who stepped forward from the onlookers. Matthew recognized the twisted-lip face of Ebenezer Grooder, a notorious pickpocket. Grooder's mouth was full of broken teeth, and he sprayed spittle when he spoke. "Does I earn meself a reward?"

"You surely do," said Greathouse, who then hit the man so hard in the mouth that the remaining stubs of Grooder's teeth flew from his head and he went out of one of his stolen boots on his way to an unconscious landing.

"Hold! Hold!" Lillehorne shrieked, like the high register of a little pipe-organ. He had no hope of holding Hudson Greathouse and neither did any other man present. But several men did take the opportunity of picking up Grooder's limp carcass and tossing him aside, but not before one of them got a few coins and an engraved silver ring out of the unfortunate's pocket. "Greathouse, mind you don't end up behind bars tonight!" Lillehorne warned, because his position demanded it. He then quickly returned his attention to the roof's underside. Matthew was still staring up at his own name, trying to figure out why the Mallorys had done it. Because Matthew had refused—and still refused—their invitation to dinner?

"It makes no sense," said Matthew.

"No sense, agreed," said Lillehorne, "yet there it is. What's the message here, I wonder?"

"I don't know." Yet Matthew was beginning to get an idea of it. *Come to us or we will turn this town to ashes.*

He looked around for the doctor and his wife, but they had slunk away. Probably in triumph, Matthew thought. He was aware of others coming forward to see what was to be seen: Effrem did, and left without a word; Marmaduke Grigsby did, and made a sound that reminded Matthew of an inkstamp hitting paper; Berry did, and she bit her lower lip for a moment and gazed at him with sorrowful eyes before she withdrew; and then others came and went, until it seemed to Matthew that the whole town had peered under the roof of this well, and at last Gilliam Vincent thrust his bewigged head forward to take a gander and then regarded Matthew as one would look smelling a piece of spoiled cheese. Matthew came very near playing out the role of Hudson Greathouse and knocking Vincent wig over tailbone, but he restrained himself.

"I didn't do anything!" Matthew said; he was speaking to Lillehorne, yet pleading his innocence to the whole of New York.

"Of course you didn't!" said Greathouse. And then to the high constable: "Damned if you believe he did! What do you think, he's causing these fires and *signing* his work?"

"I think," replied Lillehorne, in a weary tone, "that I will soon be summoned before Lord Cornbury again. Dear me." He aimed his lantern at Matthew's face. "All right, then. I know you didn't do this. Why would you, unless...your recent adventures with a madman scrambled your brains?" He let that hang in the air for a few seconds before he continued. "Tell me: do you know any *reason* this is being done? Do you know any *person* who might be doing this? Speak up, Corbett! Obviously these buildings are being destroyed in your name. Do you have anything to say?"

"He's not on trial!" Greathouse fired back, with rising heat.

"Hold," said Lillehorne, "your temper and your fists. Please." His small black eyes found Matthew once more. "I asked you three questions. Do you have at least *one* answer?"

Matthew thought, *Not one answer, but two suspects.* He frowned in the candlelight. There was no way to link the Mallorys with this. Not yet, at least. And to reveal what he felt true about the connection between Jason and Rebecca Mallory and Professor Fell…no, he wasn't ready for that yet either. Therefore he looked the high constable square in the goateed and sharp-nosed face and said calmly, "I do not."

"No opinion? *Nothing?*"

"Nothing," said Matthew, and he made it sound very believeable.

Lillehorne pulled the lantern's light away. "Damn me," he said. "Corbett, you must be ill. Perhaps you really did scramble your brains out there in the wilderness? Well, you can wager that if Cornbury summons me again, I'm summoning you again. I shall not look upon that countenance alone. Do you hear me?"

"We hear you," Greathouse answered, in a gravelly voice.

"That's all I have with you, then." Lillehorne gave the name one more appraisal. "Someone find me some whitewash!" he shouted toward the commonfolk. "I'll paint this out myself, if I must!"

Matthew and Greathouse took the moment to get away. They slid through the crowd. On the other side they walked east the rest of the way along Crown to the waterfront, where they turned south on Queen Street with the cold salt breeze in their faces.

"You're keeping something back," said Greathouse after they'd gotten clear of all listening ears. "You might throw a frog into Lillehorne's pocket, but you can't frog *me*. Let's have what you know."

Matthew was close to telling. He thought that with the next stride he would tell his friend everything, but…he did not. To pull Hudson into this, when there was no proof? To rouse the man up to action against…what? Shadows? Or against a perceived smirk on the faces of Jason and Rebecca Mallory? No, he couldn't do it. This was a personal duel, himself versus them, and he would have to fight this particular battle quietly and alone.

"I don't know anything," he replied.

Greathouse stopped. In the faint light from the lanterns of New York, his expression was impassive and yet the intelligent coal-black eyes knew. "You're lying," he said. "I don't take kindly to lies."

Matthew said nothing. How could he? There was no use flinging another lie at the truth.

"I'm going home," Greathouse announced after another moment. Home being the boarding-house on Nassau Street operated by the kindly but rather nosy Madam Belovaire. Matthew had already wondered if Greathouse was sneaking the widow Donovan into his abode, or if she was sneaking him into hers. Whichever, there was likely a lot of sneaking going on. *"Home,"* Greathouse repeated for emphasis. He drew the collar of his coat up around his neck. "When you decide to stop lying, let me know. Will you?" He took a stride in the direction of Nassau Street before he turned toward Matthew again, and Matthew was amazed to see on the great one's face a mixture of anger and hurt. "Remember," Greathouse said, "I'm always on your side." And then he walked away with stiff-backed dignity, following the stick that tapped lightly on the earth.

Matthew stood as a solitary figure against the wind.

His thoughts were jumbled. They were as confused as he felt his life to be in the present. He began walking home, north on Queen Street. He passed by the masted ships and the slave market. The wind, stronger and colder, came at him from different angles as if to upset his balance on the world. Passing the last of the docked ships, his shoulders hunched forward and his chin tucked in, he cast his gaze toward the darkness of the sea. So much darkness, he thought. It was an immense dark, and he felt it pulling at his soul. He felt it grasping at him, taunting him, making a mockery of his name and a falsehood of his desire for truth.

And that darkness also had a name, he mused.

That name was: Professor Fell.

He stopped abruptly, and peered out into the black.

What had that been? Just that quick flash of red? Far, far out, it had been. If it had really been, at all. Was he seeing red signal lamps in his mind? Was he going the path of Hooper Gillespie, and the next step would be muttering to himself in the aloneness of his mind? He waited, watching, but the red lamp—whatever it had been, *if* so—did not reappear.

He recalled what Hudson Greathouse had told him about Professor Fell. *It may be that by now Fell is on the cusp of creating what we think he desires: a criminal empire that spans the continents. All the smaller sharks—deadly enough in their own oceans—have gathered around the big shark, and so they have swum even here...*

This big shark, Matthew thought, had big teeth and big eyes. It saw everything, and it wanted to eat everything. Even—perhaps most especially—the heart of a young man who had begun life born to a Massachusetts plowman and his wife, both dead early, and then sent to the pig farm of an aunt and uncle on Manhattan island. Escaping that prison of pigshit and drunken abuse on a haywagon, he had fallen in with a group of urchins on the waterfront, later to be caught literally in the net of the law and bound over to the town's orphanage. There he had been educated by an intelligent and kindly headmaster, yet there was more misery to come. Of course, more misery...such was the essence of life. It either built or broke a character. And then finding himself clerk for two magistrates, and at last being offered the position of problem-solver for the Herrald Agency by none other than Katherine Herrald herself. *At last?* No, Matthew was certain the story of his life was far from being finished, yet at the moment he felt himself lost in a kind of limbo, a gray kingdom that demanded the right choice and proper action for his release yet he knew not what that was to be.

And swimming out there in the dark sea, the big shark. Circling and circling, getting ever closer.

A hand touched his shoulder. He almost shot out of his boots.

"I'm sorry!" said Berry, drawing back. She was wearing a black coat with a hood, and nearly was one with the night. "Were you thinking?"

"I *was*," he managed to answer, when he was certain he could speak intelligibly. His heart was still a snare drum being whacked by a madman's fist. "Don't you know better than to sneak up on a person?"

"Sorry," she said, and added with a touch of hot pepper, "*again.*"

Matthew nodded. It was best to retreat a bit rather than risk the wrath of a redhead. "All right, then. It's done." He shrugged; his heartbeat was settling down, more of a trot now than a gallop, which made him think he could use a good drink of ale from that so-named tavern on Crown Street if Felix Sudbury had opened up for business from the bucket brigaders and fire-watchers. New York was truly becoming a town that seemingly never slept. Very soundly, at least.

"Matthew?"

"Yes?" He'd been looking at the ground, and now he raised his eyes to hers.

"Do you have any ideas? I mean...*really.* Do you?"

"None," he answered, a little too quickly.

She came a step closer. Her gaze was intense and no-nonsense and she would not take *none* for an answer. "That's not like you," she told him. "You always have ideas. Some perhaps better than others…" She paused. He knew she was thinking of a certain trick involving horse manure they'd used to avoid having their faces ripped off by hawks in a rather frightening experience last summer. "Some *much* better than others," she went on. "But you always have ideas. If you didn't, you wouldn't be…" She paused again, thinking. "Who you are," she decided to say. "So if you do. Have any ideas, I mean. I would care to hear them, if you would care to tell."

He stared at her, from a distance that seemed both terribly long and at the moment uncomfortably close. She was asking him to trust her, he realized. Because she could look into his eyes and see that he had something hidden there, in that brain of his, and she was wanting to be part of it.

For a few seconds many things went through Matthew's mind. What he might say. The right choice of words, the proper tone of voice. A complicated sentence that skirted the truth, to hold her curiosity at bay and certainly keep her out of danger. But what he came up with was as simple as two words.

"I can't."

Then he turned away from her and walked toward Crown Street and the Trot in search of a late-night drink.

Berry remained where she was. The wind seemed colder; she drew her coat tighter around herself. *Oh Matthew*, she thought. *Where are you going?*

It seemed he was always going somewhere. Always on the move. Always away from where she stood, it seemed. She would never tell him that sometimes in the morning she watched through the kitchen window to see him come out his door. That she marked always how fresh-scrubbed he was, and clean-shaven, and ready for the world. Except since coming back from the wilderness, he did not seem so ready for the world. He was different, and he would not talk about it but she could tell his step was slowed and his back always slightly hunched as if expecting a blow. Perhaps not talking about it was killing him, very slowly, inside. Perhaps, she thought, if he could trust her enough to tell her...then he could truly come back from the wilderness, for some sweet and innocent part of him had been left there, and she greatly missed it.

She wished very much that she might tell him her theory of her bad luck. She'd had several suitors, of course, who'd fallen under the spell of her bad luck. And poor Effrem, always stepping into a gopher hole or a mud puddle when walking beside her. Poor Ashton, trying to be so collected and worldly when he first came calling for her, and then breaking the heel of his shoe within the next few minutes. It had become a little joke between them, how many heels he'd broken at her side.

But Berry remembered a day in the summer when she'd been sketching at the end of a long pier. The pier she'd chosen had been a horror of worm-eaten boards and gaps and damage caused by the progress of the elements and boats with unproficient captains. She'd chosen that place because she'd wished not to be bothered.

Then *he'd* come along.

May I come out? he'd asked.

And she'd said, *As you wish*, and thought he was asking for a certain swim in the drink.

She'd kept drawing on her sketchpad and waiting to hear him holler as he fell. Because surely her bad luck would be the bedlam queen of this rotten wharf, and he wouldn't make it halfway to her before he went down.

Waiting...waiting...

And then, quite suddenly, he was standing at her side. She'd heard him breathe a sigh of relief, and she might have released her own sigh of relief from under her straw hat, and she'd said with a mischievous smile, *Nice morning for a walk, isn't it, Mr. Corbett?*

His answer, somewhat shaky, had been: *Invigorating.*

And turning back to her work, which was to capture the colorful essence of a Breuckelen pasture, she'd thought *Any other man would have fallen. Why didn't* he?

That was still her question.

Because her theory of her so-called bad luck, at least as regards young men, was that it steered her in the right direction as much as a compass steered any adventurous ship. Yet Matthew's destination was unknown to her. Surely it seemed he often looked right through her, as if she existed only as a mist he might brush away like silken cobwebs.

I want to mean something to you, she said silently to him, wherever he was on his journey into the dark. *Please...will you let me?*

But on this night there was no answer. There was the just the winter wind, touching with cold fingers the face of a hopeful young girl.

He was not coming back this way anytime soon, she decided. Therefore she left her position of watchful waiting, and she went back home to go to bed.

SIX

WHEN a knock came at his door Matthew was in the midst of shaving. He looked away from his mirror, which displayed the rather pale visage of a tired young man, and called to the door, "Who is it?" The door being only six feet away from where he presently stood.

No one answered. Except here came another knock, strong and insistent.

"Yes?" Matthew asked heatedly; he was in no mood for games this early in the morning. Was it Berry, making merry? No, she'd not been in such a mood last night and wouldn't be this morning, either. It was just after seven by the candle clock on the wall, which was a candle in a metal holder marked with bars to indicate the hours. "Can I help you?" Matthew inquired, his razor ready for another stroke along his chin.

"I am here," said the voice of a man beyond the door, "to speak to Mr. Matthew Corbett."

It was not a voice Matthew recognized. Muffled by the door, yes, but still…it was an odd accent. He put his razor down on the tabletop, next to the dish of soapcream and the bowl of water. "Who are you?"

"A visitor," said the voice, "of great importance to you."

Matthew had never heard an accent like that before. English, yes, but with a definite…what would it be termed? A lilt? A strange softness? It held a slight rolling of the 'r' but it was certainly not Scottish. His curiosity took hold. He pulled a gray cloak around his bedclothes, quickly washed the rest of the soap from his face, and then he unlocked and opened the door.

He found himself staring at a white sash that crossed the white blouse covering a massive chest. On this sash was centered an ornament studded with pearls and turquoise stones. The man wore baggy white pantaloons and black boots. A multicolored cloak edged with lamb's wool was draped loosely over his shoulders, which appeared to be as wide as the doorway. The man, who must have been at least six and a half feet tall, leaned down to show his face. He was wearing a white turban, its wrapping also secured by a pearl-and-turquoise ornament.

"My name is Sirki," said the thin-lipped mouth under the hooked nose in the broad brown face. "May I enter?"

Matthew felt what could only be termed a tremor of terror. It tingled across the back of his neck and along his arms. It travelled down his legs and rooted his feet to the floor. This was because he knew the name. *Sirki*. He remembered it well, and for good reason.

After he had killed Mrs. Sutch, he'd found in her possession a letter written in a flowing script that had been cited and dated *Boston, the fifteenth of August*, and that had read: *Dear Mrs. Sutch, Please carry out the usual preparations regarding one Matthew Corbett, of New York town in the New York colony. Be advised that Mr. Corbett resides on Queen Street, in—and I fear this is no jest—a dairyhouse behind the residence of one Mr. Grigsby, the local printmaster. Also be advised that the professor has been here lately in the aftermath of the unfortunate Chapel project, and will be returning to the island toward mid-September.*

The professor requires resolution of this matter by the final week of November, as Mr. Corbett has been deemed a potentially-dangerous distraction. As always, we bow before your experience in these matters of honor.

And the letter had been signed, *Sirki*.

Rebecca Mallory had stolen this letter from Number Seven Stone Street, and may have destroyed it. Matthew had known that the letter concerned the whys and hows and whens of murder: his own. And now here stood in his doorway the man who'd composed that letter, and who had sent it to the murderous Mrs. Sutch on behalf of Professor Fell.

"Don't be afraid," said Sirki. His dark brown eyes under thick, arched black brows were calm and untroubled by any idea of violence. Unless the man was a very good actor or under supreme self-control, Matthew thought. He glanced quickly toward the razor. Six feet had never seemed so far.

"Oh," said Sirki, his voice soft and serene for a man of his gargantuan size, "I could kill you long before you might reach *that*, young sir."

Matthew had no doubt of it. He let go all thoughts of heroics with a razor.

The question was calmly repeated: "May I enter?"

Matthew was at a loss for words. He wished he could conjure up something wicked and cutting, but all he could find was, "Do I have a choice?" Even then, his voice trembled. This man was of a monstrous construction.

"Certainly you do." Sirki offered a pleasant-enough smile. He had what appeared to be two small diamonds fitted into his front teeth. "You always have a choice, young sir. I trust you will make the right one now."

Matthew decided, in the presence of this obvious killer, that it was good to be trusted. He stepped back, and as Sirki bent over and entered the dairyhouse Matthew saw the man's eyes mark both the whereabouts of the razor and the position of Matthew's hands.

"May I close the door?" Sirki asked. He waited politely for a response. When Matthew nodded, Sirki closed the door. He did not lock it. "Cold outside today," Sirki said. "A bitter wind is blowing in from the sea. I don't care for cold weather. Do you?"

"The weather doesn't care for my opinion," Matthew said.

"Ah. Yes. Correctly so." Again there was a restrained smile and the flash of diamonds in the teeth. Matthew had taken note of three small gold rings in each of Sirki's earlobes. He was a well-ornamented East Indian, for Matthew knew this man had to have come from a country where turbans were as common as tricorns. The manner of dress, the accent—though Matthew had never heard such an accent before—originated from the land of Akbar

The Great. Also an indicator was the cloyingly-sweet aroma of sandalwood incense that had arrived in the man's clothing.

"I may sit?" Sirki motioned to a chair. Matthew nodded again, though he was concerned about the chair's survival. Sirki eased himself into it and stretched out his long legs. "Ah. Now, I'm in... how would you say?...pig's paradise?"

"Hog heaven," Matthew suggested.

"Exactly. Let me show you I have no weapons." Sirki lifted his arms, shrugged off his cloak and patted around his midsection.

"Do you need any?"

This time a grin burst forth. "No, I do not."

Matthew reasoned it was time to keep his mouth shut. He backed away until he met a wall, which still put him within a dangerous arm's length of Sirki.

"I mean you no harm," came the quiet voice. "Neither does the individual I represent."

"Who might that be?"

Sirki's smile now became a bit chilly. "Young sir, let's be adults here. I've come a long way to speak to you. And I speak to you in the voice of the individual I represent."

Matthew said nothing; he waited, though he was thinking that the last time he heard from Professor Fell it was in the form of the "death card," a vow that whoever received the bloody fingerprint would be—as Sirki's letter to Sutch had said—a matter requiring resolution.

"He wishes to meet you," said Sirki.

Matthew didn't know how to respond. Should he be terrified? Or flattered?

"He wishes you to come to him," said Sirki. "Or, rather...be *brought* to him."

It was doubly difficult now for Matthew to speak, but he forced the obvious question: "Where is he?"

"A short sea voyage away." Sirki placed his elbows upon the arm rests and steepled his brown fingers. "A journey of—weather permitting—three weeks."

Matthew had to laugh. It sounded harsh. Whether it was the release of tension or not, he didn't know. But this entire scene was ridiculous, a comedy farce. "Three weeks by sea to meet *him*?

And my return voyage, I assume, would be in a casket? Or...more likely...a basket?"

"Neither, young sir. You would be returned promptly and safely." Sirki paused for a moment, gazing around the neatly-kept but cramped confines of Matthew's home. "I should think you'd enjoy a sea voyage, after living here." Another two inches and Sirki's boots would be scraping the opposite wall. He frowned. "Can't you afford anymore space?"

"My space is fine as it is."

"Ah, but you're incorrect there. Your space—and I mean by that the distance you've chosen to keep between yourself and the two persons who approached you in the autumn regarding a dinner invitation—is *not* fine. It is not fine with them, with me, or with *him*. In fact, it is offensive to him that you won't have dinner with such noble citizens."

"Noble citizens?" Matthew would have laughed again, if he hadn't thought it might be his last laugh. "I imagine they're criminals. Part of Fell's pool of sharks? And I'm guessing those are not their true names, either. Is he really a *doctor*?"

"Yes, he's a doctor," came the tranquil reply. "Quite a good one, in London some years ago. His speciality is a knowledge of poisons. But when he is required to don the guise of a practising physician again, he does."

"A question for you," Matthew ventured. "What is Fell a professor of?"

A slight smile worked across the thin lips and then vanished. "Life," said Sirki, "in all its many forms."

Matthew couldn't let this chance go past. He said, "You mean... *taking* life in all its many forms?"

"No, I mean what I said. The professor is a sterling disciple of life, young sir. When you meet him, ask him to explain his interest. He'll be happy to educate you."

"I don't think I could stand such education."

"But the truth," said Sirki, his gaze fixed on Matthew, "is that sometimes the education we do not want is precisely the education we need, and that will benefit us the most." He shifted his position in the chair and again glanced left and right, at the walls, and then up toward the ceiling. Matthew saw a hint of disturbance ripple across his features. "This is almost like a *cave* in here, isn't it? I wouldn't be able to live in a place like this. I would value my sanity too much."

"I'm perfectly sane," said Matthew.

"That remains to be seen. Twice now you've been offered an invitation." Sirki slowly pulled his legs in, like an animal about to leap upon its prey. Matthew tensed and wished he could get to the door but the East Indian giant was in the way. "You will note there have been some incidents in your town just lately. Involving fire? The destruction of property? And your name being prominently displayed? Those are *reminders*, young sir, that time is growing short. The professor's patience is also growing short. If I were you, I wouldn't wish to dawdle very much longer."

"Who's burning those buildings and painting my name there? *You?*"

Sirki smiled like a cat and touched a finger to his lips.

"Why does Fell want to see me, if he doesn't want to *kill* me?"

"You," said Sirki, "are needed."

"Needed? How?"

"I will leave that for your dinner hosts to explain. They also will explain the arrangements for transportation. Now, listen to me carefully. As I said, I speak in the voice of the individual I represent. You are to go to the Mallorys' house tonight, at seven o'clock. Mark it: *tonight*. You will enjoy a very fine dinner—for Aria is an excellent cook—and you will be told the particulars. But not *everything*, you understand." The front teeth diamonds sparkled with candlelight. "Some things are best left unknown, until you need to know. I will tell you that no harm will come to you. He vows this. Unless, of course, an act of God sinks the ship and then his vow would not be valid. But we have an able captain and crew standing by. The ship is…" He waved a hand in the direction of the sea, "out there. It comes closer to shore by night."

Aria, Matthew was thinking. Rebecca Mallory's real Christian name. And what might the surname be? "You haven't told me why he wants me. Until I hear that, I'll give no thought to going anywhere. Certainly not to have dinner with those snakes."

Sirki was silent, staring at Matthew. Obviously, he was thinking it over. His face was as expressionless as a burnished mask.

"Professor Fell," Sirki said at last, "has a problem. He is in need of a problem-solver. What did he tell me, *exactly*? He said... he wishes for the service of a providence rider. A scout, he said. Someone to forge ahead and mark a trail. That would be an apt description of you and your work, would it not?"

Matthew was dazed. He couldn't believe what he was hearing. "Fell wants to *hire* me?"

"It's somewhat more complicated than that. Your dinner hosts will explain further." The huge man suddenly got up from his chair and seemingly filled half the room. Really, he literally *did* fill half the room. He had to bend a little at the waist to keep his turban from brushing the ceiling. "Pardon my intrusion," he said, "but I did want to keep you on the right progression, young sir." As Sirki moved toward the door, Matthew pressed himself against the wall to stay out of his way.

Matthew considered himself courageous enough, but not fool-hardy. He let Sirki get to the door and open it before he spoke again. "What if I choose not to go? Another building will burn and my name will be on prominent display?"

"What you don't grasp," came the smooth reply, "is that the professor can do wonderful things *for* you...and terrible things *to* you. I would not push his patience, young—" He stopped himself. "May I call you *Matthew*? It seems we should be on more friendly terms, if we're to work together."

"You can call me the young sir who follows you to wherever you're going and then proceeds to the high constable's office. After which I expect there'll be a visit to Lord Cornbury. You won't be very difficult to find, I'm sure."

"No, not difficult at all," Sirki agreed with a quick and completely insincere smile. "I'm at the Dock House Inn. Room number four. And I've already met both those gentlemen. I introduced myself several days ago, as a businessman from Delhi interested in furthering friendship and direct trade between my country and the town of New York. I believe I impressed them. And *no*, Matthew, I'm neither starting the fires nor writing your name. That's being handled by persons of less status than myself. It wouldn't do to dirty my robes with powder and paint, would it?"

"Gunpowder, you mean? That's what causes the explosions?"

"The *professor* causes the explosions," Sirki said, with a slight lifting of the thick black eyebrows. "Even as far away as he is, he is entirely capable of destroying your world, Matthew. He wants a providence rider. He wants especially *you.*" Sirki paused to let that take deep root. "I should give the professor what he wants, my friend. Otherwise…" He clasped his huge hands together and then abruptly drew them apart.

"Boom," Sirki said, and with a sweep of his multicolored cloak he left the dairyhouse and closed the door firmly behind him.

Matthew didn't know if that last gesture was supposed to convey another explosion of a building or his own destruction, but its point was well met. He saw no need to follow Sirki; he had no doubt the giant had lodgings at the Dock House Inn and that he'd made the acquaintances of both Lillehorne and Cornbury. Both of those individuals would listen to him for perhaps ten seconds before he was thrown out of the office. Actually, they wouldn't even deign to hear him. *What possible reason might there be for a businessman from Delhi to be involved in this?* Lillehorne would ask. And for that, Matthew would have no answer. Without the letter bearing Sirki's name, he had nothing.

Which put him back at the beginning.

He ran a hand over his face. He had to get to Number Seven Stone Street. There was nothing pressing at the moment, but there was some correspondence to attend to. He went to the water basin to reapply shaving soap and finish the job. He wasn't aware that his hand was shaking until the first stroke along his chin produced crimson. He stared into his own dark-shadowed eyes in the mirror. How to get proper rest these nights was the question. He dabbed at the cut on his chin with a handkerchief. He was getting used to the sight of his own blood, which further disturbed him.

Another disturbance had happened at the Trot Then Gallop last night, when Matthew had gone in to have a cup of ale along with some of the other regulars and men who'd manned the bucket brigades. He'd found himself the focus of several curious stares and passing whispers, even from those he knew well. Felix Sudbury was kind enough, but even the Trot's owner seemed to want to draw away from him, to keep him at arm's length. Perhaps, Matthew wondered, did Sudbury fear an explosion and burning of the Trot, simply because Matthew had marked the place with his presence? Israel Brandier was the same, and also Tobias Winekoop the stable owner. Did Winekoop fear that by speaking to Matthew too cordially, his horses might go up in flames? Therefore Winekoop too kept his distance, and over in the corner the Dock Ward alderman Josiah Whittaker and the North Ward alderman Peter Conradt sat talking quietly and now and then spearing Matthew with a glance that said *Whatever you're doing or causing to be done...cease it.*

Matthew had taken his ale and sat down before the chessboard. It was still set up from the last game he'd played with Effrem several nights before, but of course on this cold black morning Effrem had other concerns on his mind rather than pawns and knights. So Matthew had not touched the pieces, but rather played the game out in his mind, taking up both sides and being fair about it. No one had approached him in his hour there. No one had spoken to him, though it was apparent in the strained quiet that some were speaking *about* him. And when he'd finished his ale and the mental game was done to his satisfaction he'd returned the cup to the bar, said good morning to Felix—who was cleaning out cups and did not answer—and then he left the Trot for home.

It had seemed a very long walk, the air he breathed still stained with smoke and smelling of burned dreams and collapsed industry.

And now this. Sirki.

And behind Sirki, the professor.

Matthew finished his shaving. He washed his face and dressed in a dark suit, befitting his mood. Actually, he only had two suits and both were dark, one black and one brown. So much for the young dandy who'd strutted through the town in the autumn. No matter; there was this thing to deal with now.

But *how?*

They were expecting him tonight at seven o'clock. A wonderful dinner, prepared by a woman named Aria. *Your dinner hosts will explain further.*

Matthew thought of Hudson Greathouse, and what the great one might say to this. There was no need in getting him involved; Matthew had nearly gotten his friend killed once before. This time might finish him off. Professor Fell needed one problem-solver—or

providence rider, as he termed it—and there would be no room for
Hudson on this journey, unless it was into a grave.

What to do? Matthew asked the image in the glass. What to *do*?

He recalled on the back of the letter from Sirki that the rubbing of a pencil lead had brought up the imprint of a wax stamp: the
many-tentacled octopus symbol of Fell's desire for criminal domi-
nation. The letter, written and signed by Sirki.

Where might that letter be now, months after the falsely-
named Rebecca Mallory had stolen it from Matthew's office?
Destroyed? Burned in a fireplace? Or might it still be in the house
that sheltered them? Tucked in a drawer somewhere, or put into a
box that might be locked yet a key could be found if one searched
diligently enough?

Matthew thought if he could get hold of that letter, he could
take it to both Greathouse and Lillehorne as hard evidence. Sirki
and the false Mallorys would find themselves behind the same bars
where the young assassin-in-training Ripley had sat in eerie and
unbroken silence before he was sentenced to London's Newgate
prison by Lord Cornbury and sent off aboard ship in December. *If*
the letter had survived, and *if* it could be found.

Was it worth the try?

Matthew put on his woolen cap, his gloves and his black fearnaught coat. It was time to leave his cave. He blew out the candles,
and with much on his mind he strode purposefully out the door into
a snow-dusted scene of winter.

SEVEN

WITH a gust of icy wind, seven o'clock had arrived.
Matthew Corbett stood outside a small whitewashed house on
Nassau Street, between Golden Hill and Maiden Lane. He could
see candlelight through the windows. Many candles were lighted in
there, it appeared. The false Mallorys obviously saw no need to limit
their illumination for the sake of their pocketbooks. He pressed his
side against the darkness of a wall in a short alley between two houses
across the way, lest someone peer out the candle-bloomed windows and
see him trying to decide just what in the name of God he ought to do.

God, unfortunately, was silent on the issue. Matthew pulled his
coat tighter about himself, as if more warmth might help his mental
processes; it did not, nor was it in truth much warmer. He rubbed
his gloved hands together, and still he paused and pondered the
situation. To enter that house, where they waited for him...or not?
A constable walked past, following his green-glassed lantern, and
never looked right nor left.

Matthew knew of the professor's penchant for poisons. It
would be simple for a debilitating drug to be put into the food or

drink, and then where would Matthew find himself at first light? He saw a figure pull aside a gauzy window curtain and look out upon the street, but whether it was the man or woman he didn't know. He remained perfectly still until the curtain was dropped and the figure gone, and then he released in a white mist the breath he'd been holding.

By his reckoning it was now ten minutes or so past seven. They would be wondering if he was coming or not. All those candles, burning in expectation of a visitor. He had to go, he decided. How else to possibly learn where the letter might be, if indeed it still survived? No, he couldn't do it, he decided in the next moment. It was too dangerous. But if he didn't go…what would be the next tragedy inflicted upon New York—and his friends—in his name?

He had to go.

No…wait…think it out a little more. Once inside that house, he was at their mercy.

Damn it, he thought. They've got me in a trap.

He had to go.

He started to leave his position of relative safety. He saw a figure come to that window again, peer between the curtains and then withdraw. He took a step forward, toward whatever fate awaited him.

"What are you *doing* out here, Matthew?"

He nearly cried out in alarm, and spinning around he found a dark-garbed figure standing a few feet behind him. But he knew the voice, and once past the shock he realized Berry Grigsby must've come through the alley from the opposite end. She was wrapped in her black coat and hood but the red tresses flowed free and he could make out her face by the reflected candlelight of the house across the way.

"Oh my *God*!" he was able to croak. That wasn't enough. "Oh *Jesus*!" he said, his face still contorted with pure fear. "Are you *insane*? What are *you* doing here?"

"I'm following *you*," she said, with a defiant note. She lifted her chin like a weapon. "I know…it was wrong. Possibly. But I saw you leave your house and I saw you turn to the left when you usually turn to the right. So I knew you weren't going to the Trot. Or to Sally Almond's. Or to anywhere you usually go. I know it was wrong. Possibly," she repeated, as if asking for his understanding.

"Matthew, I'm worried about you. I mean…I'm *concerned*. As a friend. You see?"

"I see you shouldn't be here!" He glanced quickly over his shoulder at the house. Oh, they were starting to grit their teeth in there by now. They were starting to sharpen their knives and pour out their gunpowder. He couldn't believe how stupid he was getting. His lack of attention could have been his finish, if she'd been one of Fell's killers. "Step back," he told her. "Step *back*!" She obeyed, and he stepped toward her to make up for the pace he'd taken to break his cover. "Are you spying on me? Is that it? Berry, I have a dangerous job to do! You can't be coming up behind me like this!"

"*Dangerous?*" Her voice tightened, and instantly he knew he should not have said that. "Dangerous how?" She looked past him, across Nassau Street. "That's Dr. Mallory's house. What's the danger here?"

"I can't explain it."

"Yes," she said. "You can."

"Go home," he told her.

"I wouldn't leave now if…if…" She mentally searched for a fearsome image and found it. "If Brutus the bull came charging down this alley. No! You can't tell me something is—"

"Keep your voice down," he cautioned.

"Is dangerous and then tell me to go home, like a child," she finished, adjusting her volume to nearly a whisper. She saw a movement in the Mallory house. Someone was looking out the window. Then whoever it was retreated. She aimed her gaze at Matthew. "What's going on?"

"My business. I told you to—"

Berry took a step forward and suddenly they were standing face-to-face. Matthew smelled her: an aroma like cinnamon and roses, even on a frigid night like this. Her eyes never left his. "You," she said quietly but firmly, "are not my keeper. Sometimes I wonder if you are even my friend. Well…I'm *your* friend, whether you want me or not. I care about you, and if that causes you discomfort, sir, you will have to be discomforted. Do I make myself—"

The word *clear* never was uttered.

For Matthew Corbett felt a wall within him crack and give way, just a little, and the sliver of warm light that came through that crack caused him to put his hand to the back of Berry's neck and kiss her full upon the lips.

It was a scandalous moment. Such things were just not done, in this sudden uncomplicated way. But Berry did not retreat, and her lips softened beneath Matthew's, and perhaps her mouth responded and urged the kiss to be longer and deeper than Matthew had first intended. However it happened, the kiss went on. Matthew felt a thrill of excitement. His heart was pounding, and he wondered if she felt the same. When his lips at last left hers she made a soft whisper that might have been either a breathy exhalation of surprise or an entreaty for continuation of this intimate discussion. He looked into her eyes and saw the sparkle of diamonds. She wore a sleepy expression, as if she suddenly was in need of the bed.

It hit him what he'd just done. He removed his hand from the back of Berry's neck, but she didn't move away. He was appalled at his adventurous conduct; it was terribly wrong, and terribly ungentlemanly of him. He had the sensation, however, that Berry did not share his inexactitudes, for she gazed upon him as if he had just stepped down from a star.

He did it to silence her, he decided. Yes. She was getting a little too loud, and her voice might have carried to the house across the way. Yes. That's why he'd done it. No other reason. And now he was shamed by it, but it had served his purpose.

"Be *quiet*," he said, though he didn't know why he said that since Berry wasn't speaking and it seemed she couldn't find her voice anyway.

A latch was thrown. Matthew looked over his shoulder and saw the door opening. Instinctively, he put an arm across Berry to shield her from injury. Someone was leaving the house. It was the woman. Aria To-Be-Named-Later. She wore a full-skirted gown under a purple cloak, and on her head was a matching purple hat with mink earmuffs. She turned to the right and walked briskly away from the house, following Nassau Street toward town. Her boots crunched on the hammered bits of oyster shells that covered the street, for Lord Cornbury had not yet seen fit to release public money for the laying of cobblestones in this area.

Over oyster shells, cobblestones or horse figs, Aria Whomever was walking as if she had somewhere very important to go. Matthew reasoned her destination was likely the Dock House Inn, where she might give a message to Gilliam Vincent for the East Indian giant in room number four. However it was coded, the message would be: *Matthew Corbett did not obey.*

Good for Matthew Corbett, he thought. But possibly bad for the building owners of New York?

Berry grasped his hand. "What *is* it?" She was whispering, for she'd also caught the scent of danger. "Are the Mallorys involved?"

"Involved in what?" His own whisper equalled hers.

"I don't know, that's what I'm asking. What are they involved in?"

Matthew watched the door. It didn't open again. The doctor was staying inside on such a wintry night. Best to let the female snake slither along Nassau Steeet to do this job.

"The Mallorys," Berry insisted. "Are you listening to me?"

"No," he said, and caught himself. "*Yes.* I mean..." He looked into her eyes once more. The diamonds had diminished; an excitement not for him but for the intrigue of the evening had for the moment pushed everything else aside. It was, however, equally as intense. "I can't tell you why," he said, "but I know the Mallorys have something to do with those fires. And with my name being painted around, to cause me trouble."

"But *why*, Matthew? It makes no sense!"

"Not to you, no. Nor to anyone else. But to me, it makes perfect sense." He regarded the house again. Fine if the letter was in there, but if so...how was he going to get it? Of course, there were two major problems: he had to get into the house when the snakes weren't coiled up in there and he had to find the letter. If it had not been destroyed. If, if and if. This plan, he thought, might have been hatched from the inmates at Bedlam.

"That way," Matthew said, motioning toward the other end of the alley. He followed Berry, hoping in this darkness he didn't complete his current stay in the Gray Kingdom by twisting a foot on a loose stone. But they made it through the alley onto Smith Street without incident, and there they turned to the right onto Fair Street and then onward toward Queen and the Grigsby property.

"I think," said Berry as they neared the house, "that you owe me an explanation. I can make you a pot of tea. Will you tell me?"

"Your grandfather has the biggest ears in town," he reminded her. "And even when he pretends to be sleeping, he's listening. So… no, I will not."

She stopped walking, turned toward him and actually grasped a handful of his coat. "Listen to me, Matthew Corbett!" she said, and she cast off some heat which was fine for Matthew because he was near freezing. "When are you going to trust me?"

When I don't have to fear for your life, he thought. But he kept his expression stolid and his voice as cold as he felt when he said, "My business is *my* business. That's how it has to be."

"No," she answered without hesitation, "that's how you want it to be."

"Yes," he said.

"You just kissed me. Or did I imagine that?"

And then he said the thing that he had to say, but that cut him like a knife across the throat: "I was confused."

The statement lingered in the air. The words, once released, came back upon the one who'd uttered them and added a stab to the heart to the already-cut throat. For Matthew saw in Berry's face how much she was hurt, and she blinked quickly before any tears could rise up and so they did not, and by force of will she kept her face composed and her eyes clear. And she said, in a voice that seemed already distant, "I see."

They were two words that Matthew would never forget, for they meant that Berry saw nothing, and that he could not correct her vision.

She released her hold upon his coat. She drew herself tall; taller than he, it seemed. She said, "Goodnight, Matthew," and she left him. He watched her walk with great dignity toward her grandfather's house, where a lantern showed in a window. She entered the house without a backwards glance, and Matthew drew a long, deep breath of freezing air and continued on to his own abode, which had never felt smaller nor more common.

EIGHT

MATTHEW again stood in the cold. It seemed that everywhere now was cold to him. It was a chilly world these days, and not just by the weather. He was again in the alley opposite the house occupied by the false Mallorys. Three nights had passed since his encounter there with Berry. He'd not set eyes upon her since. All to the best, he thought. This business was indeed dangerous, for tonight he was determined to get inside there and find that letter, if indeed it still existed.

The house was dark. Not a candle showed. Matthew had been standing here as last night, about the same hour after midnight, but tonight there was a major difference. Nearly forty minutes ago, he'd seen a coach drawn by four horses pull up before the house. Lashed atop the coach had been a black-painted wooden box about five feet in length, three feet wide and the same deep. A sea chest, Matthew had thought it might be. The kind that might be found in a captain's cabin. Two burly men serving the coach had struggled to get the chest down, and both the false Mallorys had emerged from the house to help them. In time the chest was lugged into the house, and the door closed. Lanterns had moved about inside. Then Matthew had waited to see what developed, his senses keen on the fact that whatever was going on, the false Mallorys wished no one to be witness.

On the gray morning after his brusque dismissal of Berry, Matthew had gone to work at Number Seven Stone Street with a mission in mind. He had climbed the steep and narrow stairs to the loft that housed the office of the two New York problem-solvers and also—if one believed such stories—the ghosts of two coffee merchants who had killed each other on this side of the darkened glass and now on the other side continued their eternal feud. If one believed such stories. And in truth Matthew had heard numerous bumps and thumps and the occasional echo of muffled curses floating through the air, but it was all in a day's work at Number Seven. Besides, Matthew had gotten used to the spirits, if indeed they still lingered and fought here over the respective sizes of their coffee beans, and all one had to do to stop the noises was say, *"Silence!"* good and loud, and order was restored for a while.

On this morning Matthew had not been interested in any spirit but the live one of oversized build and sometimes bullying nature sitting behind his desk writing a letter to a certain Mr. Sedgeworth Prisskitt of Charles Town who—

"—is asking for a courier to escort his daughter Pandora to the annual Cicero Society Ball at the end of March," Hudson explained. "She must be—shall we say—not so much in the area of looks, if her father has to pay for an escort." He frowned. "I wonder what the Cicero Society is. Ever heard of it?"

"No, I haven't." Matthew busied himself hanging his fear-naught up on a hook.

"Want to take this one on? The money's good."

"No."

"Not at all curious?"

Of course he was, but he was on a mission. "Not at all," he lied.

"Liar!" Greathouse put his quill into its rest. "All right then, what's on *your* mind?"

"Nothing in particular. Other than buildings being burned and my name being painted around."

Greathouse grunted and grinned. "At least they got the spelling right! So pull your face off the floor and smile sometime, won't you?"

Matthew walked past the polite fire that crackled in the small hearth of rough gray and tan stones. He went to the pair of windows that afforded a view of New York to the northwest, the wide river and the brown cliffs and gray hills of New Jersey. A boat loaded with crates of cargo on its deck was moving north along the river, the wind spreading its brown sails wide. Another smaller boat held two fishermen, sitting back-to-back. *Like Hudson and myself*, he thought as he surveyed the scene. *Our hooks in the water, and we have no idea what's down there waiting to bite.*

"This is becoming a habit," Greathouse observed.

"What is?"

"Your lack of joy. Why don't you go to Charles Town? Take the packet boat. Escort Pandora Prisskitt to the ball. Eh? Go have some fun for a change."

Matthew heard a murmur, but no words. He was watching the fishermen, and he was deciding how to begin what he had planned to say to his friend. He decided it was to be: *The Mallorys are behind the burnings. I know this to be true. And I didn't want to drag you into this, but—*

"Matthew!" said Greathouse emphatically, and the younger man redirected his attention. "Let me ask you. What do you think of Abby Donovan?"

The question was so unexpected that Matthew could think of no possible response.

"Go ahead," Greathouse urged. "Tell me what you honestly think." He nodded when Matthew yet hesitated. "Go ahead!"

"Well...I think she's—"

"Yes, and you would be correct!" If possible, Greathouse's grin broadened. He leaned back, precariously so, in his chair. "She is one *hell* of a woman!" Matthew thought the great one might be in danger of breaking his jaw if he grinned much broader. "Yes, she is! And *kind*, Matthew. Really she is. An angel. But...she's a devil when she needs to be, I'll tell you."

"I don't think I want to hear this."

"Oh, don't be such a prude! Are you twenty-three or fifty-three? Sometimes I can't tell. But listen...about Abby. She and I are getting along very well, Matthew. *Very* well. I'm saying, sometimes when I'm with her I'm not quite sure where she stops and I begin. Do you know what I mean?"

Looking into Hudson Greathouse's grinning face, with its left charcoal-gray eyebrow sliced by a jagged scar, Matthew knew all too well what his companion in problem-solving meant. Though Greathouse had already had his share of women, and perhaps many other men's shares too, he was falling in love with Abby Donovan. Not to be bothered that the scar through his left eyebrow had been made by a broken teacup thrown by his third wife. Not to be bothered that there were likely scars on his heart made by several women, and more scars on their hearts than his. Not to be bothered by any of that, because Hudson was falling in love.

"I do know," said Matthew, and with that short sentence he put aside what he was going to tell the great one, for this was not Hudson's business. No, today—and perhaps tomorrow too, and the day after that—the man's business was *love*.

"Things may happen," was the next comment, made by an excitable boy where a rough-assed man had been sitting a moment before. "Really, Matthew. I mean it. Things may happen."

"You mean…*marriage?*"

The sound of that word in the room seemed to knock a little of the wind from his sails, and he blinked as if he'd just been slapped with a wet rag but quickly he recovered from whatever thought of reality had intruded. "She is one *hell* of a woman," he repeated, as if Matthew needed to hear that again.

But the hellish woman and her equally hellish male partner down at the end of Nassau Street still had to be dealt with. Perhaps a cloud passed over Matthew's face, because Greathouse's mood changed just as quickly and he asked with true concern, "Is there anything else you wanted to talk about?"

Matthew shook his head.

"This thing will clear up, don't worry yourself." Greathouse picked up his quill and started to continue with his letter of regret to Mr. Sedgeworth Prisskitt. "It's a lunatic, I think. Or someone with an axe to grind against you. Now…I don't know how they're blowing those buildings to pieces, but don't let it burden you because that's exactly what they want."

"Agreed," said Matthew, in a quiet voice.

"I doubt there'll be any more of that. The point's been made, I suppose. Some lunatic doesn't like you. Maybe because of all that hero-worship the *Earwig* gave you last summer. *Oh.*" A thought hit him like a musket ball from the blue. The lines across his forehead deepened. "You don't think it could be one of Fell's people, do you?"

The moment of truth, Matthew thought. It stretched, as he wondered if the truth was worth putting at risk the life of a man who was so enamored of one hell of a woman. *Marriage*, indeed!

"I think it's a lunatic," spoke Matthew, "just as you say."

"Right. Probably one of your friends escaped from the asylum down there." Greathouse blew a breath of relief, now that Matthew had turned the discussion away from Professor Fell. "Don't fret, the constables are on watch."

"Now I *will* fret," Matthew said.

"Absolutely positive you don't wish to meet Pandora Prisskitt?"

"Absolutely," he said, "and pardon me, but I'm going to go to Sally Almond's for breakfast."

"But you just got here!"

"True, but my correspondence can wait and besides, I'm hungry."

"I'll go with you, then."

"No," said Matthew, as gently as he could. "I have some things to think about. I believe this morning I should secure a table for one."

Greathouse shrugged. "Suit yourself. And don't be running up a bill over there, hear me?"

"Yes, father," Matthew replied dryly, and when Greathouse gave him a startled look the younger problem-solver took his black coat from its hook, threw it over his shoulders like the wings of a raven and left the office for the street below.

Matthew shivered a little, in the cold alley across from the darkened house. After the sea chest had been lugged in, the two burly men had emerged from the house followed by the so-called Mallorys. Doctor Jason was carrying a leather case and a fabric bag, and Aria a larger fabric bag. Their belongings? Matthew wondered. Were they leaving for good? They had talked for a few minutes, and one of the men had motioned in the direction of the sea. Matthew could hear no words, only the hushed current of conversation. He couldn't see everything because the coach and horses were in the way. But then the two men had gotten back up on the driver's bench of the coach, the false Mallorys had climbed into the more comfortable seats, and the coach had been driven off. His teeth near chattering, Matthew longed for the mercies of a warm blanket, yet if the snakes had departed—even for a short time—this was the night to search for a letter.

Matthew found it hard to believe that they weren't coming back at some point. Though possibly not tonight? He had the sensation of emptiness about the house. Of desolation. And…something else, as well?

Tonight, as last night, he'd brought a shielded lantern, its candleglow guarded by metal ribs that could be folded down or pushed open over the glass. He picked it up from the alley's ground and pressed a spring-driven lever that made the ribs open like the petals of a flower. Illumination spread. The lantern was held by a polished walnut pistol-grip at its base. In fact, it *was* a flintlock pistol, and could fire a ball through a barrel secured underneath the candle. It was currently loaded and powdered, ready for firing. A very nice invention, purchased from Oliver Quisenhunt of Philadelphia, among other items of interest to problem-solvers who might need to extricate themselves from problems of a particularly dangerous nature.

His heartbeat had quickened. He knew what his next move must be. He would have to leave his place of relative safety, cross Nassau Street and go to the door of that darkened house. He looked along the street, in search of the coach returning, but there was no sign of it. Time was not to be wasted. As he approached the door he was thinking how he might get inside. He could break a window on the other side of the house, he decided. But first he must try the door. He hadn't been able to see if the Mallorys had used a key or not. Because life in New York was not a idyllic paradise all locks were used quite regularly, unlike the situation that had existed in that paragon of community virtue called Fount Royal. But still, the door must be tried.

It was, as he'd expected, locked tight. Matthew walked around the house and behind a shoulder-high white picket fence. He was searching for a window to break with the pistol grip of his lantern. Have to be careful with that, as the sound of breaking glass would carry. Already a dog was barking stridently a few houses away. He managed a grim smile against the cold that pressed at his face; he was about to add *house-breaker* to his list of accomplishments.

On the other side of the house was a short flight of wooden stairs leading to a narrow back door. A window was set on either side of the door. One of those appeared a likely candidate for breakage. Matthew went up the stairs and chose the window on his right. He hesitated, listening. Did he hear the sound of horse hooves on oyster shells? No, it was his imagination. His heartbeat pounded in his ears, enough to make him hear horse hooves that were not there.

A quick pop with the grip and it would be done. Careful not to shoot oneself with this device, though the hammer was not cocked. Before Matthew took aim at the glass he reached out with his other hand to try the door...

...and the knob easily turned. The door opened, and it seemed to Matthew that darkness rolled out to meet him.

He held the lantern before him and entered the house, closing the door at his back. Now his heart was a true runaway. Steady, he told himself. *Steady.* He breathed in and out a few times. He smelled pipe smoke and perfume. Smelled things that had a medicinal odor, as this dwelling also held the doctor's treatment room. Matthew crossed the planked floor of a nicely-ordered kitchen. Yes, Aria would be an orderly cook, would she not? Ashes in the kitchen hearth still smelled of a fire not long past. A hallway beckoned on the left. Matthew eased into it, and the lantern's glow showed a trio of doors, one on the right and two on the left. The doctor's office was what Matthew sought. Anywhere there might be papers. Of course, the letter he was looking for might have been ashes in that kitchen hearth months ago, but still he had to seek. It was his nature.

He opened the first door on the left. Candlelight fell upon a bedroom. A woman's frills and finery. A little writing desk and a broad chest of drawers, upon which were several bottles of what Matthew assumed was fragrance. The bedspread of woven pink and lavender. Aria sleeps alone? Matthew wondered, noting the bed for one. He went to the writing desk and found the solitary top drawer was empty. The chest of drawers likewise held nothing but some woolen lint. Matthew opened a closet and found three very lovely and intricately-fashioned gowns hanging there on pegs. Also two pairs of Aria's shoes remained on the floor. So…were the snakes slithering back tonight, or not?

He crossed the hall to the door on the right. The treatment room with a trio of beds. No windows in here. Matthew recalled this room; he'd been in here in the autumn, laid low from a poison dart. He had sweated rivers in the third bed, having consumed a thick coca-based concoction Doctor Jason had given him to defeat South American frog venom. A long story, that had been, with a happy ending: he had survived. Various vials of medicines and what-not stood on shelves, along with several important-looking leatherbound tomes. Matthew turned his attention toward the doctor's desk that stood across the room. As he walked toward it, following his candle, the toe of his right boot hit something that nearly tripped him. He aimed the light downward. A small red throwrug was crumpled up around an object of some kind. Matthew pushed the rug aside with his boot and stood staring down at an iron ring. It lifted, he saw, a wooden trapdoor set in the floor, which in this room was made of brown bricks. He grasped the ring and pulled up; the trapdoor opened with a creak of hinges, and there yawned a square of more darkness. A ladder led down. How far down, and what was down there? His light couldn't tell. But that was best saved for later. He left the trapdoor open and continued on to the desk.

Again, hands had not been idle in this house. The desk was nearly empty but for a few squares of paper. Upon examination, they appeared to be bills for treatments signed by various personages. Nothing unusual about them, save for the one signed by Edward Hyde, Lord Cornbury for the admininistration of medicine for… did that scribbling say *anal warts?*

Matthew returned the bills to the desk and wiped his fingers on his coat. Then he took stock of the trapdoor once again. What was down there, and why? Old files, perhaps? A bundle of letters? Perhaps the letter he sought?

Possibly. And possibly he had best check the next room on the left first, before he started descending ladders into dark holes. He had a sense of urgency now, and he was listening intently for the sound of horse hooves and coach wheels. He left the trapdoor open and went to the next chamber.

One step in, and a shiver of fear paralyzed him.

This obviously was Doctor Jason's bedroom. It held a black chest of drawers, an oval full-length mirror on small wheels, a black leather chair and a canopied bed.

And on that bed lay, pressed together side-by-side, two naked bodies.

It suddenly occurred to Matthew what had been inside the sea chest.

He caught his breath and stepped forward. His light revealed gray flesh. The bodies were of a man and a woman. The woman's sagging breasts and dark-haired vagina were pitiful. It was a skinny corpse, each rib showing. The man's body was also ill-fed, and had the tattoo of an eagle just below the collarbone. Two toes were missing from the left foot. The hands were stiffened into claws, which seemed to be reaching in agony toward the canopy above.

But the thing that made Matthew recoil in true horror was that neither corpse had a head.

The heads had been cut off. The neckstumps were all ragged flesh and old brown crust. Matthew smelled the dried blood and the dusty sweet reek of flesh on the edge of decay, yet it was obvious these souls were not very long-departed from this earthly realm. He wanted to lower the lantern, yet lowering the lantern meant he would be giving the corpses over to the dark and if he imagined that one of them gave a sudden jerk of arm or leg he would puddle himself quite soggily.

He backed away, keeping the lantern up and the flintlock's barrel aimed at the dead as if he might have to kill them again. Where were the heads? he wondered. In the leather case carried out by Doctor Jason? And what in the name of God were two headless bodies doing lying in the man's *bed*?

"...pay for this dirty business," someone said.

Matthew's hair might have stood up under his cap. He froze at the doorway, a heart-pounding, vein-throbbing, near-puddling wreck of nerves.

Two men were speaking in the kitchen. "Should've got more, I say. Dirty and dangerous, too. You saw them shorts on there!"

"Aw, shut your hole! Bullett knows his trade."

Matthew heard footsteps. Rough men wearing rough-heeled boots. They were coming back along the hallway. He peered through the door's crack and there they were, each carrying a lantern. One man was lugging a burlap sack over his shoulder.

"Damnable job, this is," said the complainer with the burden, who was met with a snort either of derision or accord.

Matthew realized with a fresh start of alarm that they were coming to this room. He saw only one place to retreat to: the other side of the bed, where he might lie flat on the floor. He quickly got into position and pressed the lever that dropped the lantern's ribs and closed off all illumination.

"You hear that?"

"Hear what?"

"Somethin' made a noise."

They pushed through the door. "It's the echo inside your fuckin' head," came the retort. Then: "Ewww, ain't they pretty all laid out like lovers? Kinda tugs at your heart-strings, don't it?"

"It *don't*. Help me with these and let's get out."

Matthew heard the *thump* as the sack was laid down on the floor perhaps five feet from his hiding-place. Something was dumped out, and made its own noise. He heard one of the men say, "Come on, hurry it up!" after which there was a hissing sound. A second hissing followed. Truly, this was a den of snakes. Acrid smoke stung Matthew's nostrils. *You saw them shorts on there*, the complainer had said.

Shorts? It dawned on him that the meaning must be *short fuses*.

The men were lighting fuses with their candle flames, and whatever they were preparing was about to blow the house to pieces.

He swallowed hard and stood up. As he came off the floor, he cocked the pistol and opened his lantern. Light streamed out, catching one of the jackadaws lighting the last of four fuses that went into the same number of black cylindrical objects about a foot in length.

"Stop that," Matthew said. The men fairly leapt from the floor. One gave his own explosion in the form of a fart. Matthew aimed his flintlock between them. The four fuses hissed and smoked, throwing blue sparks in their progress. "Stomp those out!" Matthew commanded.

"Who the *hell* are you?" the farter asked.

"Stomp those out!" Matthew repeated. The fuses were burning dangerously near their entrance holes into the cylinders, which appeared to be wrapped in oily black leather. *"Now!"*

"Sure, sure," said one man, lifting his hand to show Matthew his palm. Then, as if they'd practiced this cue for just such a predicament, the second man threw his lantern at Matthew's head. It hit Matthew's shoulder as he twisted aside, and the flintlock pistol went off from a convulsive twitch of the trigger finger. Smoke bloomed, the bullet smacked into the opposite wall, and the concussion made the ribs of Oliver Quisenhunt's device snap shut, cutting off Matthew's light. It occurred to him, as the men rushed from the room and smoke whirled around him, that the apparatus needed more testing.

It then occurred to him, quite sharply, that the fuses were burning into their bombs, and though he was able to crush out two with his boot the other two snaked away and flared brightly as they entered the cylinders.

Matthew ran.

Through the door into the hallway, and just as he got out the Devil shouted in his ears and a fierce hot wave of Hell picked him up off his feet and flung him like a ragdoll through the doorway into the doctor's treatment room.

NINE

S OMETIME in the next few seconds, as Matthew lay crumpled on the brick floor and the whirlwinds of flame gnawed at his coat, he realized that if he was going to live he would have to get out of this house.

He thought the roof might have blown off already, or at least a goodly portion of it. Pieces of fiery wood were falling about him. His ears made a roaring sound, but hollow as if he were in an underwater cavern. Everything hurt: shoulders, knees, backbone, neck, jaw, teeth. He felt as if his muscles and sinews had been stretched long and then jammed tight. There was a red haze before his eyes; he thought they might be swollen with blood. He swallowed blood and felt it streaming from his nose, which might have been broken in his collision with the bricks. Already the fire was surrounding him. It was a hydra-headed beast, growing bright orange horns, talons and teeth and tearing through the house. A piece of flaming timber crashed down on the floor about three feet from his right thigh. Cinders stung his face. He was at the center of a world full of red-hot hornets. Then he was aware that his fearnaught was on fire, and his own coat was going to eat him alive.

He gritted his teeth and with the effort of the damned began to roll to get the fire out. Whether he was successful or not, he didn't know, but for the moment he was alive. Was his cap aflame too? He snatched it off. It glowed with a dozen red cinders but it was not yet burning.

He began to crawl. To where?

To anywhere but here.

And now the real Matthew Corbett emerged. It took hold of the young man who had found himself in a gray kingdom of indecision and regret, whose mind had become a sluggish set of gears that did not mesh, whose spirit had been pummelled and thrashed by the memory of murder in the wilderness. The real Matthew Corbett peered out from desperate red eyes in a bloodied face. The real Matthew Corbett, who had survived so much pain and hardship and dangers that might have put any other man on his knees or in his grave, recognized that he was in the burning wreckage of Doctor Jason's treatment room. He saw the ceiling, riddled with tentacles of fire like Professor Fell's octopus, beginning to collapse. He saw the open trapdoor on the floor.

He saw a way out.

Mindless of all sensation but the need to survive, he began to pull himself toward the open square in the bricks.

Once there, he did not hesitate. He turned himself to descend the ladder into the pool of darkness below, and reaching up he got hold of the trapdoor's inner ring and slammed it shut over his head just as a new rain of cinders fell from above.

Then he lost both grip and balance, and he tumbled downward into what might have been a hundred-foot hole.

But more like ten feet. He recalled the breath whooshing from his lungs, though by this point any more pain was simply a proof of life. He was on his back in the dark. No, not quite dark; he could see the glow of flames through small cracks in the trapdoor. Would the fire eat through it? He didn't know. Would it steal his air? He didn't know. Was he burned and smoking? Didn't know that, either. He was in, as Hudson Greathouse might have said, one shit of a pickle.

He faded in and out. Fire sounds, burning away. The smell of smoke, scorched cloth and blood. He began to laugh at something, though he wasn't sure what it was. Maybe he was weeping; again, he didn't know. But at the center of his mind the real Matthew Corbett held rule, and that calm personage said *Hold on*.

Definitely he was laughing, he decided. Chuckling, really. The way those two bastards had jumped off the floor. And then he thought of Berry and his cold voice saying *I was confused* and the bitter tears watered his face.

No, he realized. Not bitter tears.

It was actually water, and it was streaming down through the cracks in the trapdoor.

The bucket brigade at work, he realized. Fighting to save the Mallorys' house. And perhaps they could save what was left of it, for this time not all the firebombs had ignited. Did he call out *Help me*? Or was it just *Me*? For he *was* himself, found once more in fire and blood, and he thought *My name is Matthew Corbett, and by God I am going to live.*

He thought the worst of the explosion had gone upward or been absorbed by the walls of Doctor Jason's bedroom. The thing was, he had not resisted the blast. He had not had time to resist, and though he was in pain he didn't think he had suffered any broken bones.

There was a lesson to be had there, he decided. He vowed to decipher its meaning later, if he survived to do so. At the moment he had more important and more strenuous work to do. And it was going to hurt, but it had to be done.

He turned himself over on the cellar's dirt, found his way to the bottom of the ladder, and began to pull himself up.

At last—somehow, with a will to live that rivalled his episode in the well at Fort Laurens—Matthew reached the top. He placed a hand against the trapdoor. It was not hot, but it was going to be an effort. He was stewing in sweat, he had very little strength and what remained was departing on a fast horse. He pushed. And pushed. And pushed some more. "Help me!" he shouted, but could he be heard? He had to keep pushing.

The trapdoor opened a crack. Matthew got the fingers of his left hand into it and kept the pressure—a dubious term, in this instance—up with his right hand. He put the back of his head against the trapdoor and shoved upward with everything he had, and suddenly the trapdoor came open with a crisp *crackle* and *slam*.

Climb up, he told himself. *And stand up*.

He entered a smoking, still-burning ruin where a house had been. The flames were low, however, having been for the most part bested by the bucket brigade. Matthew climbed out and sat on his knees, his head lowered; he was trying to make sense of what he should do next. *Ah, yes!* he recalled. *Stand up!*

He got to his feet by the shakiest of efforts. Instantly he threw up what tasted like a sick man's portion of smoke. Then he began to stumble through the wreckage, his fearnaught hanging in burned tatters from his shoulders and his face freighted with blood. He became aware of shadows in the smoke, moving hither and yon with their lanterns through this new world of burned and broken timbers, smoking piles of rubble and things that had melted and reformed into objects unrecognizable as being of the earth and possessions of man. Matthew staggered toward one of the shadows and said—or thought he said, because of the shrill ringing in his ears— "Do you have some water?" He had no idea why he said that, other than he was terribly thirsty.

The shadow came forward and became a shape that became a man that became Marco Ross, the blacksmith. Ash-blackened and filthy, he was...but then again Marco Ross was usually ash-blackened and filthy, so it was all the same.

The blacksmith, a big enough man for his job, stopped in his tracks and gave a gasp like a weakling woman who is in need of air lest she faint dead away.

"*Corbett?*" he whispered.

It is I, Matthew thought, before his knees collapsed and he went down like a brain-hammered bull.

⟩•⟨

"News," said Hudson Greathouse, pulling the visitor's chair closer to Matthew's bedside. He went on without waiting for an invitation from the grape-colored lips in a face mottled with black bruises. "McCaggers has found the corpses. At least...some of what could be found. He's got two blankets over there with the...uh... remains laid out. It's not pretty."

Matthew thought it must be terribly ugly. And horrible for Ashton McCaggers, whose gorge rose at the sight of a bloodied finger. Piecing together two charred bodies would be a scene plucked from McCaggers' worst nightmares. For the eccentric and soft-stomached coroner, it would be at least a four bucket day. And without Zed to help him, the more the worse!

"I'll say it again." Greathouse stared out the window at the late-afternoon sunlight. "Everyone has a time. This wasn't yours...but it was a damned close call." His deepset black eyes left the window and found Matthew's red-shot swollen eyes. "When are you going to tell me what you were doing in there?"

Two days of soup for every meal had left Matthew in a less-than-cheerful mood. Add to that the plaster-covered gash that had taken eight horse-gut stitches under his left eye, sundry other cuts and scrapes on forehead and chin, a nose that had nearly been broken but was so sore now even the flutter of a nostril was pure agony, and enough bruises on face, arms, legs, chest and back to make him appear a spotted beast from the heart of Zed's homeland, and he was a bedful of joy. But he was greatly thankful for a certain trapdoor and cellar, which had held at its dirt-floored bottom some items of broken furniture and a few shelves holding bottles of murky liquid probably used by the doctor in his treatments.

"Tell McCaggers he won't find the heads," said Matthew, in a voice that still sounded smoke-choked.

"I'll tell him," Greathouse said after a short pause.

"The Mallorys," Matthew went on, "wanted to appear to be dead. They got the corpses from somewhere. God only knows."

"*I* believe you," Greathouse said after a longer pause.

Matthew nodded, but gingerly because any movement yet pained his multitude of strained muscles. He knew exactly what his friend meant. He could still see Gardner Lillehorne standing over his bed, yesterday morning here at the Publick Hospital on King Street. The high constable in his cardinal-red suit and red tricorn, with the same crimson glare at the center of his small ebony eyes and his teeth on edge.

"You have secured your place in infamy now, Mr. Corbett," said the offended redbird. "Staggering out of that burning ruin? With your name painted on the alley wall across the street? And here you're telling me there were two naked and headless corpses in the bed of Dr. Jason Mallory? My Christ, boy! I thought I was talking nonsense when I said you were addle-brained after that misadventure in Pennsylvania, but I'm thinking now you *must* be half-crazy." He let that linger for a few seconds before he darted in again with, "And the other half *insane*. Do you wish to tell me how you were to be in that house, or shall we hear that in Cornbury's office?"

Matthew had not answered. It seemed to be too much effort, and anyway even the muscles of his jaws were hurting.

"You are in a *situation*." Lillehorne had leaned over the bed like a threatening bonfire, ready to catch sheets and bedclothes burning. "You are going to have to explain yourself, sir. If not to me and to Lord Cornbury, then before a court of law."

"I'm being arrested?" Matthew had managed to ask.

"Consider yourself so. I'll think up some appropriate charges. Breaking and entering would be the first."

"The back door was open," Matthew reminded him.

"Unlawful *entrance*, then. Mark it. Criminal mischief. Unwillingness to aid an official investigation. Mark those as well. Do I make myself clear?"

"In a muddy way," Matthew said, his tone as dry as October's leaves. His face, too, was a study in mottled stone. He left it at that, and after another moment the high constable made a low noise in his throat, gave a pinched expression that conveyed volumes of both frustration and disgust, and strode out of the hospital's wardroom with the lion's-head ornament of his cane slapping against his red-gloved palm.

And good riddance, you bastard, Matthew had thought.

"McCaggers," said Hudson Greathouse, as he stretched his legs out before him, "believes the corpses to be those of a man and a woman. Just as you've said. Only he's of the belief that they're the Mallorys, caught in the blast and fire."

"What they wished him to believe," was Matthew's terse reply.

"McCaggers has found fragments of women's clothing and the heel of a shoe. His question is: if the Mallorys were leaving for good—sneaking away in the middle of the night, as you've put it— why wouldn't Rebecca have taken her gowns?"

"What they wished him to question," said Matthew.

Greathouse tapped a finger against the musketball-sized cleft in his chin. "Yes," he said. "All right, then. But…" And here Greathouse's brow knit, and Matthew knew his friend was struggling to make sense of what could not possibly make sense. "But *why*, Matthew?" came the most urgent question. "Tell me. *Why?*"

"I can tell you why the corpses have no heads," Matthew ventured. "Because if the heads were found, McCaggers might determine the bodies were not those of the doctor and the damsel. By some remnant of hair or the facial bones, I would think. Possibly one or both of the murder victims had rotten teeth. They wanted to be careful, lest McCaggers find something that would throw their plot off its course."

Greathouse did not speak for a time. He seemed to be watching the crawl of sunlight across a green-painted wall. "Murder victims," he repeated, tonelessly. "Their plot."

"Correct. Two people were murdered and decapitated to serve as stand-ins." Matthew thought better of that last term. *"Lie-ins,"* he amended, with a small, tight and painful smile. "I imagine the victims were plucked off the street in some nearby town. Probably a beggar and a prostitute, who would not be easily missed."

"A beggar and a prostitute." Greathouse sounded as if he were standing in a church reciting a particularly uncomfortable Bible passage.

"Look at me," Matthew directed.

Greathouse did.

But in his eyes Matthew saw the blankness of the green-painted wall, and with that came the realization that even such a friend as Greathouse had his limits of belief. Or perhaps it was just that, to save the situation, Greathouse had simply ceased thinking.

"They put the corpses in the house," Matthew said, a little unsteadily, "to make it appear that they are dead."

"They *were*, you said."

"What?"

"The corpses. They were already dead. I would think so, if they were headless."

"The *Mallorys*," said Matthew. "Or whoever they are."

"A beggar and a prostitute, you said."

"No! The Mallorys. They put the corpses in the bed knowing they would be blown to pieces and burned to crisps. Then they could make it look as if I had something to do with it, by painting my name on the alley wall."

"And why would you have something to do with it?" The eyes narrowed, just a dangerous fraction. "You didn't, did you? I mean... I *believe* you."

"It's a plot," said Matthew, who felt himself spinning away from the world, "to draw me in."

"Draw you into *what*?"

"The plan. The...summons. I can't..." Matthew leaned his head against the pillow. He had to close his eyes for a few seconds. When he opened them again, nothing had changed. Or had Greathouse quietly moved his chair back a few inches from the bedside?

"I'll go fetch the doctor," Greathouse offered, in as sympathetic a voice as Matthew had ever heard.

"*No,*" Matthew said, and the power of his declaration stopped Greathouse from leaving his chair.

Then the great one—the man of action, the lover of wild widows, the swordsman scarred by battles and life—looked at Matthew with something like pity in eyes gone sad.

He reached out to grasp his friend's shoulder, and he said quietly, "I know you went through tribulations in that Slaughter incident. I know...they must have been terrible. And even about those, you won't tell me. But I know, Matthew. Because I see how you've been..." Here he paused to agonizingly search for the proper word, neither too hard nor too soft. "*Affected*," he went on. "By what happened. So who could blame you, for...suffering. For—"

"Imagining murders and plots?" Matthew interrupted, in a tone *descrescendo*.

"I don't understand any of this," Greathouse continued, as if the question had never been spoken, "but I do believe someone is trying to...further affect you. For whatever reason, I don't know. I believe *you* know, but you're not going to tell me, are you?"

Matthew said nothing; he, too, had begun to watch sunlight crawl across the wall, and with it the waning afternoon.

"I can help," said Greathouse. "I *will* help. I swear it."

It was close. So very close. Matthew felt it behind his clenched teeth, wanting to get out. Therefore he clenched his teeth just the harder, which further pained the bruises on his face.

After a while, Greathouse removed his hand from Matthew's shoulder.

He stood up from his chair. "I'd better be getting along. Having dinner tonight with Abby. I've never known a woman who enjoys meat so much." He took his coat and tricorn from their wallpegs. Slowly, he shrugged into the coat and positoned the tricorn just so upon his head, as if to give Matthew more time. He grasped his walking-stick and put its tip on the planks before him in preparation of his first troubled step. "I'll be back first thing in the morning. Agreeable?"

"Not necessary," Matthew said, "but appreciated." He offered Hudson as much of a genuine smile as he could muster. "Thank you. And I hope you also enjoy your banquet. But do tell McCaggers he won't find the heads."

Greathouse nodded. He strode a few paces away and then stopped once more. In the row of five narrow beds across from Matthew lay the elderly Edde van Evers, a onetime Dutch frigate captain now frail and dying of perhaps too much landsickness. To Matthew's left, in the last bed in the room, was Gideon Bloomensord, a farmer laid low when he had fallen down a rocky embankment and broken both legs. This morning the body of Martin Brinker had been removed from the bed directly to Matthew's right and bound in shroud wrappings for deposit in the cemetery, the patient having not responded well to Dr. Quail Polliver's leech treatment. Of the three remaining patients Matthew was certainly the most alert, as the first was heading silently for his last voyage and the other was raving in fevered pain that the opium had not yet diminished.

"I'll be back first thing," Greathouse repeated, as possibly a draught of medicine to himself at leaving Matthew between creeping death and inescapable agony. Then he pulled his coat collar up around his neck and went through the hallway toward the front door and—most likely—the warm and welcoming embrace of womanflesh.

Matthew rested his head against the pillow and closed his eyes. He was very tired. The two attendants, the two-hundred-pound Mrs. Sifford and the ninety-pound Mr. Dupee, would be coming around soon to offer up some kind of soup, for better or for worse. The sunlight moved, and moved some more. The afternoon dimmed and darkened into blue evening, and in the glow of lanterns hanging from their pegs Edde van Evers breathed heavily as if inhaling the salt air of seven seas, Gideon Bloomensord gasped in his opium-induced slumber, and Matthew Corbett slept uneasily with the taste of lukewarm codfish soup still in his mouth.

He tossed and turned a bit, expecting to be roused by Hudson Greathouse first thing in the morning, or—before that—by Gardner Lillehorne with more questions.

Therefore when he was shaken awake by the pain of his bruises and sore muscles he was quite surprised to see night still hard black against the windows. One might further say he was *shocked* to see standing over his bed, washed in the golden lamplight, a giant from East India.

The diamonds in the front teeth sparkled. "Matthew?" said Sirki in his soft and easy lilt. "It's time now, please."

"*Time?*" Matthew sat up, which caused him further pain but there was no avoiding it. The hospital was silent. Either Van Evers had passed onto the leeward side of this world or he was sleeping like a newborn, and Bloomensord had also sunken into perfect peace. "Time for *what*?"

"Your decision," said Sirki, his brown face pleasantly composed. "Which will be destroyed next? Tobias Winekoop's stable, with all those beautiful and noble horses? Or the boarding house run by Madam Belovaire, with its boarders now fast asleep? Most of them, that is." He gave a small, polite smile. "Your decision, please. And don't concern yourself about me. I am content to wait."

TEN

ET out of here," Matthew answered. His heart had seemingly tied itself into a Gordian Knot. "I'll call for help."

"You might," Sirki answered back, with a brief nod of his turbanned head. "But you will find that no help arrives. And yet...I *do* have help."

As if emerging from the giant's body, two men came forward from behind him to stand at the foot of Matthew's bed. Matthew instantly recognized the pair of scoundrels who'd lighted the fuses in the house of the so-called Mallorys. One of them carried a rolled-up item with wooden rods protruding from it. A stretcher, Matthew realized.

"We have come to carry you in comfort to your appointed destination," said Sirki. "Unless you had rather witness another example of our new gunpowder?"

"With me unable to walk, my name written on a wall will make no sense."

"Ah!" Sirki aimed a long forefinger toward the ceiling. "But did it ever make sense, young sir? I believe by now that your compatriots in this town—even your closest friends, perhaps—have begun to doubt your word and your sanity. It may make sense to no one, yet either a stable or a boarding house will burn to the ground this night…if you refuse this hospitable invitation." Whether he'd intended the near-pun or not was unknown, since his face remained expressionless. But the dark eyes beneath the thick, arched black brows were intense and watchful, and they were aimed upon Matthew like musket barrels.

Matthew may have shivered. He wasn't sure, but it was cold in here and the blanket was thin. "How did you get in?"

One of the men, the very same who'd thrown his lantern at Matthew's head, gave a little chuckle. Prideful, Matthew thought. "Lockpicking is Croydon's claim to art," Sirki said. "A low claim, but there it is anyway. As for the two unfortunates who spend the night here watching over their charges, the fat woman and the thin man are both sleeping soundly."

"You've killed them?"

"Not at all! Unless a gift of tea from India could be considered deathly. I had occasion to speak to Dr. Polliver this afternoon. I offered up this gift as a token of friendship. Also the tea has healing powers I thought he might care to try. Possibly he's sleeping very soundly in his bed at home."

Drugged tea, Matthew thought. Of course. Fell's people relied on drugs to move their mountains.

"The professor," said Sirki, "wants *you*. He needs you, really. Because you seem to…um…get results, shall we say. And you've impressed him, Matthew. So now I shall tell you that it is time for your choice. One of three. Yourself, the stable or the boarding house. And *yourself* shall be returned here after this business is completed, whereas the others…sadly beyond the point of return. We have the key to your house, taken from Dr. Polliver's safebox. Croydon will go to your miniature abode and remove whatever clothing you might need. You will be taken to a waiting boat, to be rowed out to meet the larger vessel. All we require you to do at the moment is roll onto this stretcher."

At that pronouncement, Croydon and the other jackal unrolled the brown cloth and held the stretcher between them. Sirki moved aside so Matthew could do as instructed.

Matthew hesitated. He swallowed hard. His bruises pulsed, and his pulse felt bruised. For all the fear that danced its Mad Robin within him, he couldn't suppress a grim smile. How many times had he felt alone at midnight, with the hard dark pressing in and no sign of morning? Many times before, and with luck he would survive this one as he had survived the others.

No, he decided. With more than luck.

With every skill of reasoning and power of concentration he had. That, plus some good old fashioned lowdown strength of will.

He glared into Sirki's eyes. "Get out of the way," he told the giant. "I'll walk."

Sirki obeyed at once. "I thought you would, young sir. That is why I placed your boots and clothing on the floor before I woke you." The dark eyes darted toward Croydon's fart-partner. "Squibbs, find Matthew a cloak or a blanket worth its weight in wool. A heavy coat might do, which you'll find hanging in the room where the sleepers doze. Move, please. It disturbs me to think my voice goes unheard."

The way the East Indian killer said that, Squibbs might well have let loose another buttock-blast. However, Squibbs moved forthwith at the speed of terror.

Matthew eased himself to a sitting position on the side of the bed. The pain came up his sides like metal clamps snapping shut rib-by-rib. A red haze whirled before his eyes. Damned if he'd let himself pass out. He bit his lower lip until the blood nearly oozed.

"Croydon," said Sirki. "Help the young gentleman put his boots on, and then hand him his clothes."

Croydon wasted no time in following the command, and Matthew realized a Corbett had suddenly become royalty, of a strange kind.

The boots were struggled into, the smoke-pungent clothing put on, and then it was time to stand up. Matthew took a long, deep breath. He slid off the bed and took the weight on his legs and his knees ached and his thigh muscles tightened and shrieked for a few agonizing seconds but then he was up and, after wavering ever so slightly, had secured his balance in an insane world.

"Very good," was the killer's comment.

Squibbs returned with a brown coat and, in addition, a gray blanket. He helped Matthew get the coat on and then wrapped the blanket around him with the care of a man who suddenly wanted to seem excellently careful. Sirki tucked the stretcher up under one long and dangerous arm. He spoke Croydon's name, and Croydon was off with a lantern in hand, obviously heading for Matthew's dairyhouse to fetch more clothes for the young sir's journey.

"Where are we going?" Matthew asked as he hobbled out onto the bracing cold of King Street, with Squibbs holding a lantern on one side and Sirki on the other.

"To a ship that will deliver you to an island," Sirki answered. "You will find the weather much more pleasant there. Step lightly, young sir. We don't wish you to sprain anything."

Between them, they steered Matthew's path toward the waterfront, and soon they were only two gleams of yellow lamplight in the dark and sleeping town.

➤•◀

Because she was still angry at Matthew Corbett, she had not gone to visit him today. Because she had not gone to visit him today, she missed seeing him and was in turn angry at herself for missing him. Because she was angry in so many areas at once, she could not sleep very soundly. And so because she could not sleep very soundly and had gotten out of bed to have a cup of water and eat a corn muffin, Berry Grigsby saw through the kitchen window the glimmer of light as someone carrying a lantern came out of Matthew's house.

Her first thought, unladylike as it might have been, was: *Damn! What's this about?* She blew out her own candle to avoid being seen. Her heartbeat had quickened and she felt the breath rasp in her lungs. She watched as the figure strode away, carrying what might have been a bundle of some kind.

Carrying it to where? she wondered. And to whom? To *Matthew?* At this time of night? It must have been Hudson Greathouse, she reasoned. Yes. Of course. Hudson Greathouse. *Go back to bed*, she told herself.

She could still see the swing of the man's lantern as he walked south along Queen Street. Heading toward the King Street Publick Hospital, of course.

But…at *this* time of night?

Was someone *robbing* Matthew's house?

She only had a few seconds to decide what to do. Her decision was rapidly made, and though she thought it might be the wrong one in the light of day it was perfectly right by the dark of night.

She rushed into her bedroom, where she knocked her knee on a table in her haste to get dressed. In her hurry, she pulled on a shift, then a petticoat and an old blue dress trimmed with yellow that she often wore when she was painting. Her stockings and shoes went on, also in a hurry, and then a dark blue woolen cloak and cap of the same color and material. Mittens for her hands, and she was ready. Her intent was to catch up with the thief, if at all possible, and then start calling for a constable. She lit a lantern from the steadily-burning candle in her bedroom and on the way to the front door had a thought to awaken Marmaduke, but her grandfather's snoring buzzed behind his own bedroom door and she decided enough time had been lost. This was her...*adventure*, perhaps? Yes, she thought. And never let it be said that the high-and-mighty Matthew Corbett would not appreciate her coming to the rescue of his stolen items.

So there.

Berry left the house, and stepped into bitter cold.

She followed her lantern's glow along Queen Street, heading south in the same direction as the thief. It crossed her mind that she was foolish out here in the wintry dark, chasing what was most likely Hudson Greathouse fetching some item of clothing for Matthew, but still...if one could not be foolish sometimes, what was the point of life? And...if it wasn't Greathouse, then...who? Well, she would see what she would see, and furthermore she was determined to show Matthew she could be a help to him and not a hindrance.

For not so very far ahead, closer toward the masted ships that sat moored to the harbor, three lantern lights were showing. She slowed her pace as she approached. If she were an animal, she would be sniffing the wind for the smells of thievery, but she could only trust what she could see. At each street corner she passed she looked in vain for the green lantern of a constable; no, they were all warming themselves before fires somewhere, so in essence Berry Grigsby was her own constable this frigid midnight.

She got close enough to make out four figures at the wharf-side, and one of them a giant wearing a multi-colored coat or robe of some fashion and a turban. The figures all had their backs to her. They were walking out along a pier. And…in the middle there, the third figure…yes, it *was*. She would know his walk anywhere. He was walking stiffly, still in pain, and he was bundled up in what appeared to be a gray blanket. He was following the giant, and behind him was a man holding a bundle of clothes under one arm and in the opposite hand a lantern. They were going toward a small skiff tied to the pier.

She didn't like the looks of this.

A wind had picked up, bringing a touch of ice. Or she felt an icy touch at her heart, for she had the sure feeling Matthew was being taken where he did not wish to go. She looked desperately for any sign of a constable's lantern, but there was no green glow to be seen. No, this night she was on her own.

As was Matthew. Or so he might think. He was being guided into the skiff, which was big enough for five or six men unless one of them was a turbaned giant. Matthew had his head down. In concentration or defeat? she wondered. Whichever…she wasn't going to let him be taken away like this, in the dead of night by villains unknown. For they had to be villains, to be stealing away from her the man she loved.

She started forward. One step at first—a cautious step—and then the others came faster, for she saw her time was running out, and Matthew was being put into the boat and in another moment one of the men was going to cast off the lines and then the oars would be put into their locks and…

"Matthew!" she called to him, before this terrible journey could begin. And louder still: *"Matthew!"*

The giant, still on the dock's planks, whirled toward her. Matthew stood up, his face ashen beneath the bruises. The other two men lifted their lanterns to catch her with their dirty light.

"Go back!" Matthew shouted. He nearly choked on the two words. *"Go back!"*

"Ah!" Sirki's voice was soft and smooth. He smiled; he was already moving to cross the forty paces between them. "Miss Beryl Grigsby, isn't it?"

"Berry!" Matthew couldn't communicate his fear for her loudly enough: *"Run!"*

"No need for that," said Sirki, as he came forward upon her with the sleek swiftness of a cobra. She backed away a few steps, but she realized as soon as she turned to run the giant would be at her back. "No need," he repeated. "We're friends here, you see."

"Matthew! What's going on?"

Sirki kept himself between them, a huge obstacle. "Matthew," he answered as he steadily advanced, "is about to take a sea voyage. It is his own decision." He came up within arm's length. His smile broadened, but in it there was no joy. "I think you might *also* enjoy a sea voyage, miss. Is that correct?"

"I'll scream," she said, for it seemed the thing to say with the blood beating in her cheeks.

"Croydon?" Sirki spoke over his shoulder, but kept his eyes on Berry. "If this young woman screams, I want you to strike Matthew as hard as you can across the face. Do you understand?"

"Gladly!" Croydon said, and he meant it.

"He's bluffing!" Matthew called out. He heard the weariness in his voice; his strength was departing him once more, and he knew that in his present state of disrepair there was nothing he could do to help her.

"I understand," said Sirki, close now upon Berry. She could smell the sandalwood incense from his clothing. The lantern light gleamed off the pearl-and-turquoise ornament that secured his turban. His voice was a soft murmur, as if heard through the veil of sleep. "You wish no harm to come to your friend. And he *is* your friend, yes?"

"Berry! Get away!" Matthew urged her, with the last of his strength. Croydon clamped a hand on his shoulder that said *Shut your mouth.*

"Your friend," Sirki repeated. "You know, I have the gift of seeing to the heart of matters. The *heart*," he said, for emphasis. "You wouldn't be here unless you were concerned for him, would you? And such concern should not be taken lightly. I would like for you to join us on our journey, miss. Walk before me to the boat, would you please?"

"I'm going for a constable," she told him.

But she did not move, and neither did the giant.

He stared into her eyes, his mouth wearing a little amused half-smile.

"Walk before me to the boat," he repeated. "I would appreciate your compliance."

Berry caught a movement to her right. She looked to the west along Wall Street, and saw at the intersection of Wall and Smith streets the green-glassed lantern of a passing constable.

"I promise," said Sirki in a cool, even tone, "to return you and Matthew safely here after his job is done. But if you cry for help or run, I will kill you before the cry leaves your lips and before you take two steps. I will deposit your corpse in the sea, where it shall never be found." He waited, silently, for her to make her decision.

Matthew was listening also. He couldn't help her, and he damned himself for it.

Berry watched the lantern's green glimmer pass away. The cry was so near to bursting free...yet she knew this man standing before her would do exactly as he said, and there was no point in meeting her death this night. She turned her gaze back upon him. "What job does Matthew have to do?" Her voice was shaky, yet she was holding herself together with all the willpower she could muster.

"What he *does*," Sirki answered. "Solving a problem. Will you walk before me to the boat, please? This cold can be doing you no good."

She had an instant of thinking she might smash him in the face with the lantern. But he reached out and grasped her wrist, as if reading her thought as soon as it was born, and with a strangely gentle touch he led her out along the pier to the skiff where Matthew was pushed back down to a sitting position by Croydon's rough hand.

"Squibbs," said Sirki when Berry had been gotten aboard and situated, "cast off our lines, please." It was done, and Squibbs stepped back onto the boat. Lanterns were placed on hooks at bow and stern. Two sets of oars went into their locks. Croydon and Squibbs went to work, rowing out into the dark, while Sirki took a seat between Matthew and Berry.

"Where are you taking us?" she asked the giant, and now her willpower was showing cracks and her voice did indeed tremble.

"First, the place you call Oyster Island. We'll give a signal from there to the ship. Then...outward bound." When he smiled, the diamonds in his front teeth glittered.

"Why?" Matthew whispered huskily. The question was directed at Berry, who did not answer. Therefore he asked again, from the bruised lips in his battered face. *"Why?"*

She couldn't answer, for she knew he didn't really wish to hear why a woman—any woman—would leave her safe abode in the cold midnight and undertake a journey at the side of a man she desired more than anything in the world. If she might be able to keep him safe...or keep him *alive*...then that was her own job, worth doing. Hang New York, she thought. Hang the world of safe abodes and warm beds. Hang the past, and what used to be. The future lay ahead for both of them, and though it was for now a forbidding place of dark water and uncertain destiny, Berry Grigsby felt more vital and more *needed* in this moment than ever before in her life.

The oars shifted water. The skiff moved steadily toward the black shape of Oyster Island, and Matthew Corbett the problem-solver could not for the life of him solve the problem of how to get Berry out of this.

ELEVEN

T HE skiff's bottom scraped rocks. "Out," said
Sirki, and at this command Croydon and Squibbs—two obedient
seadogs—fairly leapt from the boat into the icy knee-deep water
and dragged the skiff onto shore.

"Gentleman and lady?" Sirki made an expansive gesture with
one arm and gave a bow, whether in mockery or with serious intent
Matthew couldn't tell. "We'll be here only a short while," the giant
explained as he lifted his lantern to shine upon their faces. "I regret
the cold and the circumstances. Step out, please, and do mind your
footing on the stones."

So land was reached with a stumble from Berry and a muttered
curse from Matthew that would have gained approval at the rough-
est tavern in New York. Matthew caught her elbow and guided her
onward over rocks, loose gravel and the ubiquitous pieces of oyster
shells that crunched underfoot.

Standing amid the dead weeds and wild grass of shore, Sirki
busied himself opening a leather pouch, from which he removed
squares of red-tinted glass. He deftly removed the clear glass insets

of his lantern and, shielding the candle's guttering wick with his formidable body, he then slid the red glass squares into place. "Watch them," he told the two mongrels, and then he strode off in the direction of the watchtower, which perhaps was only a hundred yards or so distant through the woods.

A signal was about to be given and the ship alerted that this scheme was underway, Matthew thought. He felt Berry shiver beside him, and he put his arm and part of the gray blanket around her.

Lights from the two lanterns held by Croydon and Squibbs wandered over Berry's body. A bad sign, Matthew thought. "Where are we going?" he asked them, if just to divert their minds from their present—and highly disturbing—destination.

"Somewhere warmer than *this*," said Croydon. "Thank Christ."

"A three weeks voyage? To a warmer clime?" Matthew considered the geography; he put a map of the Atlantic in his mind and sought a harbor. "Not the Florida territory, I'm betting. Not into Spanish country. So..." *Outward bound*, Sirki had said. "The Bermuda islands," Matthew announced. "Is that right?"

"You are a pretty thing," said Squibbs, putting his light on Berry's face. "Take off that cap and let your hair loose."

"No," Matthew answered. "She *won't*."

"Here, now!" Croydon stepped forward and fairly sizzled Matthew's eyebrows by putting the lamp's hot glass right up in his face. "No one's talkin' to you, are they? Squibbs is just askin' her to be *friendly*, is all. A cold night and such...what's the harm of being a little friendly?" He turned the light upon Berry, who couldn't help but shrink back a step, for she realized these two were not so well-controlled without the East Indian giant giving them orders.

"Let your hair loose," Squibbs repeated. His mouth sounded thick and wet.

"Sirki will be back any minute," said Matthew. His body was a tense mass of bruised pain; in his present state he could neither deliver a blow nor take one.

"Any minute ain't *now*," was Squibbs' reply. He reached out, grasped Berry's cap and pulled it off, and her coppery-red tresses flowed free down her shoulders. "Pretty hair," Squibbs said after a moment of deliberation. "Bet it *smells* nice."

"Long time," said Croydon, "since I smelled me a woman's hair."

Matthew took a position between the two men and Berry. He thrust his chin forward, daring a strike. "Sirki won't like this. We're supposed to be *guests*." He spoke the word with dripping sarcasm.

"Ain't doin' nothin' wrong," Squibbs answered, his eyes narrowed and his gaze focused beyond Matthew on the true object of his attention. "Just wantin' to *smell*. Step aside."

Matthew balled up his fists, for all the good that would do. His arms were leaden lengths of ache. "I'll call him," he promised. "He won't—"

"Hear you," said Croydon. "Be a good little shit and step aside."

"I'm not moving."

"Oh yes, you are," said Squibbs, and with a quick powerful motion he grasped the front of Matthew's coat and flung him aside. Matthew stumbled over his own legs and went down amid the weeds and brush, and once out of the way and out of the light he was a forgotten man.

Squibbs and Croydon pushed forward, and though Berry retreated another step she realized there was nowhere else to go, and perhaps she ought to stand perfectly still and get this over with for surely the giant would be back at any minute. But, as the one man had said, one minute wasn't now.

They got on either side of her. Matthew said, "Stop it!" and tried to struggle out of what felt like a cluster of thorns. His legs would not obey. The two men got their faces up against Berry's hair, and as they drew in draughts of woman-perfume she smelled their unwashed odor of dried sweat, salt and old fish.

"Nice," Croydon breathed, and his free hand came up to stroke Berry's cheek. "Real fuckin' nice."

Matthew tried to get up. His legs betrayed him yet again. "Stop it!" he repeated, but he might have been speaking to the hard stones on the ground beneath him. Squibbs was starting to draw his unshaven face slowly down along Berry's throat. She made a noise of disgust with a frantic edge in it, and she pushed against Squibbs' shoulder but he was going nowhere, and now Croydon's gray-coated tongue flicked out and darted here and there amid the freckles on Berry's left cheek.

Matthew could bear no more of this. He desperately searched about in the dark for a small rock, a stick, whatever he could get his hands on to throw at the two ruffians. He struggled to stand, and in further desperation he opened his mouth to shout for help from the East Indian giant.

Before he could deliver that shout, Matthew was yanked backward through the brush by a hand that closed on his coat's collar.

At the same time, another hand that felt as rough as treebark clamped over his mouth, sealing shut all proposed shouts. He was dragged back and further back, the weeds and sawgrass and thorns tearing at his clothes, and then he was tossed unceremoniously aside, more like a beatup sack that needed to be gotten out of the way. A finger pressed hard to his mouth. The message was: *Silence.*

And Matthew knew, even in his state of brain-blasted befuddlement.

Here was the phantom of Oyster Island.

"What in bleedin' hell was that noise?" Squibbs directed his light into the underbrush. "Hey now! Where'd that boy go to?"

"Shit!" Croydon had almost hollered it. His attention had left Berry's freckles and was fixed on the empty place where Matthew Corbett had been a few seconds before. "He's fuckin' gone!"

"I know he's fuckin' gone!" Squibbs sounded near crying. "You don't have to tell me he's fuckin' gone!"

"Run off! God blast it! That ape'll have your head for this!"

"*My* head? You was supposed to be watchin' him!"

"I *was* watchin' him, 'til you started this shit with the girl!" Croydon backed away from Berry, sensing a terrible streak of bad luck coming his way. "Get in there and find that damned boy! He couldn't have gone far!"

Squibbs surveyed the dark and forbidding expanse of forest. "In *there*?"

"Go on, man! You owe me for that last mess in London!"

Berry saw Squibbs give a little shrug of resignation, as if that last mess in London had forever enslaved him to his partner. Then the hideous man whose breath smelled like spoiled onions and horse dung—and she would *always* unfortunately remember that odor—followed his lantern's light into the woods.

A few seconds of silence followed. "You got him, Squibbs?" Croydon called.

There was a *smack.*

A quick but brutal sound. Berry thought it sounded like a fist plowing into a bucket of mud. Maybe there was the *crunch* of a bone breaking in there, as well. She winced and tears burned her eyes, for she knew that Matthew could hardly survive a blow like that.

A body came flying out of the woods like dirty laundry being thrown from a hamper.

It landed nearly at Croydon's slime-crusted boots. "Jesus!" Croydon yelled, for his light fell upon Squibbs' face and the knot that was already turning purple at the center of the forehead. Squibbs' eyes had rolled back and showed the whites; he was not dead, for his chest heaved in ragged inhalations of troubled air, but his life-candle had nearly been knocked cold.

And then the phantom of Oyster Island, followed closely by Matthew Corbett, stepped out of the darkness into the quivering orbit of Croydon's lamp.

The massive freed slave Zed wore a ragged black coat over the same baggy brown breeches he'd worn when he'd leaped off a pier into the water back in November, and had last been seen swimming in the direction of Africa. He wore no shoes. A slice of bare chest showed between the straining buttons of his too-small coat. In the light from Croydon's lantern, Zed was even more fearsome a figure than three months before. Though he had lost some muscle in his hulking shoulders, he had gained a wild black beard. His skull was still perfectly bald, having been scraped clean with perhaps a sharpened shell, and across his broad ebony face—imprinted upon cheeks, forehead and chin—were tribal scars that lay upraised on the flesh, and in these were the stylized Z, E, and D by which Ashton McCaggers had named him.

Now, however, Zed's master was no longer Ashton McCaggers. A writ of manumission from Lord Cornbury had secured Zed's freedom. This stony and wooded patch of earth might well have been the ex-slave's kingdom, if he could not yet reach the golden shore of Africa. In any case, the scowling expression on Zed's face spoke to Croydon, and it said in no uncertain terms: *Get off my land or pay in blood.*

Croydon understood that message, for he turned tail and fled for the skiff. Unfortunately for Croydon, the king of Oyster Island was not in a mood to treat a trespasser with a welcome hand. Even as Croydon reached the skiff and clambered into it, Zed was upon him. The flat of a hand against the back of Croydon's head sent a spray of saliva from the man's mouth and perhaps caused the teeth to snap shut on the tongue because there was a plume also of scarlet liquid. Then Zed followed that with a fist to the middle of the forehead, same as had been delivered to Squibbs. As Croydon slithered down like a gutted fish, Zed picked him up bodily from the boat and swung him onto the shoreline's rocks, where the body made a hideous series of crunching sounds and began to twitch as if Croydon were dancing to Gilliam Vincent's abusive direction.

"Ah!" came a voice with a quiet lilt. "What is *this*?"

Matthew and Berry saw that Sirki had returned from his task. Bloody light from his red-glassed lantern had fallen upon Zed, whose fathomless black eyes took in this new intruder and seemed to glow with centers of fire.

"A *Ga*," said Sirki, with a note of true admiration. Obviously he knew the origin of the tattoos and the reputation of the Ga as supreme warriors. "I am pleased," he went on, "to make your acquaintance. I see you have taken up for my guests. And now," he said with a red-sparkly smile, "I suppose I shall have to kill you." He hooked the lantern's wire handle over a low-hanging tree branch, which would have been out of the reach of normal-sized men. Then he reached into his cloak and brought out a curved dagger whose grip gleamed with various precious stones. Its outer slashing edge was formed of vicious saw-teeth. Matthew wondered if Sirki would have used it on Mrs. Sifford and Mr. Dupee if the tea had failed to put them under. Still smiling with murderous intention and delight, Sirki advanced upon Zed, who plucked up an oar, thrust out his chest and stood his ground.

There was nothing either Matthew or Berry could do. Sirki kept striding forward, now through the ankle-deep water, as if on a simple mission to cut open an extra-large grouper.

By the red light, the two forces neared conflict. Zed waited with the oar ready to strike, and Sirki's blade made circles in the air.

Suddenly they were upon each other, with the same swiftness in the same second; whoever had made the first move was impossible to tell. Sirki dodged a swing of the oar and came up underneath it, his knife's point going for Zed's belly. But Zed retreated through the shallow water and turned aside, and the knife did no more damage than popping a button from his coat. When the energy of the thrust had

been expended, Zed brought the oar's handle up to slam against Sirki's shoulder. The East Indian giant gave a hiss of pain, but no more than that, and as he staggered back to get out of range he was already swinging the blade at Zed's face to imprint another initial upon the flesh.

Zed was faster still. The sawteeth missed his nose by an African whisker. The oar was in action again, coming at Sirki's head. The giant threw up an arm and the oar's shaft cracked and shattered across it, bringing from Sirki a small grunt as one might make stubbing a toe on a garden stone. The knife's angle changed direction in midair and what had begun as a strike to the shoulder now became a quest for throat's flesh. Zed's free hand caught the wrist. A fist slammed into Zed's jaw and made his knees wobbly but he stayed on his feet and thrust into Sirki's midsection with the oar's jagged end.

A sudden twist of the body and the oar tore through cloth underneath Sirki's right arm. Sirki's fist shot out again, catching Zed square in the mouth and rocking his head back. Still the massive black warrior did not fall, and now he squeezed Sirki's wrist with a desire to burst bones and Sirki fought back by hammering at Zed's skull with his fist. Zed's concentration was complete; the blows to his head may have been painful but he shook them off like beats to a tribal drum, and letting go of the oar's splintered shaft he grasped Sirki's knifehand and began to squeeze those bones with the tenacity and power of a python.

Sirki resisted as long as he could, and then with a muffled gasp his fingers opened and the fearsome knife fell into the water. He was no longer smiling. He jabbed the fingers of his other hand into Zed's eyes. Zed gave out a tongueless roar of pain and swung Sirki around in preparation to throw him sprawling into the rocky drink, but Sirki held tight to him and both the giants staggered and fell together into the water. They struck and splashed and kicked and grappled, rolling over stones layered with oyster shells. Zed got hold of Sirki's turban and it came undone, revealing a brown scalp bald except for a thick strip of black hair down the middle. Then Sirki chopped the edge of a hand into Zed's throat and Zed gurgled and fell back, and as Matthew and Berry watched in horror the East Indian killer got on top of the Ga warrior and, grasping the throat with both hands, forced the bearded face underwater. Zed thrashed to escape. Sirki's arms quivered with the effort of holding him under.

Matthew saw the other oars in the skiff. He roused himself to action and started out over the rocks to get an oar and beat Sirki upon the head with it, but suddenly there was an upheaval of water and Zed came up with his teeth gritted and his eyes full of Hell. He took hold of Sirki's throat with both hands and with a single powerful thrust he was suddenly on top of Sirki, whose face was sinking beneath the foam.

Now it was Sirki's time to wildly thrash. The muscles of Zed's shoulders and back bunched and twisted under the sopping-wet coat. Sirki's hands came up, the fingers clawing at Zed's tattoos. Zed's body shook with the effort; Sirki was fighting for his life, and his strength was yet undiminished by the process of drowning.

In all this violence, the rowboat that slid onto the shore with a lantern at its prow hardly caused a ripple. Matthew saw it contained five men. And one woman. The woman being Rebecca Mallory, real name Aria Something. One of the men being Doctor Jason Mallory, real name unknown. But both certainly alive and well and unburnt to crisps as had been their unfortunate lie-ins.

"Stop that!" Doctor Jason shouted. Two of the men, having realized their stately champion was being defeated by this black misfit in drenched rags, were already clambering from the boat. They grabbed hold of Zed from either side and tried to pin his arms. That lasted only a few seconds before a Herculean shrug sent them flying, one to land in the water and one in the weeds.

"Mister Grimmer!" Doctor Jason was directing his shout to another man in the boat. "Run him through!"

A thin man in a brown tricorn and a dirty brown suit with ruffles of grimy lace at the sleeves and throat stood up, drew a rapier from its sheath and stepped into the water. He approached Zed with no hesitation, and raised the sword to drive it into the black warrior's back.

"No!" Berry cried out. "Please! No!" She ran into the water to get between Grimmer and Zed, and the sallow swordsman looked for further instructions from the false Doctor Jason. Berry didn't wait. She knew the next word would be her friend's death. "Zed!" she said, with raw force in her voice. "Zed, listen to me! Let him go! Do you hear?"

His head turned. The bloodshot eyes found her, and read her fear for him. Still holding the flailing giant down, he turned his head to the other side and saw the swordsman standing there, ready to put the rapier to use.

Berry put her hand on Zed's shoulder. "No," she said, shaking her head. *"No."*

Zed hesitated only a few seconds longer. He brought his right hand up and with it made a flattening motion. *All right*, he had answered. He released Sirki, stood up and stepped back, and Sirki burst from the briny coughing and gasping and then turning over and throwing up his last New York dinner into the sea to be consumed by the small fishes of the night.

"Shall I kill him anyway, sir?" asked Grimmer, in a low sad voice that seemed to suit his name.

"I'll kill him!" Sirki had found his curved dagger. He and his clothing were a mess. He was trying to wind his sodden turban back onto his head. The furious expression on his face made him appear to be not so much a giant as a big infant angry at being deprived of a sweet. "I'll kill him this *minute!*" he nearly shrieked, and he lifted the sawtoothed blade and sloshed toward Zed, who stood immobile at the rapier's point.

"You will not *touch* him!" This announcement had not come from Doctor Jason, but from the raven-haired, blue-eyed and fiercely beautiful Aria. She stood up in the boat; over a black gown she was wearing a dark purple cloak and on her head was a woolen cap the same color. "Sirki, put your knife down!" Her voice carried the promise of dire consequences if he did not obey; he did obey, almost immediately. Matthew watched this with great interest, getting the order of masters and followers in its proper perspective. "I see you have the *girl*," Aria went on, with the slightest edge of irritation. "That may be for the best, despite all appearances. You see, the black crow means something to the girl, and the girl means something to Matthew. So no one is going to be stabbed or otherwise harmed this night, Sirki. We can use what we can use. Do you understand?"

"He's nearly killed Croydon and Squibbs! And these other two! *And* he's a Ga! A danger to *everyone!*"

"Danger," said Aria, with a faint smile in the lamplight, "can be easily controlled, if one knows the right throat to pressure. Grimmer, put the tip of your sword against Miss Grigsby's neck, please."

Grimmer did so. Zed gave a warning rumble deep in his chest.

Matthew own throat had tightened. "There's no need for that. I said I'm coming along."

"Miss Grigsby," said Aria, "inform your black prince—however you can—that your life depends on his good behavior. That we wish him to be meek and mild and for that he shall have a good dinner and a warm blanket in a ship's brig tonight."

"A ship's brig?"

"Just inform him, however you are able. And you might tell him you will be in the next cell, so he won't feel so lonely."

Now came Berry's challenge to communicate to Zed without benefit of the drawings they used to do together, which had served as a bridge between them. Zed was watching her intently, knowing that some message had been delivered to her from the black-haired woman and now was poised in his direction. Berry understood that he did know some of the English language, but how much she couldn't tell since silence had been thrust upon him with the cutting out of his tongue, and silence also was his armor.

But it was true that Berry and Zed had spent much time together, at the behest of Ashton McCaggers, for whether Zed goeth so went his master at that time and McCaggers did enjoy Berry's company, broken shoe heel or not. And in that time Berry had begun to "hear" Zed, in a fashion. It was a hearing of the senses and the mind. She could "hear" his voice in a gesture of the hand, a shrug of the shoulder, a fleeting expression. If it had been a spoken voice, it would have sounded a little low and gutteral, a little snarly as suited Zed's view of the world that held him captive.

Now Berry stared into Zed's eyes and held her hand out before him, palm outward. She spoke two words: "Do nothing."

He looked at her hand, then at her face. Then at her hand again. He turned his head to take in the scene where unconscious men were coming back to their senses. He took in the woman on the boat and then the giant he'd just nearly drowned. He took in the sight of Matthew Corbett wrapped in a blanket, the young man's face bruised by some incident beyond his understanding. He looked again at Berry Grigsby, his friend, and his lifting of the eyebrows and the slight twist of his mouth said, *I will do nothing… for the moment.*

"Good," she answered, with the rapier's tip nearly nicking her throat. She aimed her angry eyes at Grimmer. "You can put that down now."

Grimmer waited for Aria to nod, and the rapier was lowered.

But not yet lowered was the heat of rage that steamed from Sirki, who pressed forward with his knife in hand. "I'll kill you yet," he promised Zed. The ex-slave understood the meaning quite well, and he gave a square-toothed grin that almost drove Sirki into a maddened fit.

"We have a tide to catch," Aria announced. "Anyone who cannot walk will be staying here. Gentlemen, board your boats. Matthew, would you please come get into this one? I've saved you a place." She sat down and patted the plank seat at her side.

The woman's directions continued. Berry and Zed were put into the other boat, with Grimmer holding the sword ready and Sirki anxious with his knife. Everyone, it seemed, who had been knocked woozy could at least walk, and they returned to the boats. Squibbs seemed only to be able to walk in circles, however, and Croydon winced and grasped at his back with every step.

Matthew took his place beside Aria Whomever, and Doctor Jason sat facing him. The two boats were pushed off and the oarsmen went to work.

"You have made the right decision," said Doctor Jason, when they were out on the choppy water away from Oyster Island.

Matthew watched the lamps of the second boat following. "I presume no harm will come to either Berry or Zed?" He stared into Aria's intense sapphire-blue eyes, for she was the captain of this craft. "In fact, I insist on it."

The woman gave a small laugh that might have been edged with cruelty. "Oh, you're too cute," she said.

"I imagine I'm going also into a cell in the ship's brig?"

"Not at all. They will be, yes, because they are uninvited guests. But you, dear Matthew, will have a cabin of honor aboard the *Nightflyer*." She motioned out into the dark. "We'll be there in a few minutes."

He had to ask the next question, if just to salve his curiosity. "What's your real name? And *his* real name?"

"I am Aria Chillany," she answered. "He is Jonathan Gentry."

"At your service," said Gentry, with a nod and a devilish smile.

Matthew grunted. Even the grunting hurt. He recalled something Hudson had told him, back in the summer, concerning Professor Fell's criminal network: *We know the names of the most vile elements. Gentleman Jackie Blue. The Thacker Brothers. Augustus Pons. Madam Chillany. They're in the business of counterfeiting, forgery, theft of both state and private papers, blackmail, kidnapping, arson, murder for hire, and whatever else offers them a profit.*

He felt Madam Chillany's fingers at the back of his neck.

"You're thinking of something important?" she inquired.

How to survive, madam, he thought. *And how to keep Berry and Zed alive, too.*

"We're going to become very good friends, Matthew," she said. "Poor boy." She pursed her lips in a pout and now her fingers travelled over the tender terrain of his cheek. "All those bruises and scrapes. But you enjoy close scrapes, don't you?"

"Not the scraping," Matthew said. "The escaping."

A ship's bell rang, out in the distance. Suddenly a wet wall of black timbers was standing before them. Lanterns moved above. Men shouted back and forth. A rope ladder was lowered, and Aria Chillany said to Matthew, "You up first, darling. I'll be right behind you."

"Watch her, Matthew," Gentry cautioned. His smile had gone a bit crooked. "When she gets behind you, you might find something thrust into your—"

"But don't listen to him," she interrupted. "He's all talk, and precious little action."

Matthew was beginning to think these two had so tired of their roles of loving husband and doting wife that they could've broken each others' necks. Or, at least, stabbed each other below the waist. In any case, no wonder the false lovebirds had separate beds. The only fire in that house had been made by the bombs going off.

Now, though, as Matthew forced himself up the ladder—and no one else was going to help him up, for certainty—he felt Aria Chillany's hand slide across his rump, and he thought that some wells in this vicinity were in desperate need of being pumped.

The sun was beginning to turn the eastern sky pale gray as Berry and Zed came aboard. They were quickly taken away belowdecks, without a chance for Matthew to speak or be spoken to. Sirki slinked along behind them, his turban still in disarray and his clothing dirtied by shore rocks and oyster shit. The two rowboats were hoisted up by men who looked as hard as New York cobblestones. Though Matthew was not overly familiar with the many types of ships and seacraft, he thought the *Nightflyer* might be considered a brigantine, having two masts with square sails on the foremast and fore-and-aft sails on the mainmast. It looked to be a low-slung, fast vessel, and its crew appeared highly efficient at their tasks. Orders were given, the *Nightflyer* turned to catch the wind, the sails filled and the spray began to hiss along the hull. A hand touched his arm as he stood at the starboard railing in the strengthening light. Madam Chillany regarded him with narrowed eyes. "I'm to show you to your cabin now. You'll meet Captain Falco later. You'll be served breakfast presently, and a large glass of wine to help you sleep."

"Drugged wine?" Matthew asked.

"Would you prefer?"

He almost said *yes*. Maybe he *would* say yes, if he thought about it long enough. He was almost too tired to sleep of his own will, and who could sleep when they were summoned across the Atlantic to be Professor Fell's personal providence rider?

Matthew saw the town of New York fading away behind them. It did appear gray, at this distance and in this light.

Farewell to the gray kingdom, he thought. For whatever he used to be and whoever he once was, he could no longer be. He had thought himself having to grow solid stones to meet the threat and violence of Tyranthus Slaughter. But now he realized that grisly adventure might have been a garden walk compared to this journey.

So farewell to the gray kingdom, for his mind must be clear and his vision sharp. He must be more Matthew Corbett than ever before. And, he thought grimly, God help Matthew Corbett.

The *Nightflyer* turned to secure its course. A dolphin leaped before the bow. Rays of sunlight streamed through the clouds to brighten the sea, and Matthew hobbled behind Madam Chillany in search of a good breakfast and a glass of sleep.

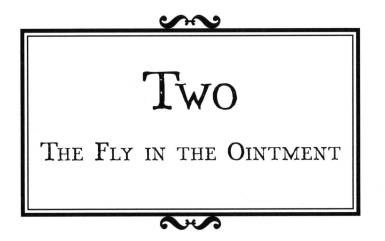

Two

The Fly in the Ointment

TWELVE

As the days passed, as the ship sailed across an ocean that might be both calm and turbulent in the same day, as the rain showered down from dark clouds and then the sun burst forth from the midst of darkness, as the pallid moonlight glittered upon the luminous waves and the bright blue ribbons of sea creatures moved on their errands of life and death, Matthew felt himself healing.

He was aided in this regard by the doctor, Jonathan Gentry by name. Gentry came by his cabin to see him in the mornings after breakfast and in the evenings before supper was served. Sometimes medicinal tea was brought, sometimes Gentry unpeeled the plaster under Matthew's left eye to check the stitches, and then he applied a green salve and put the plaster back as it was. The doctor gave him a cake of grassy-smelling soap and told him to keep everything clean, for this Atlantic travel was a nasty business and all sorts of mold grew from the grime a ship carried. Not to mention the rats that crawled about so freely they were given pet names by the sailors.

Matthew always posed the same three questions to Dr. Gentry. One being, "Are Berry and Zed well-treated?"

And the answer to that, always the same: "Certainly they are."

The next question following: "May I see them?"

"Not quite yet."

The third question: "When am I to hear what Fell's problem is?"

And its answer: "In time, Matthew." Then: "Make sure you get out on the deck for your walk. Yes?"

Matthew always nodded. In fact, he greatly looked forward to his walks on the deck. No matter if it was raining or the sun shone, Matthew walked 'round and 'round the ship, taking in the tasks being performed and the occasional glimpse of Captain Jerrell Falco, an austere figure in black suit, black cloak and black tricorn to match the blue-black sheen of his ebony flesh. The captain had a white goatee, and he carried a twisted cane that he had no qualms about using across the back of a slow seaman. Matthew had noted there were several Africans or black Caribees among the crew, as well as a few yellow skins from the Far East. If anything, the ship was worldly. Matthew found himself with books to read. They were delivered in a basket to his cabin, and they carried the faint hint of a woman's perfume. It seemed to him that either Aria Chillany liked the idea of bruised flesh under her hands, or she was toying with him. The books were Shakespeare's *The Tempest*, *King Lear* and *Julius Caesar*, a philosophical tome concerning the earth's place at the center of the universe, and a fearsomely blasphemous book explaining how God was a creation of the mind of Man. Matthew figured just opening that book in some communities might earn a backburn of whiplashes if not a noose around the neck. Still, he thought he might read it. After all, the books aboard this ship had to have earned the approval of Professor Fell, therefore some view of Fell's mental state might be gleaned from the reading.

To be sure, Matthew found no fault with his cabin or with the way he was being pampered. And pampered was indeed the correct word. Though no human element could correct the roll of the ship, the drumming of waves against the hull or the constant creaking and crying of timbers, every human element aboard the *Nightflyer* seemed intent on treating Matthew as a valued guest. A glass of wine—drugged or non-drugged, as he wished—was only the ringing of a silver bell away. His food was not only palatable, it was damned good. Yet he might tire of fish, the daily catch was spiced to his liking. His clothing had been washed and pressed by a hot iron. His boots wore a shine. As much as was possible aboard an ocean-going vessel, his cabin was spacious and clean. His bed was a four-poster, the legs pegged down to prevent movement with the ship. The person who came in to change the candles did so on a daily basis and was not stingy with the wax. And, most tellingly, the door to Matthew's cabin was never locked from the outside. If he required privacy and latched it himself, that was fine, yet he was never forced to feel like a prisoner. One afternoon a knock at his door introduced him to an elderly man who came in with a measuring stick and piece of chalk and proceeded to take his measurements of arm, leg, chest and so forth and then left without a word.

Of course there were some places Matthew could not go. He was cautioned by Gentry not to wander around belowdecks, as he might pick up some unfortunate fungus or infection that would not do his condition any good. Also, there were several locked doors he came to that were obviously not going to be opened for him, and he presumed one of those led down to the brig. But as long as he stayed out of the way he was encouraged to be up on the deck, and several times Gentry had shared dinner with him in the doctor's own cabin, which was perhaps one half the size of Matthew's and not nearly so well-fashioned. Gentry was an interesting conversationalist, focusing mostly on his travels through South America, the Caribbean, Italy, Prussia, China, Japan and elsewhere, but not a word would come from him regarding either the professor or the reason behind this endeavor.

And so it was with real interest that after the passage of six days, and after Matthew had made his morning rounds of the deck under a blue sunlit sky that projected an amazing warmth for this time of year, he returned to his cabin to continue his reading of *The Tempest* and was roused from his comfortable chair by a rap at the door.

"Yes?" he asked mildly, for he had learned there was no sense or need to be rude in this situation.

"Dear Matthew," said the raven-tressed woman on the other side, "I've brought you something."

It had been several days since he'd laid eyes upon Aria Chillany. He had to admit she was an intensely beautiful woman and his eyes had missed such beauty in the midst of all these ragged and hard-bitten sailors. Therefore he put the folio aside, got to his feet and—marking the fact that this cabin made at least two of his dairyhouse home—he crossed to the door and opened it.

"Good morning," she said with an honest smile, yet the sapphire-colored eyes were always wary. "May I come in?"

He stepped back and motioned her to enter, and she closed the door at her back.

She was wearing a lilac-hued gown and a dark blue jacket trimmed with black leather. Her hair copiously cascaded along her shoulders and down her back. She smelled of an exotic incense, with an undertone rather like a sugared, hot and slightly burned coffee. She took him in with her direct stare. "You're mending nicely."

Was some witticsm called for here? He decided to say only, "Thank you." He also had realized that the shaving mirror was becoming kinder to him. The worst of the bruises only showed faint blue, the cuts were scabbed over and this woman's ex-false-husband was coming in the afternoon to remove the plaster and the stitches. Matthew was free of pain and everything seemed to have settled back where it needed to be. This was, he'd decided, more of the effects of deep and healing sleep brought on by the drugged wine than any other of Gentry's ministrations.

"Here," she said, and gave him a rolled-up parchment secured with a black cord.

"What is this?"

"Your future," she told him. Her gaze wandered over to the dresser and atop it the brown clay bowl holding two apples, an orange and a lemon that were brought to him on a daily basis. Without asking, she moved to the bowl with a crisp rustle of under-clothes, selected an apple and bit into it. She chewed and watched him as he opened the parchment.

Matthew saw it was someone's life history, scribed in black ink by a steady and very disciplined hand. The title was *The Life And Times Of Nathan Spade*.

"And exactly who is Nathan Spade?" Matthew asked.

"That would be *you*," said Madam Chillany, as she crunched another bite of apple.

He scanned the document. It proclaimed a false birthday, and a birth year that made Nathan two years the elder. It described a hard-scrabble childhood on a farm in Surrey. A younger brother, Peter, died as an infant. Mother—Rose by name—perished from consumption. Father Edward was ambushed by a highwayman and his throat slashed for a palm's weight of measly coins. Therefore Nathan went into the world as a bitter twelve-year-old with many miles to walk and many scores to settle against the whole of humankind. His first occupation: rolling the drunks at a London dockside bordello and cleaning up the mess they left—whether vomit, blood or other.

"Charming," said Matthew. He stared into the woman's eyes, forcing his expression to remain stony and unflinching. "What is this *about*?"

"Obviously," she answered, "your new identity."

"And why would I need one?"

She continued to eat her apple with leisurely bites. She smiled faintly, the smile of a predator. She came around behind him, and he allowed it. She leaned forward and said quietly into his right ear, "Because being Matthew Corbett, problem-solver for the Herrald Agency, would hasten your death where we are going. You would not last a day, darling Matthew." Her forefinger, wet with juice, played with his hair. "Some of the personages you are going to meet knew Lyra Sutch. They would not like to know the part you played in her tragedy. Your name is already being bandied about. Therefore the professor wishes to protect you...from them, and from *yourself.*" The last word was concluded with a nip to Matthew's ear. Playful or not, she had sharp teeth.

He decided it was best, after all, not to let her get behind him, and therefore he turned to face her and backed away a pace.

"Oh," Aria said, her face placid and self-composed but her eyes on him as if he were the most luscious apple to be plucked, "you shouldn't be afraid of me, darling. It's those others you should fear. The ones you're going to meet."

"Who are they, exactly?"

"Associates. And friends of associates." She came toward him a step, and again he retreated. "You have been invited to a gathering,

Matthew. A...*festivity*, if you will. That's why you need the new identity. So you will...shall we say...fit in."

He read a few more lines of the document. "Hm," he said. "Spade murdered his first victim at the age of fourteen? He was involved with one of the prostitutes and he killed a jayhawk?" A jayhawk, in this instance, being a man who attempts to remove a prostitute from one ill abode to another, using either flattery or force.

"Yes," said Aria. "The jayhawk beat her terribly one night. Broke her beautiful nose and vowed to cut her open and watch her guts slide out upon the floor. And do you know what, dear Matthew? Her name might have been Rebecca."

That took a few seconds to sink in. He held up the parchment. "I thought this was a work of fiction."

"Fiction is often the echo of truth," she answered, her focus steady upon him. "Don't you think?"

Matthew studied her face. Her nose was indeed a little crooked, yet still beautiful. He wondered what those eyes had seen. Or perhaps he really did not wish to know.

But one bit of information he did desire. He decided now was the moment to reach for it. "I'm presuming you were the woman with the blue parasol that day at Chapel's estate? When he put his birds on us?" He was speaking here of an incident that had occurred during the summer, in his investigation concerning the so-called Queen of Bedlam.

"I was. And happy we all are now that you did not succumb to that fate."

"I'm presuming also you got out through the hidden tunnel? The one that wound down to the river?" He waited for her to nod. "Tell me this, then. What happened to the swordsman? The Prussian," Matthew emphasized. "He called himself Count Dahlgren." Matthew and the count had been locked in deadly combat, and but for a silver fruit tray one young problem-solver would have found himself run through by a wicked dagger. Though Dahlgren had been wrapped in a pair of curtains and clouted into a goldfish pond, his left arm broken at the wrist, still the enigmatic Prussian had escaped capture that day, and had disappeared.

"I have no idea," Aria answered. "That's the truth."

Matthew believed her. He hated loose ends. Dahlgren was definitely a loose end. Moreover, Dahlgren was a loose end who could still manage a sword and surely bore a Prussia-sized grudge against the adversary who'd bested him. The question was still unanswered: where had Dahlgren gone, and where was he now?

Surely the count was not waiting for him at the end of this voyage, Matthew mused. But he felt sure that somewhere, at sometime, he would meet Dahlgren again.

Matthew decided to try another angle to one of his three questions, now that he had this parchment and some idea that he was being required to playact the part of a rather nasty young killer. Obviously, a great deal of thought and preparation had been put into the professor's plan...whatever it was. "I want to see Berry and Zed."

"That's not possible. I believe that Gentry has assured you—"

"You're speaking when you should be listening," Matthew interrupted. "You must not have heard. I'm not asking, I'm telling." He rolled up the parchment and wrapped it with the black cord. "I want to see Berry and Zed. *Now.*"

"No," she said.

"And why not? Because if I see what condition they're being kept in, I may refuse to go along with this...*nonsense?*" He flung the parchment across the room to land in the far corner. "All right, then. You go tell Sirki I refuse to leave the ship when we dock wherever we're going. Tell him they'll have to carry me out on a stretcher, after all. Tell him—"

"I'll tell him," Aria agreed, "to kill them. Starting with the girl."

Matthew forced a harsh laugh. He and the woman might not have swords, but they were fencing all the same, and damned if she wasn't as good at using her own weapon as Dahlgren had been with his. "You will not," said Matthew, and now he approached her. She stood her ground and lifted her chin. "Sirki vowed Berry would be returned safely to New York, and myself as well. His anger toward Zed will have passed by now. I have the feeling he might be an honorable man, in his own way." *And you a dishonorable woman in all ways,* he might have added. He continued right up to her, as if he owned the very air she breathed. He had already decided he had very little to lose in this situation, and he must show himself to be a powerful force. As much force as he could masquerade under, to be honest. A look of uncertainty passed only briefly across Aria's face before she righted her ship. She stood firm and defiant before him, and she started to take another bite of the dwindling apple.

"If I'm going to be Nathan Spade," said Matthew, "I'm starting now. *Rebecca*," he added with a faint sneer. "And who gave you permission to steal my apples?" He took it from her before it reached her mouth, and then he took a bite from it. A bit green and sour, but there it was. "I said I want to see Berry and Zed today," he told her as he chewed. "This moment. Is that clear enough for you?"

She didn't answer. She stood expressionless, like a cypher, perhaps revealing her lack of soul. Or, possibly, she was simply struggling to control a scene that had gotten away from its playwright.

"All right, then. I'll find them on my own." Matthew picked up the bowl to prevent further thievery, and also to take the fruit to Berry and Zed for he fully intended to either find someone to unlock the necessary door or he was going to kick it down.

She let him get a grip on the door's handle before he spoke. "You can only spend a few minutes with them. *If* I take you."

He turned upon her as if determining where to thrust the sword, now that her defenses had been cracked. "You'll take me," he said. "And I'll spend as much time with them as I please."

She hesitated. Then, with a small cat-like smile, "I'm not sure I approve of this Nathan Spade so very much. He does seem to like to give commands, when he's in no position to—"

"Be silent," Matthew said flatly. "I didn't ask to be here. Neither did my friends. So take me or step aside or do whatever you need to do, madam. But I'm done listening to you prattle."

A hint of red crept across Aria Chillany's cheeks. She blinked as if she'd been struck. But the damnedest thing, Matthew thought, was that the look in her eyes was not so much temper as tempest, and she began to chew on her lower lip as if it might spring forth a wine of rare vintage.

"I'll take you," she said quietly.

Good enough, Matthew thought, and if the woman had not been as near he would have heaved a sigh of relief so gusty the sails might have blown from their masts.

He followed her along the corridor. She took a key from an inner pocket of her jacket and started to unlock a narrow door about thirty feet from Matthew's cabin, but she found the door already unlocked; its grip turned smoothly beneath her hand. She returned the key to its place. "It seems your friends already have a visitor this morning," she told him.

The door opened on stairs that descended between two oil lamps hanging from ceiling hooks. At the bottom was a second door. Down here, nearer to the sea and the mollusks that likely clung by the hundreds to the hull, the aromas of tar, fish and old wet timbers were nearly overpowering. The constant low thunder of the waves was bad enough, but the creaking of the *Nightflyer* made it sound as if the vessel was coming apart at pegs, nails and seams. At this level the ship also rolled like a little bitch. Matthew was certain he would face Berry's wrath about this, at some point to come. Yet it was he who should feel wrath, for who had asked her to stick her nose into this? Who had asked her to creep along and appear there on the dock, apparently in an effort to save him? Who had asked her?

Not I, Matthew thought, and didn't realize he'd said it aloud until Aria Chillany looked over her shoulder and inquired, "What was that?"

He shook his head. She took him through the second door, and into the brig.

He had a moment of feeling he was back in time, entering the dingy gaol in the town of Fount Royal to hear a witchcraft case as a magistrate's clerk. This might be a shipborne brig, yet the four cells were familiar and the iron bars as forbidding as any landlocked cages for human beings. Several dirty lanterns hung from hooks, illuminating the scene with a murky yellow light. A rat skittered across the floor at Matthew's feet. It was chasing a cockroach as big as a crab. The smells of foulness commingled with the odors of musty wet wood and the fishy bowels of the ship were nothing short of an apocalyptic assault. Matthew felt rage rising in him, as he saw Zed confined in one cell to the left and Berry—a poor moldy ragamuffin with a tangled mass of red hair, she appeared to be—confined in the furtherest one to the right. They had straw mattresses and buckets, and that was the extent of the hospitality offered here.

"God *blast* it!" Matthew nearly shouted. His throat had almost seized shut. "Get them out of there!"

A man stepped from a pool of shadows in front of Zed's cell. "Sir, please restrain yourself."

"*Restrain* myself? Good Christ!" Red-faced and steaming, Matthew was on a tear. As a matter of truth, he felt he could tear the head from the neck of any sonofabitch who defied him. Even if it was the white-goateed and austere Captain Jerrell Falco who stood before him, armed with his twisted cane, and staring at him with steady and rather frightening amber-colored eyes. "These are my friends!" Matthew said into Falco's face. "They're not animals, and they've done nothing wrong!"

"Oh my," said Madam Chillany, who wore a thin smirk that very nearly was her last, "I knew this was a bad idea."

"Matthew!" Berry was calling for him. She sounded weak and sick. And who wouldn't be, Matthew thought, in this undersea tomb that smelled of tar and dead fish, with the ship rolling enough to tear a person's internals loose.

"*Get them out!*" Matthew roared, at both the woman and the captain. The smirk melted from her face and Falco's goatee may have smoked a bit as well.

The twisted cane was laid softly but firmly upon Matthew's right shoulder.

"Calmness," said the captain, "in a situation of pressure is a virtue, young man. I suggest you become more virtuous in speaking with me, beginning with your next word." He had a deep, resonant voice that Matthew thought any church pastor would sell his soul to possess. And then Falco's head turned and he said something in a rough dialect to Zed. Matthew, to his everlasting amazement, heard Zed give a throaty chuckle.

"You can...*speak* to him?" Matthew asked, feeling the sweat of rage start to evaporate from his brow. "He *understands* you?"

"I speak the Ga language," Falco answered. "Also five other languages. I read and write ten languages in all. I was educated in Paris, and I have lived on three continents. Why would I not have taken benefit of my travels?"

"He understands you," Matthew repeated, this time as a statement.

"I believe that fact has been demonstrated." Falco frowned. His eyebrows were graying, but had not yet turned as snowy as his chin-hair. Gray also was the hair that could be seen beneath his brown leather tricorn. "What are you doing down here?" The amber eyes shifted to Madam Chillany. "Why did you allow this?"

"He insisted."

"If I insist you jump to the sharks wearing a necklace of fish guts, would you do so?" He gave her a stare that would have buckled the knees of any ordinary woman, but Aria Chillany was nearly a witch herself, it seemed, so it had little effect.

Matthew strode past them and went to Berry's cell. To say she was a sad-looking mess was to say that the sun did not shine at night. And truly her sunny disposition had been darkened by this perpetual gloom, enough that Matthew felt tears of new anger squeezing past his eyeballs. "Damn this!" he said. He put one hand around the bars, the other still gripping the bowl of apple, orange and lime. They built these brigs to keep mutineers and madmen at bay, and surely the iron that would not surrender to a Ga warrior would not be moved by a problem-solver. Berry came up close to him, her hair in her face and her eyes as murky as the light. "Can you get me some fresh water?" she asked him. "I'm very thirsty."

"Yes," he said through gritted teeth. "I'll get you some fresh water. First, take this." He pushed the orange between the bars, and she took it and bit into it peel and all as if this were her first food since leaving New York. He turned toward Falco and Madam Chillany with something near murder glowering in his eyes. "I want my friends out of here. Captain, I implore you. They've done no crime to fit this punishment. I want them freed from this place and given decent cabins."

"Impossible," said the woman. "Everything is taken."

"It seems to me that one uses what can be used," Matthew said. "For instance, *your* cabin might be freed if you were to take habitation with your husband. I mean to say, the man who *posed* as your husband. A few more nights of sleeping with him and you might fall in loving bliss all over again."

"I'd rather die!" shrieked the harpy.

Matthew ignored her. "Captain, could you find a bunk for a Ga? Perhaps give him some work to do, after he's been decently fed and allowed to breathe healthy air?"

"He stays here!" said Madam Chillany. "It's safer for all!"

Captain Falco had been staring fixedly at Matthew. Now his amber gaze settled upon the woman. "Do I hear," he said quietly, "you making decisions concerning my ship and my crew, madam? Because if I do, I will remind you that I am indeed the master of this vessel—"

"I'm just saying it's better he stays locked—"

"I hear what you're saying," the captain continued, "and I appreciate your opinion." He looked again at Zed and fired off some statement that made Zed shrug. "I don't think he's a danger," Falco said, addressing Matthew. "The girl is certainly no danger."

"They should be freed from this place," Matthew said. "The sooner, the better."

"I disagree." Madam Chillany stepped between Matthew and Falco to disrupt their burgeoning accord. "Captain, I will remind you that you are being paid very well by your employer to—"

"Madam, you are not my employer," he said, with a hint of a curled lip. "Yes, I am being paid very well. I am loyal to my employer, as long as he pays well. I always do my job to the best of my ability…but my job, madam, is to make the best decisions possible under the shadow of the sails above our heads. Now, I've been coming down here for several days to speak to the Ga. And to the girl as well. I was simply told when they were brought aboard that for the sake of security and simplicity they should be caged here, and I agreed with your position. At *that time* I agreed," he added. "But now, having spoken to both of them and gained a bit more… shall we say…understanding of the issues involved, I see no point in having them remain in these cells." He reached for the wall, where a ring of keys hung from a hook. "After all, where are they going to *go*? And I believe the swords and pistols aboard this ship can handle a Ga if he loses his temper." He spoke again to Zed, who answered with a chest-deep grunt and a shake of his bald head. "Madam," Falco translated, "he vows not to lose his temper."

"The professor won't care for this," she warned as Falco slid a key into the lock on Zed's cell, and instantly Matthew knew she'd gone a threat too far.

Falco unlocked the cell and opened the door with a creak of sea-rusted hinges. He motioned Zed out. "I believe our young guest has a good idea," said Falco. "Concerning the arrangement of quarters.

I think our Ga here can be given tasks to perform and therefore rate at least a blanket on the deck, if not a hammock." He strolled past Matthew to slide a second key into the lock on Berry's cell door. "As for *her*, I believe she should rest in some comfort, to make amends for this affront to her dignity. Madam, I expect you to move into the doctor's cabin within the hour. If he has any problem with this, he'll know where to find me."

"No!" The woman had a voice on her. It nearly shook the oaken beams at the ceiling. Her eyes blazed. She was one mad madam. "I *refuse*! He snores to high heaven and his feet stink like the devil's ass!"

The key turned. The lock was sprung. Falco opened the door and Matthew was there to catch Berry when she staggered out.

"I'll be glad to provide you with wads of cotton," Falco told Aria Chillany. "Two for the ears and two for the nose. Shall we all go up now and enjoy a little sunshine?"

THIRTEEN

MATTHEW was not himself today. On this thirteenth morn of sailing aboard the *Nightflyer*, he was restless and irritable and felt he would soon jump from his skin if harbor was not presently reached. Of course, reaching harbor would offer its own set of pressures. He pitied the crews and passengers of ships bound from England to the colonies. But he did have an escape from this constant roll of ship upon sea and vista of sun's glare off dark blue water. He was becoming Nathan Spade.

Madam Chillany had told him, very coldly, the same afternoon of the day that Berry and Zed had been released from their cages: *I assume you're proud of yourself, that you won the little skirmish? But there are real battles ahead of you, Matthew, and I hope you are up to fighting them so valiantly for you might be fighting for your life. I would suggest you pick up that parchment you so carelessly tossed aside and read the entire document. It was prepared for you by Professor Fell, so it's not to be taken lightly. Consign the life and times of Nathan Spade to your memory, dear one. Become him, if you value your neck...and, by reason of association, the necks of your lady friend and the black crow. We will be*

*making harbor toward the end of another week. By that time, you should
be* Nathan Spade. *Mark this advice well, won't you?*

I shall, Matthew had replied. *I do hope you enjoy your new quarters, and thank you for your hospitality to Miss Grigsby.*

There had been a definite chill in the air when that woman left
his door.

Why he had to become Nathan Spade, he had no idea. But it
seemed the right thing to do, since Aria Chillany was so insistent
upon his no longer being Matthew Corbett when they docked. And
as for her statement that *Some of the personages you are going to meet
knew Lyra Sutch*…well, long live Nathan Spade.

Whether Nathan Spade had ever really lived or not was a
question Matthew considered, and then decided upon not asking
Madam Chillany, as such a creature in this world further darkened his view of God's control over Evil on this side of Heaven. As
Matthew walked the deck on this thirteenth morn, with the sun
out in full force and Berry walking at his side refreshed and wellfed and free of shipboard mold, he speculated with an uneasy mind
upon the life and times of Master Spade.

From one murder to the next, Nathan Spade travelled as if
on a mission of discovery to reach the wretched bottom of the
human soul. It seemed that Spade had become very proficient
at murder, having hired himself out to a gang of London thugs
called the Last Chancers, and having killed—and pray to God
this was Professor Fell's attempt at fiction—eight men by the age
of twenty. And an additional two on his twentieth birthday, seemingly for the sport of it. He was called 'The Pepper Kid' for his
method of throwing a handful of ground pepper into the eyes of
his victims before he either slashed open their stomachs or their
throats with a hooked blade, depending on how fast or how slowly
he wished them to die. Then he became a jayhawk of the most
sterling quality, and secured for the Last Chancers the gin-sodden
wenches they desired to fill the rooms of their house of ill-repute
on Blue Anchor Road in Southwark. He fulfilled this role to the
best of any bastard's dark ambitions, having impressed upon the
Last Chancers the fact that little girls and virgins always sold well
in any economic climate, and that there were always little girls
lost or thrown out upon the London streets, and there were always

doctors ready for an amount of cash to restore with needle and stitches the pride of a wholesome virgin.

"I wish you wouldn't tell me these things," Berry said, as they walked the deck and Matthew recited this particular element of Nathan Spade's charm. Then she corrected herself: "But I do want to know. Why do they need you to pretend to *be* him? And what does this Professor Fell *want* with you?"

Matthew had had no choice but to tell her everything, as he knew it to be. He saw her daily, during these outings, but had seen Zed only a few times as Zed was usually working belowdecks. Matthew had decided that keeping Berry in the dark was no longer a noble endeavor, but was in fact an act of cruelty. "As I said," he told her, "he wants me to work for him. To solve some unknown problem. But I do trust his word to return us to New York after we're done."

"And why should you trust his word?"

Matthew looked at her. He noted she was getting sun on her face. Her freckles were emphasized by her freshened coloring. In the last few days the sun had made the weather as warm as April in New York. They were nearing the Bermuda islands and Matthew reasoned they couldn't be more than a few days out. "I *have* to," he replied. "Though I've...shall we say...disturbed his plans on more than one occasion, I believe he considers me to be..." He hesitated, pondering the end of that thought. "Of worth to him," he finished.

"I still don't understand why you didn't tell someone, Matthew! About the Mallorys! I mean...Doctor Gentry and that *woman*." She spoke the word with supreme disdain. "You could have told Hudson! Why didn't you?"

"For the same reason I didn't tell you," he reminded her. "I want no one dead on my behalf. If Hudson had interfered with this, they might have killed him. Because it wasn't he they wanted. The same with you. And, of course...here you are, and look what's happened. Now not only do they have *me*, they have Zed to be held as a sword over your head and *you* to be held as a sword over mine."

"As you've said," she answered with a quick flash of blue-eyed anger, "many times before."

"And I'll say it many times hence before I'm done." His anger was not so flashy, but mayhaps burned deeper. Still, there was no use in hitting her over the head with her own obstinacy, for he shared that same particular quality and it had certainly hit him over the head a few times.

They walked a distance further, completing one circuit of the deck and watching their step for coiled ropes and the numerous seamen scrubbing the wetted planks with holystones, before Matthew said, "All right, then. Continuing on about Master Spade, if you wish to hear anymore."

Berry hesitated only briefly. Her gentle sensibilities were no match for the power of her curiosity. "Go on."

Matthew did. Nathan Spade—if this indeed had been a living person—had evidently done a robust job as a jayhawk and thus at the age of twenty-two he had graduated to running the Blue Anchor bordello for the Last Chancers. Clock forward six months, and the Pepper Kid was put in charge also of a second Southwark whorehouse on Long Lane. And then at the age of twenty-four, his reputation both for discovering new talent and putting knives in the bellies of competitors was such that he was contacted by a certain Doctor Jonathan Gentry on behalf of a certain professor who wished to know if the aforementioned Master Spade might wish to come up in the world? Namely by managing a new house nearly in the shadow of Parliament, where men of good breeding and excellent funds mixed and mingled with the women of bad breeding who were determined to remove some of those funds from the overstuffed pockets? And suffice it to say, the women should be beautiful and rather ruthless in gaining information from their sex-stunned or love-struck lotharios, the better to share that information with Nathan Spade on its progress to Doctor Gentry and the professor's ear.

So be it.

The Pepper Kid had arrived in his own personal land of Milk and Honey. Now he no longer needed the pepper nor the knives, for he had the professor's killers to do that work if needed, and these days he wore expensive Italian suits and strolled the halls of diplomacy as an equal among the other moneyed and well-placed scoundrels.

"Disgusting," was Berry's comment when the tale was done.

"I agree," Matthew said, and yet he was becoming Nathan Spade and so he felt compelled to add, "But one must admire ambition."

Spoken, he realized, from a knowledge of what it took for a farmer's son to rise above a mountain of pigshit.

A commotion among a group of sailors snagged the attention of Matthew and Berry as they came around the starboard side, and following the pointed fingers and eager grins of these men brought their view up into the *Nightflyer's* intricate rigging. Up there two figures were climbing and leaping amid the jungle of ropes and netting, even as the sails blew wide and tight with captured wind and strained against their masts. Matthew saw, at the deck level, some of the crew coming forward to drop coins into a black box held by a surly-looking seaman and beside him one of studious demeanor marking in a ledger book. Up above, the two figures grasped ropes and swung from mast to mast, and on the deck some of the sailors hollered with glee and some catcalled with derision. Matthew realized he was witnessing not only a race between men in the rigging but also a bet in progress as to who would win, yet it wasn't clear what finish line one had to cross first in order to claim the prize. He wondered, from the shouts and rather crude encouragements of the gamblers, if several circuits of the masts had to be made, and so it was not only a contest of speed and dexterity but also of endurance.

He was struck with a sudden remembrance.

It had to do with the Iroquois tracker Walker In Two Worlds, who had been so vital in helping him in his hunt for Tyranthus Slaughter. Walker was telling Matthew about an arrangement that had been made, for a group of wealthy Englishmen to—

Pick three children, Walker had said, *and see them off on one of the flying canoe clouds that rested on the waters of Philadelphia. Nimble Climber was chosen, Pretty Girl Who Sits Alone was another, and I was the third. We three children, and the tribe, were told we would see the world of England and the city of London for ourselves and when we were returned—within two years—we would be able to explain to our people what we had witnessed. In hopes, the men said, of forming closer ties as brothers.*

But Matthew recalled that had only been part of the story.

My soul withers at the memory of that trip, Walker had said.

Watching the men race through the rigging high above his and Berry's heads, Matthew realized what had lit the fuse on this line of thought.

Nimble Climber did not survive, Walker had told him. *The sailors begin a wagering game, betting how fast he could get up the rigging to fetch a gull feather fixed to the mast with a leather strap. And they kept putting it higher and higher. They were paying him with peppermint candies. He had one in his mouth when he fell.*

The sailors hollered. One of the racers had slipped but had caught himself in the safety netting. He clambered up again to the nearest rope, undaunted by his brush with death.

When we reached England, Matthew remembered Walker saying, *Pretty Girl Who Sits Alone was taken away by two men. I held onto her hand as long as I could, but they pulled us apart. They put her in a horse box. A coach. She was carried off, somewhere. I never found out. Some men put me into another coach, and I was not to see my people again for almost ten years.*

Matthew recalled the rest of Walker's story, that the Indian had been put into several plays as the 'Noble Young Savage,' and then— as his fortunes had dwindled and the novelty of an American red-skin on a London stage had faded—he had found himself as the Demon Indian in a broken-down travelling fair and later returned to his tribe sadder, wiser, and—as he put it—insane.

The racers went around and around. A foot slipped on a mast. A rope was grabbed. The two men, having landed face-to-face on the same beam, wrestled with each other for a moment with no lack of effort. One fell, causing a mighty uproar. He toppled into a safety net ten feet above the deck and so no blood was spilled nor bones broken in this display of rough skill amid the ropes. It seemed also that throwing one's opponent off the mast was part of the game, as another uproar ascended for the victor and a crowd of men began to gather to claim their payouts from the black box.

"Skylarking," said a voice behind Matthew and Berry. There was only one voice like that aboard the *Nightflyer.* "That's what it's called," Captain Falco said when they looked to him for explanation. "A time-honored tradition. We're close enough to harbor now that I thought they should have a little reward."

"How close to harbor?" Matthew asked.

"Two days distant." The amber eyes scanned the sky. "The weather will hold. The wind favors us. Yes, two days."

"Thank God," said Berry, with a sigh of relief albeit premature. "I can't wait to walk on land again!" Though this trip had been nothing like the agony of her journey from England to New York on the ill-fated *Sarah Embry* last summer.

"Soon enough, miss." Falco regarded Matthew for a silent moment. Matthew thought he was trying to come to a decision. "Mr. Corbett," the captain said at last, "would you do me the courtesy of having a drink with me this evening? Say eight bells, in my cabin? I have something to discuss with you."

"Concerning what, if I might ask?"

"Concerning your presence here. And I would appreciate your not mentioning this visit with any of your other friends."

"Oh. I see."

"No, you *don't* see," Falco corrected, in a tone that was becoming a shade harsh. He looked up, as he did more than a hundred times a day, to measure the progress of wind in the sails. "Two days distant," he repeated. And then, to Matthew: "Eight bells, sharp." He turned away, and went about his business of managing a sailing ship under the charter of the emperor of crime.

FOURTEEN

"ENTER," said Captain Falco when eight bells had been struck on the deck above. Matthew had just knocked at the door decorated with the carved face of a lion. He turned the door's handle and half expected the lion to let out a roar. Then he stepped into the captain's cabin, where Falco was sitting at a table lighting a clay pipe with a candle's flame.

"Sit," came the next invitation, which sounded like a command. Falco blew out a gust of smoke and motioned toward the chair on the other side of the table.

Matthew obeyed. He saw that fish bones littered Falco's dinner plate, along with the remnants of biscuits and brown gravy. A smaller plate held slices of lime. Also on the table were two wooden cups and a squat "onion"-style bottle of black glass. Matthew had a quick look around at the ship master's quarters. Situated at the *Nightflyer*'s stern, it had six shuttered windows that, now opened, gave a view of the sea and star-spangled sky. The cabin, however, was not so very much larger than Matthew's. There was an oak chest of drawers with a mirror and water basin sitting atop it. A writing desk held a gray blotter and a quill pen and inkpot at the ready. A bed—more of a thin-mattressed cot, really—was made up so tautly its brown fabric covering looked to be in agony. Several lanterns hung from hooks in the overhead beams to give light to the captain's world. Falco smoked his pipe and Matthew smelled the rich, fragrant tang of Virginia tobacco.

"Pour yourself a drink."

Matthew again obeyed. What flowed from the black bottle and into his cup was a clear, golden liquor.

"Brandy," said the captain. "I decided to uncork something decent."

"Thank you." Matthew took a taste and found it considerably better than decent, but not so strong as to cause the eye-watering reaction he'd been expecting.

"It's a civilized drink." Falco poured himself a cupful. "For civilized men. Eh?"

"Yes," Matthew answered, for Falco seemed to expect a comment.

The captain offered Matthew the plate of lime slices, but Matthew shook his head. Falco chewed one of the slices, rind and all. He had a high, heavily-creased forehead and a widow's-peak of iron-gray hair. The upper portion of his left ear was missing. Matthew wondered if he'd ever met a swordsman named Dahlgren. In this light Falco's flesh appeared the hue of the deepest blue-black ink, which made the amber eyes both lighter and more powerful in their unwavering appraisal of his guest.

Falco finished the lime before he spoke again. "What in God's name have you gotten yourself into?"

The question was so direct it stunned Matthew for a few seconds. "Sir?"

"I don't repeat myself." Smoke roiled through the air.

A silence stretched, as one waited and one considered.

At last Matthew said, "I really don't know yet."

"You'd best find out in a hurry. Day after tomorrow, we reach Pendulum."

Matthew wasn't sure he'd heard correctly. He frowned. "Pendulum?"

"Pendulum Island. One of the Bermudas. It belongs to…but you know who it belongs to. Don't you?"

"I do."

Falco nodded, the pipe's stem clenched between his teeth. The eyes had an expression in them both sinister and jovial. *Mocking, it might be*, Matthew thought. *Or carefully curious.* "Are you afraid?" Falco asked.

There was no sense in lying to the lion. "Yes."

"And you should be. My employer, I understand, is to be feared."

"You *understand*? You've never met him?"

"Never met him. Never seen him. I take my orders from him through Sirki." The eyes had become heavy-lidded, and smoke swirled between the captain and Matthew. Falco poured himself a drink and removed the pipe from his mouth to take a sip. "I know he…commands many people, and directs many things. Some I've heard about, but I have ears that can remain closed when I choose. Also, my mouth can remain closed when need be. Which is most of the time." Another drink of copious strength went down the hatch, and then the pipe's stem was returned between the teeth.

"You're not one of his criminals, then?" It was a daring question, but Matthew felt it was the right thing to ask.

"I am the captain of my ship," came the measured reply. "How long I wished to be a captain, I cannot tell you. How long I labored for this position, again…a long time. He has given me the *Nightflyer*. He has placed me in the position I desired," Falco amended. "And pays me what I am worth."

"To do what, exactly? Sail from where to where?"

"From here to there and everywhere. To ferry passengers and carry cargo and pouches of letters. You see, I'm not like those others."

"What others?"

Falco spewed smoke in a long stream toward the ceiling. He took another drink. "His other captains. The ones who—" He paused, with his head slightly cocked to one side and his gaze sharp once again. "The ones who do more than ferry passengers," he finished.

"What more would there be?" Matthew asked, hungry for as much information concerning Professor Fell as he could consume. He reasoned that the more he knew, the stronger his armor.

"More," said Falco, with a faint and passing smile his eyes did not share. "But I asked you here because I wished to know what your purpose is on Pendulum Island. I wasn't told. My orders were to expect a passenger. *One* passenger, not three. Then there was some business with the signal lamp, and I saw fires burning in your town. Evidently the gunpowder bombs Sirki brought along in a wooden crate were put to use. I chose not to know anything further."

"But you're curious about my reason for being here?" Matthew prodded. "Why is that?"

Falco drew in more smoke and released it. He drank again before he answered. "You are out of place here. You are not..." He hesitated, hunting the rest of what he was trying to express. "The type I usually see," he said. "Far from it. And the young girl and the Ga warrior? They shouldn't be here. I can't understand this picture I'm seeing. You stood up to that woman in the brig. And you stood up to her for the right reason. *My friends*, you said. You see, this is what puzzles me: the kind of person I ferry for my employer *has* no friends, young man. To risk *anything* for anyone else...well, I've never seen that happen before on this ship. So I have to wonder... what in God's name have you gotten yourself into?"

Matthew pondered the question. His reply was, "I'm a problem-solver. I've been summoned by Professor Fell to solve a problem for him. Do you have any idea what that might be?"

"No. And why would I? I keep out of his business." Falco nodded at some inner comment he'd made to himself. "There. You see? I knew you were different. You're not of his world, if you get my meaning. But take care that his world doesn't get into you, because there's a lot of money in it."

"Dirty money, to be sure."

"Clean or dirty, it buys what you please *when* you please. It'll buy me a ship of my own one day. I'll start my own cargo business. That's what I'm in it for."

"A reasonable plan," said Matthew. He decided to try again at a question he wanted answered: "What do the other captains do? Besides ferrying passengers?"

For a time Falco did not answer, instead relighting his pipe from the candleflame. Matthew thought the question was going to go unheeded, and then Falco said, "There are four others. A very nice fleet, the professor has. The other ships carry cannons, which I have said I will not do. I want a clean and fast ship, unburdened by that heavy iron. But the others are also in the business of taking prizes on the high seas."

"Pirates?"

"They fly no flag," Falco corrected. "They are in the professor's employ."

This scheme was becoming clearer to Matthew, and the picture fascinated him. "So the professor gets a major portion of the prize for affording these...um...other captains a safe harbor?"

"As I said, he pays well. And lately the prizes have been something he obviously finds of great value."

"What? Treasure boxes of gold coins?"

"Not at all." Falco drew on his pipe and the blue-tinged Virginia fumes rolled from a corner of his mouth. "In the past few months the professor has been interested in ships carrying loads of sugar from the Caribbean."

"Sugar?" Matthew had to sit back in his chair on that one, for he'd had the image of Solomon Tully having a temper fit on the Great Dock, and asking the question of Matthew and Hudson Greathouse: *What kind of pirate is it that steals a cargo of sugar but leaves everything else untouched?*

The third shipment in as many months, Tully had moaned in his disconsolate agony of lost commerce. *And I'm not the only one affected by this either! It's happened to Micah Bergman in Philadelphia and the brothers Pallister in Charles Town!*

Professor Fell at work, Matthew thought. Sending his captains out to the trade routes to intercept the sugar boats.

"Why?" Matthew asked, through the smoke that hung in layers between himself and Captain Falco.

"I have no idea. I only know the sugar is brought into that harbor on the northernmost point and taken away in wagons." He offered Matthew a thin smile that looked like a razor cut. "Possibly this is also of interest to a problem-solver?"

Matthew remembered something else Solomon Tully had said, that cold day there on the Great Dock: *There's something wicked afoot with this constant stealing of sugar! I don't know where it's going, or why, and it troubles me no end! Haven't you two ever faced something you* had *to know, and it was just grinding your guts to find out?*

Looking across the table at Jerrell Falco, Matthew realized the *Nightflyer's* captain was also troubled by this unanswered question.

Perhaps Falco had sensed a change in the wind, or a shift in the direction of his life toward darker and deeper currents.

And, perhaps, he had decided…far down in his soul, where every man lived…that he didn't wish to go there.

He was asking Matthew to find out what was happening to the sugar. Because he too, like Solomon Tully, was confronted with something he felt had to be tinged with evil, and if Professor Fell desired shipload after shipload of it…was there any doubt?

"I may look into it," said Matthew.

"As you please," said the captain. "With one eye forward and one eye behind, I trust?"

"Always," Matthew answered.

"Finish your drink," Falco advised. "Take a slice of lime if you like."

Matthew drank the rest of the very good brandy. He chose a slice of lime and, like the captain, chewed it down rind and all. Then, realizing he was being dismissed, he stood up from his chair and said goodnight.

"Goodnight, Mr. Corbett," Falco answered, behind his swirling screen of smoke. "I do hope you solve the problems facing you."

Matthew nodded. It was a sincere wish, and certainly Matthew shared it. He left the cabin and walked back along the corridor to his own little room on the sea.

Upon opening the door, he found three people waiting for him by the light of the hanging lanterns. Sirki and Jonathan Gentry occupied chairs in his chamber, while Aria Chillany lounged on the edge of the bed. They were sitting as if waiting for a concert or theater program to begin, and the show being a bit late Doctor Gentry was playing a solitaire version of cat's-cradle with string between his fingers. The giant Sirki stood up, tall and dignified in his white turban and robes, as Matthew entered the room, and the madam pursed her lips and seemed to stretch her legs out a little as if to trip Matthew as he passed.

Matthew only needed a few seconds to compose himself, though seeing these three in his room had given him a severe jolt. "Good evening," he said, his face expressionless. No need to let them see any hint of nerves. Nathan Spade surely wouldn't have broken a sweat. "Making yourselves comfortable?" He closed the door at his back, a further sign of confidence he did not entirely embrace.

"Yes," Sirki said to the question. "Very. So good to see you. I presume you've been walking the deck?"

"I fear there's not much else to do for amusement aboard this ship. I've finished the books."

"Ah." Sirki nodded. Matthew felt the eyes of the other two on him. "Amusement," Sirki repeated, in a dry voice. "We are here just in time, it seems, to amuse you. Also to *instruct*. We shall be reaching our…will you *stop* that?" Sirki had shot a glare at Gentry, who was still playing with his cat's-cradle. The hands went down into Gentry's lap, while the doctor's mouth crimped with sullen indignation. To further the indignity, Madam Chillany gave a hard little laugh that sounded like clippers snipping off a pair of balls.

Matthew thought that the sea voyage was wearing on his hosts just as it wore on himself. He crossed to his dresser and poured himself a cup of fresh water from the pitcher there. Would Nathan Spade offer his guests a drink? No.

Sirki softly cleared his throat before he spoke again. "Have you been smoking?"

Matthew waited until he'd finished his water, taking leisurely sips in order to prepare his mind. He didn't really want these three to know he'd been talking to Captain Falco, in case they decided to find out exactly *why* Falco had summoned him. Falco's sudden discovery of curiosity and, perhaps, a desire to know the depth of his employer's evil would not go well for him with this triad of terror-makers. Matthew asked, "Excuse me?"

"Smoking." Sirki came upon him, nostrils flared. "I smell tobacco smoke on you."

"Hm," said Matthew, with raised brows. "I suppose I walked through a cloud or two."

"On deck? It seems a windy night for smoke clouds."

"It seems," Matthew said, meeting Sirki's dark stare with as much willpower and steadiness as he could find in an otherwise trembly soul, "windy in *here*. What's this about?"

"For fuck's sake!" squalled the woman, reduced to her true sensibilities due to either the buzz of snoring in her ears or the noxious aromas of her cabin companion. "Tell him!"

Sirki paid her no attention, but kept his focus solely on Matthew. "In the morning," he said after a pause, "the tailor will bring you two suits. Both will fit you very finely. You will wear one of them—your choice—when we dock at Pendulum and leave this ship. From that moment on, you will be Nathan Spade. There will be no more Matthew Corbett until you reboard this ship to be taken back to New York. Is that understood?"

"Somewhat," Matthew said, with a disinterested shrug to hide his seething curiosity.

Sirki took a stride forward and closed his hand upon Matthew's collar. "Listen to me, young sir," said the quiet and deathly voice. "There will be no mistakes made. No slips." The eyes bored into Matthew's. "Too much money has been spent to secure you to allow for a mistake. And bear this in mind: you will be a small fish in a pool of predators when you leave this ship. They can *smell* weakness. Just as I smell tobacco smoke in your clothes, and wonder who you've been spending time with tonight and why. They can smell...how shall I put this?...blood in the water. They will eagerly eat you alive, if you show any part of yourself that is not Nathan Spade. Now: is *that* understood?" Sirki released his grip on Matthew's collar, and though Matthew's first impulse was to put his back against a wall he instead set his chin and stood his ground.

"No," said Matthew. "I don't understand any of it. So tell me right *now*. What am I getting into?"

It was Madam Chillany's cool, rather taunting voice that replied: "Dearest boy, you are entering the professor's world as one of his own. You are going to attend a gathering. A business meeting, I suppose you'd call it. The professor's associates from England and Europe are coming to Pendulum Island for a...a..." Here she lost her power of description.

"Conference," Sirki supplied. "Some have already been there several weeks, waiting for the others to arrive. This has been planned for many months. Your inability to follow directions has made us late to the party, but it can't begin without you."

Matthew was still trying to get past the sentence about the professor's associates from England and Europe coming to Pendulum Island. He felt as if he'd taken a blow to the basket. A convergence of Fell's criminals, with Matthew Corbett—no, make that Nathan Spade—among the dishonorable guests.

My God, Matthew thought. I've stepped into deep—

"Water," said the woman languidly. "Matthew, would you pour me a cup?"

He did so, as he was not so far gone as to be heedless to good manners. And as Matthew offered the cup to Madam Chillany, Sirki swept it disdainfully from his hand and the cup broke to pieces against strong oak planking that bore the heelmarks of many passengers before himself.

"It's time," said Sirki, his glare like embers about to burst into dangerous flames, "that you learned to answer *only* to the name *Nathan.*"

Matthew regarded the bits of broken clay. He said easily, "That was a damned fine cup. I presume you'll bring me yours to correct this unfortunate situation?" He turned his own hot gaze upon Sirki, and let it burn. "In fact, I insist on it."

"You're a cocky little bastard!" sneered Doctor Gentry, but there was some humorous admiration in it.

"Oh, now *that's* my Nathan!" came Aria's voice. Her admiration seemed a bit lower. "Give him room, Sirki. I think he's big enough for the part."

Matthew had no comment on that remark, but he wondered if his parts were big enough to make a whole.

Sirki smiled faintly, enough to display a glimmer of diamonds. "I think you're right, Aria." The smile vanished, like a busker's conjuring trick. "But so much remains to be seen." He pulled toward himself the chair he'd vacated, turned it around and sat astride it. "I'll tell you," he said, addressing Matthew, "that when we dock, your beauty and her beast will be kept aboard this ship after you have left it. When darkness falls, so as not to draw any undue attention, they will be put into a carriage and taken to a place of confinement. It would not do for any of the other associates to see them, and wonder who they might be. The type of person we're dealing with here has a high degree of suspicion and a higher degree of cunning. We want no questions left in the air."

"A place of confinement?" Matthew frowned. "I don't like the sound of that."

"Whether you do or not is of no concern to me, but I'll tell you also that they will be in comfort and well looked-after."

"Behind bars, I take it?"

"No bars. But locks and a guard or two, yes. I'll see to that arrangement. They'll be near the main house and out of the way, but they'll also be out of danger."

"What kind of danger?"

"The same that faces you if anyone discovers you are an imposter. Some of these people make Nathan Spade appear a saint. They kill for sport. And trust me, I can think of two or three who will be doing their best to unravel your rope."

"This sounds less like a conference as it sounds to be a gathering of..." *Sharks*, Matthew was about to say. *All the smaller sharks—deadly enough in their own oceans—have gathered around the big shark, and so they have swum even here...*

Well said, Hudson, he thought. Well said.

"Do not push anyone," Aria offered, standing up from the bed. She came to Matthew's side. He thought she smelled of fire and brimstone. Smiling—if that could be called so—she pushed a finger into his right cheek. "But do not let yourself be pushed, either." Her finger moved to gently trace the outline of the wound underneath his left eye, where the traces of stitchery could still be seen. "This will do you splendidly. They like evidences of violence. It makes them feel all warm inside."

How does it make you *feel?* he nearly asked. But he reckoned that she was waiting for him to ask that question, and he was not that much Nathan Spade. Yet. God forbid.

"If these associates are so cunning," Matthew said, looking at the woman but speaking to the East Indian giant, "then they'll soon find out I'm not the blackhearted whoremonger I'm supposed to be. A few questions regarding my relations with the Last Chancers and the...um...ins and outs of my particular business, and—"

"No one will ask those questions," Sirki interrupted. "They know *not* to know too much. Consider the professor's organization like a ship. Everyone is on board, yet all have their cabins."

"*Not* a good example," sniffed the woman.

"All have their cabins," Sirki repeated, "and their responsibilities. Yes, I'm certain some of them will have *heard* of Nathan Spade, but none will have ever met him or had any business with him. That's not how it's done."

Matthew grunted softly and moved his attention from Aria to Sirki. Gentry, in his own defiance of being told what to do, was playing again with the cat's-cradle, keeping his hands low and his movements tightly controlled. "I see," said Matthew. "It's a security measure, yes? Also to keep any one person from knowing how everything works?"

"I know how everything works," Sirki reminded him. "Then next would be the madam, and after her would be the good doctor, who has the bad habit of losing his power of concentration due to the many exotic elixirs he has inhaled or imbibed. Isn't that right, Jonathan?"

"As rain at a funeral," said Gentry. A crooked half-smile stole across the devilishly-handsome face. "But oh what colors I have seen."

"I wish you would see less colors and more soap," Aria said. "You *stink*."

"Ha," Gentry replied, a humorless laugh, as he applied all his brain to the pattern of strings between his fingers. Matthew wondered if a particularly strong and exotic elixir, possibly one made from the jungle mushrooms of South America, had been the doctor's companion this evening.

"No one will want to know too much about Nathan Spade," Sirki continued. "It would be bad behavior and a violation of rules. But you can be sure the professor has made your name and reputation known to one and all."

"Grand," said Matthew, with a bitter edge. "May I ask if there really is—or was—a Nathan Spade? And if he *is*, where he is, and if he *was*, what was his fate?"

"Oh, Nathan was very real." Aria's fingers stroked Matthew's cheek. She stared deeply into his eyes. "But Nathan became weak, with his position and his money. He let himself falter. He became too comfortable." The fingers went back and forth across Matthew's flesh. "He *forgot* who made him, as made all of us."

"God?" Matthew asked.

"Oh," she said with a quick smile though the sapphire-colored eyes remained dead, "you are so *cute*."

"For a dead man? I'm assuming he's no longer on this side of Hades?"

Sirki rose to his feet, an ominous sign. The chair creaked with relief. "Madam Chillany shot Nathan Spade in the head last year."

"Almost a year ago exactly," she added. The fingers moved, stroking from chin to ear and back again.

"Nathan Spade became a liability," Sirki went on. "He went into the business of selling information to foreign interests. That conflicted with the professor's aims. No one you're going to meet will know that, nor that Master Spade is deceased. The body was cut to pieces, burned, and the remnants—"

"Dumped from a basket into the Thames," said the woman, nearly whispering it. Whether she was choked with emotion or pride, Matthew couldn't tell. "He deserved what he got," she murmured. The fingers abruptly stopped moving. The nails pressed against Matthew's flesh. Harder, and harder still. She smiled, her eyes glassy. "Such is life," she said.

Her hand left his face.

She turned away.

Matthew watched her back stiffen as she walked past Sirki and Doctor Gentry. She resumed her casual position on the bed. Perhaps it was the position she was most comfortable with. There was something remote and even desperate about her blank expression, and Matthew didn't care to look too long upon it because he had left the desolation of winter in New York.

He regarded Sirki once more. "I still don't understand my purpose. What does the professor expect me to *do?*"

"Professor Fell," said the giant, "wants the pleasure of informing you in person."

Matthew had no response to this. He wished he had put down a second cup of brandy in Falco's cabin. He wished he had a bottle of rum to keep him company tonight. He wished he could see Berry, who was down the corridor in a locked cabin. He wished he was still a magistrate's clerk, whose responsibilities began and ended with a quill.

But no, he was *somebody* now. Someone special in this world.

And for that, he must pay the price.

"Those suits," he managed to say, "better fit me perfectly. If I'm to play the part, I will look the part."

"Naturally," Sirki agreed. "And well spoken, sir." He spoke then to his companions in crime: "We should leave Mr. Spade to his deliberations, and his rest."

Aria Chillany left the cabin first, seemingly still in a trance of her own making, followed by the cat's-cradle devotee. Sirki paused at the door.

"It occurs to me that Captain Falco smokes," he said.

"Does he?" Matthew offered not a hint of reaction. "I'd say there are at least twenty others aboard who also smoke."

"True, but the fragrant Virginia weed is more expensive than most, and I think beyond the means of ordinary swabbies. Be careful whose smoke you collect, young sir. It can get in the eyes and make one blind as to their purpose here." He let that linger in the air, like its own stinging fumes. Then: "Goodnight." Matthew didn't return the comment. Sirki left the cabin, and instantly Matthew threw the latch on the door. The horses had already left the barn, yes, but he didn't want any more manure on his floor. As he readied himself for what he presumed would be a troubled night's sleep, he could almost sense the *Nightflyer* approaching Pendulum Island. The brigantine with full sails stretched wide, a few lamps burning on deck, the wake bluish-white under the silver moon and lacy clouds moving slowly across the dark. And the lair of Professor Fell, becoming closer with each wave crossed and each slow roll of the ship. He wondered if Sirki knew Captain Falco was starting to question his lot in life. If maybe Falco had expressed some misgiving to someone who told someone else, who told an ear that led to a voice cautioning the East Indian giant: *Falco knows too much, and he thinks too much.*

It occurred to Matthew that the captain's days might be numbered. This might be Falco's final voyage. Payment in full, when they made landfall.

What would Nathan Spade do?

Laugh and say *Good riddance*?

Yes. But what was Matthew Corbett to do?

He had a head full of problems, but—sadly—no solutions.

Yet, he thought.

And then he extinguished his lanterns except for one candle left burning, and he took to bed in the *Nightflyer*'s creaking belly.

FIFTEEN

MATTHEW had expected to hear a shouted "Land ho," but instead the note of a trumpet signalled the sighting of Pendulum Island.

There was a rushing forward of sailors eager to set foot onto solid earth. Matthew stood among them in the bright warm morning sun and watched the island take shape.

Possibly by the eye of a gull it had the shape of a pendulum, but from this vantage point it was a mass of jagged black rocks and broken gray cliffs with a sparse covering of moss and brown lichens. Inland there looked to be a verdant wilderness, which did not soothe Matthew's soul. He yet saw no sign of manmade structures, and had to wonder if Professor Fell's domain lay somewhere within the very rock itself.

He was dressed for Nathan Spade's success. His charcoal-gray suit with thin stripes in a hue of lighter gray fit him like a prison cell. His pale blue shirt was adorned with ruffles at collar and cuffs, which seemed to Matthew to be a little precious for an ex-jayhawk, but then again it was likely perfect for a genteel whoremaster-around-town. His stockings were chalky-white and his black boots buffed to an admirable shine; they gleamed with every step. He was clean-shaven and ruddy-cheeked, his hair was brushed back and—by Aria Chillany's insistence this morning—put under strict control with two fingers of pomade that smelled of sandalwood and another sweetly pungent scent that made him think of the incense curling from a Turkish lamp in Polly Blossom's parlor. Call it, he decided, the smell of 'vice.'

It made sense to him that such an aroma would be leaking from Nathan Spade's pores.

"It doesn't look like much, does it?"

"No, it doesn't." Matthew was aware that Berry—freed from the confines of her cabin during the daylight hours—had come up beside him. The sailors gathered around were also aware of her presence, and seemed to bend toward her like saplings in a strong wind to get the womanly perfume of her hair and flesh. But one glance from the false Nathan Spade and they straightened their backs and went about their business, for they knew the young man had favor of the master of Pendulum.

Matthew saw Captain Falco at the wheel, turning the *Nightflyer* a few degrees to port. He took stock of the sun and reasoned they were making a course to the southeast. "Not much," he said to Berry, continuing her statement, "but obviously it's an important destination." He examined Berry's face, and found her eager-eyed and nearly as sun-ruddy as himself. Her freckles had emerged by the dozens across her cheeks and the bridge of her nose, and her curly hair flowed free in the breeze and seemed the color of some kind of tawny-red candy sold by the handful to sweet-toothed children. *She is on a grand adventure,* he thought. *She is all kite and no string.*

For all his masquerade of courage and fortitude in the faces of Madam Chillany and the giant Sirki, he had not been able to bring himself to tell Berry that she and Zed were destined for lock-and-key upon landfall. He trusted Sirki, that they would be well-cared for. He really had no choice but to trust Sirki. But as he stood beside Berry her hand suddenly came out and searched for his. He took it firmly, and she looked him in the face and asked, "Are we going to be all right?"

"Yes, we are," he answered without hesitation.

The island grew nearer. Waves crashed against the rocks and white foam spewed up. A whirring of gulls thrashed the air.

"Are you afraid?" Berry asked, in a quiet voice.

"Yes," Matthew said, "I am." But he recovered from this spillage of truth long enough to give her a sturdy smile with no lack of false bravado at its center, and he added, "But before this is done, they're going to fear *me*."

And though he only half-believed it, he fully meant it.

The *Nightflyer* was going to pass this northernmost point of Pendulum Island on its starboard side. Matthew and Berry still held hands as the first sign of human life came into view, and mayhaps they clasped hands harder at the sight. Two masted ships of dark design were moored to a wharf. Dark design, due to the gunports along the hulls. Matthew thought that here were two of Fell's plunderers used to raid the sugar merchants. One look at the snouts of cannons protruding from those ports, and any issue of resistance was ended. Just beyond the wharf was a low-slung wooden building that likely was a warehouse for nautical goods storage. A dirt road curved away from the wharf and entered the forest, where it disappeared among green fronds and the thick walls of trees. And up above, perched atop a gray cliff but partly hidden by vegetation, was the stone wall of a fort also guarded by cannons on its parapets. The professor's estate? Matthew wondered.

Onward the *Nightflyer* sailed, sliding over blue sea and white swirling foam. Captain Falco had a sure touch on the wheel. At his urging the ship moved between fangs of black rock. To starboard Matthew and Berry saw another pier come into view, this one tucked into a small cove where the waves were more gracious and the rocks less fangly. More cliffs of some thirty or forty feet faced the sea, and along them was a road that followed their ascent. Before the road disappeared around a bend, Matthew figured it was nearly a hundred feet above the water. A pair of coaches, each with four horses, waited alongside the pier. Evidently someone had come to witness the arrival of that notable black-hearted scoundrel Nathan Spade.

"Miss Grigsby, I would ask that you return to your cabin."

The voice, so close to their ears, startled them both. Sirki was watching the pier. "A spyglass might be in use," he said. "We wish no one to inquire about the red-haired girl." He took Berry's elbow. "Come below, please."

"What?" She resisted his pull, showing remarkable strength. In truth, her heart had leaped to her throat and she could hardly speak. She looked to Matthew for aid, and when she spoke again she forced the words out one by one: "Why do I have to go to my cabin?"

"A moment," Matthew said to Sirki, and the East Indian giant withdrew his hand and also his presence by a few paces. Matthew stared intensely into Berry's eyes. "Listen to me," he said quietly, even as the gulls croaked and called above. "You can't be seen by anyone on the island. Nor can Zed. Sirki's going to take you somewhere for… safekeeping," he decided to say. "It won't be a cell. *Will* it?" He darted a glance at Sirki, long enough for the giant to shake his turbanned head. Then back to Berry's eyes again. He saw fear in them, and the wet beginnings of tears. *"Listen."* He took both her hands. "In this case, I agree with Sirki. I don't want you or Zed to be seen by any of the…the creatures I'm going to meet. I want you out of the way." She started to protest, but a finger went to her lips. *"No,"* he said. "Don't speak. When this is done, we'll go home. All of us, safe and sound. But for that to happen, you're going to have to trust me to do my job."

"I can *help* you," she said, with a note of pleading.

"No you cannot. Not in the way you wish. You can *really* help me by going with Sirki to your cabin, and waiting there until he summons you to leave the ship. Also by controlling Zed, if you can. Let him know that he needs to lie low for a time. Both of you do. Sirki!" Matthew's voice was harsher than he'd intended, but it caused the giant to step forward with something like obedience. "Where will they be taken? Tell me now, and tell me the truth."

"Of course. They will be taken to the village of Templeton on the east side of the island. Many people live there, but none who will be a danger to your friends. Miss Grigsby and the Ga will be afforded quarters at the Templeton Inn, run by a very efficient Scotsman who knows to ask no questions. The inn is used primarily for the professor's guests, when not invited to the castle. And I can tell you that the innkeeper's wife is a very excellent cook." He paused for a few seconds before continuing. "I will say also that two guards will always be present, and if Miss Grigsby and the Ga desire to walk about the village they will never walk alone. Is that truth enough for you?"

"Sufficent," came the curt answer. Matthew was in no mood for niceties; this subject was disagreeable to him to an extreme, yet he knew how necessary—and unavoidable—was the outcome. "You have to go," he told Berry.

"*Now*," Sirki added, with a glance at the oncoming wharf. Captain Falco had given the order to drop sails, and weighted ropes had been thrown over the sides to reduce their speed into the cove.

Berry realized she had no choice. Ordinarily this would have made her temper flare, but she knew that to let herself be angry here was pointless. Matthew was doing what he needed to do, and indeed she had to trust him. She nodded. "All right." She was still holding one of Matthew's hands, and this she released. She turned away from him without another word, and Sirki followed her across the deck to the stairway down.

Matthew started to call *It won't be for long* after her, but he didn't wish to lie so he kept his mouth closed. He had no idea how long it might be. Several days? Weeks? A month or more? He dreaded to think, therefore he shut away all thoughts to that regard.

The *Nightflyer's* speed had slowed dramatically, and the brigantine was now mostly drifting. The ship's course was met by four longboats that had set off from the wharf. Ropes were thrown from ship to boats, and now the crews on the smaller craft had the work of rowing the *Nightflyer* in the rest of the way and securing Captain Falco's vessel to her mooring bollards. Falco strode forward to the bow and nearly rode the sprit in his intense watch over the task at hand. He gave a few commands which were relayed to the seaman at the wheel, but otherwise he was silent.

So it was done within another twenty minutes, the ship being moored to the wharf and the longboats withdrawing. Matthew noted Jonathan Gentry and Aria Chillany on deck, dressed in their finest for the landing. A couple of unfortunate and weary-looking sailors had been impressed to carry their luggage. Matthew also saw Croydon and Squibbs wandering about, but they cared not to cast a glance in Matthew's direction and that likewise was fine with him.

The gangplank was lowered. "All ashore!" came a sea-fevered cry, yet there was no rush for the crew to leave the ship for there was still work to be done before the *Nightflyer* could be considered well-and-truly arrived. Falco stood on the poop deck, casting a long shadow. Matthew saw that the two black coaches waiting at the head of the wharf was manned by two drivers, and looked to be a type he knew to be called a *berline*, enclosed with room for four passengers, the driver sitting on a forward perch. But atop one of the coaches sat a pair of men in gray suits. They both had bright shocks of orange hair, and were sunning themselves as they presumably waited for the *Nightflyer*'s passengers to disembark. The lithe figure of a young woman with short-trimmed blonde hair stood in a casual attitude beside the second coach. She was a sight to behold and would have caused jaws to drop in New York, for she was wearing a man's brown breeches, high-topped brown boots, and a deep purple waistcoat over a cream-colored blouse.

Whoever they were, Matthew reasoned they had come to see Nathan Spade set foot on Pendulum Island. Either that, or the amusements on Pendulum were so lacking they had little else to do.

"Are you ready?"

Matthew looked to his left, into the sapphire-blue eyes of Aria Chillany. Gentry stood a few feet behind her. His eyes were bloodshot. He wore a stupid smile directed at no one. Though the *Nightflyer* had docked, the doctor was still flying. Matthew wondered if Gentry's proclivity for his potions had to do with the fact that he would soon be hearing his master's voice, and this paragon of handsome charm was unnerved by that oncoming certainty. In any event, Gentry was skunked.

"I'm ready," Matthew managed to answer.

"You know your subject, then?" Her mouth was very close to his.

"I said I'm ready." Spoken with fortitude, but little surety.

"Your luggage is here." She motioned toward a seaman who stood nearby shouldering a brown canvas bag. Matthew had been given it this morning, and had dutifully packed away his belongings. "You should be first off the ship. I'll follow along."

He nodded. It was time for the grand entrance, and this particular—and peculiar—play to commence. He crossed the deck to the gangplank, gave a glance at the two men and the woman who watched the wharf, and then he puffed out his chest and determined to put a little strut in his stride, as befitting a big cock-of-the-walk.

Matthew started across the gangplank, taking long strides as if he owned the world and everyone else was just a passing visitor.

Suddenly his world tipped over on its side. He realized his sea-legs were still measuring the roll of a ship after three weeks on the Atlantic. He staggered left and staggered right, drunk with solidity. On the third stagger he reached for the handrail but there was no handrail to be gripped, and he gave a curse to both Nathan Spade's vanity and the fact that God was a more mischievious trickster than ever any preacher imagined in a sonorous Sabbath's speech.

Then he went right off the gangplank, splashing headlong into the drink between the wharf and the *Nightflyer*'s hull.

The water was far warmer than Manhattan's winter harbor yet still cool enough to make swimming uncomfortable about the family jewels. He reckoned he might have shouted underwater, for an explosion of bubbles hit him in the face and following that was a rush of saltwater into his mouth. *There goes the hair pomade*, he thought either grimly or crazily. Then he realized he had better kick to the surface and get out of here, for it was a shame for his fine suit to be so soaked.

His next thought was: *Damn, I've made a mess of this already!*

He came up to the noise of hooting and cat-calling, and some-one yelling with unbridled mirth, *"Man overboard!"* He pushed the hair out of his face and saw Aria making her way unsteadily down the gangplank, but she had prepared for this moment by taking small steps. She speared him with her eyes as one might spear a fat-bellied bottom feeder. A sailor appeared holding a long wooden pole with a leather-wrapped hook on one end, which he offered to Matthew. The hook having been taken, Matthew was pulled up until he could get a grip on the edge of the wharf, and so struggling and scrabbling like a dumb, doomed crab for a moment he at last hauled himself up onto the hardwood.

Oh, the laughter! The hilarity! The horror of it all! Even Captain Falco had his hand strategically to his face, and was examining some point of interest up on the mainmast.

He got himself up on his feet and stood dripping. He heard the harsh, rasping laughter of the two orange-haired gents coil-ing toward him like whips. The young blonde woman—bless her—watched in silence.

Matthew felt a box closing around him. It might be a coffin. He decided he would not let it close. It was time—oh, *yes*—for Nathan Spade to speak out.

He looked up at the grinning crew of the *Nightflyer*. He looked up into the laughter, and he brought a wide grin of his own up from somewhere, and he puffed his chest out again like a banty rooster and he hollered at the top of his salty lungs, "Fuck all! I've wet my fuckin' britches, haven't I?"

The words did not taste very good, but the sentiment was delicious.

The laughter changed; it was difficult to tell exactly how, but it did. For Matthew began to laugh too, and now the joke was not just about one strutting man who'd taken a dive into the drink, but about all men who cast their fate upon a treacherous path and find themselves quite unexpectedly falling from grace.

They grinned and nodded and nearly cheered him, and then Matthew turned away with a sweeping flourish of his arm that said *I am the same as you, only better dressed.* In his squishy boots he strode past Aria Chillany, who moved to give him way, and on his purposeful yet still dizzied walk up the wharf he saw that the two orange-haired men were no longer laughing but watching him with narrowed eyes from fox-like faces, and that the blonde woman had climbed into her berline and could no longer be seen.

He continued onward, leaving puddles of the Atlantic in his footsteps. Madam Chillany caught up with him and said in a guarded voice, "Careful of those two. Jack and Mack Thacker. You don't want to turn your back on them."

The Thacker brothers. Matthew recalled hearing mention of them from Hudson. And here they were, in the ugly flesh. They sprawled atop the coach, each wearing an identical gray suit, white shirt, white stockings and black boots. In fact, they were identical twins, or nearly much so. They looked like lazy animals taking the morning sun. One spoke to the other and the other spoke back, but the eyes in their granite-jawed and sharp-nosed faces never left the person of Nathan Spade. They looked to be in their early forties, short and compact like rowdy tavern brawlers ready to bet a coin on a mouth of broken teeth. Someone else's broken teeth, of course, because the Thackers had thick forearms and shoulders, legs like squat treetrunks and necks that could burst a hangman's noose. Their faces were flushed with the blood that pulsed just beneath the skin's surface, or perhaps they didn't take the sun very well. As Matthew approached the berlines, he saw that one of the twins had a streak of gray at the front of the orange hair, which was brushed back from the forehead and shiny with pomade; the other twin did not share this mark, and so it was the only thing Matthew could see different about them. They had small deepset eyes that looked to be pale green, like sharp splinters of glass.

They did not speak or move from their languid positions as Matthew approached.

"Nathan!" said the woman behind him. "We'll take the other coach."

Matthew changed his direction. He heard the brothers snicker at almost the same time.

The one with the gray streak said in a heavy Irish brogue, "Go on with ya! Listen to your—"

"Mama!" said the second, and they both snickered again.

Matthew shot them a dark look, but he also offered a thin smile. He stopped in his wet tracks. Now was as good a time as any to display his mettle, though it be fashioned from the cheapest tin. "Should I know you gentlemen?"

"I don't know," said one, and the other added, "Should ya?"

Interesting, Matthew thought. They finished each others' sentences. They wore identical smirks. The coachman of their berline kept his head down and his attention forward, as if fearful of imminent violence. Matthew could feel it in the air. These two liked to bloody up a victim, and maybe they were sizing him up as fodder for their fists.

"My name is Nathan Spade," said Matthew. "Do you have names?"

One of them answered with an outthrust chin, "I think your name is—"

"Soggy Ass," said the one with the gray streak, and both of them grinned tightly, with no humor on their faces.

"Nathan?" Aria's voice had also tightened. "Come along. Yes?"

"Hold her petticoat, Nathan!" said the gray-streaker.

"Go on with ya!" said the second, who perhaps had larger ears than his brother.

But Matthew stood his ground. "Oh," he said easily, though his heart was pounding, "I've heard of you two. The Thackers. Which is Jack and which is Mack? Or have you forgotten?"

Their grins began to slowly fade.

A movement within their coach caught Matthew's attention.

He saw someone lean forward to peer through the door's open window. It was a woman. He met her eyes, and he felt turned inside-out.

She stared at him only briefly, possibly five seconds before she leaned back into the seat once more. But Matthew was left with the stunned impression of one of the most beautiful women he'd ever seen. She had tawny flesh that seemed almost radiant. Her long ebony hair, topped by a gray hat tilted to one side with a spill of black lace across her forehead, flowed down about her shoulders in rich waves. She had an oval face with high cheekbones, a straight and narrow-bridged nose, and a full-lipped mouth that seemed to Matthew to be crimped tightly on many secrets. Her eyes were very dark, perhaps as ebony as her hair, and they had regarded Matthew in passing, without life or fire or spirit.

Whoever she was, she was not altogether there. In just the instant of seeing her, Matthew thought this lovely creature was terribly, heartbreakingly lonely. And he thought it was a shame, that such a pretty girl should sit alone.

"What're ya lookin' at..."

"...boyo?"

The two brothers slid off the coach. They stood a few feet distant from each other, one to Matthew's left and one to the right. They had lost their grins. Their faces were impassive, and brutal in their lack of expression.

"The woman in the coach—" Matthew began.

"Never ya mind her," said the gray-streaker.

"Go 'bout your business," said the other. It was no doubt a warning.

"Nathan?" Aria's voice held a hard edge. "To our coach, please." Gentry was staggering toward them, whether by nature or by naturalist potion difficult to tell. Behind him came the sailors bearing their luggage.

The two brothers were silent. They were waiting, it seemed, for Nathan Spade's next move in this small but potentially deadly game. Matthew realized the stocky pair were about as tall as the point of his nose. He said, "Good to meet you gentlemen," and turned toward Aria. He had taken two strides when one of the Thackers let out the sound of a wet and nasty fart and the other gave a quick grating laugh that made the flesh on the back of Matthew's neck crawl.

"Let's keep moving," said Aria in a hushed voice, her face frozen in a smile but her dark blue eyes glittering with either repressed rage or something akin to fear, if she knew what that was. It was clear that the Thacker twins were no devotees of good manners, and Matthew figured his masquerade—and usefulness—might have ended here at the head of this wharf if those two had been incited to explosive riot. And it seemed the Indian girl might be their powderkeg.

There it was, Matthew thought as he opened the berline's door. The beautiful woman in the other coach was most decidedly an Indian...not of Sirki's nationality, but of the tribe of Walker In Two Worlds.

He slid along the leather bench seat and found himself sitting across from the blonde-haired woman dressed in the male finery.

She aimed at him a pair of eyes the color of golden ale. "You're dripping on my boots," she said, her voice low and controlled and not lacking in menace.

"Pardon me." Instantly he shifted his position, which he figured was not what Nathan Spade would have done, but he was still Matthew Corbett at heart and in manners. Something to work on, he decided. He looked at the third occupant of their berline, a rotund bald-headed man with three chins. This individual, dressed in a beige suit and a dark green blouse with lavender ruffles, was taking a pinch of snuff from a gold box. He wore round spectacles that magnified his watery blue eyes and made the small red veins in them jump out. Adorning the edge of his right ear were seven small gold ornaments of varying geometric shapes. His lips were as thin as a pauper's wallet, his bulbous nose as large as Lord Cornbury's ambitions. Matthew guessed his age at around fifty. "Good morning," the man said when the two huge nostrils had taken their drink of whuffie-dust. "I am Augustus Pons. You are Nathan Spade." It was a statement, not a question.

"I am." No hand was offered from either man.

"Ah," said Pons, with a slight nod. The eyelids blinked drowsily. When he spoke, his jowls danced. "We have been awaiting your arrival. I have been on this island for nearly one month. Why is it, may I ask, that it took so long for you to join us?"

"Complications," said Aria as she entered the coach and sat beside Matthew. She offered nothing else, but stared at Augustus Pons in a way that told him to ask no more questions. Pons smiled wanly, showing small nuggets of brown teeth, and visibly retreated as if going down a hole and pulling it in after himself.

Evidently the luggage had been loaded in the berline's cargo compartment at the rear and Jonathan Gentry had found a seat in the other coach, as there was only room for four here. Aria rapped on the wall behind her as a signal to the driver. A whip cracked and the team set off.

"Nathan Spade," said the blonde woman. She was staring intently at him, her head cocked slightly to one side as if trying to make up her mind about something. "Where did you sail from?"

"New York," Matthew said before Aria could speak. He'd decided it was time for him to chart his own course. "I had business there."

"Don't we all?" she asked, with a half-smile and a lift of a thick blonde brow. Then she said, "I'm Minx Cutter. Pleased to meet you." She offered a hand, which Matthew took. "Welcome to Pendulum," she offered, with a squeeze before releasing him.

"Thank you. I believe those other two don't welcome me quite as graciously."

"Jack and Mack Thacker," she said. "They go everywhere together. I understand Jack is the elder by a few minutes. He has the streak of gray."

"Ah." Matthew paused for a few seconds before asking the question that followed: "And who is the young Indian woman?" Minx Cutter shrugged. "They call her Fancy." The coach was climbing the cliffside road. Matthew glanced to the right, out the window past Aria, and saw their height increasing over the sunlit blue cove. His drenched clothes were a nuisance, but he'd suffered worse. He made a show of examining his fingernails, which were perfectly clean, while he gathered impressions of Minx Cutter.

She had a hard quality of beauty. There was nothing soft about her except possibly the curly ringlets of her hair. Even those might have been thorny to the touch. She had a firm jawline and a square chin, a tight-lipped mouth and a nose that appeared to have been broken and improperly repaired, for it bore a small bump in the middle and crooked slightly to the left. She was slimly-built, but far from being frail. Matthew thought she was built for speed and agility. She held herself with calm composure and obvious high regard. Her intelligent eyes, light brown with a golden element in their hue, feigned disinterest, but Matthew had the sense that she was also sizing him up. She might have been anywhere from twenty to twenty-five, as her peach-toned flesh was unlined; she appeared to Matthew to not have much practice in smiling. So young to be so deeply in the professor's pocket, he thought. Therefore he had to wonder exactly what Minx Cutter did for the emperor of crime and the owner of Pendulum Island.

He was mulling over the possiblities when he heard a man's scream. Looking out his own window to the left, he was uncomfortably aware that the four horses of the second berline were thundering up nearly wheel-to-wheel of their own coach and that this precarious path was suited only for one set of wheels at a time. He saw that the coachman had been removed by force, and sitting with reins in hand was Mack Thacker, while Jack swung the whip with mad abandon over the rumps of their team.

"Oh my!" croaked Augustus Pons. His eyes were gigantic. "I fear those two are up to—"

The whip cracked against the side of their coach, causing Pons to jump and spill most of the snuff from his open box. As the brown dust swirled around, Matthew saw Jack Thacker grit his teeth and swing the whip to connect with their own driver, who must have been stung by the blow because there was a strident cry of pain. The next whipstrike did something particularly nasty, for both brothers grinned and jostled each other with their elbows.

Matthew sensed uneasily that their speed was becoming dangerous on this already-dangerous road. There were no walls nor railings; if two wheels on the cliffside went off, so would follow the berline.

And then Jack Thacker in a red-cheeked frenzy began to whip the team of Matthew's coach to more reckless speed. Matthew realized with a start of fear that their whipstruck driver must have abandoned his seat and reins. They were sitting in a runaway coach only a few inches from disaster. Minx Cutter realized it at nearly the same time because she cried out a most unladylike *"Shit!"* and Matthew reckoned that under the circumstances it could be a command.

SIXTEEN

AN enraged cry flew from Aria Chillany's mouth toward the boisterous brothers: "Stop it!"

But that, Matthew reasoned in his cool center at this moment of heat, was like asking the breeze to cease blowing and the ocean to quit waving, for the Irish twins were now both red-faced and crazed in this drama of their own making and there was no stopping them until...*what*? Nathan Spade's coach went over the cliff?

As if to emphasize this thought, the whip struck out again and hit the edge of Matthew's window, knocking loose a chip of black paint.

The runaway horses surged forward at an even more frantic gallop, and now the wheels of the Thackers' speeding coach hit those of Matthew's berline, rim to rim, and a shudder passed through the framework that made the joints moan.

"Those bastards!" Aria seethed. She thrust herself across Matthew's lap and halfway out the window. "Stop it!" she screamed at the brothers. "Stop it or you're *dead*, do you hear?"

It occurred to Matthew that threatening the Thackers with death was not quite the way to resolve this problem, particularly from the way they laughed and snorted at this pronouncement and also due to the fact that they were not in the coach on the cliff's edge. Now the road was curving. The coach began to swing to the right and the precipice just beyond. Aria pulled herself back in and looked into Matthew's face, her eyes wild and black hair wind-blown. "Do *something!*" she shrieked.

"For the sake of *Christ* do something!" Pons implored with a similar shriek, the lines of his face brown with whuffie-dust and his eyes wet with terror behind the magnifiers.

There was a crash up underneath the coach on the right rear side. Matthew was sure one of the wheels had left the road. The berline shook so hard Pons' spectacles vibrated off his face and hung by his ornamented ear. His jowls nearly slapped him silly. Matthew's heart was a constant drummer. He felt the coach leaning toward the gates of heaven...or wherever this bunch would end up. Jack Thacker swung his whip back and forth between the two teams, absorbed in a race that seemed to Matthew to be wholly and terribly one-sided, and as a flame of anger burst into barely-controlled rage he realized that if he went over the side in this shuddering berline he would never set eyes upon Professor Fell and never know why he'd been brought here, and both Berry and Zed would likely be murdered and buried somewhere on this island, and everything—his entire life and all his struggles—had been for naught.

"The hell you say," he spoke to himself, in a voice that seemed torn from the throat of Nathan Spade.

He was going to have to get up there, find the reins and take control of the team. And he had to go *now*.

He couldn't get the berline's left-side door open, for the wheels of the other coach were already scraping the paint away. As if reading his mind and intent, Jack cracked the whip nearly through Matthew's window into his face; the smell of burned air rushed past his nose. Matthew countered by angling his body to the right and kicking the opposite door open. Then he pushed himself past the two women and grabbed hold of the open door in an effort to climb atop the berline. The sea glistened sixty feet below his boots. The right rear wheel was balanced on the precipice. He started climbing up the coach's side and saw the driver clinging to dear life on top, arms and legs spread out and fingers grasping anything that afforded a grip. How fast the horses were going now, Matthew didn't dare guess but the wind of progress up here was terrific. The road was curving again. There was a high thin skreeling sound of contact as the wheels of the Thackers' coach once more gouged paint and wood splinters. Matthew's coach lurched further to the right and he heard Augustus Pons give his own high thin skreel of terror from within.

Matthew crawled over the trembling driver, who bore a bright scarlet welt across the side of his face. Then the whip came at Matthew, striking left and right, as Jack Thacker aimed to knock Nathan Spade off his perch. "Stop it, you damned fool!" Aria shouted through the left-side window, but the stridency of her voice only added more cotton to Jack's tinderbox. He began whipping the runaways as Mack gave a shrill laugh and popped the traces on their own team. Matthew kept his head down and inched toward the driver's seat; he figured it was all a ghastly joke to those two, but the way the berline was rocking back and forth, the joke might be on himself, Aria, Pons and Minx Cutter. He could imagine the Indian girl frozen in her seat in an attitude of silent acceptance, while Jonathan Gentry might be curled up on the floorboard singing a song of sixpence.

Well, Matthew thought grimly, it was time to show what a Soggy Ass could do.

He reached the driver's seat and got up on his knees. But where the hell were the reins? Dragging somewhere beneath the horses? The team was throwing up dust and gravel from under their hooves. Matthew saw the road ahead continuing to curve, and now once more the coach was sliding toward the bitter edge.

He heard the crack of Jack Thacker's whip almost in his ear. At the same time, a searing pain striped across the left side of his neck. It was enough for him to lose his senses and his position on the seat, and suddenly he was falling to the right in a wild flailing of arms and legs.

Even in his pain and panic Matthew realized the only thing between him and the sea below was the berline's open door, and it was swinging erratically. He reached out for it as if trying to grasp

God's own hand. He caught the windowframe and clung desperately to it as his boots dangled over the edge. He heard what sounded like pistol shots: the spokes of the right rear wheel breaking loose.

"Here!" came a woman's shout. "Grab hold!"

He looked up at Minx Cutter, who stood crouched over and braced in the coach's doorway. Her right arm was outstretched toward him, her fingers clawing at the air in an effort to reach his.

He hooked one arm through the window and with the other hand grasped Minx's. She pulled him toward her but he decided he was not going back into the coach, but rather back into the fray, and the bully boys be damned. He let go of her fingers when he could get his boots on the doorframe's edge. Then he climbed back up the berline's side and hauled himself to the top where the coachman still sprawled in abject terror. It occurred to Matthew, as he fought off the pain of his whipstung neck, that working for Professor Fell in any capacity was an exercise in throwing caution to the wind.

Jack's whip searched for his skin as Matthew crawled once more toward the driver's seat. What these two were trying to prove was beyond reckoning, or perhaps they simply delighted in deadly games. Call it life-or-death chess, Matthew thought. Fair enough.

The coach suddenly tilted to the right, and both Matthew and the driver had to grab hold of anything their fingers could latch onto. There was a grinding, shrieking noise under the berline. Matthew thought that both right-side wheels had gone off the edge. The horses were fighting to keep from being pulled over by the berline's weight. For a few horrific seconds it seemed the horses were going to lose, but then they righted the coach and the terrible enterprise kept on shuddering at breakneck speed along the hellish road with the demonic Thackers grinning from crimson faces.

Matthew continued his crawl for the driver's seat as the whip cracked over his head. Again he searched for the reins, and determined that indeed they were down amid the horses somewhere. His mind deserted him; he had no idea what to do. Without the reins, the horses were beyond control. He thought he must do *something* to slow the berline, but what it was he *could* do was another matter. The whip came at him once more, and he ducked to avoid having an eye extinguished.

"Get out of the way!"

Matthew looked over his shoulder. Minx Cutter was on her feet atop the coach, daring Jack Thacker to strike at her. "Get out of the way!" she repeated in a shout, her curly hair flying in the wind and her face a firm-jawed, rather frightening visage of raw determination.

He drew himself aside so she could get past him. A glance at Jack Thacker showed the elder brother with his teeth clenched, and rearing his arm back to swing the lash again upon either Matthew or the young woman.

But Minx Cutter was faster.

In a blur, her hand went into her waistcoat. It reappeared with an extra finger of sharp silver. She turned the knife in her hand to seize the grip. She hardly seemed to take aim. Her throw of the knife across the distance between the coaches, taking into account the speed, the whirling dust and the shuddering of the damaged berline, was nothing short of awesome. The blade flashed with sunlight on its arrow-straight path to the hand that held the whip, and when it pierced the flesh between forefinger and thumb Jack Thacker's fingers opened and he howled like a dog.

Then Minx Cutter leaped past Matthew and landed upon the back of the first horse on the right. She grabbed hold of the flying mane and leaned down so far Matthew thought surely her legs would lose their grip and she would be lost beneath hooves and wheels. But then she came up with dust on her face and the reins in her hand. She put her shoulders and back into slowing the team, all the time shouting, "Whoa! Whoa!" in a voice that made Matthew think her lungs must be made of leather.

Within ten seconds of her handling the reins and shouting for order in this scene of chaos, Minx Cutter was obeyed. The horses began to slow. The offending coach sped on past with a final scraping of wheels, as Mack slapped the reins and Jack held his bleeding hand to his chest like a wounded dove.

Minx stayed aboard her horse until the berline had rolled to a creaking and clattering stop. It sounded to Matthew as if the entire framework was about to fall to pieces, yet miraculously it held together. The horses nickered and jostled each other, still nervous from their run, but Minx held them with a steady hand. When she was satisfied, she slid off her mount to the ground and walked around to look at the battered right-side wheels, her own boots about three inches from the precipice.

"My God!" Matthew had to say. He was nearly sputtering with admiration. "How did you *do* that?"

She gave him a narrow-eyed glance that said she didn't suffer fools, and that she ranked him highly on that low list.

"Get out! Get out!" Aria Chillany shouted. In response, Augustus Pons made it out of the coach before tossing his breakfast in long streams over the cliff. His face had taken on a green cast to match his blouse. Minx Cutter aimed her most reproachful gaze at him, hard enough to slap his jowls without lifting a finger, and then she called for the coachman, who peered over the berline's side like a terrified child.

"Come down here and look at these wheels!" she commanded. "Can we keep going or not?"

The coachman, a sweating bundle of raw nerves, obeyed in spite of his obvious desire to cling to safety as long as possible. Matthew eased himself off the driver's seat to the ground, where his knees begged to give way. Yet he thought that one stumble and fall today was already one too many, and to show weakness before the formidable presence of Minx Cutter would not do honor to the dirty reputation of Nathan Spade.

"I'll have them killed!" seethed Madam Chillany as she staggered from the coach. She stared along the dusty road in the direction the Thackers had gone. "No matter who they think they are, they are *dead*!"

"I believe...we can go on," said the coachman, which might have been the most difficult six words he had ever spoken. He followed this statement with a more cautious, "If we go slow."

"Just get us to the castle as quick as you can!" Aria blotted her face with a frilly handkerchief. Her eyes were ablaze. "Pons, stop that! Wipe your mouth and get back inside!"

The fat man, whose legs were almost freakishly short, crawled into the berline as if he were closing about himself the spiky confines of an Iron Maiden. He sat with his head tilted back, his eyes squeezed shut and both hands clasped to his mouth.

"Nathan!" Aria snapped, to coax Matthew from his reverie. "Get in!"

Matthew's knees were still trembly. "When I'm ready!" he snapped back, only half-acting. He had a hand on the whip's sting to his neck; the pain had eased a little, but the welt was going to be worthy of some soothing ointment. He planted himself in front of Minx, aware that one step to his left would send him to find out how his old employer, Magistrate Isaac Woodward, fared in the Great Courthouse Beyond. "I asked you how you *did* that," he said.

"I jumped," she replied cooly. "How else?"

"Not that. *Anyone* could've done that," he lied. "I was about to do the same thing."

"Really?"

"Really," he answered, feeling his oats. "I mean with the knife. How did you throw the knife like that?"

She got up close to him and stared him in the eyes. Her golden-hued gaze was both solemn and yet touched with a shade of humor, though the expression on her face remained absolutely impassive. She let a few seconds expire, during which Matthew began to feel extremely uncomfortable. Then she said, nearly in a whisper, "It's all in the wrist." She strode past him and swung herself up into the coach.

Matthew had the thought he was still in the water, and maybe in far too great a depth for either comfort or safety. He had the feeling of being a small fish at the mercy of any number of predators. But where was there to go from here, except deeper still? He waited until the coachman had secured the reins, positioned himself back in his seat and the horses were ready, as much as they could be after that wild frenzy of whipping and the pounding of hooves. Then Matthew got into the coach and after a bemused and careful glance at Minx Cutter closed his eyes to think more clearly. But just before his eyes shut he saw her turn her head to take him in, and he had the distinct feeling that she would be examining him as he sat drowsing, and—a dangerous feeling—she might be thinking she knew him from somewhere yet could not decide where the meeting had taken place.

In any event, he could feel her watching him. Taking him apart, as it were.

And suddenly he thought he was becoming more Nathan Spadish by the moment, for he reckoned he wouldn't be averse to being taken apart by a woman like her.

No, not in the least.

"Giddup!" said the coachman, almost apologetically, and the injured berline rolled on up the road like a Saturday-night drunk determined to get home before cock's crow.

In a few moments Matthew gave up his pretense of rest to mark their progress. The road turned away from the cliffs. It went inland through a thick forest where moss hung from trees like banners of emerald-colored lace and flowers of intense purples, reds and yellows burned the eyes. The smells of strange fruit both sweetened and soured the air. Occasionally a black person or two in bright clothing and straw hats could be seen picking such fruit and putting them in a basket. Matthew noted that the citizens of color here were not the true deep ebony of Zed, but rather the shade of milk in strong tea. It was obvious that, at least from these few examples, interbreeding between the races had gone on here for many years. He wondered if such might be the result of long-forgotten shipwrecks that had thrown slaves and Englishmen together on what probably was an unhospitable chunk of rock. The questions were, then: how old was the settlement on Pendulum Island and of course how long had Professor Fell been its...what would be the correct term? *Benefactor?*

Just two questions of many in Matthew's mind, and here came another one as the road emerged from the forest onto a plain of wild grasses swept by the seabreeze: how much money had *that* thing cost?

That thing being the castle of white stone that came into view on the right-hand side, perched on the cliff overlooking a turbulent cauldron of Atlantic foam. It was a massive monument to the power of a wallet...and also, possibly, to the power of power itself. In any case, Matthew suddenly felt very small indeed. Turrets roofed with red slate stood like cobra heads. Arched windows and doorways called attention to the art of a highly-talented architect. The road continued on, but a gravel driveway curved from the road to the castle's entrance, and passed between stands of wind-sculpted pines, thatches of palmettos and ornamental flower gardens. Outbuildings stood to either side of the main structure, possibly stables or servants' quarters. The whole picture was one of serenity and removal from the world beyond. This truly was Professor Fell's kingdom, and one would have to be very stupid not to be awed by it. Not being by any means stupid, Matthew was sufficiently awed; yet he did not let anyone see this register on his face, for the masquerade was underway and much depended on the power of his mask.

The berline turned on the driveway. The team followed the orderly path until they reached a porte-cochere supported by thick white columns, and there stood the offending coach driven by the Thacker brothers. A pair of native servants wearing sea-blue uniforms and elaborate white wigs were removing Gentry's luggage from the baggage compartment while two more in the same colored clothing and ridiculous wigs waited to transfer it beyond a massive oak door. The Thackers were waiting beside the coach, one having removed his shirt and using it to wrap around a bleeding hand. His blood-spattered coat was draped over his shoulders. Jack Thacker's chest looked like a squat wall of reddened brick. Both brothers eyed the approaching berline with barely-concealed loathing.

As Matthew's coach pulled up under the porte-cochere, Jonathan Gentry half-stumbled and half-fell from the passenger compartment of his own. He went down on his knees nearly under the hooves of the approaching horses, which had to be pulled up short and sharply by the beleaguered driver. "Hell's bells!" Madam Chillany snarled, and she was out of the coach like, indeed, a belle from Hell.

The chilly madam had become a redhot fire spitting a plentitude of profanities in the faces of the Thackers as Matthew disembarked the berline and strolled up beside her. The brothers looked highly disinterested, and the wounded Jack produced a yawn for her troubles. Their eyes then went to Matthew and their gazes sharpened like daggers.

"Soggy Ass," said Jack.

"In the flesh," said Mack.

"Listen to *me!*" the woman nearly screeched. Augustus Pons waddled past, his fat and florid face stricken by the need to distance himself from any impending ugliness. Aria reached out and seized Jack's chin, as he was the brother standing closer to her. "I could have you fucking killed for that! Do you hear me? I could have your fucking heads on fucking platters, you fucking assholes!"

"Such language!" said Jack.

"Tut, tut!" said Mack.

"I'll report this to *him*, you can believe it!" she threatened. "We'll see what *he* decides to do to punish you fuckers!"

"What he might decide to do," said Mack in an easy voice, his eyes on Matthew, "is punish Spadey, 'cause we've been waitin' on this fuckin' island for more than one solid *month*. And you know what he tells everybody?"

"The meetin' can't start without Spadey," said Jack, smoothly picking up the tale, "so we all have to wait. We all have to twiddle our fuckin' thumbs and play with our cocks 'til—"

"Spadey gets here," said Mack, "which was supposed to be weeks ago, as I take it. What I want to know is…what was so important, that Spadey had to make everybody wait for him—"

"And us with our business to get back to, 'cause it ain't gonna run itself!" Jack finished, with a puffing out of the brickwall chest and a defiant glare at the *faux* Nathan Spade.

This prideful puff visibly stole some of the wind from Madam Chillany, who sought to make a comeback and found nothing in her slim treasury of wit. "We'll see about that!" she managed to say. And then, back to more familiar territory: "You *assholes*!"

Matthew was suddenly aware of an additional presence.

The young Indian woman had emerged from her coach. She stepped slowly and carefully around Jonathan Gentry, who still sat on his knees blinking stupidly at the sunlit garden. She passed Matthew at a distance of three or four feet. It was near enough for Matthew to feel he was crowding her, and so he moved further aside; he also seemingly felt the hairs stir on his arms and on the back of his neck, yet he knew this must only be his imagination or some effect of gaining his landlegs.

She was a painting come to life, he thought. She was a piece of art that could never be confined by frame or glass. To his tastes she was stunningly beautiful. Her face, her hair, her body…all the creation of a master's hand. She was nearly as tall as he, and she was lithe and long-stemmed and moved with a grace that perhaps was born of silent walking in lush green forests. She wore a slate-gray gown trimmed with red, and a pale blue blouse with a boil of black lace at the throat to compliment the lace on her hat. She looked neither to right nor left as she approached the brothers. Matthew noted that she did not look directly at them either but rather seemed to be staring as if in a dreamstate through them at some scene beyond their reckoning.

Mack spoke sharply. "What're your eyes findin' so interestin'…"

"…boyo?" said Jack, just as sharply.

"A very attractive woman," Matthew answered, with a little of his own defiance in his voice. The girl obviously heard, but gave no reaction to this compliment whatsoever. Her face was slightly downcast, her attention removed from the moment. Matthew had the impression she was hearing a different voice in her head, and possibly it spoke the Iroquois language. "Where she did come from?" he asked, to whichever brother would reply first.

"She's a fuckin' *squaw*," said Jack.

"Where d'ya *think* she came from?" Mack's eyes held a dangerous glitter. "You ain't too smart, are ya?"

And so saying, Mack Thacker reached out and grasped the girl's arm, and he pulled her roughly toward him so she was between himself and his brother. Then, his dangerous eyes still focused on Matthew, he began to lick along the girl's face with a brown-coated tongue, and on the other side Jack took her free arm in a hard grip and he too began to lick the girl's face with his own ghastly tongue, his eyes also on Nathan Spade the jayhawk-turned-political pimp and purveyor of valuable state secrets.

And between these two nasty and brutish tongues, the Indian girl looked at Matthew with her sad ebony eyes. There was something crushed and defeated in her yet-beautiful face that nearly wrenched his heart out, but he had to keep his mask on and so by the most difficult effort his visage maintained its stone. The two brothers began to laugh as they marked her cheeks with their saliva, and then the girl lowered her gaze from Matthew's and she was again gone, walking silently through a forest unknown.

Minx Cutter took Matthew by the elbow and guided him toward the formidable oak door, which was being held open for the guests by a black servant in the sea-blue uniform and a powdered wig that must have been three feet tall.

"Come along," Minx told Matthew, as she linked her arm with his and held it in an unbreakable grip. "You're with me."

SEVENTEEN

U NTIL now, Matthew Corbett had thought he understood the balance of the world. Good was its own reward. Evil deeds were punished. God was in His Heaven, and the Devil was evermore forbidden to walk the streets of gold. Yet here, in the realm of Professor Fell, all such platitudes and pieties for the Sabbath pulpit were revealed to Matthew as being echoes of the hollow voices of long-dead saints.

No rich man on New York's Golden Hill had ever lived thus. He wondered what rich man in London might have earned such a monument. He was standing in what he presumed would be the Grand Entrance, and grand it was. The high arched ceiling might have been a sanctuary for angels, who could hide amid the polished oak beams with their feathered wings kissing the snow-white stones. The flags of many nations hung on poles that protruded from walls on either side, among them the white banner of France, the crowned eagle of Prussia, the tricolor of the Netherlands, and the Spanish arms of Bourbon-Anjou. Matthew noted that none of them were afforded a central location or a height that would emphasize one above the other, not even the English Union Jack. Matthew reasoned that to Professor Fell all countries were meant to be equally plundered.

A marbled floor of black and white squares made Matthew wonder if the professor was a chess player. But of course he was, Matthew decided. Who else would he be if he did not recognize the value of helpless pawns, black knights, crooked bishops, and an errant queen or two in his malignant view of life?

The Grand Entrance opened onto a Great Hallway and Glorious Staircase. White trimmed in gold seemed to be the color of the professor's love. Well, Matthew mused as he followed Minx Cutter toward the stairs, the professor was his own God, so why not create for himself his own Heaven on earth?

"I'll show you to your room," Minx said, her voice echoing amid the ceiling's beams.

"*I'll* show him to his room." This was spoken by Aria Chillany, who had come up behind the pair and now caught Matthew by the arm that Minx did not hold.

Minx levelled a calm but icy stare at the interloper. "I should think," she said, "that you are very tired from your journey, and that a woman of your age needs her rest. So, as we have a dinner tonight and much to prepare for, I suggest you go to your own room and get your…shall I say…*beauty* sleep?" Her hand tightened on Matthew's limb, and he thought if it got much tighter he would lose the circulation in his arm. She flashed a quick and totally insincere smile into Aria's stony and—one might say—stunned face. "I'll show you to your room, Nathan," she said, a statement of power as well as of fact, and without a second's more of hesitation she led him up the staircase with a stride that left a woman of a certain age at her bootheels.

Matthew had just time enough to glance back at Aria, who had recovered her composure to offer him a look that might have said *Careful with this one, and guard your throat*. He did not have to be so warned, but he was truly on his own now and whatever this game was, he was in deep.

They passed a stained-glass window overlooking the staircase that caught the morning sun and burst it into jewels of yellow, gold, blue and scarlet. It depicted what Matthew had first thought was the image of a suffering saint, but then he saw that it was the portrait of a young boy possibly ten or twelve years of age, his hands folded against the side of his face and tears of blood dripping from his haunted eyes. It was a strange decoration to be a centerpiece of Professor Fell's paradise, and Matthew wanted to ask who that person might be but then they were past it and climbing up and he let the question go.

Though the stairway continued up to a third floor, Minx guided Matthew into the second floor's hallway, lined with doors and hung with various tapestries that showed intricately-woven hunting scenes. Matthew thought they must date from medieval times or else be very convincing reproductions. Minx stopped at a white door about midway along the hall. "This is yours," she told him, and opened the door for his entrance. The room had a canopied bed done up in black. Again, the floor was made up of the black-and-white chessboard squares. An iron chandelier and eight candles awaited his tinderbox flame, and on a white dresser stood another three-wicked candelabra. There was a small writing desk and a chair before it. On the desk was a key, presumably to his door, and a candle clock. Next to the bed was a white high-backed chair with black stitches woven through it in an abstract design. A white ceramic washbasin stood on iron legs with a supply of folded towels as well as a pearl-handled razor and a small round mirror. Matthew picked up the cake of soap next to the mirror and smelled limes. He noted that his baggage had been brought in and placed at the foot of the bed. He wondered if there might be a solid gold chamberpot under the bed, for surely here even the nuggets were worth something. "You might enjoy this," said Minx, as she opened a pair of louvered doors. The warm seabreeze rushed in, bringing the salt tang of the Atlantic. A small balcony with a black iron railing overlooked the sea that thrashed itself into foam sixty feet below. Matthew had a view to the horizon, which was all empty blue ocean and sparkling waves.

"Very nice," he agreed, uncomfortably aware that this young woman who was so good with knives had retreated a few paces to stand at his back. He turned to face her. When he did, he was startled to find that she had come up upon him as silently as a cat and was standing only inches away.

Minx peered into his eyes as if studying items for sale beyond a window. She said, "Have you ever seen me before?"

Matthew felt a small tremor. Was this a trick question? Was he *supposed* to have seen her before? He decided to play this safely. "No," he answered, "I think not."

"And I've never seen you before, either," she said, with an arched eyebrow. "You're a handsome man, I should have remembered you."

"Oh." Did he blush a bit? Possibly. "Well, then…thank you."

"Soft hands, though," she said, and took his right hand in hers. "You're not much for handling horses, are you?"

"I haven't much need to handle them."

"Hm," she replied. Her gold-touched eyes had taken on a certain ferocity. "Are you and Madam Chillany together?"

"Together?"

"An *item*," she clarified.

"Oh. No…we're not."

"You may not think so," she answered. Then she let his hand go. "If you'd like some lessons, I'd be glad to offer them."

"Lessons?"

"In handling horses. The professor keeps a very fine stable. I might show you the island, if you'd like."

"Yes," he agreed, and gave her a wisp of a smile. "I would like." Immediately he thought he had just taken a plunge into the deepest water yet, but still…such a sea should be explored.

"Meet me downstairs in one hour." She was already moving toward the door. Yet she paused on the threshold. "That is," she said, "if you can manage a tour. After your voyage, I mean."

"I can always sleep tonight." As soon as he voiced this, he noted an expression on her face that said he might be wrong about this as well as wrong about Aria Chillany's interest in him.

"All right." Minx gave him back his wispy smile. "One hour then." And she added his name after the briefest of pauses: "Nathan."

When the girl had gone and the door closed behind her, Matthew let out a long exhalation of breath and had to sit down on the bed, damp breeches be damned. The room seemed to be rocking on the Atlantic waves. He had his doubts about staying aboard a horse very long, but the offer of a guided tour of Pendulum Island was too good to reject. If he toppled from horseback, at least his excuse would pass Minx Cutter's judgment. He stood up, went to the washbasin, poured water into it from a pitcher and splashed some into his face. Then he wet a portion of a towel and used it to cool the hot whipsting on his neck. It wasn't so bad, but he could do with a little poultice of honeysuckle to calm the fever. He needed to get out of these clothes and...what?...send them downstairs to be cleaned? He imagined it would be that simple.

He thought of how many things could go wrong on his excursion with the girl. But then again...he had to have faith in himself. He had played parts before, notably as Michael Shayne with Lyra Sutch or, more corrrectly, in her own guise as Gemini Lovejoy. It occurred to him that Professor Fell had faith in him. Then he thought he must be going mad to be affirming the professor's questionable attributes, or possibly it was the island's sultry air clouding his mind.

He dressed in his other suit, this one of a velvety forest green, with a white shirt and white stockings. When he'd finished fastening the last shirt button he was aware of a shrill calling of seagulls from outside, and therefore he strolled out upon the balcony to have a look at what was stirring the birds up.

She was sitting cross-legged atop a large rock in the sea, her perch some twenty feet above the waves. Over her shining black hair the gulls spun around and around, perhaps disturbed at their roost being claimed by a human. She was entirely nude, her brown skin wet and glistening in the sunlight. Matthew grasped the balcony's railing with both hands. She was sitting about forty feet below him, her chin resting on her folded hands, her face aimed seaward, her attitude remote and absolutely solitudinous in her nudity. Matthew could only stare at this display of removal from the world. Where had she disrobed and left her clothes? Obviously she was unconcerned about being an object of attention from any of the other guests...or, Matthew thought after another moment, she simply had ceased to care.

They call her Fancy, Minx had said.

Of course that was a made-up name, Matthew reasoned. A nearly-sarcastic name imposed upon her if not by the Thacker brothers then by whoever else had lured her over the Atlantic from her tribal home. He wondered how she'd fallen into their hands, and wound up between their dirty tongues.

She was such a beautiful girl, he thought. And there she sat, still alone.

He very suddenly had the sensation that the balcony had given way beneath his feet and he was falling, and yet he gripped the railing harder and he was not falling at all but still…he thought that in the space of a few startling seconds he had indeed travelled from one risky position to another equally as dangerous.

"Oh my God," he said quietly, to himself and to whomever might be listening, even here in this place of Professor Fell's self-worship.

He had already voiced the thought in his head, when he'd first seen the Indian girl in the coach.

It was a shame, that such a pretty girl should sit alone.

He recalled the tale of his Indian friend, Walker In Two Worlds, who had departed from this life and gone to walk the Sky Road. Walker had told him about the Indian girl called Pretty Girl Who Sits Alone. The girl who had been taken from her tribe and accompanied him and the doomed Nimble Climber in their journey across the Atlantic to England, where she had been seized by two men and put into a coach while he went on to portray a parody of the savage redskin on the lamplit English stage.

"Oh my God," Matthew repeated, in case that entreaty to hear him had been missed the first time.

He had no idea how old the girl was who sat upon the rock below him, under her moving crown of seagulls. Walker had not told him exactly how old the girl was when they left the tribe together. *We three children*, Walker had said. Matthew had judged Walker's age at around twenty-six or twenty-seven. Therefore…if this indeed *might* be the same Pretty Girl Who Sits Alone, then she could be the same age or younger by a few years. Or, perhaps, she was the same age as Matthew, twenty-three. In any case, it was possible…just possible…that before him was the very same Indian girl who had made that daunting voyage with Walker, and who had been removed by rough hands into a rough life that led her here, between two orange-haired ruffians who thought themselves the owners of a beautiful…yes, the word that Mack Thacker had used…*squaw*.

But still…certainly other Indian maidens had been brought over from the New World in all the many years since Walker's journey. Of course. Many of them, brought over to be curiosities or servants or…whatever.

That this young woman could be the same one…

It boggled the mind.

Suddenly she must have caught a prickling sense of Matthew's mental thornpatch, for she turned her head toward him as surely as if she had heard her name spoken, and they stared at each other seemingly not only across space, but also across time.

Fancy stood up. She rose to her full height. Brown and gleaming she took one step forward and flung herself into the air like one of Walker's arrows leaving his bow, and as she came down into the sea she tightened her body and narrowed it and entered the churning foam with the bravery and ease of a creature born to be part of nature and perhaps desirous of a return to the childhood dream.

She did not surface. Though Matthew stood for several minutes scanning the boisterous waves there was no sign of her reemergence to the realm of air-breathers. He wondered if she was part fish, and once in the security of the blue world her fins and gills had grown, her tail had taken shape, and she had gone down with vigorous strokes to the silent bottom of the bay, where a pretty girl might once again sit alone. He had a moment of panic, thinking he should call someone to help her. But it occurred to him that no one without Indian courage would dare a dive into that deep, and if she would rather dream in the peaceful solitude of an ocean grave than be called Fancy and be tossed about like a ragdoll between two scums of the earth, then so be it.

Matthew left the balcony and closed the louvered doors. He took the key, went out of his room and locked it, then he walked along the corridor back to the stairs. A tall, slim and hollow-cheeked man with a trimmed gray beard and a smooth sheen of gray hair tied back in a queue was coming up. He was dressed in a black suit and smoking a clay pipe. The man's eyes, equally gray in a heavily-lined and craggy face, barely registered Matthew's presence. But Matthew registered the distinct odor of unwashed flesh.

Another bad ingredient in this odious stewpot, Matthew thought as he descended the stairs. Who might that be, and what was his role for Professor Fell?

Or…had it *been* Professor Fell?

Keep going, he told himself. Whatever you do, don't look back. We don't wish to become a pillar of salt today.

Minx was waiting for him under the flags of many plundered nations. She still wore the man's brown breeches, the cream-colored blouse and the high-topped brown boots, but had put on a tan waistcoat decorated with small gold-colored paisleys. Matthew wondered how many knives were concealed underneath there. Her first expression upon seeing him was a frown, followed by the question, "Don't you have any riding clothes?"

"This will have to do," he answered, and decided to add: "Unless you'd like to loan me some of yours?"

"Hm," she said, with a darting glance at his crotch. "No, I think you'd be too small for my breeches. Shall we go?"

It was a brief walk to a very well-appointed stable, where a black attendant saddled their horses and wished them pleasantries for a good ride. Then they were off, Minx on a sleek black mare the attendant had called Esmerelda and Matthew on a broader-chested sorrel mare called Athena. Minx took the lead and obviously knew where she was going, guiding her horse onto a trail that crossed the estate in the direction of the road. Matthew dutifully followed, finding Athena not too hard to handle in spite of her namesake being a Greek goddess of war. The trail led them across the road and onto the plain of windswept seagrass. But a verdant green wilderness awaited a hundred yards beyond, and they entered it and rode for a while without speaking as the sunlight streamed down through the treelimbs overhead and strange birds called in the ferns.

At last, as they plodded along, Matthew decided it was time to voice a question. He urged Athena up alongside Minx's horse. "May I ask," he said, "what you do for the professor?"

She stared straight ahead. "You know better than to pose a question like that."

"Ah, yes." He nodded. "No one should know anyone else's business, of course. Pardon my curiosity." His curiosity, he thought, had been cursed before but never pardoned.

They went on a distance further, past a small lake where white egrets searched for fish in the shallows. Here and there treacherous brown thornplants reached out from the softer green growth on either side of the trail to snare the clothes of unaware riders, and they made Matthew think of the dangerous predicament that Berry and Zed had constructed for themselves. *I can help you*, she'd told him. Yes, he thought; help them all into unmarked graves. And that night she'd shown up in the alley opposite the house on Nassau Street and nearly scared his tenor into a permanent falsetto. My God, the cheek of that girl! he thought. She had lovely cheeks, it was true, but her curiosity was likewise to be cursed and not pardoned. Who did she think she was? A female version of himself?

And now he had not only to watch his own step in this beautiful morass, but to keep Berry and Zed from plunging into quicksand… and at a distance, no less.

"I will overlook your lack of propriety," Minx suddenly announced, as the horses walked along side by side. "Because this is your first conference. And I suspect you're curious about the other guests."

"I am." He paused for a few seconds before he went on. "Is it true that the professor has told the others a little about me?"

"A little. A *small* amount." She held up two fingers pressed nearly together to show how small.

"But enough to let them know who I am and what I do for him?" He was amazed how easily this flowed, even as he thought how easily the quicksand pit might suck him under.

"Yes," she answered, still staring straight ahead as the trail led them through a grove of spidery trees with leaves like miniature green fans.

"I am at a disadvantage then. I don't like to be disadvantaged." He smiled to himself. *Well said, Nathan!*

They went on perhaps forty more yards before Minx shifted in her saddle and spoke again.

"I'm an expert on handwriting. Forgeries, in four different languages," she emphasized, as if he didn't understand: "I oversee three apprentices to the craft. You've seen Augustus Pons. He's a blackmail specialist. You may have seen Edgar Smythe on the stairs. He has something to do with weapons, I'm not quite sure what. Then there's Adam Wilson, who does something with finances. Cesar Sabroso is a Spaniard who has influence with King Philip the Fifth. You'll also meet Miriam Deare at dinner tonight. She prefers to be called 'Mother Deare.' What she does, I don't know, but she is one of the professor's oldest associates. You might already know that Jonathan Gentry is an expert on poisons, and that Aria Chillany has a position of responsibility concerning murders-for-hire. Lastly but not leastly, we come to the Thacker brothers, who hold themselves in high regard for their persuasive abilities in the area of extortion. Then there's you…the whoremaster who steals state secrets."

"Yes," Matthew agreed. "Whenever I get the opportunity, that is."

"You sound proud of that."

"I am." Lies came so fluidly they frightened him. "As I'm sure *you're* proud of the work you do?"

"I'm proud of my abilities. They are hard-earned."

"Your talent with a knife speaks for itself. Is that ability also hard-earned?"

Minx gave him a little sidelong smile, as they passed beneath the branches of trees draped with curtains of green moss. "I was born into a circus family," she said. "I had to do something to earn my keep. For some reason, I was drawn to the knives. You know. Throwing them at moving targets. Including my own mother and father. I was quite the attraction, at twelve years of age taking aim with a knife in each hand, and outlining with the blades my mother's body as she whirled around on a spinning wheel. Or splitting an apple on my father's head while I wore a blindfold."

"The art of dexterity," Matthew said. "And a solid measure of self-confidence, I'm sure. Did you ever miss?"

"My mother and father are still circus performers. They may have a few more white hairs than they should. But no, I never missed."

"For that, I'm grateful." He fired a quick glance at her. "As should be everyone in our coach. But don't you think Jack Thacker might hold a grudge? After all, you gave him something more than a quill's prick."

"He might hold a grudge," Minx agreed, "but it is just because of the quill's prick that he knows to leave me alone. My dexterity as a forger is more important to the professor than my ability with the throwing knife."

Matthew made no comment. He was thinking, and being drawn along a wilderness path as surely as the horses followed their own. *I oversee three apprentices to the craft*, Minx had said.

It stood to reason that the others—Pons, Smythe, Wilson, Sabroso, Mother Deare and of course the handsome Thackers—were also the heads of their respective departments, rather than being lone wolves. Each one might oversee several—or dozens—of other lowlier lowlifes. Just as he, Nathan Spade, had a network of prostitutes and well-groomed grabbers of Parliament's finest whispers. So when he looked at one of these so-called associates, he was looking at a single cog of what might be a truly vast criminal machine.

"What are you thinking?"

He brought himself back. On either side the forest was dense and dark, and birds called out in harsh voices from the tangled limbs. "Only about the conference," he said, and just that quickly he decided to venture out on his own dangerous limb. "The why of it."

"This being your first, I should suspect so. I attended the conference two years ago, which was my first. We are all used to being summoned by now. Some more than others."

"And it is for the purpose of...?" He let the rest of it hang.

"It is for the purpose," Minx said firmly, "of obeying the professor. Also he enjoys hearing in person reports of progress from his associates. It *is* a business, you know."

"Of course it is. Otherwise, what would be the point of any of it?"

Minx suddenly kicked Esmerelda forward and then sharply reined the horse in, turning the animal so Matthew's path was blocked. Matthew also reined in Athena, and he and Minx stared at each other as motes of dust drifted through the sun's streamers and dark-colored butterflies flew back and forth between them.

"What is it?" Matthew asked, his heart pounding, when Minx remained silent a bit too long for his comfort. Her eyes were likewise too sharp for his skin.

"You intrigue me," she answered. "And *puzzle* me."

He forced a smile. "An intriguing puzzle. I am flattered to be so."

"Don't flatter yourself. I mean to say that I can't quite get the sense of you. Your manner of speaking...the way you present yourself..." She frowned and shook her head. "It isn't what one would expect, after *hearing* about you."

Matthew said with a shrug, "Possibly if I heard about your exploits in forgery, I'd never expect you to have been a child of the circus. Meaning that there are many sides to a person. Yes?"

"Yes," she agreed, in a careful voice, "but even so…I think you are a puzzle with many pieces, and not all of them seem to fit."

With that, Matthew felt the best course of action was silence lest he reveal another piece of his puzzle not meant for Minx's sharp eyes and senses. She turned her horse to follow the trail again, and now she gave Esmerelda's sides a kick and the animal took off at a brisk trot. Matthew likewise urged Athena forward and in another moment caught up behind the black mare's flowing tail.

Presently they emerged from the forest trail onto another road. A horse-drawn wagon was trundling past, carrying a load of various brightly-colored fruits. Minx turned her mount in the direction the wagon was travelling, and left the fruit-vendor in her dust. Matthew urged Athena to speed but this time was unable to catch Lady Cutter. Soon, however, their progress was slowed by a sign on the roadside whose green-painted letters read: *Welcome To Templeton*.

Stood the village as quaint as a Quaker's bonnet and as tidy as a Presbyterian's soul. The small houses were all painted white with green trim. There were white picket fences and shade trees aplenty. The street led past a number of shops: a bakery, a wig-maker, an apothecary, a shoemaker, a general goods store and the like. People were out and about on this sunny morning. Most of them were the cream-colored locals in their vivid hues and straw hats, yet there were a few whites in their more restrained English or European clothing. On the right, behind a dark green iron gate and fence, stood a two-story yellow-bricked structure that Matthew took note of: *The Templeton Inn*, read a small sign above the front door. There appeared to be a tiled courtyard with a small circular pond at its center. Curtained windows looked down upon the street, and doors opened onto green wrought-iron balconies. Matthew wondered if Berry and Zed had been taken yet from the ship. This would be their final destination for a while. It seemed to be a pleasant enough prison. He figured the guards would not be too very obtrusive, but then again this was Fell's kingdom so who was going to complain?

The street continued past a farmers' market that was doing a brisk business in the sale of fruits and vegetables. On the left, further along, was a stable and on the right a series of corrals holding cattle and hogs. Here the air glistened with dust and smelled like New York in midsummer. Then after a few more unremarkable houses the village of Templeton passed away and the forest again took hold on either side. Minx and Esmerelda kept going, and Matthew and Athena kept following.

"Shouldn't we turn around?" Matthew asked presently, as the sun was warming toward noon and the sweat had begun to prickle his neck.

"I want to show you something," Minx answered. "It's not far."

Indeed it wasn't. Minx guided Matthew to the edge of a cliff with the glittering expanse of the sea spread out below. "Wait," Minx told him, as he scanned the rolling waves. "Ah!" she said suddenly, and pointed. "There they are!"

A geyser of water marked the surfacing of a number of whales. They rolled about each other like children at play. They flapped their tails and created their own foamy surf. They dove down and rose up again, breaking the sea into shards of rainbow glass. Matthew looked at Minx and saw she was smiling as she watched the cavorting of the leviathans, and he thought that the circus might be very far from the girl but the girl was never very far from the circus.

Something else caught his eye. It was the fort situated up on the northern point of Pendulum Island. There were several buildings within the cannon-guarded walls, and a pall of gray smoke hung over the area. A little fluttering of smoke rose from a chimney on a squat building to the far right.

"What's that?" Matthew asked. He nodded toward it.

Minx's smile went away. "The professor's property."

"I *know* that. But...a fort, yes?"

"His concern, not ours," she replied. The air had become frosty on this sunny noon. She urged Esmerelda away from the cliffside, and the moment of watching whales at play had passed. Matthew followed back to the main road, feeling he had stepped on something that stuck to his bootsole. The fort was lost to sight by another dense thicket, but presently the two riders crossed in front of a secondary road that cut through the forest toward what Matthew presumed was the very place he'd just seen. He noted the ruts of wagon wheels in the dirt. The road to the fort had seen many comings and goings. And there on either side of the road was to him an interesting element to this new puzzle of Pendulum Island: hanging from leather cords on two poles were two human skulls painted with vivid stripes of color.

There was no need to ask Minx what that meant. Matthew knew. It was a warning of death, made cheerful by the stripings but no less serious. In fact, Matthew thought, there was a twisted sense of humor on display here. The entire message seemed to be: *No Entry Without Permission, Or You Will Wear Your Bright Colors To Your Grave.* He wondered if there were any guards nearby, watching the road, to enforce that particular threat. He decided that there probably were, hidden in the foliage somewhere. He didn't care to test his question.

Not today, at least.

For it seemed to Matthew that a cannon-guarded, walled fort on the island owned by Professor Fell must hold something the emperor of crime did not care to be viewed by the inhabitants of his drowsy dreamworld.

Well, Matthew thought, there was always tomorrow. By now he was used to kicking over ordinary rocks and finding extraordinary horrors scuttling from underneath them in a desperate search for the protective dark. He reined Athena in and sat for a moment staring down the road that sat between two poles and two skulls. He marked that this place was about four miles from the professor's castle, by the route they'd taken. Within him his sense of curiosity and desire for discovery began to vibrate; he was attuned to a question that needed to be answered.

Minx said firmly, "Come along. We shouldn't linger here."

Indeed not, Matthew thought as he got Athena moving again. For he had the sure sensation that they were being watched from somewhere in the trees, and even the guests at this strange conference of criminals could find their skulls separated from their necks by following that particular road into the unknown.

But, of course, following the unknown road was part of his business. His nature, also.

Another time, he promised himself.

And he knew that, whatever dangers and intrigues he might face at this bizarre dinner planned for tonight, his promises were for keeping.

EIGHTEEN

CAUTION doubled. And redoubled. A bell was being rung by a servant who walked along the hallway. It was time for dinner. Time for Matthew to slip into the skin of Nathan Spade and button himself up in it, just as now he buttoned his shirt. When he was done, he slipped into the coat of his forest-green suit and also buttoned that up. It seemed he could not have enough security, nor buttons enough. One popped off as he was wrestling it. The bell called him to hurry. He appraised his look in the mirror. His face had become darkened by the sun, which made the bear-claw scar on his forehead stand out as a pinker line. Also more on the pinkish side was the newer and smaller mark under his left eye, put there by his adventure in the exploding house on Nassau Street. His hair was brushed, his teeth were cleaned, he was freshly-shaved and he was ready for the moment. Yet...there was something about himself that was a recent arrival, he thought. It was a steely glint in his eyes that had not been there before...what? The last gasp of Tyranthus Slaughter? It was the glint of a sword ready to parry another, or quickly strike if need be. It was the steel of survival, forged from his experiences to the point of standing here before this mirror.

The sound of the calling bell had receded.

Dinner was ready. And so was Matthew Corbett.

He pulled in one long breath, let it slowly out, and then he left his room.

In the hallway, a woman glided up beside him and took his right arm. Aria Chillany pressed close against him, her fragrance like the last embers of a smoky fire. She was wearing a black gown trimmed with red lace. Her ebony hair flowed down in brushed waves and her sapphire eyes sparkled, yet her beautiful face was tight and her mouth a hard line. "Nathan," she said quietly as they walked, "do you know your part?"

"I do," he answered, just as quietly. These doors they were passing might have ears.

"Let us hope," she said, and added: "Dear boy."

They descended the stairs like criminal royalty. Matthew allowed the woman to guide him, as he was certainly a stranger here. They walked through a hallway that held alcoves displaying what appeared to be the skeletons of various types of fish mounted on stands. Then the hallway ended at a short staircase descending to a large banquet room with blue-painted walls and ceiling and, upon that ceiling, painted clouds with painted cherubs gazing down upon the denizens of earth.

The assembled group of six sat before silver placesettings at a polished table that seemed to Matthew as long as a New York block. Above it was a brass chandelier ablaze with candles, as the night had fallen over Fell's festival, and also spaced along the table were brass candelabras that gave off a lovely light upon the unlovely throng.

Where to begin? It was Matthew's question to himself, as he and Madam Chillany came down the stairs and their presence brought to a halt the banquet room's already-restrained conversation. He was wondering where to begin gathering impressions, and was aided in this regard when Aria announced to the group, "Let me introduce our new arrival, Nathan Spade."

No one sat at the foot of the table, nor at the head. The first person seated on the left was a dashing-looking gentleman in a shimmery gray suit and a vivid scarlet neckscarf, his age probably in the late forties, his hair black and gleaming except for streaks of gray along the temples, his chin sharp, nose narrow and his deep-set eyes dark brown beneath arched black brows. He stood up, smiled showing good white teeth, gave a crisp bow and extended a hand. "Cesar Sabroso," he said, in a voice that made Matthew think of warm oil at the bottom of a lamp. The better to lubricate a monarch's imagination so as to get at the Spanish treasury beyond it, Matthew thought. He shook the man's hand and then gave his attention to the person seated on the right.

"Adam Wilson," spoke this slight, pale and nearly invisible creature, who wore small square-lensed spectacles and had a long, somber and horse-like face. His voice was like the echo of another voice spoken in another room. He wore a baggy suit the shade of bleached-out hay, and his tight cap of hair pulled back into a painful-looking queue was nearly the same color. His pallid blue eyes refused to meet Matthew's, but rather angled off a few inches to the side even as he offered a hand the size of a child's. Matthew's impression was that this man could sit in a corner without moving for a time and be forgotten by everyone else in the room, and therefore he carried around with him his own disguise.

"Edgar Smythe," announced the next gent on the left, in a voice like a bucket of gravel being pounded by an iron mallet. It made Matthew's eardrums throb. Smythe, the selfsame gray-bearded and gray-haired man who had climbed the stairs past Matthew this morning, looked supremely bored. He was again in his black suit, with a ruffled blue shirt. He neither rose from his chair nor offered a hand, but immediately returned his attention to a glass of red wine he was nursing like a beloved child.

Matthew noted gold-lettered placecards on the table. The one across from Smythe read *Dr. Jonathan Gentry*, but the seat was empty. The physician, Matthew mused, was yet upstairs healing himself. Then next to Smythe was another empty chair and the placecard for *Minx Cutter*, who likewise had not yet arrived. Across from Minx's chair, the card read *Nathan Spade*, and next to that place *Aria Chillany*. Next to Minx were three empty chairs, the closest to her being for *Mack Thacker*, the next for *Miss Fancy*, and the third for *Jack Thacker*. This will be a lovely scene, Matthew thought grimly.

"Our daring savior!" said Augustus Pons, who sat one chair down from Aria's place. The triple-chinned face grinned, as candlelight played on the lenses of his spectacles and gleamed upon his bald pate. "You and Miss Cutter taught those bad boys a lesson, eh?" He opened his mouth and the twig-thin young man with curly brown hair who sat between him and Madam Chillany's chair tipped a glass of the red wine over lips that glistened like garden slugs. The young man wore a powder-blue suit and had ruddy cheeks like those of the painted cherubs gamboling above. His eyes were bright blue, and they sparkled merrily for his master.

"Thank you, Toy," said the fat man, when the glass had been lowered and the young man had blotted Pons's third chin with a napkin. "Mr. Spade, do sit down and tell us all about your escapades in London!"

"Keep your business to yourself, Mr. Spade," said the white-haired woman who sat on the other side of Pons. "His mouth has been known to get people into trouble."

"It is other people's mouths that get *me* into trouble," Pons protested, without much vehemence. "Isn't that right, Toy?"

Toy giggled, a nasty sound.

"Come speak to me, Mr. Spade," said Mother Deare. "Let me take your measure." She was a broad-shouldered, thickly-set woman in a copper-colored gown with frills of red and blue lace at the neck and cuffs. Matthew thought the gown fit her as much as two pairs of silk slippers fit a drayhorse. He went to her side, as she pushed her chair back from the table and turned it to regard him with froggish brown eyes in a wide, square-chinned face. Matthew reasoned she was likely sixty years old or thereabouts, with deep lines across her forehead and radiating from the corners of her eyes. She appeared to have known a life of hard work, probably performed outside under a hot sun. She wore red lace gloves, perhaps to hide hands that had been worked to the point of broken knuckles. The cloud of her cottony hair was done up with golden pins. She smiled at him, in a motherly way. Matthew had the desire to step back a pace or two at the sight of this peg-toothed smile, but he held himself in check as he thought rudeness here would be an unforgiven sin.

"A handsome young lad," Mother Deare decided. She had a quiet voice, yet there was some element of the bludgeon in it. "I suspect you are no stranger to the wiles of women."

The moment of real truth had arrived. Everyone was listening. Matthew's heart was pounding, for he thought surely this bulgeous-eyed woman was able to see through his mask. He kept his face composed and reached deep for a reply. "The wiles of women," he said, "are my business. And in *my* business, the stranger the better."

Pons gave an amused little laugh. Aria Chillany followed that one with her own. Mother Deare's smile was unbroken, but she nodded ever so slightly. "Well said," she told him. She motioned toward his chair. "Join us."

Matthew took his place.

Aria sat to his right. A black servant in the sea-blue uniform and high wig emerged from a door artfully concealed in a wall at the far end of the room, bringing a basket full of various kinds of freshly-baked bread cut into slices. After he had served these to whomever desired them, he went around the table refilling wine glasses from bottles of red and white already on display. Matthew chose a glass of red, as that seemed to be the drink of choice among this bunch. When he took his first sip a thrill of terror shot through him...not at the sense that he might be taking a sip of poison, but at the fact that suddenly he was so damned comfortable in this masquerade. It astounded him, how far he had come from being a lowly law clerk, to being...what? It seemed to him that he wasn't quite sure what he was on his way to being. And that too caused a kink of unease down where the red wine drifted.

Descending the stairs to the banquet room came Minx Cutter, wearing tan trousers, a dark blue waistcoat and a white blouse. She took her time about it, and then she seated herself directly across from Matthew as per her placecard. She nodded at Mother Deare and Pons but directed her attention to her choice of wine from the servant instead of to any of the other guests, and to his surprise Matthew felt a pang of envy toward the bottled grape.

A minute or so after Minx's arrival, came a bellow of noise and the slamming of bootheels on the stairs and thus the Thackers arrived with Fancy held fast by either arm and pressed between them. The brothers wore identical red suits—a shock to any civilized eyeball—with black waistcoats and gray shirts. Fancy was draped in a dark green gown with a black bodice, and she wore elbow-length gloves of black cloth. She was manhandled along until she was shoved down in the chair between the Thackers, and they were laughing like hyenas and snorting like bulls all the way. Matthew noted with a certain satisfaction that Jack's right hand was bound up with a cloth bandage. The two brothers took their places and sprawled in their chairs, and Fancy wore a blank stare on her lovely face and kept her head lowered.

Mack and Jack went after the bread and spilled as much wine as they poured. When Minx reached for the bread basket the servant had left on the table, Jack suddenly reached into his coat with his left hand, brought out a knife crusted with blood and, standing up and leaning forward, plunged it into the basket's contents.

"There ya go," he said sweetly to Minx. "Wanted to return what ya gave to me—"

"—so kindly," Mack finished, and then he swigged a glass of red.

Minx's expression remained placid. She pulled the basket toward her, removed the knife and chose a slice of bread marred by Jack's crusty lifejuice. She ate it while staring at Matthew, after which she calmly slid the blade into her waistcoat.

The eyes of the Thackers settled on Nathan Spade.

"Hey, boyo!" Jack called. "Enjoy your coach ride?"

"Thrilling," Matthew replied. "Thank you."

"We wasn't tryin' to *thrill* ya," said Mack, as he dipped bread into a bowl of brown sauce the servant had left. "We was tryin' to—"

"—*kill* ya!" Jack finished, and he gave a harsh chortle. "Naw, just jokin' there, boyo! We knew you wasn't gonna go off the edge!"

"And how did you know that, please?" Madam Chillany had regained the fire in her eyes and the ice in her voice.

Mack answered, "Somebody as smart as he's supposed to be, playin' with the whores and all, he ain't gonna go so easy as that! Naw, ma'am! 'Course, it helped him to have—"

"—a knife-thrower at his side," said Jack, with a quick and disdainful glance at Minx. "Problem is, maybe she ain't always gonna *be* at his side!"

"Maybe not." Matthew took another drink of his wine before he spoke again. "What do you two gents have against me? You're simply angry because I made you wait a few weeks?"

"They don't like anyone with three attributes they don't have," said Mother Deare. "Good manners, good looks, and good sense.

Pay them no further attention. You are feeding a fire that should be left untamped."

"Listen to her, Spadey," said Mack, with brown sauce on his chin.

"Yeah, she's big enough to fight your battles for ya, ain't she?" Jack grinned in the most sarcastic way. Then his eyes flared like flaming tinderboxes, he grabbed Fancy by the hair and kissed her mouth, Augustus Pons said, "Oh my God," Toy squirmed in his chair, and Mack then grasped Fancy's chin and smashed her lips with his own. After the bully-boys' statement of ownership was done, they went back to their drinking and Fancy again lowered her head and stared at the surface of the table as if it were a new world she was fixated on either exploring or escaping to.

"Well, *I* don't enjoy having to wait for anyone!" It was spoken by the hammer-crushing-gravel voice of Edgar Smythe. His face was a wrinkled mass of barely-confined anger. "Here nearly a month! After that damnable voyage from Plymouth! The seas so high I was swimming in my fucking bed! And then I get here and am told I have to wait for *him* before we can start our business?" A finger stabbed toward Matthew. "A damned *boy*?"

"Watch your words, please," Mother Deare advised. "We are all equals here."

"The money I bring in *has* no equal," Smythe fired back, his bearded chin lifted in defiance. "You know that's true, and so does *he*!"

He meaning the professor, Matthew surmised.

"Settle yourself," Mother Deare said quietly, but the bludgeon was ready. "Have another glass of wine, breathe deeply of this exalted air, and remark to yourself how fortunate you are—as we *all* are—to be at this table.

"One month of waiting *bothers* you, Mr. Smythe? Here on this warm island? Really it does? My, my!" She touched her throat. "Such ingratitude, I would be ashamed."

"Ingratitude my ass," Smythe growled. He reached to refill his glass, which evidently had already been refilled several times. "I know my place here, and it's far better than *his*!"

"I want to know," spoke the soft and echoey voice of the nearly-invisible Adam Wilson, "when Matthew Corbett is going to be killed."

Matthew had been lifting the glass to his mouth. The jolt that went through him almost caused a regrettable spillage.

"That Chapel disaster lost us all some fine young recruits," Wilson went on. "He had a hand in that, and he caused the loss of one of my best men. I want to know when revenge will be delivered."

Matthew was thinking furiously. Ah yes! He remembered! One of the older men captured at the Chapel estate during the Queen of Bedlam affair had been an expert on finances, and had been serving as an instructor.

Mother Deare's voice was as steady and direct as her fierce stare: "The professor decides that, Mr. Wilson. Not *you*."

"I'm only voicing my wishes, Mother Deare," spoke the slender man, who even as he shrugged his shoulders seemed again to be vanishing away.

A clattering on the stairs announced the arrival of Jonathan Gentry, clad in a dark blue suit with a white shirt and stockings. Unfortunately he appeared to be under the influence of his own making, for his face was flushed and sparkling with sweat and the tail of his shirt was hanging out beneath his waistcoat. He came staggering down the staircase, gripping hard to the oak bannister, and at the bottom he hesitated and felt forward with one shoe as if he feared the floor was made of ice and might crack under his weight.

"Oh Christ," Madam Chillany breathed beside Matthew. "He's in one of his states."

Assured that the floor would hold him, Gentry released his death-grip on the bannister and approached the table, in a circuitous sort of way. He walked as if he were dancing to an unheard tune. Matthew thought Gentry's steps would be appreciated by Gilliam Vincent.

Mack said, "Come on and sit your arse down—"

"Ya stumblin' arsehole!" Jack supplied, and the two brothers laughed as if they were the very kings of wit.

The devilishly-handsome though nearly-incapacitated Gentry just gave a feeble smile, a comma of dark brown hair sweat-stuck to his forehead. His remarkable green eyes were not so luminous; tonight they were darkened and bloodshot. Matthew watched as Gentry searched for his place at the table, and no one helped him. Matthew thought that whatever freight the doctor was carrying, the castle of Professor Fell must weigh most heavily upon him for he had surely drunk or inhaled something potent to deaden his nerves.

"You're next to me," Matthew spoke up, and Gentry narrowed his eyes to focus and came staggering around the table to claim his place.

"Thank you, M—" Gentry caught himself and smiled dazedly. "My friend," he said, as he lowered himself into the chair.

Sirki emerged from the door at the far end of the room, presumably to make sure everyone had arrived, and then he went away again without a word to the guests. Matthew noted the East Indian giant was wearing black robes and a black turban tonight, and for some reason that fact sent a disturbance rippling slowly through him like a wave about to shatter itself against a rock.

In a few minutes the feast began to arrive, brought in by a squadron of servants. The theme—no surprise here to Matthew—was nautical. Seafood stew was served in clay bowls shaped like boats. Platters of clams wafted steam up through the candlelight. A glass bowl contained bits of raw fish mingled with onions and small red peppers that nearly seared Matthew's tongue off at first taste. Puff pastries filled with crabmeat and a white wine cream sauce came piled on a blue plate and were quickly gobbled down by the Thackers before anyone else could get their fair share. Then came whole fish grilled, baked and steamed. A swordfish laid out on a wooden slab still had its beak and eyeballs. The pink tentacles of an octopus dripped puddles of butter. The wine flowed and the guests consumed. Matthew watched Mother Deare watching everyone else. From time to time someone gave a grunt as they ate something particularly pleasing to them, but otherwise there was no conversation.

Then Jonathan Gentry, his face and suit jacket smeared with oil and butter, withdrew from a pocket a small bottle of green liquid and poured it into his wine. He drank it down with relish, after which he began trying to carve a piece of mackerel with the edge of a spoon.

"What are you drinking?" Aria asked him, with notes of both wariness and disgust in her voice. "Something of your own making, I presume?"

"My own making," he said, and nodded. "Yes, my own." He smiled at nothing, his eyes heavy-lidded. "I am a *doctor*, you know.

I am a *physician*. And a very able one, in fact." He turned the heavy lids toward Matthew. "You tell her."

"Leave *Mr. Spade* alone," came Aria's quiet command, emphasizing the name.

"What's he saying?" Mother Deare asked, interrupting her consumption of tentacles.

"He's sayin' he's a fuckin' asshole," said Jack Thacker, and he grinned drunkenly at Fancy, who had eaten half of a boatbowl of seafood stew before she had again left the room on her silent voyage.

"I'm saying I am a doctor. A *healer*," Gentry replied, with as much dignity as a grease-smeared drug fiend could muster. "That is who I am. And this," here he held up the bottle, which still contained a few drops of green, "is the medicine I have given myself tonight. I call it..." He paused, seemingly searching for what he called it. "Ah, yes. Juice of Absence."

"Shut the fuck up," Mack muttered in his wine, and then he took hold of Fancy's hair and began to gnaw on her throat. Not to be outdone, Jack attacked the other side of her neck.

"Oh dear me," said Pons, who had been fed his entire meal and had his mouth and chin wiped by his special Toy.

"Juice of Absence," Gentry repeated, his face slack. His eyes appeared to be sliding inward. "It removes one. Takes him away. It eases the mind and deadens the nerves. It causes one to leave this realm of unhappy discord, and enter another more pleasant. Yes, it is of my own making." He stared blankly at Aria. "Somewhat like my life, isn't it?"

"A disgusting mess, you mean?" she asked, her brows uplifted.

Gentry nodded. Suddenly there was nothing handsome about him at all. He just looked to Matthew like a pitiful man trying to hold onto something that had perhaps slipped his grip many years before. Down the table, Pons was being fed by Toy, Mother Deare was carefully watching Gentry, the Thackers were feasting on Fancy's throat, and Minx was sipping her wine in stiff-backed silence. Up the table, Smythe was tearing into a piece of swordfish, Wilson ate small bites of the raw fish concoction and kept pushing his glasses up because the peppers were making his face glisten with sweat, and Sabroso leaned back in his chair and drank not from a glass but from a fresh bottle of red wine that he had uncorked with his teeth.

But Gentry in a way sat alone, and Matthew found he could no longer look at the man.

Instead Matthew stared across at the Thackers, and seeing the suffering expression on Fancy's beautiful and tortured face as the two brutes ravished her he felt the words come up from his soul to his throat and he was powerless to secure them from leaving his mouth.

He said, *"Stop that."*

They continued on, unhearing.

"You two!" Matthew said, louder, with the flush of righteous anger and redhot peppers in his cheeks. "I said..." And again, louder still: *"Stop that!"*

This time they heard. Their mouths left the Indian girl's throat, leaving red suction marks and grease trails. Their glittering eyes in the foxlike faces found him, and yet they grinned stupidly as if they had never in their lives heard anyone give them a command and really mean it.

"Nathan?" Aria's voice was very small and very tight. "I think—"

"Hush," he told her, and she hushed. He focused his attention on the girl, who just that quickly had begun to leave the room once more. There was something he had to find out, and it had to be now. "I saw you sitting on the rock today. I thought...that's a pretty girl, who sits alone."

There was no response whatsoever. Her face was downcast, her disarrayed hair hanging in her eyes.

"A pretty girl shouldn't sit alone," Matthew continued. He felt sweat gathering at his temples. It was hard to avoid the deadly stares of the Thacker brothers; their silence seemed equally as deadly. "You know," Matthew said with an air of desperation, "coming from New York's winter to this island, I feel like a walker in two worlds."

Again...nothing.

Mack's mouth opened: "What *shit* are ya goin' on about—"

"—boyo?" Jack finished, and he started to rise threateningly from his chair.

It was wrong, Matthew thought. Something was wrong. What was it? *Think!* he told himself. She didn't respond to the name Walker In Two Worlds. Why not? If she was the same girl who'd crossed the Atlantic on the ship with he and Nimble Climber, then...why not?

"I think your head needs fixin'," said Mack Thacker, who likewise started to slide from his chair.

"Straightenin' out," said the brother with the gray wisp in his hair, his teeth clenched and his fists the same. "Gentlemen! Please restrain yourselves!" Mother Deare's voice was a shade shrill.

"Let them fight!" said Smythe, with a satisfied grunt. "Give us some entertainment while we wait!"

Matthew was the only one who saw Minx Cutter slide the knife out from under her waistcoat. He was feverishly fixated on something he was trying his damnedest to recall. It was Walker's name. Something…something…

He caught it. Walker In Two Worlds had not been called that when the Indian crossed the Atlantic. As a child, he'd been known as—

"He Runs Fast, Too," said Matthew, staring at the girl. And then, realizing he sounded like a complete fool but not caring very much: "Speaking of Indians."

Fancy lifted her head, and she looked not only across the table at him but across a divide of space and time. For a brief few seconds their eyes met and held, and he thought he saw something within hers awaken like a brief flicker of flame or the dance of a spark. Then she gazed down upon the table once more, and whatever there had been—*might* have been, Matthew thought—was gone.

The Thackers appeared about to climb over the plates and glasses to get at their victim of the evening. They glared at him like dumb beasts, their faces reddened and eyes glinting green. They were done with fish, and now they wanted meat.

Matthew lifted his chin and awaited what was to come. He was ready to do whatever was needed to survive, which meant using a knife, a broken bottle, a chair, a candelabra. But he thought that indeed Fancy had shown a reaction to that name, and if this was the same girl who had crossed the ocean with Walker he reasoned that he owed his departed friend a final favor.

He decided that if it was the last thing on earth he did, he would free Pretty Girl Who Sits Alone from these two animals.

The room shook.

Just a fraction, perhaps. Overhead the chandelier swayed an inch or so, back and forth. Matthew saw the wine in his glass tremble. It was over and done within a couple of seconds, but Matthew was left with a sick feeling of motion in his gut.

"Damn it!" growled Smythe. "There's another one!"

The concealed door in the wall at the far end of the room opened. Sirki emerged, pushing before him something covered up with a brown tarpaulin. There was the noise of rollers on the chessboard floor.

"Gentlemen!" Mother Deare was addressing the unruly Thackers. Her voice was hard, the voice of a woman who has known plenty of hardship and has dealt it out aplenty herself. "Be seated before Professor Fell!" she commanded.

NINETEEN

SIRKI pushed the covered object to the head of the
table. By the time he'd reached it, the Thackers had grumbled curses
at Matthew and resumed their seats. Matthew saw Minx return
the knife to its safe place beneath her waistcoat. Jonathan Gentry
poured the last few drops of Juice of Absence into his wine and
drank the concoction down, thirsty perhaps for a sense of removal
from the scene before him. Cesar Sabroso quietly cleared his throat.
Adam Wilson seemed to be there even less than before. Fancy darted a quick glance across the table at Matthew. Toy blotted Augustus
Pons's lips and whispered something into one of the blackmailer's
ears, which surely had heard their share of secrets.

Matthew waited, his eyes slightly narrowed and his jaw set.

Sirki whipped the brown tarpaulin off. Revealed underneath
was a man in a chair, set upon a polished wooden platform with
rollers on the bottom.

But yet not a man, Matthew realized.

It was the image of a man. A portrayal of a man. A facsimile,
and that was all.

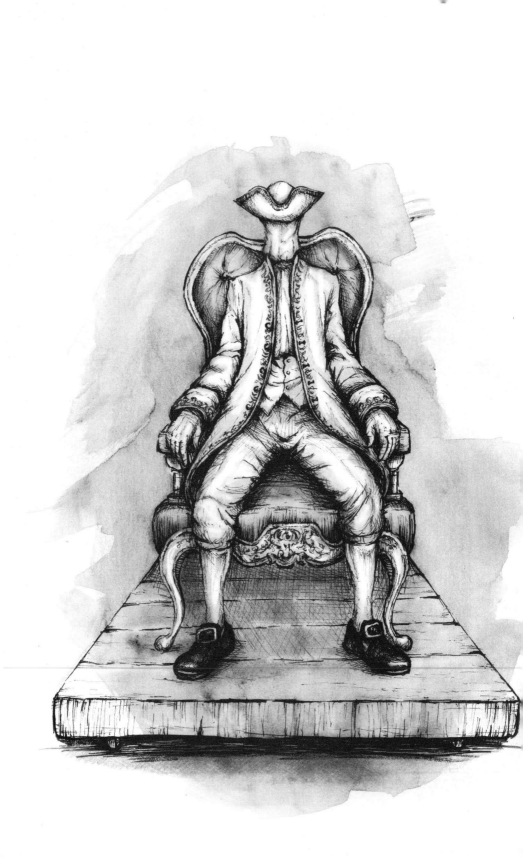

The chair was made of red leather, with gold-colored nailheads decorating the armrests. The man was made of...who could say? Certainly not flesh and blood, for the stillness of the figure. It was a dummy, Matthew thought. A life-sized poppet. Likely stuffed with hay and sawdust?

This figure of Professor Fell sat stiffly upright with its arms upon the rests and its feet spaced equidistantly upon the platform. It was a thin and wiry-looking construction, dressed in a white suit with gold trim and whorls of gold upon the suit jacket and breeches legs. It wore also a white tricorn, likewise trimmed in gold, white stockings and shiny black shoes with gold buckles. It wore flesh-colored fabric gloves and—most remarkably and startling—a flesh-colored fabric cowl that covered the face and head, yet showed the faintest impression of nosetip, cheekbones and eyesockets.

Matthew's thought was: *What the hell is this about?*

He was answered in another few seconds, when Sirki removed a rather large key from a pocket of his robe. He inserted it into some opening at the back of the chair and turned it a dozen times. He threw a lever. With a sound of meshing gears and the rattling of a greased chain, the figure in the chair began to move.

It was a smooth motion, for a machine. For Matthew realized it was a majestic and almost-unbelievable creation he'd read about in his newspapers from London but had never seen or thought he would ever see. It was something called an automaton.

The right hand came up to press an index finger against the chin, as if measuring a thought before speaking. The right hand came down again, upon the armrest. Was there a twitch of the head, as a few ragged gearteeth moved through their circles? Yes, now the head was turning...slowly...left to right and back again, taking view of everyone at the table.

"*Welcome,*" spoke the automaton, in a tinny voice with a hint of a rasp and a whine, "*to my home.*"

No one responded. Did the machine have human ears? No.

Matthew realized he was gripping his wine glass so hard he was either about to break the glass or his knuckles. Everyone else was taking this in stride; they had been here before and obviously seen this machine in action.

The left hand rose, fluttered up into the air with a racheting of gears and then settled back once more. *"There are important things to discuss,"* the machine said, with a slight tilting of the masked face.

Did the mouth move behind that opaque cowl? It was hard to tell in the flicker of the candlelight. The voice was high and metallic and otherworldly, and Matthew felt a chill skitter up along his spine.

"I shall hear your reports at the proper time," spoke the automaton, as Sirki stood several feet behind it and to one side. *"For now, with you all together, I have a request."*

A silence stretched. Had the gears run their course? Then the chain rattled and the head moved again and the right hand came up to press the index finger a second time against the chin, as if in studious contemplation.

"I am searching for a man," said the image of Professor Fell. *"His name is Brazio Valeriani. He was last seen one year ago in Florence, and has since vanished. I seek this man. That for the present is all you need to know."* The finger left the chin and the head moved slowly from left to right. *"I shall pay five thousand pounds to the person who locates Brazio Valeriani,"* said the voice of the machine. *"I shall pay ten thousand pounds to the person who brings him to me. Force may be necessary. You are my eyes and my hands. Seek,"* it spoke, *"and ye shall find."*

"Pardon, sir," said Mack Thacker, suddenly a docile child, "but who is he?"

"All you need to know I have told you." Once more the faceless head tilted to one side. *"That concludes my request."*

Matthew was amazed. It appeared the construction had human ears after all. And the figures the machine had just offered were incredible. At once new questions burned his brain. Who was this Brazio Valeriani, and why was he so immensely valuable to Professor Fell?

The automaton was still. The silence was heavy. Suddenly it was broken by the clatter of a glass overturning on the table, which made Matthew almost jump out of his chair. Jonathan Gentry's hand must have gone nerveless due to the Juice of Absence, and now the good and drug-addled doctor held the offending hand before his face and examined the fingers as if they belonged to someone he did not know.

The gearteeth moved again. So did the head, tilting backward a few degrees.

"*One of you,*" said the voice of the machine, "*has been brought here to die.*"

Matthew was near wetting his pants. If his heart was running any faster it was going to tear from his chest and roll across the room.

"*To be punished for your sin,*" the automaton continued. "*You know what you have done.*" The right hand lifted, the index finger beckoned, and Sirki withdrew from his black robes the wicked curved dagger with the sawtoothed edge. Then the East Indian giant strode forward, walking slowly and leisurely behind those guests sitting on the side opposite Matthew. "*You have betrayed me,*" spoke the tinny tongue of metal. "*For this you shall not leave the room alive.*"

Sirki continued his stroll, candlelight gleaming from the knife's inset jewels and edge of horror.

"*I offer you a chance to speak. To confess your sin before me. In so doing, you will receive a quick and merciful end.*"

No one spoke. No one moved but Sirki, who now rounded the foot of the table and crossed behind Adam Wilson.

"*Speak,*" said the machine. "*I will not abide a traitor. Speak, while you have life in your veins.*"

There was no speaking, though Aria Chillany drew in her breath as Sirki passed behind her, and already Matthew's nuts had seemingly pulled themselves up into his groin.

Sirki continued onward. Behind Mother Deare he stopped, turned and began to retrace his steps. The knife was held low, at the ready.

"*This involves the Cymbeline,*" came the hideous voice, which now held a note of taunting. "*You know nothing can be kept from me. Confess it now.*"

No tongue moved, though perhaps even in this rough company hearts pounded and pee puddled.

"*Alas,*" spoke the machine, "*your moment of redemption has passed.*" And then it added: "*Doctor Gentry.*"

"What?" Gentry asked, his eyes bleary and saliva breaking over his lower lip.

Sirki's progress stopped. Standing behind the good, drug-addled and doomed doctor, the giant swung his arm back and with tremendous force smacked the sawtoothed blade into the right side of Gentry's neck.

He gripped Gentry's hair with his free hand. And then he began to saw the blade, back and forth.

Matthew flinched as the blood jumped upon him. In truth, in any other arena he might have let out a bleat of terror but in this room it might be another kiss of death. But horror came quickly upon horror, as Gentry turned his head toward Matthew even as it was being sawed from his neck, and there was more puzzlement upon Gentry's face than pain as the crimson blood flowed from the deepening wound. Matthew realized that the Juice of Absence was at work, and perhaps too well it had deadened the nerves and taken the doctor to a distant room.

But *this* room, unfortunately, was where his head was being methodically—and somewhat joyfully, it must be said from the grim smile on Sirki's face—cut off.

Augustus Pons gave a strangled gasp, though it was not his throat being opened. Toy was pressed up against his master like a second skin, or at least a second suit. The blood leaped and sprayed from the wound in Gentry's neck, and though the body began to tremble and the hands to grasp and claw at the table yet the doctor's face was placid and composed as if he were hearing the voice of a patient sitting at his knee.

And indeed, in the next moment Gentry asked Matthew with the gore dripping from his lips, "Tell me. What ails you?"

Across the table, Jack Thacker had recovered his nerve enough for a hollow laugh that Mack Thacker finished, with a ghastly chuckle. Between them, Fancy's hair was in her face but her gaze was riveted to the tides of blood that flowed between the glasses and platters.

The right side of Gentry's neck and his shoulder were both masses of red connected by darker threads and clumps, like a hideous suit coming apart at a crucial seam. The wound had the appearance of a gaping, toothless mouth. Matthew, to his absolute terror, could not look away.

Gentry's eyes had seemingly sunken into a once devilishly-handsome face, now gone suddenly gaunt and sallow. When he spoke again, his voice was a hollow rasp. "Papa?" he said, addressing Matthew. "I've finished my lessons."

The blade sawed back and forth, and forth and back. A sheen of sweat had risen upon the giant's cheeks.

Aria gave the first burst of a scream but she choked it down. Her eyes were wide. The sapphires had turned to onyx. Toward the foot of the table, Adam Wilson leaned forward toward the carnage, his eyes alight behind his spectacles and his nostrils twitching as if entranced by the smell of so much blood. Cesar Sabroso, his mouth slack and eyes deadened, had hold of a wine bottle in each hand, gripping them like life itself.

Suddenly Gentry seemed to realize what was happening to him and he gave a shuddering cry and tried to rise but the giant's hand was firm in his hair and just that quickly all of the doctor's ebbing strength had run its course. The Juice of Absence was obviously a very potent formula. Gentry collapsed back into the chair, his head hanging to the left, and his hands twitched and jerked on the armrests as his legs kicked underneath the table and tried to run. Yet there was nowhere to run to.

"Oh," moaned the mangled voice of a dead man, as the body whipped and spasmed, "Papa…I kissed…kissed Sarah today."

A gush of nearly black blood met the next tearing of sawteeth. What came from the center of the thick red flood issuing out of Gentry's straining mouth might have been a voice, and it might have been a pitiful cry for a life lost or a small handsome boy's last boast: *"I think she likes me."*

The sawblade met bone and scraped with a noise that made Matthew's hair stand on end. There was a crash as Minx Cutter's chair went over; she had risen to her feet and was backing away. It appeared that she had reached her fill of this particular dinner.

"Leave here if you're going to be ill!" Mother Deare snapped at her, in a not-very-motherly way at all. Minx took the stairs, but she did it at her own speed: a deliberate and almost disdainful walk.

Sawblade on bone. The kicking of Gentry's heels against the bloodied floor. Matthew nearly rose to his feet and also departed the room, but it seemed to him that the tough-minded and grim-hearted Nathan Spade would have stayed it out, and so then should he.

But by the hardest effort did he remain in his place, for in the next excruciating moments Sirki cracked through the vertebrae and cut through enough flesh to tear the head off its streaming stalk. Sirki deposited the head of the formerly-living Jonathan Gentry upon the table in front of its former body, and as the sallow and sunken-eyed face continued to grimace and contort in its agonies of dying nerves the body slithered down under the table with all the boneless grace of a raw oyster.

There was silence, but for the dripping.

"Thus endeth the lesson," said the automaton, its right index finger pointed into the air.

It was Jack Thacker who spoke next.

"Professor sir?" he asked, in his nasally brogue. "Don't we get dessert?"

The automaton's hand lowered. With a noise of moving chains the mechanical head turned from side to side, as if seeking the speaker.

"Certainly you do," came the eerie metallic voice, *"and you have earned it. On the patio you shall find vanilla cake, sugared almonds and some very fine bottles of Chateau d'Yquem. My best for my best."* The head nodded slightly, and the voice added, *"And I shall say goodnight."*

Sirki had wrapped the gory knife in double napkins. Now he came around behind the automaton and threw the lever that presumably turned it off. The noise of gears and chains ceased. The figure was motionless, returned to exactly the posture in which it had first appeared. Sirki put the tarpaulin back over it and wheeled it away toward the concealed door.

Gentry's face had ceased its spasms. The good doctor had gone, quite messily, to either the Celestial Apothecary or the Hellpit of Incurable Diseases. Matthew pressed his napkin against his mouth, realizing how much blood had spattered his suit. It seemed that Pendulum Island was not only death to people, but murder on men's wear. He realized also who and what had severed the heads from the two bodies in the house on Nassau Street. The neck stump was similarly ragged to those. A point of observation that only he would have made, and yet he clung to his powers as a problem-solver to make certain he did not completely fall into the tarpit that was the soul of his masquerade.

Said Mack, with a hand to his belly, "I'm for gettin' me some vanilla cake."

Evidently this drama had caused the Thackers to, for the moment, put aside their animosity toward Spadey. They got to their feet, hauled Fancy up between them, and sauntered up the stairs as if they'd just witnessed a particularly stirring ballroom dance...or, in their case, barroom fight.

Somehow, and he didn't know how long this took him to do so, Matthew got out of his chair and, slipping on the bloody floor, made his way to the steps. He didn't care to look at anyone else, nor did they care to look at him. He did have the impression that Adam Wilson wore a barely-concealed grin of delight, for it seemed the invisible finance-man had a taste for gory violence. On his ascent, Matthew wondered who was going to take the head off the table, remove the corpse and clean up the Godawful mess. One would have to need a job terribly much to do such work as that, it seemed to him.

Or possibly the servants in this house were used to anything.

Matthew's knees were weak as he walked unsteadily toward the main staircase. He had no taste for vanilla cake, sugared almonds and dessert wine. Halfway up the stairs he felt something break within him and very suddenly his skin prickled with cold sweat. He had to grip hard to the bannister for fear of being flung off the world. Then he righted himself, as strongly as he was able, and pulled his body up the stairs using the bannister as much as any man would haul himself up a lifeline.

He entered his room and, still sweating and with the smell of blood up his nose, closed the door at his back. He latched it. He noted on the white dresser the three tapers of the triple-wicked candelabra still burning, as he'd left them. His first impulse was to relieve his bladder in the chamberpot, but instead he staggered toward the louvered doors to breathe deeply of sea air and perhaps clear his head of the bloodied fog.

And that was when he saw the automaton of Professor Fell sitting next to the bed in the white high-backed chair with the black stitching. The automaton had one thin leg crossed over another at the knee.

"Hello, Matthew," said the construction, in a voice no longer metallic or high-pitched yet still eerie in its quiet, mechanical delivery. "I believe we should talk."

TWENTY

ID the earth cease its spinning? Did the floor give way beneath Matthew? Did a firepit of demons laugh, or a wing of angels cry?

No. But Matthew nearly fell down, all the same, and his heart nearly exploded and his mind reeled with the knowledge that Professor Fell's automaton was not a machine at all but the real version.

The creature was dressed exactly the same, in the white suit with the gold trim and decorative gold whorls. The head was topped by the gold-trimmed tricorn. Same as well were the flesh-colored cloth gloves, covering long-fingered hands, and the flesh-colored cowl over head and face that showed the faintest impression of nosetip, cheekbones and eyesockets.

When the figure spoke again, Matthew saw the barest fluttering of cloth over the mouth. "Yes," Professor Fell said, "I do enjoy my games."

Matthew could not speak. As much as Gentry's bodiless face had struggled to make sense of the where and the how and the why, so did Matthew's face contort with the exact questions.

"You're so young," said the professor. "I wasn't prepared for that."

Matthew gasped a few more times, and then he found his voice. "I'm...as old...as I need to be."

"Older, perhaps, than you *ought* to be." The gloved fingers steepled together. "You have seen some disturbing sights."

Matthew forced himself to nod. He didn't have to force his reply. "Tonight...was possibly the worst."

"I would apologize, but that scene was necessary. It served many purposes."

His mouth dry, Matthew said, "It certainly served to spoil my appetite for dessert."

"There will be other dinners," the professor answered. "Other desserts."

"Other heads to be sawed off?"

Did the cowl hide a quick smile? "Perhaps. But not at the dinner table."

Dare he ask the question? He did: "Whose?"

"I don't yet know. I will wait for *you* to tell *me*."

Matthew thought he had walked into the middle of a bad dream. Was this real, or had he eaten a corrupted clam? He wished for more light in this room, though the candles burned merrily. He wished for more distance from Professor Fell. He wished he might be anywhere but here, with the emperor of crime and the nemesis of Katherine Herrald sitting four paces from him. "Me?" he asked. "Tell *you*?" He already wore a frown, and now it deepened. "Tell you what?"

"Who is to be executed," said the professor, "as a traitor."

"A *traitor*?" Matthew wondered why in moments of extreme stress he wound up sounding like a drunk parrot. "Doctor Gentry was just executed as a traitor."

"That is corrrect...yet not entirely correct."

Matthew couldn't make heads or tails of this. His mind felt overwhelmed. He backed away from the masked figure in the chair. When he bumped into the iron legs of the ceramic washbasin he reached back at a clumsy angle, scooped water up in his hands and wet his face. Water dripped from his chin and he blinked like a sea-turtle.

"Take your time," the professor advised. "I'm sure you have questions."

Matthew found his way to the chair at the writing-desk and sank into it. He certainly did have questions...so many, in fact, that they were tangled together like a multitude of fast carriages trying to jam themselves through a tunnel.

"Let me begin, then." The cowled head tilted a fraction to one side. "My little game at dinner. Pretending to be an automaton. I'm fascinated by those mechanicals. Sirki knows the truth, as does Mother Deare...and now you. My charade is useful in keeping a suitable distance between myself and my associates."

Matthew thought he nodded, but he wasn't certain. "May I ask...how that works? I heard the machinery...and your voice."

"Oh, there *is* machinery in the chair. I operate it by pressure on the nailheads in the armrests. As for the voice." The right hand slid into a pocket and emerged with a small metal object that resembled the miniature pipes of a pipe organ. "This fits my mouth. Not so comfortable, and yet a challenge. I had to learn to alter my breathing. It is designed to give the effect I wished." He returned the mouth-organ to its pocket, and then he sat without moving or speaking for a time as if to demonstrate his ability to mimic a construction of gears and chains.

"I don't..." Matthew shook his head. The fog was closing in again. Surely the gray kingdom had not followed him here. "Am I drugged?" he asked.

"Only by your own mind," came the reply.

Matthew was trying to examine the voice. What age? It was hard to tell. Possibly a man in his late forties or early fifties? It was soft and smooth and entirely without malice. It carried the sheen of education and abundance. It was supremely confident, and had the power of pulling the listener toward the speaker as any warm flame would pull a moth from the dark.

This was the man who had wished to kill him, Matthew thought. This was the man who never forgot, who ordered death like a delicacy at dinner and who had organized a criminal parliament beyond Matthew's comprehension. This was the destroyer of lives and fortunes and souls. This was Fear Itself, and Matthew felt terribly small in its presence...and yet...this was an educated and literate man behind that mask, and Matthew's curiosity—his innate need for answers—had burst into an absolute conflagration.

"You remind me of someone," said Professor Fell, quietly.

"Who might that be?"

"My son," was the answer, delivered more quietly still. "Well… who he *might* have been, had he lived. Did you note the stained-glass on the staircase? Of course you did. That is a depiction of my son, Templeton. I named the village for him. My dearest Temple." There was a soft laugh that held a sad edge. "The things a father will do, to perpetuate a memory."

"What happened to him?" Matthew asked.

There was no immediate response. Then the masked figure released a sigh that sounded like the wind at the end of the world. "Let me tell you why you are here," he said. "You call yourself a problem-solver. I call you a providence rider, for I need a scout to go ahead. To find the trail that shall be followed. Much depends upon this, Matthew. Much expense and…difficulty…has been paid to bring you here, as you certainly know."

"I know many people have suffered."

"They have, yes. But that was *your* doing. You declined an invitation to dinner, did you not? You must realize, Matthew…that no one says *no* to me."

Spoken like a man who believed himself to be in no need of a greater god, Matthew thought…but he decided it unwise to turn that thought into words.

The professor said, "You are here *now*. That is the important thing. You've seen part of my world. What I have achieved. And *me*…from academic beginnings. It boggles the mind, doesn't it?"

"Yes, it does."

"Sensibly agreed. I have brought you here because there is a fly in the ointment of what I have achieved. A small little fly that bothers me, day and night. Jonathan Gentry was *not* a traitor. At least, not to me. To himself, possibly, with his worsening addictions. I persuaded him some time ago to fill a notebook with his formulas for poisons and other drugs of usefulness, and therefore *he* became useless. Except…tonight, he was *very* useful."

Matthew said nothing. Better not to walk upon a garden made of quicksand.

"He was useful," Professor Fell continued, "in that his death may have made the *real* traitor think he's gotten away with his sin against me. There *is* a traitor among them, Matthew. I suspect three men, one of whom is the irritating fly: Adam Wilson, Cesar Sabroso and Edgar Smythe. Any one of them had opportunity—and perhaps motive—to do what was done to me last summer." The figure leaned slightly forward, gloved hands gripping the armrests. Matthew had the impression that behind the mask the face was still calm yet perhaps the mouth had drawn tight and the eyes held a seething ferocity.

"I need your abilities to uncover this traitor," said the mouth, which fluttered the cloth ever so faintly. "I could in my rights as their lord execute all three of my suspects, but that would be counterproductive. Therefore...I need one name. Better still, I want to see some proof of this treachery, if it exists and is in the hands of its creator. So, as you ask...there is only one more head to saw off, and *you* will tell me whose head that is to be."

Matthew almost laughed. Almost, but then he imagined his own head sitting on a table. "What you're asking...it's *impossible*. I would have to know so much more. And I'm not sure I want to know, just as I'm sure you wouldn't wish to tell me." In spite of his predicament, a sudden heat flamed his cheeks. He stood up. "I can't believe this! You've brought me here to uncover a traitor, yet I have no way of knowing even how to begin! All right, then, tell me this: what did the traitor do?"

"He caused a ship to be seized off Portsmouth by the Royal Navy. It was on its way to a meeting at sea with another ship."

"And I'm presuming the cargo was important? What was it?"

"You have no need to know that."

"Of course not!" Matthew gave a half-crazed, half-terrified grin. "What was the nationality of the ship being met at sea?"

"You have no need to know that, either."

"Oh, certainly not!" Matthew threw out a line, angling for a different fish. "What's the Cymbeline you mentioned at the table? You said, *This involves the Cymbeline*. Was that the name of the ship?"

"It's the name," said Professor Fell, in his maddeningly soft and calm voice, "of a play by William Shakespeare. You know his work, perhaps?"

"I do. And that play, as well. But you see, you tell me nothing. How can I uncover a traitor without knowing the details of the betrayal?"

The fingers steepled again. The masked face aimed at Matthew for a long while without speaking. Then: "You call yourself a problem-solver, is that not true? And you indeed have solved quite a few problems in that little town of yours? Don't you by now have an instinct for lies? Can't you read a face or a voice for the truth? Can't you read guilt or innocence in a man's teacup? In the way he holds himself before others? In the way he handles questions, and pressure? I give you leave to ask questions and to apply pressure. Knowing, of course, that you must maintain your disguise as Nathan Spade, for your own safety."

"My *safety*? I think the Thacker brothers would treat Matthew Corbett a shade better than they do Nathan Spade."

"They're testing you. That's their nature."

"Oh, all right." Matthew nodded, with the distorted grin still on his face. "Just so they're not *killing* me!"

"Their enthusiasm for bullying will pass, if you stand up to them."

"I say this is impossible," Matthew told him. "How long would I have for this traitor-uncovering? A week or two?"

"Three days," said Professor Fell. "After the reports are given, the conference comes to an end."

Three days, Matthew almost repeated incredulously, but he wished his emulation of a drunk parrot to cease. "Impossible," he breathed. "No one could do what you're asking!"

"Do you think Katherine Herrald couldn't do it?" the professor asked, silkily.

Matthew was silent. He stared at the floor, which seemed their board for this grand game of chess they were playing. Unfortunately he could think of no brilliant move.

"Let us talk of money," Professor Fell said. "Let us talk of *reward*s, Matthew. Here is what I propose. If you fail to produce the traitor in the next three days, I will pay you three hundred pounds and send you, your lady friend and the blackbird back to New York. If, however, you do produce the traitor and some evidence of treachery, I will pay you three *thousand* pounds before sending you home. Also, your death card is burned to ashes and so is the death card of your friend Nathaniel Powers in the Carolina colony. All grievances against you and Powers will be forgiven. Does this still sound impossible?"

Matthew had to spend a few seconds recovering from the sound of that much money. And the fact that ex-magistrate Powers would no longer fear the man who never forgets. "Maybe not impossible," Matthew answered. "But nearly so. What would I have to work on?"

"Your instincts. Your intelligence. Your experience. Your... *guess*, if it comes to that. I will provide a key for you to use in entering the rooms of our three suspects. Sirki will inform you when the time is right to do so. I also will empower him to answer any further questions, within reason. Perhaps you'll discover for yourself what the betrayal was, but I shall inform you of this: if I sat here and told you exactly the facts of the matter, I should have to prevent you and your charges from ever leaving this island again. So...I am asking you to use your *skills*, Matthew. Are they sufficient for this task, or not?"

The answer was truthful enough. "I don't know."

"Know by morning. Sirki will come to your door before breakfast."

"Give me this, then," Matthew said. "Does this involve the man you're seeking? Brazio Valeriani?"

"No. That is a different matter. Yet I will say that if you are successful in this situation, I should think of sending you to Italy to search Valeriani out. And if you found him I would pay you enough to own that little town of yours."

"Ownership of a town is not my ambition."

"Hm," said the professor, and Matthew thought that small unspoken comment was *Ownership of the world is mine.*

"I'll come to some decision by morning," Matthew replied, though he knew what the decision must be. He was going to be working blind, but he had to try.

Professor Fell suddenly stood up. He was about two inches taller than Matthew and nearly frail but he moved with graceful strength. "I shall trust that you trust yourself. I know what you're capable of. After all, we have a *history*, don't we?"

The Black Plague had a history too, Matthew thought.

"I'll speak to you again," the professor promised. He walked to the door and paused with his hand on the polished knob. "This is important to me, Matthew. It is *vital*. Find this traitor, and you may be assured of a very bright future."

As Matthew hoped to be assured of *any* future, he chose to let that observation pass. But he had another question: "Before you entered the room, there was a small…jolt, it felt to be. A movement. What was that?"

"An earth tremor. We get them occasionally, but nothing to be alarmed about."

"This castle is on the edge of a cliff and you say an earth tremor is nothing to be alarmed about?"

"The tremors are mild and the castle is sturdy," said the professor. "I know, because I had it rebuilt when I claimed the island as my birthright. This is the house I was born in. My father was the governor here."

"The governor? Of Templeton?"

"It is time for you to rest," came the soft reply. "I wish you pleasant dreams."

"Thank you, but aren't you worried about running into one of your associates in the hallway? That wouldn't do for your pretense as an automaton, would it?"

"No, it would not. That is why the vanilla cake, the sugared almonds and the wine have been treated with a potent sleep drug. I believe the others are likely resting in the comfortable patio chairs by now. I doubt that Miss Cutter will be leaving her room to wander the hallways tonight. Madam Chillany is also behind a locked door, and she won't be coming out either."

"But you knew I wouldn't want any of that dubious dessert?"

"Not after the dinner, no. But just in case, Mother Deare was watching you, ready to intercede, and Sirki was going to summon you from the patio. In any case, I did not come up by the main staircase and I shall not be going down them."

"No secret passages here?" Matthew dared ask, with a trace of improvidence.

"None," said Professor Fell, "that you shall know about. Oh… you do realize you have wet your breeches, don't you? Leave your suit outside the door. I'll have it cleaned for you." Matthew didn't have to look. It was a little too late for the chamberpot. "Goodnight." The cowled figure opened the door, paused only briefly to regard the corridor, and then left Matthew's room. The door closed behind Professor Fell with nearly the same sound as the breath leaving Matthew's lungs a few seconds later.

Matthew got his legs moving. He went out onto the balcony to listen to the waves against the rocks. Stars filled the sky in the utter black. It was majestic but also seemed desolate and dangerous. Many things whirled through his mind. He concentrated on keeping the vision of Jonathan Gentry's yellowing face out of his brain, but it was a hard order. He knew that when he attempted sleep it would all come back upon him, and therefore he would surely end up flaming the eight tapers in the overhead chandelier as well as keeping the candelabra burning all night.

What a day this had been! He wondered how Berry and Zed had survived it, and what their present situation was. He wondered at the mysterious fort and the brightly-colored skulls that served as warnings of death. He wondered at the fate of Captain Jerrell Falco, and how he was going to deliver Fancy—if she was indeed who he thought she was—from the rude clutches of the Thacker brothers.

He wondered who Brazio Valeriani was, and what was the Cymbeline. He wondered how he was going to uncover a traitor in three days. And mostly he wondered how the hell he'd gotten into this predicament.

But the fact was…he was here. Up to his neck in a sea of predators, and him wearing a suit that smelled of blood.

I wish you pleasant dreams, the professor had said.

Not to be had this night, Matthew thought.

But in another moment he would take off his blood-spattered suit, fold it and put it outside the door and he would stretch himself out in the bed in the room in the castle of Professor Fell, and he would seek some kind of rest because he needed a fresh mind in the morning when Sirki came to call.

He was who he was. And as Katherine Herrald had once told him regarding his position at the Herrald Agency: *We need you, Matthew. You'll be well-paid and well-challenged. Probably well-travelled too, before long. Certainly well-educated in the complexities of life, and of the criminal mind. Have I frightened you off?*

Matthew stared into the deeper darkness, and he answered aloud as he had answered the woman in person.

"No, madam. Not in the least."

But then again, there was always tomorrow.

THREE

THE WORLD TURNED UPSIDE DOWN

TWENTY-ONE

BERRY awakened in the light of the candle at her bedside. She lay still, listening. A dog was barking out in the town. Another answered from a different direction. She wasn't sure it was the noise that had roused her from her troubled sleep. No, there was something else…

An object clinked against one of the windows that overlooked the courtyard. She sat up. A second object hit the glass. There was no doubt. Someone was throwing pebbles from below. She rubbed the sleep from her eyes and got out of the comfortable goose-down bed, with its rose-colored canopy. She pulled her dark blue sleeping-gown a little closer about herself, and taking the candle in its pewter holder she walked toward the door that opened onto her balcony.

It had been a day she would never forget. For that matter, what day lately—since being taken from the Great Dock pier by the East Indian giant with diamonds in his front teeth—had been forgettable? But at least the ordeal in the *Nightflyer*'s brig was far behind her, though not very far from her memory. She and Zed had been removed from the ship after nightfall, put into a closed carriage and driven to this inn, where again under cover of the night they were brought in through the dark green gate. Once inside they were separated, and Berry ushered to this room by a heavy-set Scotsman with a red tuft of hair atop his dome and a red tuft of hair on his chin while two husky men with muskets took Zed away. A meal of baked fish, corncakes, some kind of green melon and black tea had arrived at her room on a tray borne by a young woman with long ebony hair and coffee-colored skin. The door had been locked from the outside when the young woman departed. Later on, she had returned with the sleeping-gown, which she lay upon the bed for Berry. Again, upon leaving she locked the door. Berry had stepped outside onto the balcony and seen by torchlight the two tough-looking men with muskets talking in the courtyard below. Another movement had caught her attention and she'd seen Zed standing on a balcony one room over from hers. Zed had not paid her a penny of attention, but had been focused on watching the musket-men.

Though her mind was concerned with thoughts of what might be happening to Matthew—and her fears, she realized, were likely much more treacherous than the reality, since Matthew was a sort of guest here—she found sleep easily enough when she donned the nightgown and slipped into bed, simply because she was exhausted. But now, with the clinking of pebbles against the glass, Berry was fully awake as she followed the candle's glow to the balcony door.

The night was still and warm, and down in the courtyard the torches were still burning. She didn't know how long she'd been asleep. Two or three hours, possibly? But something was missing. She leaned carefully over the railing. Where were the armed guards, who looked as if they'd never skipped a meal of hog's fat, horse meat and baby's bones?

A shadow moved. It became a huge bearded black man, baldheaded, with massive shoulders jammed into a clean yellow shirt. He wore his baggy brown breeches and had on scuffed black boots. His tribal-scarred face peered up at Berry and he made a motion with his arms that Berry could read as if he were speaking to her.

He said, *Jump*.

"I can't!" she whispered, before she realized he couldn't understand. Yet it was clear he understood her facial expression, because he repeated the motion and then held his arms out.

I'll catch you, he promised.

"Where are the guards?" she asked, again more to herself rather than to him. Zed stared up at her for a few seconds more in the orange torchlight, and then he shook his hands back and forth at chest-level seemingly to get the blood flowing.

She thought she understood what that meant. *I took care of them.*

It was about a twelve-foot drop. Could he catch her, if she jumped? Of course. "My shoes," she said, and started to go back for them. Zed quickly popped his palms together.

No time, he said.

She understood that completely. But if they left the Templeton Inn, where would they go? And if they did get away, would that put Matthew in more danger, or less? She thought that Zed wasn't as concerned with Matthew as he was with finding a boat to cast off from this island and continue on his own personal journey. She had to worry about Matthew's safety, first and foremost, and maybe she should remain here in this velvet cage, but still…

She did not like cages, velvet or otherwise.

Zed was waiting, and the seconds were going past.

Berry thought he wished to escape this night, and in so doing escape from the confinement of the past into the freedom of the future. If he could find the local fisherman's harbor, secure a small sailboat and possibly a net or some fishing equipment…but, how far might he get? It seemed to her that even if Zed perished at sea, without provisions or plan other than setting his face toward Africa, it was how he wanted to leave this earth. And he, too, could no longer abide the cage.

She decided she would help him find a boat and see him off, and then she would return here to wait for word from Matthew.

She climbed over the railing, careful not to snag her nightgown on the wrought iron, and she jumped.

Zed easily caught her. He set her down like a feather. Then he nodded—*Yes, we're in this together*—and he held up a ring of four keys. He strode to the padlock on the gate and began to test it with first one key and then another. As Zed sought to unlock the gate, Berry looked left and right and found the bodies of the guards stacked up in some shrubbery just beyond the torchlight to the left. Their muskets appeared to be broken. One of the bodies was missing its boots. Suddenly one of the bodies shuddered and a hand lifted as if to seize the air before it fell back again, indicating that they were not dead but rather in a state of enforced sleep.

It was the last key. The gate swung open. Zed plucked a torch from its place in a wooden holder. Then they were walking into the road, Berry mindful of the small shells and pebbles that made up the surface. They had a choice to make concerning direction. They had come from the left, therefore they knew the harbor for large ships that lay over that way. Zed turned to the right and started off, seeking the local harbor, and Berry followed at his bootheels.

They seemed to be the only souls stirring at this hour. Dogs barked, but none were seen. The sky was ablaze with stars and a moon nearly full. The road left the last quiet houses of Templeton and was soon taking them through wilderness tinged blue by the moonlight. From the thicket the insects of the dark sang their songs of whirs and chitters, and Zed and Berry followed the flickering torchlight deeper into the night.

Berry wished she could ask Zed a question, but she wouldn't know how to ask it. While she'd been eating her dinner, there'd been just the slightest movement of the room. A passing tremor, there one second and gone the next. She wished she could ask Zed if he'd also felt that. But in the aftermath of the tremor, she'd realized that the walls of her room were spiderwebbed with tiny cracks. She'd meant to ask the Scotsman about it in the morning, for evidently Pendulum Island was true to its name.

The road went on, and so did the journeyers. Zed walked fast, striding forward with a purpose, and though the shells and stones were not kind to her feet Berry kept up with him. More than once she wondered what her Grandda thought of her disappearance, along with Matthew's. Were they still being searched for, after all this time? Or had her and Matthew's whereabouts become a mystery that could not be answered? Surely Hudson Greathouse hadn't given up the search! Yet...still...if there was nothing to be found of them, after so many days, then...a mystery, unanswerable.

Zed suddenly stopped so quickly Berry bumped into him. It was like hitting a stone wall. She staggered back. He didn't even seem to feel it.

"What is it?" she asked him rather sharply, for her feet were cut and now she'd bitten her lower lip when she'd plowed into his immovable mountain.

He lifted the torch higher, and she saw what the light had already revealed to him. Hanging by leather straps from two poles on either side of the road were a pair of human skulls painted with brightly-colored stripes.

Zed moved the light from one side to the other, taking stock of not only the skulls but also of the situation.

"I think we shouldn't go any—" *Further*, Berry was about to say, but Zed was already going further ahead for this road was his choice of direction and no skulls would stop his progress.

"Wait!" she called to him. And a little louder: *"Wait!"* But he was on the move, the mountain in motion. If Berry desired the comfort of the torchlight she would have to keep up. She also got herself moving, and though she imagined her feet must be leaving bloodmarks on the road she caught up with Zed and walked just behind him but within the circle of light.

Berry thought that the wilderness on either side was as thick as Matthew's stubborn nature, and equally impenetrable. But where was the local harbor? Surely it couldn't be very much further! She intended to see Zed off in whatever boat he might find, with whatever fishing tackle or net, and then get herself back to the Templeton Inn. There would be some explaining to do. And would she be punished for this transgression? Would Matthew in some way be punished? She was in this soup now and she was going to have to swim through it. Zed's freedom was worth it...she hoped.

They hadn't gone but a few minutes more when Zed stopped again. This time Berry avoided a collision. Zed stood motionlessly in the middle of the road, his torch upraised. Off to the left a bird suddenly called stridently from the dark. Zed angled his light in that direction. His head cocked back and forth. He was listening, Berry thought. But listening for *what*?

Another bird called from the right. It was a higher-pitched sound, but equally as strident. Two notes, similar to the cawing of a crow. Zed abruptly spun around, facing Berry, and offered the torchlight past her; his eyes were centers of flame, likewise trying to pierce the dark. She turned to see what he was seeing, her spine and arms having erupted into goosebumps, but all she saw was flickering firelight, an empty road and nothing more.

In the woods on the right, a small spark jumped. A torch burst into fire.

In the woods on the left, a small spark jumped. A second torch came to life.

On the road before them, a third torch exploded into flame, and behind them a fourth awakened its scarlet eye.

Four figures approached Zed and Berry, moving in silence. Firelight jumped off at least two drawn swords. Berry felt Zed's body coiling, the muscles bunching up in his shoulders. His black-bearded face looked from one point of the compass to another, and he reached out to pull Berry closer to him but she realized even he must know four men with torches and swords would be too many for one Ga to fight.

Not, however, that he wouldn't try.

"Hold still," said the one on the right as he came through the thicket. "Don't try to run, it'll go worse for you."

Zed gave a quiet grunt. Berry heard it as: *And worse for you, that I don't run.*

The four figures converged upon them. They were heavy-set, broadshouldered white men with faces as hard as chunks of granite. A couple of them had faint smiles on their twisted mouths, as if they knew what was coming and looked forward greatly to the experience.

"Who the hell are *you*?" one of them, a man with a hooked nose and a wicked cutlass, asked Berry as he got nearer.

"Who the hell are *you*?" she answered back, standing her ground as if her bare feet were rooted there. She lifted her chin in defiance and hoped they wouldn't see all the fear swimming in her eyes.

"We'll sort this out later," said the man standing behind Zed and Berry. "Take 'em, boys!"

"This is a damned big'un," said one of the boys, a mite nervously. "What're them scars on his face?"

"Damned if I know or care. Just take 'em!"

The order having been given by the man who was apparently in charge, the other three came forward with torches outthrust and swords ready to slash. Zed didn't wait for them to arrive. He sprang at them with unexpected speed, and with teeth gritted at the center of his beard he stabbed his torch into the face of the nearest man and swung flames across the head of the next, setting the unfortunate's hair on fire. At that, the proverbial hell broke loose. Two swords came at Zed from front and back, and as Zed twisted to parry the blows with his own blazing weapon he gave Berry a mighty shove toward the woods and past the man who was trying to slap out the bonfire in his hair. She staggered into the brush and almost went down before she grabbed hold of a hanging vine. There she watched Zed battling torch against swords, doing his gallant best, but then the man with the scorched face swung a leather cudgel against the back of Zed's skull. One swing wasn't enough, for Zed turned to apply torch-to-face once more but a second cudgel blow hit him squarely on the left temple. Berry saw his knees sag.

It took a third blow right in the center of his forehead to drop the torch from Zed's hand. As Zed went to his knees on the ground, one of the swordsmen started to run him through at the neck, but the other—the leader—said, "Hold that! I think he's done!"

But not quite. Zed started to get to his feet again. The leader struck him across the base of the skull with the sword's grip, and the eager swordsman hit Zed in the face with a balled-up fist. Berry heard the sound of Zed's nose bursting blood. Then the man who had half a headful of ashes came at Berry, grabbing hold of her gown with one hand and putting a sword's tip under her chin with the other.

Berry saw Zed fall. There was nothing she could do for him. It was beyond her ability to stop them if they stabbed him to death in the next few seconds. Now she had to think about herself, and about the fact that the sword's tip was just about to pierce flesh. With a harsh cry that startled her assailant into a frozen instant, she tore free from him and ran into the thicket.

"Get her, Austin!" came the shouted command, but it was already well to Berry's back. She was going through the underbrush as if her own hair was aflame. A stumble over a pod of cactus plants was not a pleasant experience, but she sucked in her breath and swallowed the pain and kept running for all she was worth, which felt at the moment like a wooden shilling. When she dared to look back she saw in the silver moonlight Austin—half-haired and sweat-faced—still after her, his torch having been lost to hand in the initial skirmish. As he lunged forward to grab at her Berry changed direction like a skittering rabbit. She heard a grunt as his feet slid one way and his body careened in another, and there was a solid and satisfying *thud* as Austin hit the ground.

Berry ran for her life, or at least her freedom. She tore through vines and thorns and disturbed beams of moonlight with her running shadow. A look behind showed her no one following…yet. She didn't slow down. God help Zed, she thought, for she could not.

She came out of the woods onto another road. To her right, a torch was visible with a man underneath it, running in her direction. The light glinted off a sword. She ran along the road, her breath coming hard and fast and the sweat standing out on her cheeks. In another few yards a cart trail led off to the right through the brush, and this she took without hesitation, feeling she was safer amid the trees. She followed the trail further on, and saw by the moonlight several houses of white stone standing ahead.

A shout caught her attention. Two torches were coming from behind. Berry ran to the first house and banged furiously at the front door. There was no response or lamplight from within. The torches were getting closer. She had a few seconds to decide whether to run for the woods again or try the door of the second house. It was a near thing, but she went to the door. A hammering this time awakened a light that moved past a window. There was not much time; the two men approaching were almost within sight. Then a bolt was drawn, the door opened a crack and a lamp was thrust into Berry's face.

"Help me," she gasped. "Please!"

There was a pause that seemed to stretch for a hundred years. "What're you *doing* out here?"

That voice. She recognized its deep, commanding resonance.

The door opened wider and the lamplight revealed the ebony, white-goateed face of Captain Jerrell Falco. The amber eyes were ablaze in the yellow light. They moved to take in the two torches coming along the trail.

"*Please*," Berry said. "They're after me."

"So they are," Falco replied, without a shred of emotion. He stared at her as if to ask why he should help. But then his mouth crimped, he blinked as if someone had slapped sense into his soul, and he said, "Get in here."

Berry entered the house like a sliding shadow. Falco reached past her, closed the door and bolted it. A movement to her left startled Berry, and when she looked in that direction she saw a young cream-colored woman in a yellow gown holding a baby in her arms.

"Saffron," Falco said, "take the child into the bedroom." The girl instantly obeyed. Another small candle was burning in the room she had entered. Falco positioned himself between Berry and the front door. "Go back in there and stand in a corner out of sight," he told her. "Go on. *Now.*"

The voice was made to give orders. Berry went into the bedroom, a small but tidy place with pale blue walls, a clean bed, a crib for the baby, a writing desk and a couple of cheap but sturdy chairs. Berry took a position with her back in a corner, while Saffron rocked the baby and stared at her with huge chocolate-colored eyes.

Falco's candlelight was blown out. Berry knew he must be standing in the dark, waiting for the insistent knock upon the door. A half-minute stretched, and then a full minute. The baby began to cry, a soft mewling sound, but Saffron crooned quietly to it and the crying ceased. Saffron's eyes never stopped examining Berry Grigsby.

Another thirty seconds passed. Saffron whispered, "You runnin' from them men?"

"Yes," Berry answered, supposing 'them men' were the same who chased her.

"Go in them woods? Where they be?"

"Yes."

"*Quiet,*" said Falco, in a low murmur.

"Them woods is death," Saffron told her. "That road, too. You go in there, you doan come out."

"Why?" Berry asked, recalling how the men had converged on Zed. "What's in there?"

"Somethin' ain't healthy to know," Saffron answered, and that was all.

Falco came into the room. In this low light he looked very old, and very weary. "I believe they've passed by," he said. "But they might yet start knocking on doors. Did anyone else see you?" Berry shook her head. "Good. Where's the Ga? They take him?"

"Yes."

"I thought so. You wouldn't have come out here alone. Miss, you should have stayed in the village. Are you so eager to be…" He stopped, measuring his words against his tongue and teeth.

"To be *what*?" she prompted.

"Made to vanish?" he asked, with a lift of his unruly gray brows. "As some curious cats have vanished before you?"

Berry swallowed. She had to ask the next question. "What will they do with Zed?"

"Whatever they wish. That's no longer your concern, if you care to keep your skin." Falco took one of the two pillows from the bed and tossed it to the floor. "Sleep there," he said. "The men might come back with their dogs. If so…we shall see." He stretched out upon the bed, his hands folded back behind his head. Saffron lay the baby in the crib and curled herself up alongside the *Nightflyer*'s captain.

Berry lay down on the floor and rested her head on the pillow. Sleep would be impossible, but this was the best place to hide. Lying on her back, she stared up at the ceiling and saw in it the small cracks that meant Pendulum's movements were felt here as well.

"Thank you," she offered, in a voice strained from the night's events.

Someone blew out the candle, and from the dark there was no answer.

TWENTY-TWO

MATTHEW was ready and waiting, dressed in his charcoal-gray suit with thin stripes in a lighter gray hue. The suit was a bit tighter than it had been before being immersed in salt water, but Matthew still wore it well. When the knock came at the door this bright and sunny hour, Matthew was quick to open it for he knew who was behind the fist.

"Good morning," said Sirki, with a slight nod of his turbanned head. Today the East Indian giant wore his white robes, spotless as new snow. A glimpse of diamond-studded front teeth sparkled. "You are well, I presume?"

"Very well," said Matthew, attempting lightness but finding it a heavy effort. "And you?" As well as can be expected, Matthew thought, for someone who delights in severing heads from their bodies.

"I am instructed," the giant replied, "to pay you." He offered a brown leather pouch tied with a cord. "Three hundred pounds in gold coins, I am told. A very sizeable sum, and one you may keep whatever your decision may be regarding the professor's problem."

"Hm," Matthew answered. He took the pouch; it was richly heavy. He noted the red wax seal that secured the cord, and the octopus symbol of the professor's ambition embossed upon it. He moved the pouch back and forth next to his right ear to hear the coins clink together. "I have questions for you before I decide," he said firmly. "Will you answer them?"

"I will do my best."

Matthew decided not to tell Sirki about his dream last night, in the midst of his troubled sleep. In the dream, which was fogged at the edges with phantasmagoria, the gasping head of Jonathan Gentry had rolled along the bloody table and fallen into his lap, and there the twisted mouth had rasped three words that Matthew now repeated to Sirki.

"Finances. Weapons. Spain." Matthew had gotten out of his bed and walked back and forth upon the balcony in the cool hour before dawn until his perception of the matter had cleared. "Those are the realms of the three men involved. I am assuming, then, that the Royal Navy intercepted a cargo of weapons meant to be handed over to the Spanish, in return for a large sum of finances to the professor?"

"Your assumption may be correct," said the giant, with an expressionless face and voice that likewise revealed nothing. "I think," he added, "I might enter your room instead of having this discussion in the hallway." When Sirki came into the room, Matthew backed cautiously away from him, reasoning that the evil sawtoothed knife was somewhere near at hand. Sirki closed the door and planted himself like an Indian ironwood tree. "Now," he said, "I will entertain more of your assumptions."

"Thank you." A small bow completed the charade of manners. "I'm thinking, then, that Professor Fell is supplying some kind of new weapon to the Spanish? And he plans to sell the same weapon to Britain as soon as Spain puts it into full production? *And* there are other countries he plans to see this weapon to?"

"Possibly correct," said Sirki.

"But someone informed the authorities, and the first shipment was waylaid on the high seas? What's the weapon, Sirki?"

"I am not allowed," came the reply.

"All right, then." Matthew nodded calmly; he'd been prepared for this. "The professor believes one man of three is the traitor. Is it possible there could be *two* traitors among the three, working together?"

"A point well taken. The professor has already considered this possibility and wished you to reach it at your own opportunity."

"So the evidence Professor Fell is looking for may be some signal or message exchanged between the two, if indeed there *are* two?"

"That may be so."

Matthew placed the pouch of gold coins upon the writing desk. He was loathe to turn his back upon Sirki, even though he trusted that today he might keep his head. Through the louvered doors that led to the balcony he could hear the shrill cries of gulls and the hammerbeat of the waves below the castle's cliff. It was going to be a warm day, a world away from New York. He devoutly wished he were walking on snowclad streets, his hand in Berry's to guide her away from trouble.

"Professor Fell," Matthew said after some consideration, "puts me in the position of being a traitor myself. A traitor to my country," he said, with a quick glance at the giant. "As I understand this, the professor is selling weaponry to England's enemies, with the expectation that England will also have to buy the devices to keep their armories current. The so-called traitor...or *traitors*, perhaps... are actually working, whether they intend to or not, for the good of England. Therefore to expose them, I also become a traitor to my country. Is that not so?" Now Matthew directed a cold stare at Sirki, awaiting a response.

Sirki didn't answer for a time. Then he said, with a shrug of his shoulders, "Money is money. Sometimes it buys patriots, and sometimes it buys traitors. Do not mislead yourself, Matthew. Both breeds of men walk the halls of Parliament. They sit in luxury and sip their wine while underneath their English wigs the worms of greed eat into their brains. But let us not use the word *greed*. Let us say...*opportunity*. That is the grease of all the great wheels that turn this world, Matthew. And I shall tell you that here you face the greatest opportunity of your life, if you take it with both hands."

"My hands should not be so covered with English blood," Matthew countered.

"But *someone's* hands shall be," said Sirki, in his silky way. "The professor is offering you many...incentives, I understand. He also wishes to see how you react under pressure."

"I float," Matthew said.

"He hopes that is so. He wishes you to float to a good conclusion here. One that benefits himself and yourself. You have no idea what he can do for you, if he perceives you are worthy."

"Worthy to him, and unworthy to myself?"

Sirki smiled thinly, and almost sadly. "Oh, Matthew. What you don't know of this world might fill the professor's library ten times over."

"Does he write all the books himself? And sign his name as 'God'?"

Sirki for a time stared at the chessboard floor without speaking. When his voice came, it was no longer silky but edged with saw-teeth like his blade. "Shall I tell the professor you are accepting or rejecting the problem to be solved?"

Now came time for Matthew's move. He saw no way to get his knight to safety; it was going to be a hard sacrifice, but one that might yet win the game for him if he had further stomach for the playing.

"Accepting," Matthew said.

"Very good. He will be pleased to know." Sirki put his hand on the door's knob, engulfing it with his grip. Matthew thought the giant could pull the door from its hinges with that one hand, if he pleased. Sirki opened the door, however, with a gentle touch. "I trust you will enjoy this day to its fullest," he said.

The meaning of that was *get to work*, Matthew thought.

"Speaking of the professor's library," Sirki said, pausing on the threshold. "It's on the third floor. You might be interested in visiting it, since it holds volumes you might find intriguing, and especially since I saw Edgar Smythe going up the stairs."

"Your direction is appreciated," said Matthew.

Sirki closed the door, and their discussion for the moment was finished.

Matthew reasoned that there was no time to lose. He had no idea how he was going to approach Edgar Smythe, the scowling weapons expert, but he decided to let that take care of itself. He left his room, locked the door, went to the main staircase and climbed it to the upper floor.

A pair of polished doors made from pale oakwood opened onto a room that nearly made Matthew's knees buckle. It was filled with shelves of books almost from the smoothly-planked floor to the vaulted ceiling. Above his head, as per the banquet room, were painted clouds and watchful cherubs. The smell of the room was, to Matthew, the delicious and fragrantly yeasty aroma of volumes of ideas, considerations and commentary. There would be enough in here to keep his candle lit for years. He actually felt his heartbeat quickening, in the presence of so much treasure. Three hundred pounds be damned; this abundance of knowledge was the gold he truly sought. He saw across the room louvered doors that must lead to a balcony, and on either side of the doors heavy wine-red drapes with yellow tie cords were drawn across windows overlooking the sea. The library held several black leather chairs and a sofa, a table bearing bottles of what appeared to be wine and spirits for the further delight of the bibliophile, and an expansive white writing desk with a green blotter. Sitting at the desk, evidently copying something down from a slim volume onto yellow parchment with a quill pen, was Edgar Smythe, his gray-bearded and heavily-lined face absorbed in his task. He was once more wearing his ebony-black suit and white shirt—perhaps he owned a half-dozen of the exact same suit, Matthew mused—and between Smythe's teeth was a clay pipe that showed a thin curl of smoke the color of the sea's waves at first light.

Matthew approached the man, stopped and cleared his throat. Smythe kept right on copying something from tome to parchment. From time to time the quill went into an ink bottle, and then returned to its industrious work.

"Are you wanting something, Mr. Spade?" Smythe asked suddenly around his pipe, without interruption of his labor. The voice was as harsh as yesterday's murder.

"Not particularly." Matthew stepped nearer. "I wanted to have a look at the library."

"Look all you please," Smythe instructed. Whatever he was copying, there was no attempt to hide the effort. "But...refrain from peering over my shoulder, would you?"

"Certainly, sir." Having said this, however, Matthew made no move to back away. "I *was* wondering, though, about something I hoped you might help me with."

"I can't help you with anything."

"That might not be exactly true." Matthew took one more step closer, which put him nearly at Smythe's elbow. In for a penny, in for a pound, Matthew thought. He said, "I was hoping you might explain to me about the Cymbeline."

The quill ceased its scratching. Matthew noted that the parchment was almost full of small but neat lines of writing, and that there were several other blank pages ready for use in the same way. Smythe's face turned and the somber gray eyes fixed on Matthew with some force. "Pardon me?"

"Cymbeline," Matthew repeated. "I'd like to hear about it."

Smythe sat stock-still for what seemed a full minute. Presently he slid his quill onto its rest and removed the pipe from its clenched-teeth grip. "*Cymbeline*," he said quietly, "is a play." He held up the volume, and stamped there upon its dark brown binding were the gold letters *The Tragedie Of Cymbeline, Five Acts By William Shakespeare*. "Shall I read you a scrap of what I've written here?" He went on without waiting. *"Fear no more the heat o' the sun, Nor the furious winter rages; Thou thy worldly task has done, Home art gone and ta'en thy wages; Golden lads and girls all must, as chimney-sweepers, come to dust."* Smythe looked up from his parchment. "Would you care for more?"

"A recitation upon death? No, thank you."

"Not just any recitation, Mr. Spade, but a grand affirmation of death. I am a great admirer of Shakespeare's plays, sir. I am a great admirer of his mind and his voice, which unfortunately I only hear in my imagination." He placed the volume down upon the desk again and drew a pull from his pipe. "This is how I've been keeping myself *sane* on this bloody island, sir. I have been dutifully copying passages from Shakespeare's plays, of which the professor thankfully has a full set. Waiting for *you* to arrive has been a strain on all of us. Therefore...this little diversion of mine, which serves to heighten my appreciation of the master's work. Do you have any complaint you'd care to commit to the air?"

"None." Matthew was desperately trying to mask his confusion. Of course *Cymbeline* was a play, about the trials and tribulations of a British king—Cymbeline—possibly based on legends of the real-life British king Cunobelinus. But what this had to do with the professor's problem, or the matter of the new weapon, Matthew had no clue. He decided he had better quit cutting bait and start to fish. "I'm presuming that's the code name for the new device the professor has created?"

"Device? What are you talking about?"

"The new *weapon*," Matthew said. "Which he is intent upon selling to Spain, and which was seized at sea by the British Navy." He decided to add, "Due to Gentry's influence."

The pipe's bowl spiralled its fumes. "Young man," said the gravel-bottomed voice, "you are wandering into dangerous territory. You know that our businesses should be kept separate, by *his* order. I don't wish to know anything about your use of whores to spear state secrets, and your desire to know about the Cymbeline is ill-met."

Matthew shrugged but held his ground. "I'm curious by nature. And my curiosity has been sharpened after that pretty scene last night. I'm just wishing to know why it's *called* Cymbeline."

"Really? And who told you that Cymbeline is a weapon?"

"Sirki did," Matthew said. "In response to my questions."

"He also told you the first shipment to Spain was captured at sea?"

"He did." Matthew thought that Nathan Spade was a very accomplished liar.

"What's his game, then?" Smythe frowned; he had once been a handsome man in his youth, but now he was just harsh and ugly.

"Did he tell me untruths?"

"No," Smythe said. "But he's violating the professor's decree. Why is that?"

"You might ask him yourself," Matthew suggested, ever the gentleman.

Edgar Smythe smoked his pipe in contemplation of that remark, and when he was wreathed by the blue fumes he seemed to diminish in size and let any idea of confronting the East Indian killer slip away like the very essence of tobacco now floating toward the louvered doors. "You are incorrect," he finally said, in a doomsday voice.

"How so?"

"Incorrect...in your statement that Professor Fell created Cymbeline. He did not. It was my idea. My creation. My unremitting labor of mind and resources. And I am very good at what I do, Mr. Spade. So that is your first error, which I am glad to adjust." He blew a small spout of smoke in Matthew's direction. "Your second error," he went on, "is that Cymbeline is a *device*. Oh, did you believe it was some kind of multiple-barrelled cannon dreamt up by an eccentric inventor?"

"Not exactly." Though the idea had crossed Matthew's mind. He had experience with multiple-barrelled guns and eccentric inventors.

"Cymbeline," said the weapons expert, "is the foundation upon which future devices shall be constructed. Whoever possesses it has a distinct advantage on any battlefield, and thus its immense worth to many countries."

"I see that, but if many countries have it...wouldn't that mean Cymbeline has become obsolete?"

"The nature of the beast," Symthe granted, with a snort of smoke through the pinched nostrils. "There will always be something beyond Cymbeline, and something beyond that, until the end of time."

Matthew brought up a thin smile. "It seems to me, sir, that your business ultimately hastens the end of time."

"That will happen after I am long gone." Smythe tapped a finger against the bowl of his pipe, whose flame had deceased. "Therefore it is not my concern. But I will inform you that it is the *professor's* business, not mine. I am the hand, he is the brain."

A simple way to seek escape from blame, Matthew thought. He wondered if indeed Edgar Smythe's brain had not begun to believe treachery against England was not worth money in the hand. "The Cymbeline," Matthew persisted bullheadedly, as was his wont. "Whatever it is...why is it called that?"

Smythe began to turn through the pages of *Cymbeline*. "Professor Fell titled it. After a line from the play. Just a moment, I'll find it. Ah...here it is. Actually a stage direction: *Jupiter descends in thunder and lightning, sitting upon an eagle; he throws a thunderbolt.*" Smythe looked up from the page with an expression that could only be bemusement, though on that sour face it was hard to tell. "The professor enjoys his drama."

"Yes," Matthew agreed. "Undoubtedly."

Smythe stood up. He gathered his sheets of parchment, took the volume and slid it back into its place on one of the shelves. "I will say good morning to you, then. And I hope your day is pleasant. I have a report to give to the professor this afternoon. When are you giving yours?"

"I don't know yet."

"You're an odd sort," Smythe said, his head tilted slightly to one side as if seeing Nathan Spade in a different light. "Are you sure you belong here?"

"I must. I'm here, aren't I?"

"So you are." Smythe started for the doors.

"Let me ask you one more question," Matthew persisted, and Smythe paused. "Who is Brazio Valeriani?"

"Someone the professor seeks. That's all I know."

"Is he connected to the Cymbeline?"

Smythe frowned; it was, in truth, a horrible sight. "I have heard things," he said, quietly. "And no, Valeriani is *not* connected to the Cymbeline. It's another matter altogether. But I have heard…" He hesitated, staring at the floor. "Unsettling things," he continued, as with an effort. The face lifted and the gray eyes were darkly-hollowed. "This is not something you should be concerned with, young man. If what I have heard is true…if any *part* of it is true… you will wish you never heard that name."

"Why does the professor seek him?"

"*No.*" Smythe shook his head. "You will get none of it from me, nor from anyone else here. That is as far as I go. Good day."

"Good day," Matthew answered, for Edgar Smythe the weapons expert was already going through the doors and gone.

Matthew was left alone in the library. Hundreds of books— large and small, thick and thin—were there before him on the shelves. Ordinarily this would have been a dream come true for him, but some element of evil lay coiled in this room and therefore it was an oppressive place, an atmosphere of dark brooding. But the books called to him nevertheless, and in another moment he was walking past the shelves looking at the titles stamped upon leather. He reached out a hand to accept Nicolaus Copernicus' *De Revolutionibus Orbium Coelestium*, but his hand then moved to touch the red spine of Homer's *Odyssey*. Next to it beckoned three thick volumes of English sea voyages and navigational studies, and next to that one...

Odd, Matthew thought.

He took the book from its place. It was a battered brown leather edition titled *The Lesser Key Of Solomon*. Matthew recalled seeing an edition of this book before, in the ruins of Simon Chapel's library just before his involvement with Tyranthus Slaughter. In a way, this book had caused him quite a lot of misery, for that copy he'd found in Chapel's library had been hollowed out and literally held a key to unlock a book—*The History of Locks As Regards The Craft of Ancient Egypt and Rome*—that had concealed a bagful of Professor Fell's money. Which had put him nearly on the road to ruin, regarding his future fate and the health of Hudson Greathouse. But now...finding a *second* copy of this book, here in the professor's own library...

Odd.

This book appeared to be only a book, not a depository. Matthew opened it and began to turn through the yellowed pages, and at once he realized that the God Professor Fell was playing to be might have another side altogether.

The Lesser Key Of Solomon was a book describing the demons of Hell.

In Latin script and prints of woodcut drawings, the descriptions of these dark dwellers were quite vivid. The demonic entities appeared as such things as animalish creatures with blade-like claws, spidery denizens of nightmare worlds and shadowy combinations of man, beast and insect. They were given titles, as befitted the nobility of the netherworld.

Matthew came upon a page depicting the stork-like Earl Malthus. The text reported this monstrosity as an expert in building towers filled with ammunition and weapons, and who was noted for speaking in a disturbingly rough voice.

He turned the pages. There was Prince Sitri and Marquis Phenex, Duke Vepar and King Belial. There was Count Renove, Prince Vassago, King Zagan and Duke Sallos. More pages were turned, and more demons revealed in all their ghastly inhuman but human-like shades: King Baal, Duke Barbatos, Prince Seere, Marquis Andras, Count Murmur, Duke Ashtaroth, President Caim, Duke Dantalion, Marquis Shax and on and on. It took a steady hand and a steely nerve to view these woodcut impressions and read this text of otherworldly horrors. Each demon had a specialty...king of liars, activator of corpses, deliverer of madness, creator of storms, destroyer of cities and the dignity of men, power over the spirits of the dead, the sowing of the bitter seeds of jealousy and discord, the transformation of men into wolves and crows and creatures of the night, the power to burn anything on earth to utter ash.

And, as he turned the pages, Matthew realized with a start of further horror that not only did this book depict the demons of Hell, but it also contained spells and rituals to call them from their caverns at the end of time to do the bidding of men.

This room suddenly seemed much too small and too terribly dark. Matthew wished to put the book away, to get it out of his hands lest it blister the flesh, and yet...

...and yet...

It had caught him. He, who had seen through the artifice of an evil man in positioning an innocent woman as a witch in a town called Fount Royal. He, who had no belief in witches and demons and things that went bump in the night. He, who viewed facts as facts and superstitions as the coinage of a past century. He, who would champion himself for that woman named Rachel Howarth but would not give a cup of warm piss to the idea of demons riding the currents of the whirlwinds. He, who did not believe in such fantasy.

But...perhaps the owner of this book did?

And he believed so strongly that he had shared another copy with his associate Simon Chapel, who had—perhaps in his own revulsion or sense of irony—turned it into a key-box?

Matthew had to get out of this room. He needed light and air. He took the *Lesser Key* with him, through the louvered doors onto the balcony. Sunlight and warm air hit him in the face. He smelled the salt of the sea and saw the bright glittering shine of morning light upon the waves below. The balcony had a white stone railing and balustrade. At both corners, just beyond the railing, were ledges upon which was situated a white stone seahorse standing up nearly as large as a real stallion, a remarkable job of sculpture. Matthew held the book at his side and drew in long draughts of the sea air to clear his head. He wasn't sure what he had stumbled upon, but he felt quite sure he had stumbled upon *something*.

And then he saw her, down below, sitting cross-legged upon her rock.

Fancy, they called her. Her body nude and brown and glistening, her long hair black as a raven's wing, her face turned toward the far horizon where the waves broke upon an unknown shore. To them, Fancy. To him…possibly Pretty Girl Who Sits Alone. And to him, another one to champion. To save. To free, if he could. It was in his nature to do so, and calling himself Nathan Spade in this vile gathering of greedy men and women did not change that. *Could* not change that. *Would* not change that.

"Mornin'," came the voice behind him.

And a second voice, following: "…boyo."

Matthew turned quickly toward the two brothers, as they came onto the balcony from shadow into sunlight that seemed suddenly blighted in its wet and sultry heat.

"Spadey himself," said Mack, with a cold grin on a face that appeared red-eyed and bloated, the same as his twin's. Both men were carrying bottles they'd picked up from the drink table in the library, and Matthew judged them to have been downing the liquor since the breaking of dawn a couple of hours ago. That, or they'd been drunk all night and had emerged to replenish their supply. Both men wore the breeches of their red suits, and both had spilled upon their wrinkled gray shirts copious amounts of liquid danger. Their sleeves were rolled up to display the thick forearms of tavern brawlers, ready to strike.

"…all *by* himself," Jack added. He stood in the doorway as Mack got up nearly chin to chin with Matthew. Yes, the breath could have knocked over one of the stone seahorses, and Matthew steeled himself not to retreat from its sour flames.

"Where's your knife-thrower now?" Mack asked.

"Ain't here," said Jack.

"'Tis a pity," said Mack.

"Solid shame," Jack lamented.

"Oh the agony of it, to be young and handsome, and so mannered and smart to boot…and yet be forgot about, up here alone."

"Way up here," Jack said, and now he drank from his uncorked bottle and came upon the balcony with his eyes narrowed into slits. "All alone."

Matthew's heart was beating hard. The sweat pulsed at his temples. By the greatest effort he kept fear out of his face, even as the Thackers positioned themselves on either side of him, shoulders pressed against his body and pinioning him in. "I was just on my way to breakfast," he said. "If you'll pardon me?"

"Mack," said Jack, and another drink went down his pipe, "I don't think Spadey likes us."

"Don't like us worth a shitty shillin'," said Mack, who also swigged from his own bottle. "And him such a *worldly* gentleman. Makes me feel like he thinks he's better than most."

"Better'n *us*, you're sayin'," Jack prodded.

"Yeah, that's what I'm sayin'."

"Said correctly, brother."

"So sad to say."

"Sad," said Jack.

"Awful most," said Mack, with his grin still in place and his green eyes showing a dull glare.

"Oh, mercy me." Jack had taken note of the figure on the rock. "Looky what Spadey's been lookin' at."

Mack saw, and nodded gravely. "Looky, looky. But don't touch the nooky."

"Think he'd like to touch it," said Jack.

"Think he'd like to roll in it," said Mack.

"Agreed, brother," they said, almost as one.

"Gentlemen," said Matthew, and perhaps now was the time to get out while he could, for he sensed violence about to rear its ugly head, "I admire your taste in women. I would ask where you found such a lovely specimen."

"*Specimen*," said Jack, with a snort that blew bits of snot from his nostrils. "Makes our Fancy sound like a fuckin' *worm*, don't he?"

"Like a bug, crawled from under a rock," Mack observed.

"No disrespect meant." Matthew realized it was a lost cause; these bully boys were wanting to thrash him, come what may, and

Matthew's plan was to get their minds on Fancy and then—igno-miniously or not—bolt from the balcony as soon as he could. "I was wondering where I might find a woman of that breed?"

"You can *buy* 'em, boyo, on the pussy market." Jack leaned in, leering, his breath smelling of whiskey sharpened by snakeheads. "I thought that was your fuckin' *business*."

"'Cept we didn't buy Fancy," Mack confided, and now he put an arm around Matthew's shoulders in a way that made Matthew's spine crawl. "We come across her owned by a gentleman gambler in Dublin. He'd won her at the faro table last year…"

"Year before that," Jack corrected.

"Whenever." Mack's grip tightened on Matthew's shoulders. "We decided we'd have her. You listenin' here? It's a good story. Wanted to teach him he couldn't play faro in that tavern without our permission or a piece of the pie, and him riggin' the box against those other poor punters. We left him crawlin', didn't we?"

"Crawlin' and pukin' blood," said Jack.

"Man with no knees left," said Mack, "has got to crawl."

"Sure as fuck can't walk," Jack added, and then he pressed the mouth of his bottle against Matthew's lips. "Have a drink with me, Spadey."

Matthew averted his face. He caught a movement, and saw that this little drama was being observed by Fancy, who had stood up upon her rock to watch.

"No, thank you," Matthew said. And he saw the Indian girl turn her back and dive from her perch into the sea, where the waves closed over her brown body and rippled white in her descent.

"You didn't hear me, boyo." Jack's voice was very quiet. "I said I want you to have a drink with me."

"And then with me." Mack's bottle also pressed against Matthew's mouth. "Wet your whistle while ya can."

"No," Matthew repeated, for his boundary had been reached. "Thank you." He started to move away from them, even as they pressed in harder on either side. "If you'll excuse me, I have to—"

Mack suddenly whipped *The Lesser Key Of Solomon* from Matthew's hand. He used it to smack Matthew hard on the nose, which caused a fierce and staggering pain and made Matthew's eyes blur with tears. In the next instant, before Matthew could right himself, Jack gripped the back of his neck and headbutted him on the forehead, sending jagged spears of light and flaming stars through Matthew's brain. His arms and legs at once became heavy dead limbs, without feeling or purpose.

"Hold him up," he heard one of them say, as if an echo in a long cavernous corridor.

"Little fucker don't weigh nothin'."

"Got me an idea. Don't let him drop."

"Want me to knee him in the balls?"

"No. Let's send him swimmin'. But first...drag him over here. Lemme get them curtain cords."

"What're ya thinkin', brother?"

"I'm thinkin' Spadey got hisself drunk, climbed up on that thing, it fell, and...over the side he went."

"You mean to *kill* him?"

"I mean to wash our hands of his shitty little self, that's what I mean. And damned to the depths for him, where he'll never be found. Come on, drag him over."

In the fog of his dazed brain and throbbing brainpan, Matthew realized this was not good for his future. In fact, it was horribly bad. He felt himself being dragged. His eyes were blinded by sunlight and black shadows that shifted in and out of his befouled vision. He tried to get his feet under himself, tried to get a hand up to protest this rough treatment.

"He's comin' round."

"Smack him again."

Another headbutt slammed into Matthew's forehead. Bright balls of light exploded behind his eyes. He felt his legs dance of their own volition for a few seconds. He thought Gilliam Vincent might commend him. Wasn't he at a dance at Sally Almond's tavern? Didn't he hear fiddle music—though terribly off-key—and the banging of a drum close to his ear?

The echoing voices returned.

"...up on that thing with him. Tie his hands behind him."

"Ain't somebody gonna miss the cords?"

"Not my concern, brother. Maybe they'll think he made himself some reins for his horse, and got tangled up in 'em."

Horse? Matthew thought, in his deep dark cave. *What horse?*

He felt pain at his shoulders. His arms had been pulled back. Tying his hands?

"Now get the other cord tied around him and the horse. Come on, hurry it!"

Horse? Matthew thought once more. It seemed very important that he figure this out, but his brain was not working too well. He felt himself being wrapped around with a rope of some kind. *Lemme get them curtain cords*, he remembered hearing.

"They'll know it was us."

"No, brother, they won't. Leave your bottle on the ledge. Help me push this bastard over. You ready?"

"Always ready."

"*Push.*"

Matthew felt himself falling. He tried to blink his light-smeared vision clear. He had a scream locked behind his lips, but his mouth would not open.

Horse, he thought.

As in...*seahorse.*

He hit the water on his side. The chill of the sea shocked some of the sense back into him. He had time to gasp a lungful of air before he went under.

I float, Matthew recalled saying to Sirki.

But he realized at once that no man tied to several hundred pounds of stone seahorse was going to float, and so with the desperate air locked in his lungs and his hands bound behind him he rode his horse beneath the waves and down and down into the blue silence below.

TWENTY-THREE

UNDERWATER, Matthew was turning as he sank. The seahorse was above him one instant, and then the next he was riding it to his death. His ears crackled with pain. He heard the air bubbles bursting from his mouth. His vision was clouded with blue. He roused himself to fight against the cords that bound his wrists together, yet his strength was already much abused and used-up. He was a dry vessel, surrounded and suffocated by the sea.

Panic set in and caused him to thrash wildly and with no purpose. More air escaped lungs and mouth. The pressure upon his ears was inescapable, as was his predicament. The roar in his head was the sound of a watery grave opening to forever hide his corpse from the sun, and yet it might be the voice of a demon from *The Lesser Key Of Solomon*, exulting in the demise of a good man.

Matthew's stone mount suddenly hit something with a sea-muffled *thud*, landing upright on its base. Its descent ceased.

He could see only smears and shadows, strange forms around him that might be angular rocks sculpted by time and currents. His heart pounded, and with the next loss of air he knew his stuttering lungs would lose their grip on life and the sea would come rushing in to complete the job the Thackers had begun.

He couldn't get free. He couldn't wrench himself loose from the seahorse. He was done, he realized. What gunpowder bombs had not stolen, the cool blue depths would take.

Finished, he thought. *But dear God…I am not ready to—*

A mouth clamped onto his. A breath of air forced itself into his lungs. Black hair swirled into his face. Something began sawing at the cord binding his wrists. A sharp edge grazed him. A piece of glass or a broken shell? He had to hold on a moment longer…just a moment, if he could…

His body shivered and jerked in involuntary battle against the oncoming dark. One moment more…just one…

He felt the cord give way, and the Indian girl had freed his hands.

There was still the rope binding body to seahorse. Wrapped around his waist. He grasped at it and pulled. Tighter than a swollen tick. Where was the knot? Somewhere underneath the horse? The girl's mouth was suddenly on his again, feeding him more breath. He felt her sharp edge at work on the cord at his left side. Sawing frantically, it seemed; as frantically as he fought the pounding and the pain and the darkness reaching for him. He looked up, silver bubbles bursting from his mouth and nostrils because he just couldn't hold the air in any longer. Sunlight shone on the surface above. How far? Thirty or forty feet? He could never make that.

She pulled at him. The cord had come loose enough for him to get free of it. He started desperately for the surface, but she yet pulled at him in another direction. Deeper, it seemed. He thought she must be insane, and he was not a merman to her mermaid; yet her pull was insistent and now she had her arm around him and was urging him to swim with her.

I am not finished, he thought in his anguished blue haze. *I have much to do. I am not finished…but I must trust this girl.*

And so he kicked forward with her as the silver bubbles bloomed from his mouth and nose, and three more kicks and the Indian girl was leading him downward still. She took him into a dark place, through some kind of opening. A cave? he thought, near letting his lungs either empty themselves or explode. But no, not a cave…

They swam a few seconds longer, and then she abruptly led him up and his head broke the surface and he tasted salty sweet air. He inhaled mightily with a shudder that racked his body and in the next instant was punished by spasms of retching. She held him up while he filled his lungs and emptied his belly. In the dark blue gloom he saw the stones of a wall to his right and two feet above his head the stones and rafters of a ceiling. He reached up with both hands to grasp hold of a rafter, finding the wood spongy but still able to bear his weight, and he hung there breathing hard, coughing viciously, and shivering with not the chill but the idea that death had been so very, very close.

"Oh my God," Matthew rasped. And again, for he knew not what else to say: "Oh my God."

"Don't let go," Fancy told him, her body pressed against his side and her own hands up to hold onto the near-rotted rafter. "Do you hear me?" Her English was perfect, not a trace of an accent.

"I hear," Matthew said; more of a frog's croak than human speech.

"Just breathe," she said.

"No instruction…necessary," he managed to answer, though he had to breathe through his mouth for his injured nostrils were nearly swollen shut. His head was still pounding, his heart about to beat through his chest, and his stomach roiling. He closed his eyes, for now a sick weakness was threatening to make his fingers open. If he slid back in just yet he was done for.

"You're going to live," she said.

He nodded, but he was thinking he would not bet on such a statement. His eyes opened and he again surveyed their surroundings. Not a cave, but…a building of some kind? "Where are we?"

"The town under the sea," Fancy answered, her black hair pushed back from her forehead and her face a blue-daubed darkness. "I found it, nearly the first day I was here."

Matthew thought his brain must still be fogged and burdened. "Town? Under the sea?"

"Yes. Many buildings. Some with air still caught in them. I swim here, many times."

"A *town*?" Matthew still couldn't make heads-or-tails of it. Possibly Fancy had seen him go over the balcony and had used broken glass from a window to cut him free. "Did they know?" He tried to clarify that: "The brothers. Did they know?"

"About this place? No. It fell away from the island in the earthquake, long years ago."

"Earthquake," he repeated, lapsing back into his parrotty pattern. That would go along with the tremors still being felt on Pendulum. He felt as if his head was full of mush. "Who told you this?"

"One of the servants. She was a child when it happened."

Matthew nodded. He still felt numb and bewildered. It occurred to him quite suddenly, as if he hadn't realized it before, that this beautiful creature pressed against him was quite naked.

"Who are you?" she asked. "You're not like the others. You're not part of them. So...who are you, really?"

"I can't explain that," he decided to say. "But I can tell you that I knew an Iroquois brave who was called He Runs Fast Too. He—"

"Came over on the ship with me," Fancy interrupted. "And with Nimble Climber. How did you know him? And what happened to him?"

"He went back to your land. Back to the tribe. He...helped me do something important."

"He's dead now," she said. "I can hear it in your voice."

"Yes, he's dead. And you were called—"

"I know what I was called. That was a long time ago."

"Those two who have you. They—"

"I don't wish to speak of them," she said. "But I will say they do not have *all* of me. I always find a place to go. As here. In the silence, I can think. I can *be*." She adjusted her grip on the beam because her fingers were sinking into the black rot. Her voice was quiet and distant when she next spoke. "I love this. This ocean. This blue world. It speaks to me. It *hides* me. It makes me feel safe."

Matthew thought this was the only girl in the world who would feel safe forty-something feet underwater, with her head in a small breathing space in the ruins of a collapsed town. But he understood exactly what she meant.

"I can never go back," Fancy told him. "Not to my land. Not to my people."

"Why not? If I could get you out of here—and away from *them*—then why not?"

"You could never get me away from them." It was said with a fair amount of smouldering anger. "They would kill you if you tried."

Matthew said with a weak grin, "They'd have to do better than this, wouldn't they?"

"They would do far better. I have seen them do…terrible things. And to me, also. I used to fight them, but I suffered for it. Now I don't fight, but I still suffer. They enjoy that. It is their great *pleasure* in living."

"I'm going to get you away from them."

"No," she answered, with the hardness of a stone that could not be moved, "you will not. Because even if you could—which you cannot—I have no place to go. Except another bed, in another room, in another house owned by another man. I am…how would you say…an item to be sought. Not so much now, as there are many others like me brought across the ocean. But I am still rare enough."

Matthew couldn't fully see her face in the blue gloom, but he had the impression of looking at someone who had long ago lost all ability to smile, and whose happiness was silence and peace taken at every possible moment. He didn't wish to think what those rough hands and biting teeth had done to her. He didn't wish to think what her eyes had seen.

"I can help you," he offered.

"I can never go back," she repeated. "Not who I am now."

It was said, Matthew noted, the Indian way: all statement of fact, all hard true reality, and not a sliver of self-pity or pretense.

"All right," Matthew said, but he knew himself. And, for better or for worse, he never surrendered.

"We should start up," Fancy told him. "Take in some breaths. Get ready. It is easy for me, but it may be difficult for you. I will hold your hand all the way."

"Thank you." Matthew thought this sounded like a casual stroll along the Great Dock, but he knew one usually did not perish on such a stroll, whereas in this instance perishing was a prominent possibility.

"Are you ready?" she asked in another moment.

The dreaded question, he thought. And the answer?

"As I'll ever be," he said, though the racing of his heart spoke otherwise.

She reached out for him and he gave her his left hand. "Stay close to me," she directed. "We will pass through a doorway and a broken window and we will be out. Mind the glass at the bottom of the window."

"I will." If it hadn't snagged him on the way in, he wasn't concerned about it on the way out. And he was determined to be her second skin, within reason.

"Take a breath and let it go," she said. He imagined he could see the gleam of her eyes as she stared at him. "Then take another breath and hold it. When you do that, we will start."

Matthew nodded. Damn, this was some deep hell he'd gotten himself into. He was scared nearly beyond his wits from the memory of his lungs spasming on the edge of drowning. He wasn't sure he had the strength or willpower to make this swim. His head still pounded and his nose sat on his face like a lump of hot tar. Was the damned thing broken? No time to fret about that now. He took the breath and let it go. He was afraid. But then he felt her hand squeeze his and he took the next breath—a deep breath, as deep as possible—and held it and instantly Fancy went under and pulled him with her. He let go his one-handed grip on the beam, and he was swimming alongside the Indian girl with terror thrumming through his veins.

He didn't know when they went through the doorway, except his right shoulder hit a hard surface that shot fresh pain through him. God blast it! he thought as he held onto his air. Fancy pulled him onward with remarkable strength. She was indeed in her element, a daughter of the blue world. Did they pass through a broken window? Matthew wasn't sure, for he could see nothing but blurs and smears. Maybe something caught at his stockings, though he wasn't sure about that either. Then the light from above brightened and they were rising. Matthew had a blurred glimpse of what might have been the white stone seahorse, perched on a crooked roof. All around were the shapes of stone buildings, with alleys and streets between them. It appeared to Matthew in this blue haze that some were intact and others fallen to ruin either by the action of the sea or the violence of the earthquake. Then he could gather no more impressions for his lungs were aching and the surface was still thirty feet above.

She took him up, their hands locked together.

Perhaps it was a swift ascent. To Matthew, as he fought to control both his spasming lungs and the terror that chewed at him, it was the journey of night into day. Never had such a distance, which could easily be walked on land, seemed so far and so horrible. Ten feet below the surface, he lost nearly all his air in an explosion of bubbles that swept past his face in silver mockery. Then his lungs desired to pull in the seawater, and yet Matthew by force of will and fear of death kept the Atlantic from invading him, and two more kicks and the surface was right there in his face and his head was breaking the surface and the foamy slop of a wave almost drowned him in his moment of victory but he opened his mouth and drew in breath after breath and felt Fancy's arms around him holding him up.

He pushed the hair back from his forehead and treaded water, his chest heaving. He looked up at the professor's castle on the cliff above, and could clearly see the third floor library's balcony and the ledge where one of the two stone seahorses had lately rested. The Thackers were long gone. If anyone else but Fancy had seen this assault, they had kept their lips sealed for there appeared to be no activity anywhere. It was just another sunny day in Fell's paradise.

Here the waves were rough, as they surged toward the base of the cliffs. Matthew could see from this vantage point where part of the island had been sheared off. He recalled the professor saying *My father was the governor here.* It was likely that his father was indeed governor when the town—whatever its name had been— had collapsed into the sea.

"Follow me," said Fancy, and she began to swim toward the cliffs not directly but at a forty-degree angle. Though weakened and certainly no champion in the water, Matthew followed as best he could. Fancy's taut bottom breaking the surface and the glistening shine of her legs made following nearly a delightful obsession.

In time they reached a cove shielded from the breakers by a series of large rocks, and Fancy could stand in hip-high water. Matthew felt more rocks under his feet and walked carefully lest a surge of waves trapped and snapped an ankle; Fancy, however, knew the territory and forged onward like a true providence rider. A beach pebbled with black stones was ahead. On a rock in the shadows lay her clothing, neatly folded, and her shoes. As Fancy hurriedly dressed herself, Matthew staggered from the sea and fell to his knees in the grainy gray sand.

"You're all right now," she told him, as she buttoned the front of her rather tight-fitting lilac-colored gown.

"I know," he answered, his face lowered. His head seemed to be full of crazy churchbells. "I'm just trying to..." He had to start again, for he was out of breath. "I'm just trying to make sure of it."

She finished dressing and smoothed her gown before she spoke again, her black hair swept back and her face beautiful and austere. "You're very brave."

"Am I?"

"Certainly you are."

"I think I'm mostly lucky."

"I think," she said, "you have earned the right to live another day."

"At least," he agreed, and he pulled himself up and got to his feet.

Her ebony eyes, full of pain and secrets, examined him from wet bottom to drenched top. "You won't tell me who you are?"

"I can't."

"But you're not one of them. Not *really*."

"No," he said, deciding she knew anyway. "Not one of them."

"Then you're here for a different reason than the others. I don't understand why. Perhaps it would be best *not* to know?"

"Yes," he answered, "that would be best."

"Ah," she said, and nodded; it was an expression that spoke volumes. Still she held him with her solemn gaze, as if reading not only his face but his soul. Then she motioned toward a rocky pathway several yards distant that led up the cliff to the highland. "It's steep and a little dangerous, but that's the only way."

Steep and dangerous, Matthew thought. Was there any other way? He followed her when she started up, the water squishing in his belabored boots.

At the top, he realized the castle was hidden from view by a patch of forest. The road to Templeton surely wasn't very far through the woods. He thought the sensible thing to do was go back to his room, collapse into bed, rest his aching noggin and possibly put a compress on his swollen nose.

But then, again, he wasn't always sensible, and the sensible thing often did not make for advancement. Templeton was a few miles along the road. Berry was being held in the Templeton Inn. It was time for Nathan Spade to walk into town and see what might be seen. Possibly his clothes would be dry, in this heat, by the time he got there. If not, not. There probably was a physcian in Templeton who might look at his beak. And who also might answer some questions about Professor Fell and the underwater town.

"The house is this way," said Fancy.

"I'm not going there yet," Matthew told her. "I trust there'll be no mention of this to the brothers? As far as they know, I'm dead. I'd like to keep it that way for a while."

"I never saw you," she said. "Not even your ghost." And then she turned away from him, walked her usual path through the forest and was gone.

Matthew walked away from the cliff. The road had to be just ahead, in the direction he was going. Birds called in exotic voices and the sun shone down through green fronds and vines.

It was a good day, he decided, to not be a ghost.

TWENTY-FOUR

I HAD an accident on the road," Matthew said to the doctor who inspected his swollen and by now purpling nose. The purple was spreading out on both sides of his face. Also, there were two frightful lumps on his forehead. "Clumsy," Matthew explained. "Tripped over my own feet."

"Happens to the best of us, Mr. Spade." The physician was a portly man with long flowing white hair and dressed in a cream-colored suit as befitted his tropical position. His name, he'd told Matthew, was Benson Britt and he and his wife had been living on Pendulum Island since the summer of 1695. Britt's hand moved to touch the whipstrike on Matthew's neck. "This was also an accident?" The doctor's dark brown eyes in the sun-wrinkled face held the question.

"Yes, that also," Matthew answered firmly. "I was hoping you might apply some ointment?"

"Certainly. I have some lemon ointment. As for your proboscis…does this hurt?" Britt gave the bridge a quick little tap with a wooden spoon. Tears came to Matthew's eyes, but the pain was not so much as to make him cry out. "Not broken," Britt observed.

"Only badly bruised. And the injuries to your forehead...not very pleasant, I'm sure, but nothing serious. Unless you have a ringing in your ears and a constant headache?"

Matthew could hardly hear him for the ringing in his ears, but at least the headache had subsided. "No," he said.

"Very good, then. I'll apply a bee's-wax lotion to your nose to draw out the sting, and then we'll bind on a poultice of seaweed and sea salt—my own remedy—to keep the swelling down and the passages open."

"Hm," said Matthew, unimpressed. There was no way to keep the passages open; his nose was blocked shut. But some sort of medical attention was needed, and this was the best—and perhaps only—Pendulum had to offer.

"Lie back on the table," Britt directed. He had a handful of grease from a small yellow jar. "Let me do my best."

"Certainly, sir." Matthew obeyed, and while he was lying on the table he noted all the crisscrossing of small cracks in the white ceiling above his head.

His journey through the forest to the road had been uneventful, except for the wobbling of his knees as he still found himself in a weakened condition. Less than a mile on his way, though, he'd gotten a ride on a passing wagon full of melons bound for the farmer's market in Templeton, and so at least for a little while he could rest and gather his strength. The wagon's driver was an elderly man who knew nothing of Professor Fell except to call him "the professor," and he had been thirty years old when the earthquake hit Pendulum and dropped the thriving community of Somers Town into the sea. At that time, the farmer recollected, Somers Town had been populated by about three thousand people and its primary business was the export of cedar boxes to England.

"Son of the governor," said the aged informant when Matthew had inquired about the professor's heritage. "Name of...hmmm... can't quite place that name no more. Forgive me, sir."

"Absolutely forgiven," Matthew had said, as his clothing dried in the bright sun and his mind formulated more questions to ask when he reached Templeton.

The good doctor Britt applied the bee's-wax lotion and then bandaged his seaweed and sea salt poultice in a thin piece of cheesecloth across the bridge of Matthew's nose, which certainly would go far in gaining Matthew attention he did not seek. Nevertheless, it was done and appreciated, and Britt informed Matthew that any guest of the professor's need not pay for treatment, as the professor had supplied himself and his wife with the house and a yearly salary.

"I'm presuming Dr. Gentry is among the guests?" Britt asked as Matthew was starting to leave. "If so, would you tell him to head my way?"

"Dr. Gentry's headings are difficult to tell," Matthew confided, "but I'll relay the message to *someone*."

On the street, Matthew followed his bandaged snoot toward the Templeton Inn. The green gate was open and the place appeared welcoming. Of a certain red-haired girl or a massive Ga there was no sign, nor did the inn seem to be guarded. Matthew crossed the tiled courtyard and opened the front door, which caused a bell above it to tinkle merrily. Matthew entered the inn's main hall, a room constructed of dark wood with a blue and yellow rug upon the floorboards and over his head a circular iron chandelier with six wicks. Past a writing desk where the guests were admitted was a narrow staircase that curved to the left. Matthew was trying to determine what to do next when a broad-shouldered and heavyset man wearing brown breeches and a white shirt with the sleeves rolled up descended the stairs.

"Mornin', sir," said the man, with a distinct Scottish brogue. He had a red tuft of hair on his otherwise bald head and a small, neatly trimmed red tuft on his chin. "Help you?"

"My name is Nathan Spade," Matthew answered with hesitation. He realized the power of his voice was less than optimal, since his nose was so stopped up. If this place had smelled either of perfume or the chamberpot he wouldn't have been able to detect a difference. "I'm a guest of Professor Fell's, staying at the castle."

"Yes, sir," said the Scotsman, as if he heard this declaration everyday.

"I'd like to see the red-haired girl who was brought here yesterday," Matthew said. "What room is she in, please?"

"Oh...sir. There's a problem, I fear." The Scotsman frowned. "Miss Grigsby is no longer—"

The bell tinkled. The Scotsman looked toward the door, as did Matthew. Sirki came in, dressed in his white robes as he'd been earlier. The East Indian giant drew up a smile that made his front teeth sparkle.

"Nathan!" he said, coming to Matthew's side like the onrush of an ocean wave. He clasped one hand to Matthew's left elbow. His smile remained radiant. "I was looking for you! And here you are!"

"Exactly as you knew I might be?"

"Exactly," said Sirki. "We missed you at breakfast. When I discovered you weren't to be found, I decided this would be the place."

The Scotsman said, "I was about to tell Mr. Spade that Miss Grigsby and the colored man are no—"

"I thank you for your efforts here, Mr. McKellan," Sirki interrupted. "I have this situation in hand now, you may go about your business."

"Yes, sir." McKellan actually gave a small bow of deference. "I *am* busy upstairs," he offered, and with that he turned away and went up the steps again.

Sirki stared coldly at Matthew. His eyes examined Matthew's face. "What in the name of mighty Shiva has happened to *you?*"

"I had an accident on the road. Tripped over myself."

"That's a lie," said the giant.

"Where are Berry and Zed?" Matthew fired back.

"Upstairs, I presume."

"That's a lie," said Matthew.

The two liars stared at each other, neither one willing to move their lie one inch.

Matthew went first. "*I'm* presuming that McKellan started to tell me that Berry and Zed are no longer here. Where are they?"

"I have a coach outside, ready to take you back." Sirki increased the pressure a fraction on Matthew's elbow. "Come on, shall we? You have much work to do."

Matthew had no choice but to be taken along, though he removed his elbow from the giant's grip as soon as they were crossing the courtyard. Ahead on the street, a black berline with the harried driver of yesterday awaited its passengers. Sirki waited for Matthew to climb in, then he pulled himself up, closed the door and settled his bottom. He tapped on the roof with a fist and they were off.

"On your desk you'll find a key and a map of who occupies which room along the corridor," Sirki said as they left Templeton. "The key will allow you entry into the rooms that Smythe, Sabroso and Wilson occupy. Smythe is giving his report to the professor at two o'clock. Sabroso is reporting tomorrow at two. Wilson tomorrow at four. You should make plans to enter those rooms and—"

"Search for what?" Matthew interrupted. "I don't have any idea what I'm looking for. Besides, if it involves some kind of information passed between two of those men, why would someone be stupid enough to write it down? Why not just whisper the information in passing and be done with it?"

"There's the matter of the authorities getting firm evidence of the next shipment of Cymbeline," Sirki replied, as he watched the countryside glide past. "They may have asked for written notification, instead of secondhand hearsay. So you might consider that you're searching for some kind of coded message."

"Hidden where? Under a pillow? Rolled up in a stocking?"

"Both good places to look, I'm sure."

"The professor didn't need me to do this," said Matthew. "Any of his thugs might've done it. Just ransacked the rooms and gone through the debris."

"Ransacking is not part of the plan. And that's exactly why the professor's thugs, as you put it, are inadequate for this task."

"No, there's some other reason he wanted me here. Isn't there?" Matthew prompted, but Sirki remained silent. "Especially *me*. Why? Because I impressed him by besting Tyranthus Slaughter and killing Lyra Sutch? And he wished to *see* me, in the flesh? To take stock of me?" Matthew nodded at the thought that was being born. "Because he wishes to test me, to see if I'm capable of finding Brazio Valeriani for him?"

"He wishes at present," Sirki replied quietly, "only to discover the name or names of a traitor or two."

Matthew was silent for a time, watching the lush green forest pass by his window. "I suppose you won't tell me where Berry and Zed are?" he asked at last. "Will you at least tell me why they were taken from the inn?"

"I will tell you that they decided to leave the inn last night. Without permission, I might add. Zed was captured and taken to a more secure place for safekeeping. The young woman…is unfortunately still missing."

"Still *missing*?" That word had caused Matthew's heart to jump into his throat.

"The island is not that large. She's being searched for, and she'll be found."

"Christ!" Matthew said forcefully. And then more quietly and mostly to himself: "Why didn't she just stay where she was? Where she was safe?"

"I'm sure you'll have the chance to ask her those questions yourself on the return voyage to New York."

Matthew was thinking of McKellan's deferential bow, and the subservient expression on the innkeeper's face. "This island is a prison, isn't it? No one comes or goes without the professor's approval?"

"It's a bit hard to call Pendulum Island a prison, as its citizens live very happy and productive lives. The second part of your statement, however, is certainly true." Sirki regarded Matthew with a baleful glare. "The professor likes *balance*, young man. He wishes to be undisturbed here. As he owns the island as an outright possession, he may limit the ships coming in and going out, to his pleasure."

"What's his first name?" Matthew decided to ask.

"The castle is within view," Sirki answered. "We should be there in just a few minutes. I trust you'll tend to your business and not go wandering on the road again? By the way, the stablemaster has been instructed to refuse your request for a horse."

"So the castle is also a prison?" Even as he presented this question, Matthew knew there would be no response and he was correct.

The coach pulled up to the entry, Matthew and Sirki disembarked, and Sirki walked with Matthew to the foot of the stairs. "You look ridiculous with that thing on your nose," was Sirki's final comment before he took his leave. Then Matthew went directly to his room, where he unlocked his door with the key that had been in his pocket in another room forty feet underwater. On the writing desk was, indeed, a second key and a piece of paper that, unfolded, showed the corridor and the names of who slept where. It was drawn precisely and written neatly, in small tight lettering, and Matthew wondered if the professor himself had done this. Smythe was far down the corridor, the very last room. Beside the key was a plate of three muffins: cornbread, cinnamon and orange. Or as best as Matthew could tell without tasting, for his nose was so much dead matter. He poured himself a glass of water from the provided pitcher and ate the presumed orange muffin, which tasted to him—lacking a sense of smell—like so much gluey wool. The cornbread was likewise tasteless and the cinnamon muffin might have been artificial for all its flavor. Yet at least he had something in his stomach. He drank down a second glass of water, and then he stretched himself out on the bed for a few minutes to rest and organize his thoughts.

Matthew mused that from the death-condemned back to the living in the matter of a few gut-wrenching minutes was not a bad way to start a day off, if one had to be condemned to death by a pair of orange-haired shits. He wished to stay out of their sight until he was ready to reveal that his watery grave had opened. The damnable thing on his mind now was Berry's fate. That girl had a habit of tearing him up. Out on the island by herself somewhere? He dreaded to consider what might have happened to her. And now add that weight to his ton of troubles, and try to balance along the professor's beam.

"Impossible," he said to the black bed canopy over his head. No god answered, not even Professor Fell.

He slept, and had some half-recalled dream about falling through the water toward a town that, while submerged in its blue aura, held the filmy spirits of citizens who walked upon the lowered lanes and streets, and drove their ghostly wagons toward a harbor swallowed by the sea. When Matthew awakened it was close enough to two o'clock to rouse himself to action. He went to the waterbasin and washed his face, musing that one pitcherful of the liquid made him the master, yet in quantity this could snuff out one's life as easily as the fire from the gunpowder bombs that had blasted New York.

He waited ten more minutes. Then he took the key and eased into the hallway, watchful for two thick-bodied redhaired shits, and he went to Smythe's door at the far end of the hall and knocked quietly and respectfully just in case. When there was no response he slid the key home and let himself in.

He was interested—and gratified, in a way—that Smythe's room was neither as spacious as his own nor did it have a balcony overlooking the ocean. Smythe's balcony faced the gardens. Perhaps Smythe had requested so, because of his late discomfort of the sea. In any case, it wasn't as fine a room as Matthew's. The problem-solver got to work, trying to solve a problem to which there were no clues. He saw the many sheets of parchment on the desktop, covered with lines not only from *Cymbeline* but other of the Bard's plays. Smythe had been a busy scribbler these last few weeks. Matthew went through the desk drawers and found nothing of interest. The chest of drawers, the same. A small collection of clay pipes drew his hand, but in their bowls and stems were no rolled-up secret messages, as far as he could tell. He went through Smythe's clothes, a delicate matter. Smythe did not wash as much as Matthew might have liked, and the clothing was stiff with sweat and the shirt collars ringed with grime. But again, nothing there but the bad habits of a dirty man.

He checked the shoes and the stockings, more items of distaste. He looked under the bed, under the mattress, and drew a chair over to peer on top of the bed canopy. He searched behind the chest of drawers and beneath the iron-legged stand that held the waterbasin. He exhausted all possible hiding places in the room, and then he took stock of the sheets of parchment.

Lying in plain sight, he thought. If a code was indeed written somewhere in those sheets, then why bother to hide them?

He picked up a few of the sheets and scanned them. Nothing remarkable that he could decipher. Just someone with time on his hands, scribing for the sake of something to do. He found the line of stage-direction from *Cymbeline* that Smythe had read to him from the play: *Jupiter descends in thunder and lightning, sitting upon an eagle; he throws a thunderbolt.*

That was the line that had prompted the professor's titling of the new weapon? How had Smythe described it? Oh, yes...*Cymbeline is the foundation upon which future devices shall be constructed.*

The foundation, Matthew thought. Something basic. Something...ordinary that now was extraordinary?

Thunder and lightning, Matthew mused. The throwing of a thunderbolt by Jupiter, king of the gods. The professor would surely identify with Jupiter. And what happens when a thunderbolt hits the earth? Matthew asked himself.

Fire, of course. No, no…wait…first, before the fire…there is…
…the explosion.

Matthew walked out upon the balcony. From this vantage point he could see, far in the distance, a thin smudge of smoke that must be rising from the fort at the far end of Pendulum. The forbidden fort, where intrusion meant death. That, Matthew surmised, must be where the Cymbeline was being created.

Because he realized what Cymbeline must be. In fact, he'd already had a taste of it. A very hot and searing taste, in fact.

The foundation of future weapons was gunpowder. Professor Fell was creating a new and more potent—certainly more powerful—kind of gunpowder. The kind that could in a fairly small quantity tear a building to pieces and hurl a roof back into Jupiter's realm. Oh yes, they were using the Cymbeline to good effect in New York, all right. Matthew nodded, watching the smoke smudge. Of course the chemicals had to be cooked. The fire kept away from the finished product. But what made it different? What ingredient made it more powerful or better in any way from the gunpowder normally created?

Matthew knew.

He recalled a certain Solomon Tully, wailing for his losses on the Great Dock.

…there's something wicked afoot with this constant stealing of sugar.

"Indeed there is," said Matthew Corbett, his eyes steel-gray and his voice grim.

For sugar was the new ingredient in the professor's formula for death. Some chemical component of sugar, cooked and introduced into the process. Professor Fell was making his Cymbeline with sugar, and it was the foundation of what the professor hoped was not only new weapons using that powder, but a source of revenue that perhaps was the greatest he'd yet known.

And here stood Matthew, seeking a traitor or two who had decided England's security was more important than Fell's power or money. Truly, for Matthew, it was the world turned upside down. He decided it was time to vacate these premises. He put everything back upon the desktop exactly as it had been, for he thought Smythe would have a sharp eye for such irregularities. The chair he'd used to perch upon also was returned to its exact position. Everything else looked right. But no evidence of a traitor was to be found in here today, and probably not any day. Matthew left the room, closed the door behind him and turned the key in the lock. "Here!" said someone down the hallway. "What are you doing?" The voice made Matthew jump. As he turned toward it, he put the key in his pocket. Adam Wilson, the invisible man, was striding toward him.

"Spade? I asked you what you're doing." The voice was as slight and vapid as its owner, yet insistent in its own way. The watery blue eyes stared at Matthew behind the square-lensed spectacles. "Were you trying to get into Edgar's room?"

Matthew recognized that the man of finances had not seen him leave Smythe's room, but had only seen him standing at the door. Possibly it looked as if Matthew was working the doorknob. "I knocked at Smythe's door, yes," he said.

"It looked to me as if you were trying to get in, sir." Wilson had small teeth that showed between the bloodless lips and came together as he spoke, as if taking small vicious bites from the air.

"I...suppose I did try the knob." Matthew shrugged, as if to say it was his nature. "Smythe and I were having a discussion in the library earlier. I'd hoped to continue it."

"Really?" It was spoken with either droll unconcern or a lingering touch of suspicion.

"Yes," Matthew answered. "Really."

"Edgar is meeting with the professor at this moment," came the reply. The eyes narrowed. "What happened to you, sir? You are much the worse for wear."

"You should have seen the horse after I beat it up."

"You were thrown from a horse?"

"Regrettably, yes. Early this morning."

"Hm." Wilson took two backward steps to look Matthew over from head to toe. "Nothing is broken, I presume?"

"My pride," said Matthew, with a tight smile that made his nose ache.

"Your sense of humor seems undamaged," said Wilson, humorlessly. "I should think you would take to bed rather than seeking companionship."

"In my line of work, those two things go together."

"Ah." A slight smile disturbed the small ugly mouth. "As you say." Wilson gave a small nod of his head and shoulder-stoop to pass for a bow of respect and started to turn away.

But the problem-solver had at last detected something, and meant to hone in upon it. "Pardon me, Mr. Wilson, but...why do you refer to Mr. Smythe by his first name?"

"Because that is his name," was the stone-faced reply.

"Of course it is, but...it indicates a certain familiarity. A friend-ship, I suppose. Or, as you put it...a *companionship*. I noted that at dinner last night there was a very strict air of formality in how everyone addressed everyone else. I suppose it's an indicator of the distance we must keep from each other regarding our businesses. So why do you call him *Edgar* and not *Mr. Smythe*? Is it because...oh... you and he communicate with each other outside the realm of the professor's view?"

"You know that would be forbidden."

"I do know. But I also know you're very comfortable calling him by his first name. Are you two friends in London?"

"No, we are not. But we have become friends here. Because as you must know, this is not the first of our conferences." The eyes took on a wicked gleam behind the square lenses. "And if we're speaking of noticing such things, Mr. Spade, I should say I heard Madam Cutter calling you *Nathan*. Does that mean, then, that you and she are...hmmmm...an *item* in London?"

"I've never met her before."

"Obviously, then, you've made an impression. Or should I say, a new *friend*." The upper lip curled. "Sometimes, Mr. Spade, a name... is only a name, and it conveys no darker meaning."

"Darker meaning? Why do you put it that way?"

"Neither Edgar—Mr. Smythe, if you please—nor I are in viola-tion of the professor's code of conduct. Now it is true I have received some messages from Mr. Smythe, regarding the Cymbeline and money needed to store it in its London warehouse. I likewise have sent messages to him, but only through a courier designated by Professor Fell. Everything, you see, is aboveboard."

That statement nearly caused Matthew to guffaw, but he swal-lowed it down. He said, "I'd hate to think of anyone here being dishonest."

"And you would be responsive to that in some way? You would make sure Edgar and I were penalized, if indeed we were enjoying a social relationship beyond the call of our professions?"

"What are you doing together?" Matthew asked. "Going to the..." He picked up the recollection of an item from one issue of his cherished *London Gazette*. "Rakehell clubs?" Where, it was written in the broadsheet, a man might have a sumptuous eight-course dinner and enjoy fine rare wines before his bottom was blistered by a woman in riding boots and spurs and whirling a bullwhip. Matthew could imagine Smythe and Wilson at these festivities, linked possibly by their purient interests. One would be bellowing as if he had a lungful of burning coals while the other smirked in the admiration of applied pain.

"Young man," said Wilson coldly, "it would be best for you to restrain your obvious penchant for fantasy. Save such suggestions for your whores and clients, won't you?" He started to turn away, his face screwed up with something that was supposed to convey either anger or disgust, and then he paused.

"You look laughable with that thing on your nose," he sniped, before he turned and stalked away to his room further along the hallway. Matthew let Wilson unlock his door and enter before he too returned to his own abode.

TWENTY-FIVE

AFTER the dinner bell had been rung up and down the hallway, Matthew gave the candle clock an extra fifteen minutes of burning before he put on the somewhat shrunken jacket of his gray-striped suit and prepared to join the party.

With any luck, the Thackers had remained drunk or been—and the thought was repugnant to him—ravishing Fancy all day in their double brotherhood and thus had no idea Nathan Spade had risen from his grave.

It was time now to display himself, in all his abundant life.

He had scrubbed himself and shaved. He had combed his hair. He was presentable. Except for one thing. When he peered into the mirror he thought he looked ridiculous with that thing on his nose, so he peeled off the poultice to reveal the swollen blue-black-and-tinged-with-green artistry of Jack and Mack. He still couldn't smell anything through this heated lump of clay, but so be it. The darkness had spread under his eyes and the two lumps on his forehead had turned dark purple. He was a real peacock, he was. And ready to strut, too.

He left his room, went down the stairs and to the banquet room where last night Jonathan Gentry had lost his head.

They were all there, minus the headless doctor. They were seated in their exact same places. They were eating from bowls of what appeared to be some kind of thick red seafood stew. Toy was feeding Augustus Pons, and giggling happily. Smythe was drinking his wine from a glass and Sabroso was drinking his from a bottle, and the nearly-invisible Wilson had his face poised over his bowl as if to inhale it up his nostrils. Minx Cutter was there, sitting rigidly in her chair. Aria Chillany looked pale and wan, as if the island's sunlight was stealing her power. Fancy's expression was blank, as she was jammed shoulder-to-shoulder between the two brothers, who were wearing orange suits to match their hair and jamming hunks of bread into their mouths. Mother Deare was eating delicately, her red lace gloves concealing the large hands of a workwoman.

Matthew came down the stairs as if he owned every riser.

Fancy looked up at him first. Her expression did not change, though her eyes may have widened only enough for him to note. Then the others saw him, and with pieces of bread stuffed in their mouths Jack and Mack Thacker made gagging noises and their green glinting eyes in the foxlike faces became huge. Jack jumped up from the table, his chair going over to the floor behind him, while Mack only half-rose before he grasped the neck of a wine bottle either to steady himself or use as a weapon.

"What the hell is wrong with you two?" Mother Deare rasped, a rough plaid of coarseness showing through her studied lace.

"Forgive me for being late." Matthew came around the table to his place across from Minx and next to Aria. He was gratified to see that not a trace of last night's murder remained. He sat down and sent a smile around the table. "Good evening to all."

The Thackers had gone as gray as wet paper. They looked at each other in wonderment, and then at Matthew with something close to fear.

"Settle yourselves, gentlemen," said Matthew. "I won't bite."

"Your *face*," Minx said. "What happened to you?"

"Small accident. I took a fall." He reached for the steaming pot of stew that sat upon the table and spooned some into his bowl. "This looks delicious." It would taste nearly of nothing, however, since he could not smell a single peppercorn nor fish fin, both of which were exposed as his spoon went to work.

"On the stairs?" Mother Deare asked. "Didn't you seek attention?"

"No, I rested in my room." He aimed his smile at the two scowling brothers. "Please, don't stand on *my* account."

Mack recovered first. He drew up a half-grin that had nothing to do with either humor nor his eyes. "Pick up your chair, Jack. Clumsy of you." Mack sank back into his seat, his teeth slightly bared. From the wine bottle he took a swallow that must have emptied it by half.

"Clumsy," Jack repeated. He sounded stunned, as if he'd been headbutted. "Damn clumsy." He righted his chair and as he sat down offered a thin and insincere smile to Mother Deare. "Pardon the fuss. I don't know what come over me."

Matthew spread his napkin across his lap. "Good manners are worth gold," he said, and regarded Mother Deare. "Wouldn't you agree?"

"I surely would. Good manners gets a person into a lot of rooms…and out of a lot of scrapes," she answered, and she gave him a nod as if she knew exactly what he meant.

"You were in your room all day?" Aria asked. She looked bleary-eyed. Though Gentry hadn't been her shining knight and hero, his death must have unnerved her at least enough to disturb her beauty-sleep.

"Not quite all day," Wilson spoke up, in his irritating near-whisper. "He was out and about for a short while. Wasn't he, Mr. Smythe?"

"That he was, Mr. Wilson," answered the barrel of gravel.

"Interested in things," said Wilson.

"Books," said Smythe. "He's a very learned fellow."

"Are these riddles?" Sabroso asked. His voice was slightly slurred. Wine spots had appeared on the jacket of his cream-colored suit.

Matthew thought that Smythe and Wilson—two brothers, perhaps, in their quest for the dirtiest hole in London to squat in and spend a few pounds for pain—were emulating the communication style of the Thackers. He said, "No riddles, I think. Just roundabouts."

"You look like ya come into some trouble, boyo," said Mack as he reached over to play his greasy fingers through Fancy's hair.

Almost as if they were connected by the same nerve endings, Jack reached over to do the same on the opposite side. Fancy stared at Matthew for a few seconds more, and then she continued silently— and with as much dignity as possible—eating her stew.

"Trouble," said Jack, with a hissy giggle.

"And ya *look* like shit, too," Mack provided.

"A turd on legs," Jack said.

"Gentlemen?" Augustus Pons had turned his face away from Toy's spoon. The young man kept trying to slide the spoon into Pons's mouth, but his efforts were waved away. "At *least*," Pons said with an air of superiority, "Mr. Spade's current hues are somewhat restrained. He wears no *orange*."

That brought a drunken laugh from Cesar Sabroso and a fleeting smile across Minx Cutter's face. But no joy from the land of the Thackers.

"Shut your hole, ya fat-assed buck!" growled Jack, who leaned toward Pons with the seething glare of murder in his eyes. Matthew was quite familiar with it.

"Mind yourself!" The voice of Mother Deare was indeed motherly, if one's mother could hammer a spike through your forehead with two words. "We are a civilized gathering, sirs! And *madams*," she added, for the sake of inclusion. "We are all brethren here, and we should act in accord with that. Understood?" She glared at the Thackers with eyes that might cut steel. And repeated the word to their silence: *"Understood?"*

Jack was the elder if one counted minutes and gray hairs, but the younger Mack seemed to be the more intelligent and diplomatic for it was he who nodded and said, "We do understand, Mother Deare."

"Is my ass so very fat?" Pons asked Toy, with a stricken expression.

The young man frowned and offered the spoon and said, "Oh, no! It's just *perfect*!" To which Pons gave a satisfied smile and accepted the offering.

Those at the table quietened down. Indeed, some sort of rough semblance of civility came upon the gathering. Most were silent, but for Pons and Toy who whispered to each other and an occasional winey laugh or exclamation directed into the air by Cesar Sabroso.

"But you're feeling all right now?" Aria Chillany had come back to life. She placed her hand upon Matthew's arm. She stared imploringly at him, the sapphire eyes wide with the just-asked question and her fingers squeezing his flesh.

"I am, yes."

"Such a fall you must've taken!" She made it sound like a hero's journey.

"Fortunately," Matthew said with a quick tight smile, "I was able to save myself from serious injury."

"*Very* fortunate." Minx was regarding him over the rim of her glass. "Nathan, you seem to have somewhat of a charmed life, don't you?"

Matthew heard Adam Wilson clear his throat down the table at the sound of the name, but he paid no heed. "Charmed? Not sure of that. But I suppose I *am* lucky."

"The Devil's luck," said Mack, into his stewbowl.

"Hell wouldn't have him," said Jack.

"Spat him out," Mack offered.

"*Shat* him out," was Jack's correction.

"You two," said Madam Chillany, "make not an ounce of fucking sense." She kept her hand on Matthew's arm, and now began to do a little rubbing. Matthew noted that both Minx and Fancy took note of this action, before they pretended not to.

The dinner went on through platters of steamed clams and grilled swordfish to its conclusion of rice pudding, sugar cookies in the shapes of various sea creatures, and offerings of sweet sherry and golden port. During this procession of edibles and potables, Aria Chillany drew herself nearer and nearer to Matthew, at one point rubbing his leg with her own while she drank her weight in wine and began to burble about that bastard Jonathan Gentry. It seemed to Matthew that Jonathan Gentry, for all his faults, might be missed by at least one person at this table, and the sudden sadness that leaped into the sapphire eyes was a pity to behold. But it didn't stay very long, for Aria was surely a woman of the moment, and Gentry's moment—even if it was brief and lackluster—had passed in a long sigh between bottles. Then her fingers found Matthew's arm again and her foot taunted his ankle beneath the table, and her laughter at Pons's gallant little attempts at joking was forced and strident and carried the note of a woman terrified of sleeping alone for fear her bedtime companion might awaken with a scream behind her teeth.

Matthew had trouble looking her in the face; in fact, he had difficulty looking at any of them, but all through the dinner he felt the eyes of Minx Cutter and Fancy upon him, one set of eyes perhaps carving him up into small pieces the easier to digest, the other set wondering what freedom would taste like in the brave new world he might present to her. At last Matthew finished a final seahorse, which he crunched noisily for the benefit of those who knew, and then excused himself from the table with a word of goodnight to Mother Deare, who seemed to rule this particular roost. It was a difficult chore getting out of Aria's claws, and she looked at him despondently over her umpteenth glass of wine. He turned his back on her and walked away from the gathering and up the stairs.

To be joined within seconds by Minx, who grasped his arm and pressed to his side and asked quietly, "What *really* happened to you?"

"Stairs," he answered. "Fall. Unfortunate."

"Bullshit," she said.

"If you lean on me any harder, I may fall down these stairs as well." He continued his ascent and she kept beside him.

"I need you," she said.

His eyes widened. "Pardon?"

"To go with me in the morning. I want to show you something. Back where the whales play. It's important. Will you meet me at the stable? Say...eight o'clock?"

"Fuckin' *impossible!*" hollered Jack Thacker, and a wine glass died a shattered death upon the floor.

Matthew kept going without a backward glance, and Minx with him. They went through the corridor of sea-skeletons toward the main staircase. "I'm not sure I can get a horse," he told her.

"Why not?"

"I've been a bad boy."

She frowned. "What're you talking about?"

"Only that I've offended someone here, and I may not be able to get a horse."

"That's more bullshit. If you need a horse, I'll get one for you."

"All right, then." He stopped at the foot of the central stairs and regarded her with a neutral expression. "Yes, I'll meet you at the stable at eight. What's this about?"

"It's about…" She glanced left and right, to make sure no one was near. Then she suddenly leaned into him and kissed him on the mouth. It was a long, lingering kiss, and though Matthew was amazed by this unexpected action he did not draw away.

"Well," said Matthew when the kiss had ended and Minx was staring at him with her slightly dewy golden eyes. "May I guess it's about…*us*?"

"Eight o'clock," she said, and she started up the stairs without waiting for him. A few risers up, she paused and turned toward him once more. "Unless," she added.

"Unless?" he asked.

"Unless I see you before then," Minx held his gaze for a few seconds longer, and then she continued on her way and out of his sight into the second-floor hallway.

Matthew's lips were burning. Now this was the damnedest thing! he thought. Who could have seen this coming? The princess of blades, attracted to *him*? He was a dull knife in this company. Still…he did have youth, and manners. He was quite simply stunned. Therefore he was doubly pole-axed when he started up the stairs and a soft feminine voice behind him said, "Nathan?"

He turned to face Fancy, who came up to stand beside him.

"I have only a minute," she said, but calmly as was her hidden spirit. "They'll be after me. I want you to know…when I saw you go into the water today…I knew I had to help you. I don't know why. I just…*had* to. I don't know who you are, or why you are here, but… I want to thank you for thinking you could help *me*."

"I *can* help you," he said. "If you allow it."

The dark eyes were fixed upon him. The beautiful face—the beautiful creature from a different world—was his, for the moment. He felt it. While she gave him every iota of her attention, she belonged to him. This would change in the next few seconds; when the sound of boots clunking through the hallway came to them, it would change, but for now…

"Perhaps you can," she said, and then they heard the boots.

Matthew had no stomach for jousting with those bastards tonight. He turned away from Fancy even as she lowered her face and turned to meet her masters, and Matthew went up the stairs two at a time sick to his heart and aching in his nose. He fished for his key to open his door but as he slid the key in, the door came ajar and that was how he knew he had a visitor this evening.

He opened the door to the ruddy light of the triple wicks atop the dresser.

From the white high-backed chair with the black abstract design, Professor Fell said, "Close the door and lock it, Matthew."

Matthew stood still for a few seconds too long.

"Go ahead," the professor urged. "It's the sensible thing."

Matthew had to agree with that. He closed the door and locked it. Then he stood with his back pressed rigidly against it, and the figure with the flesh-colored mask and flesh-colored gloves sat comfortably with legs outstretched and crossed at the ankles. The professor tonight wore a conservative dark blue suit, a white shirt with a cascade of ruffles down the front, and a dark blue tricorn with a black band.

There was a silence. Professor Fell seemed to be studying the ceiling. Regarding the small cracks there, Matthew thought. Then Professor Fell's featureless face angled toward the New York problem-solver.

"You had some trouble today." It was a statement of fact, as dry as the fish bones in the skeleton collection.

"A mite," Matthew allowed.

"Hm. One of my stone seahorses is missing from the library balcony. Also the curtain cords are gone. There is—*was*—a wine bottle on the ledge. What can you tell me about that?"

"Nothing." Matthew shrugged. His heart was a furious drummer. "Much."

"You shield your enemies. Why?"

"I take care of my own business."

"That's admirable. Stupid, possibly…but admirable. Please sit down, you're putting a crick in my neck."

Matthew seated himself in the chair at the writing-desk, the same as the evening before. He turned himself so as to have full view of the emperor of crime. A question came to him that had to be thrust into the air, like a fiery sword. "May I ask…why you never reveal your face?"

Did the mouth laugh, just a shade, behind the cowl? "I am so beautiful," said the professor, "that I might stop time itself, so the angels could adore me longer. Or I am so ugly I might stop the hearts of any beasts that lay their jaundiced eyes upon me. Or... most likely...I am simply a man who enjoys being faceless."

"Oh," said Matthew.

"Anything else you'd care to know?"

"Many things. But I don't think you'd tell me."

"You speak with certainty, though it's doubtful you understand."

"I'm ready," said Matthew, as the candles cast equal amounts of illumination and shadows, "to be enlightened."

The head nodded, ever so slightly. The gloved fingers steepled. "First, what have you learned?"

"Not much." But it occurred to him that Professor Fell valued his opinion, so he reversed himself. "A little. Concerning Adam Wilson and Edgar Smythe."

"Go on," the professor urged.

"My opinion only, of course."

"Yes. Your opinion has been paid for. Go on."

"That the former has a streak of cruelty and the latter does not wash enough." Matthew paused, his own fingers steepled, to consider his next offering. He decided to give the professor the benefit of his suspicion, and a taste of what Fell was looking to find. "I believe they have had some...association outside the realm of business. I believe they've discovered they are kindred spirits in some activity in London."

"And you say this based on *what*?"

"Based on my instincts. On my feeling that they are familiar in a way that has formed a bond between them. What that bond might be, I don't know, but it's in the way Wilson speaks of Smythe using his Christian name. And, also, the fact that they seem to be looking out for each other. Guarding their interests, possibly. Or sharing a secret." His horses were galloping now, and Matthew decided to give them free rein. "I think they have violated your decree of no association between members of your..." What was the proper word? Oh yes. "Parliament," he concluded.

Professor Fell was silent, and did not move. For a time he appeared to be what he pretended to be, an automaton dependent upon a key. Then he sat up straighter in his chair, with a motion that made Matthew think of the smooth gliding of a snake.

"I enforce that decree," said the professor, "for reasons of security. If one member of my 'Parliament,' as you so colorfully phrase it, is...shall we say...put out of business by an overzealous puppet of the law, then I do not wish that consequence to spread through my other affairs. My associates know their positions, and what is required of them. That is all they need to know. *I* take care of the..."

He hesitated, seeking the word.

Matthew supplied it. "Octopus?"

"As you please." The tricorned head bowed, with the eerie flesh-colored cowl beneath it.

"I have no proof Smythe and Wilson are meeting in violation of your decree," Matthew said. "Only a..."

"*Guess?*" Fell asked.

"Only that, yes."

"But you found nothing of interest in Smythe's room today?"

"Nothing." He frowned. "Again, I don't know what I'm looking for."

"I think you may have an idea. And...I think you may know it when you find it."

"*If* I find it," Matthew corrected. "Which may be impossible, given the situation and lack of time."

"The situation is what it is. And you may be responsible yourself for the lack of time, as you were too stubborn to attend my command in a prompt fashion."

Matthew lifted his chin. He stared into the faceless void. He brought up every ounce of courage he possessed, and he said, "I don't care to be commanded. Not by you or anyone else."

"Oh! Bravely spoken, sir. Surely then, before Mr. Matthew Corbett I must restrain the very power that has brought me from my humble beginnings to where I sit today."

"A man in a cowl," Matthew said. "His face hidden, his steps guarded, his path uncertain."

"An uncertain path? Why would that be?"

"One traitor or two," came the reply. "Double flies in the ointment, possibly. And your path so uncertain in picking them out that you have to enlist *me*? The very same man you sent a blood card to back in the summer? What if one of your thugs had killed me? Where might you be sitting today?"

"Downstairs, in my own quarters."

"And you might be walking in circles on your floor, trying to decide whose head to cut off next. It seems to me that you should be very glad I slipped the blood card. For *with* your providence rider, you have hope. Without me...an uncertain path."

The professor did not speak for a time. When he did, it was one word spoken with near-admiration for a point sufficiently made: *"Ah."*

"What do you *do* during the day, anyway?" Matthew continued, daring fate. "Do you hide away down in your quarters? Do you work on something? Surely you just don't live for these little dramas and then sleep all day."

"I rarely sleep," was the reply, spoken with no expression.

"All this treasure at your disposal, and you can't sleep?" Matthew realized he was nearing the dangerous cliff's edge of his own sharp tongue, yet he felt the need to press forward a little bit more. "You're a lurker in your own house? You must wear a mask to go out and about? Professor...I fear you're not as wealthy nor as privileged as you might believe, because even though I live in a dairyhouse half the size of this room I do sleep well—most nights—and I feel no need for a mask."

Fell grunted quietly. "You do," he said, "have a set of balls on you."

"I think they've grown since I've had this occupation."

"I could have Sirki saw them off for you, if they've grown too large to be comfortable."

"Do what you please," said Matthew, and he meant it. His heart was calming and the small beads of sweat that had risen at his temples had begun to dry. "It's your world, isn't it?"

With that, the professor leaned slightly forward. "May I tell you a little about my world, young man?"

Matthew didn't respond. Something in the soft, genteel voice had sent a cold shiver down his spine.

"I shall," Fell decided. "I told you I had a son, didn't I? Templeton, as I said. A very fine lad. Very intelligent. Curious about the world. Almost as curious as his father. Well, you do remind me of Temple. As I said...of who he might have been, had he lived. He died when he was twelve years old, you see. Twelve years old." The words had been repeated with a sad sort of passion that held restrained fury at its center. "Beaten to death by a gang of rowdies on his way to school. He wasn't a fighter, you see. He was a gentle soul. He was a very fine boy." Here the professor paused and sat in silence for a time, until Matthew nervously cleared his throat and shifted his position in the chair.

"His image," said the professor, "is the portrait in stained-glass on the staircase. My Templeton, lost to me. By the bloody fists of a gang of six. They chased him through the streets like a dog and beat him for their amusement, I understand. Oh, he was always dressed very well. Always very clean. No one tried to help him, in that London mob. No one cared. He was another show on the streets, another display of what human beings can do—and will do—for the *pleasure* of it. And the awful thing, Matthew...the awful, terrible thing...is that Temple had a premonition of his death the night before, and he asked me to walk with him to school that morning... but I, being busy in my own affairs...could not be bothered to do so. I had my research before me. My academics. So I said, Temple... you're a big boy now. You have nothing to fear. Your mother and I trust in God, and so should you. So...go along, Temple, for the school is not very far away. Not very far. Go right along, I said. Because you're a big boy now."

To the heavy silence that followed, Matthew offered, "I'm sorry."

"Don't speak," said the professor, with a soft but cutting hiss, and Matthew dared not utter another word.

They sat without speaking for a while, the professor and the problem-solver. Matthew could hear waves breaking against the rocks below, slowly beating Pendulum Island to pieces.

"I...had to do something," came the terrible and quiet voice. "Something, to ease my pain. I couldn't live like that, could I? And neither could Teressa. She was such a mild and sensitive woman. Like Temple, really. He took most of his personality from her, and he resembled her too. When I looked at her, I could see him looking back. But she cried all the time, and I couldn't sleep...and I knew... I must do *something*, to ease this pain."

One gloved hand came up, almost touched the forehead, and slowly fluttered down again like the death of an arrow-shot bird.

"I had money. My father left me wealthy. He was the governor here. Have I told you that?" He waited for Matthew to nod. "The governor of Pendulum Island and its seaport, Somers Town. Yes, I remember telling you. Well…I had money. And money is a tool, you know? It can do whatever pleases you. What pleased me then… was to find out the names of the six creatures who had beaten my son to death. After that…to go upon the streets after nightfall, out into the dark dens where the animals gather, and pushing any fear I felt down into myself I walked into places a year before would have never seen. I had money enough—and the skills of persuasion enough—to buy a gang of ruffians of my own. And pay them handsomely to kill the six boys on my death list. The youngest creature fourteen, the eldest seventeen. They never lived another month. But you know…still…it didn't suffice.

"No," the professor continued, the word like the tolling of a distant funeral bell. "The pain was still there. So…I gave the order to my gang of ruffians to kill the parents of those dead creatures, their brothers and sisters, and anyone who lived in their squalid little rooms. It cost me quite a lot of money, Matthew. But…it was worth it, because I wanted it done and it *was* done. And quite suddenly…I had power and a reputation. Quite suddenly I was known on the streets to be ruthless in my regard to life, and quite suddenly I had an interested following. And me…a lowly, bookish and reclusive academic, suddenly with a gang of…thugs, did you say?…thugs who *wanted* to work for me. And several in particular who stepped forward and gave me education and good advice. That money was to be made enforcing tribute from the carters and higglers who set up their wares on the streets. In other words, to create a territory. *My* territory, Matthew. At first a small area, then larger. And larger still, encompassing businesses that had existed long before Temple's death." The cowled head nodded. "It seems I was very good at persuasion. At…creating plans for further expansion. My thirst for knowledge grew. Only now it was beyond books. It was the desire for knowledge of how to control people, and thus control my destiny. And all that you see—and all you do *not* see—was brought about because of the savage murder of my son on a London street, when you would have been but a child.

"And now," said the professor in his smooth, quiet and terrifying voice, "here you are, before me."

Matthew feared to speak.

But the silence stretched, and at last Matthew cleared his throat to urge up the words lodged there like thorns.

"Your wife. What became of Teressa?" he dared ask.

"Ah, sweet Teressa. My gentle angel, whom I pledged to for life at the altar of a beautiful church. She could not go where I was going." Fell was silent for a moment, as if trying to control the one thing he could not: the whirlwinds within his own soul. "After the deaths of the families, I told her we were done. My love for her was gone. I saw too much of Temple in her. When I saw him looking out at me, it speared my heart. I could not abide such disturbance. Thus…I cast her away. And I recall…I recall this very vividly. When I told her we were done, that I wished never to see her face in this life again…that I was a changed man and walked a changed path she could not follow…she did not begin to cry, Matthew, but she began to *bleed*. From that stricken face I used to love…two tendrils of blood began to drip from her nostrils…slowly, very slowly. And I, being a changed man, watched that blood ooze forth, and all I wondered was…which tendril of blood would reach her upper lip first."

The last words lingered in Matthew's mind. The professor folded his hands in his lap, fingers twined.

"As I say, you do remind me of my son. I mean…of what he might have been. The thoughtful young man, who believes he has the world in his pocket. How delightful that must be. Listen to me now: tomorrow afternoon at two o'clock, Cesar Sabroso gives his report," Fell said. "At four o'clock, Adam Wilson speaks. I trust you will use the key well and wisely."

"I'll get into their rooms," Matthew replied, his voice tight.

"Very good, then." The professor rose smoothly to his feet. "Oh," he said, with an upraised finger. "I'd like you to see clearly what I am now, Matthew. I am curious about all forms of life, of course, but one of my interests is in marine life, in all its varied shapes and forms. It is the *specialized* lifeform that most intrigues me. The creature, you might say, from another world. One may say…the nightmare, formed in flesh? If you desire a further insight, you might meet one of the servants at six o'clock in the morning at the foot of the main stairs. Don't be late, please. With that, I will say goodnight."

Matthew stood up. Not necessarily out of respect, but because this was after all the man's domain. He nodded, still finding language difficult.

Professor Fell unlocked the door, opened it a crack and peered into the corridor. He waited for a moment, because perhaps someone was nearby. Before the professor slipped out, he said without looking at Matthew, "Don't fail me," and then he was gone.

Matthew relocked the door. He hadn't realized that his hands had begun to tremble. He splashed some water into his face from the basin. For a few minutes he stood outside on the balcony staring at the stars in the black sky and hearing the waves rumble.

He was himself a creature from another world, he thought. He did not belong in this one. His heart yearned for New York, his regular life and his friends. But before he, Berry and Zed could get back to that solid earth…

…he would have to present evidence of treachery to Professor Fell, the master of treason.

It was nearly too much for his mind to comprehend and his soul to bear. He drew in deep lungfuls of the salt air, but it didn't help. Then, tired to the point of desperation, he turned away from the sea that had almost claimed his life and went to bed to seek the ethereal solace of sleep.

TWENTY-SIX

A **TAPPING** at the door brought Matthew up from the pit of a fitful sleep. He hesitated, listening. And yes, there it was again. Someone definitely at the door. And what time was it? A squint at the candle clock: nearly two in the morning. Now what the hell was this? Matthew wondered. He sat up on the bed's edge. "Who is it?" he asked, but of an answer there was none. A third time: tap tap tap. Someone definitely wanting him to open that door. Matthew started to call again, but he knew it would be no use. If they had wanted to reply, a reply would have been given. Still… perhaps it was someone who didn't wish their voice to carry in the hallway. Or…more ominously…it could be one or more Thackers, wishing to finish the job they'd started yesterday. That thought made him mad. He'd had a damned gutful of those orange-haired nubbers. If they wanted some of him, they'd get it…in the form of a candle clock smashed across their skulls. He got out of bed, plucked up the candle clock and, oblivious to the wax dripping onto his right hand, went to the door, unlatched it and opened it a fraction. A caped and hooded figure was standing there, touched by the golden glow of its own candlelight. "Who are—" Matthew began, but he could not finish the question because in the next second the figure blew its candle out, pushed the door open, blew Matthew's candle out before light could reveal the face, and pressed her lips against his own. And very definitely, from the shape of the body beneath the cape, it was a *her*. He pulled back and started to speak again, to ask the same unasked question, and now in the velvet dark the figure fairly flew upon him and, dropping her own candlestick to the floor, clasped his arms to his sides and kissed him again. Whoever she was, she was strong. Lithe and nimble, he thought. Her body strained against his, a powerhouse of earthy passion.

It had to be Fancy.

He started to speak her name, and yet her mouth upon his was unrelenting in its quest to consume every word he might try to utter. She backed him across the room to the bed, proving that an Indian could see, catlike, in the dark. He fell back before her, upon that selfsame bed, and she proved also that an Indian maiden could be far from maidenly.

She began a campaign to disrobe him, if it meant tearing the nightclothes from his body. And they were not even *his* nightclothes, but provided to him from Sirki, and Matthew thought that if the East Indian giant wanted them back after this misadventure he would have to settle for the rags the West Indian girl had rent them into with fingers and teeth. Her haste was ridiculous, but also flattering.

"Wait!" he said, stunned by the speed of this disclosure of desire. He couldn't get out the second *wait*, for she clamped a hand over his mouth and bit his belly just south of the navel. With his nightclothes torn into tatters and himself nearly naked, Matthew found the girl hellbent on pinning him to the bed and having her way with him.

She kissed his mouth, grasped his tongue with her lips, and nibbled his throat. What could he do, but lie back before this onslaught? He returned her kisses and would be remiss—actually insane—if his body did not respond. And so it did.

She wore no clothing under the cape. She had no time for formalities nor foreplay; she got astride Matthew and mounted him with the dampened ease of wanton and needful urgency. He did not protest this action, but when he tried to reach up to touch her face and hair beneath the hood she gripped his arms all the harder and held them fast to the bed.

If any member of her tribe had attempted to mark time to the thrusting of her hips with a drum, his hands would've been beaten bloody within the first minute. "My God!" Matthew said, or thought he said; he wasn't sure, since his senses were beginning to fly in mad circles round the room. He thought he wouldn't be able to walk tomorrow, but what a hell of a run he intended to have tonight.

She leaned forward then and harshly bit his lips. Very harshly, in fact, and most painfully, and Matthew realized from the roughness of her toothy attention this was not Fancy at all.

It was Aria Chillany.

Of course it was. She of the cold soul and brutal demands. She was demanding of him right now and he intended to deliver. Her intention was strictly to enjoy his flesh, and all else be damned. He could bear that hardship. In fact, her soul might be cold but something else was quite hot. Quite.

He decided to give as good as he got, and so he met her halfway on each stroke and their banging together might have broken bones if it had been any more violent a wallop. His teeth cracked together in his head and he feared his eyeballs would jump from his skull. The woman was wild. She ground down on him and moved her hips around and around and Matthew who had not experienced anything like this since the episode with the sex-crazed nymph Charity LeClaire could only hang on for the pounding and try to keep the impending explosion from knocking Madam Chillany through the ceiling.

But no, no...he had to withstand this assault as long as he could. Therefore he sent his mind out on an errand of imaging himself a man swimming under the cold sea, whereas in this room the pulsing heat and violence of their frenzied encounter promised the seaman must in a short time certainly rise from the depths.

He tried to reach up for her again and was again promptly armpinned. Then her rhythm changed to a softer beat and she leaned forward and kissed him gently on the mouth, the touch of her lips stirring a not-so-distant and very pleasing memory.

It was not Aria Chillany. He realized it must be Minx Cutter.

Yes. He was sure of it. Though not entirely certain, in that he would not have bet his life upon it. Now they were meeting more gently but still with a powerful thrust, and her mouth was upon his and her tongue questing within. *Minx*, he almost said, but his mouth was no longer his own. She kissed him and bit him playfully, as her hips circled around and around and she held him tightly within. Yes. Certainly Minx Cutter, he thought. Maybe.

The problem was, he could not touch her hair or her face nor could he *smell*. His bashed and swollen nose prevented all aromas from entering. He could not tell if the woman astride him smelled of earth, of fire, or of seafoam. He tried to inhale her scent and found nothing. As the woman began to thrust down upon him harder and harder still, as she began to moan softly in a voice that could belong in its passionate strain to any one of his three suspects, Matthew was at a loss to know who it truly was. And then he met her one thrust too many, their heat blending and melding, and he could hold back no longer. He was lit up as if by a white-hot blaze, his mind was filled with a spinning of colorful wheels, and he emptied himself into her as she clutched him tighter and deeper and made noises of both passion and satisfaction that served to inflame him to a hotter candle. When Matthew was all served out, the mystery paramour gave him one slow and final grind that was pain mixed with pleasure, as love must be. Then she dismounted, grasped his most valued instrument and kissed its ticklish tip, and without a word departed from the bedside. He heard the door open and close, and that was the end of the affair.

"Damn," he managed to say, to the dark.

The dark answered, in its own way, for there was suddenly the slightest tremor of Pendulum Island shifting like a beast in its sleep, and in the castle there came a beggar's symphony of creaks, cracks and pops issuing from the walls.

Matthew got out of bed. On shaky legs he went to the door, opened it and peered into the hallway. It was, as he'd suspected, empty. Fancy...Aria Chillany...Minx Cutter. Who? He somehow doubted he might ever know. Therefore he closed and latched the door, he relit the candle clock estimating to his best judgment the amount of time that had passed, and he returned to his bed ready for sleep and whatever the next morning might bring in this strange new world he found himself a part of.

At as near to six o'clock as he could manage Matthew was dressed and waiting at the bottom of the stairs. The sun was rising over the sea, the air was still and the day vowed to be warm indeed. In a few minutes a middle-aged black servant arrived in the high powdered wig and the sea-blue uniform that seemed to suit Professor Fell's taste for drama and color. The servant held a black leather bag and wore leather gloves the same hue.

"Good mornin', sir," he said to Matthew, his face impassive. "If you'll follow me?"

Matthew followed the man out another door beyond the staircase. They walked through a manicured garden where early birds sang from the trees. Purple and yellow flowers lined the walkway, which led to a series of stone stairs going down the cliff face to the sea.

"Careful with your step," said the servant, as they started their descent.

Suddenly a voice called, "Daniel!" A second servant who'd been standing among the trees approached them as Daniel and Matthew paused. "I'll take the young man down," this second man offered.

"I was told to do it," Daniel said.

"I *know* you don't like it," was the reply. The recent arrival—or had he been waiting for them? Matthew wondered—was dressed in the usual fashion and looked to be a few years older than the first man, with a square jaw and deep-set eyes that held both sadness and determination. "I'll do it for you."

"You don't like it neither," said Daniel.

"Who does?" asked the second servant, with a lift of his eyebrows. He reached out for the bag.

Daniel removed the leather gloves and the second man put them on. Then the bag changed hands. Daniel gave a very audible sigh of relief. "Thank you, George," he said, and he nodded at Matthew, turned away and retraced his steps to the castle.

"This way, sir," said George, who started down the long and—to Matthew's eye—extremely dangerous and sea-damp stairs.

At the bottom of the cliff was a wooden platform jutting out over the sea, and low enough that some of the harder waves were smashing against it. A wide plank extended from the platform another ten or so feet over the turbulent water, and at the end of that plank was a highly-unsettling metal spike coated with what could only be dried gore. Matthew noted what appeared to be the top of a wire fence, exposed in the trough between waves, that made a circle about a hundred or more feet around. Keeping something caged, he thought. But *what*? The sweat had begun to rise under his shirt.

"If you'll stand where you are, sir," cautioned George, who set the leather bag down and opened its ram's-horn clasps. Matthew was perfectly glad to obey, as the wind and the sea spray hit him full in the face.

George reached carefully into the bag and drew out by the unruly hair the severed head of Jonathan Gentry. Matthew caught his breath and drew back another few feet. The face was gray with a touch of green on the sunken cheeks. George held the head at arm's length and walked out to the spike, where he did what Matthew feared he was going to do: he impaled the head on the spike, and then he walked back along the plank and stood looking out to sea. He removed the gloves and dropped them with the briefest shiver of revulsion into the bag, which he promptly closed once more.

They waited.

"What's in there?" Matthew dared ask, his voice pitched nearly an octave higher than normal.

"The professor's prized possession," said George. "It will show itself soon. Please don't move when it does."

"No concern there," Matthew answered, watching the blue waves and the white swirling foam within the wire enclosure, which had to be secured by chains many feet underwater.

Still they waited.

And then George lifted his chin and said, "It's coming now. Time for its breakfast."

Something was indeed rising from the depths. Matthew could see a brown shape coming up, a thing that looked to be blotched with barnacles and stained with seaweed. George stood his ground about midway on the platform, and though Matthew's brain begged him to turn tail from this ascending nightmare he was profoundly curious. His curiosity always won over his sense of impending danger, which he reasoned would someday be his undoing.

The shape hung suspended just below the churning surface. Matthew had the sense of looking at a huge mass of moving jelly.

Then a tentacle as big as a treetrunk came up through a green-foamed wave and reached upward, questing for the head of Jonathan Gentry.

Matthew did not have to be cautioned to stand perfectly still, for his blood seemed to have frozen in his veins on this warm sunny morning and his muscles turned to lumps of heavy clay.

The tentacle rubbed itself across the hair on the severed head. A second tentacle rose up, blighted with mollusks and ringed with pinkish-green suckers that pulsed and moved seemingly of their own accord. This, too, went to the head and began to caress the face with hideous anticipation.

"It is very intelligent," said George, in a hushed voice. "It's exploring its meal."

A third tentacle rose from the water, snapped like a whip toward the platform and then submerged again. The two others began to work in concert at lifting the head off its spike. Matthew thought he was a stagger and shriek away from Bedlam.

With a noise of sliding flesh the tentacles wrapped themselves around Gentry's gaping face and pulled the head upward from its mount on the plank. Then, quickly and greedily, the head was brought to the shifting mass that hung just under the waves, and as it went down Matthew could imagine he heard the crack of a skull and the crunch of facial bones under the biting beak of Professor Fell's huge and nightmarish octopus.

The creature withdrew to its lair below. There was a brown shimmer and a flail of tentacles, and it was gone.

"It usually eats horsemeat, lamb or beef," George explained, altogether too helpfully. "It does seem to like entrails and brains." He stared across the platform at Matthew, who had retreated to its far edge. "You're very pale, sir," he observed.

Matthew nodded, dazed; he was thinking that never in his worst fever-dream had Doctor Gentry ever thought that not only would his head be sawed off, but that his brain would be a sea-monster's delicacy.

George picked up the leather bag as if it carried a disease. "I need to tell you, sir," he said, "that your lady friend is currently in hiding at the house of Jerrell Falco."

Matthew blinked. *"What?"*

"Your lady friend," the servant repeated. "Her name is Berry, I believe?"

"Berry. Yes." Matthew wondered if he were still asleep and dreaming this by way of a bad oyster; yes, of course, it had to be that.

"At Captain Falco's house. His wife, Saffron, is my daughter. I was told to tell you, and as I learned you were coming here this morning I waited for you."

Matthew rubbed the lumps on his forehead with the fingers of his right hand. Surely he'd been injured more severely than he'd first imagined.

"I have a map for you." George reached into his jacket and brought out a folded piece of rough-edged paper. He offered it to Matthew, who stood dumbly staring at it. "Please, sir," said the servant. "Take it and put it away. If anyone finds that and learns I've brought it for you, I hate to think what would happen to poor George." He cast a disturbed glance over the octopus enclosure. "It shows you how to reach Falco's house from here. Please, sir…put it away, and show no one."

Matthew put the paper into his own jacket. "Thank you," he managed to say.

"I hope it will help you," George answered, with a dignified half-bow. He picked up the leather bag, now headless. "If you'll follow me up the steps, then?"

Behind the locked door of his room, Matthew studied the map and consigned it to memory before he burned it over a candle and then scattered the ashes from his balcony into the sea. Falco's house was not far from the forbidden road that led to the fort. What in the name of all the demons of Solomon's Key was Berry doing over *there*? He had to find a way to get to her, and that was the problem. And finding Zed, too, would be a problem. The largest problem looming upon him now, however, was that he was running out of time.

Don't fail me, Professor Fell had said.

This whole affair seemed to Matthew like an exercise in failure. He still had the rooms of Cesar Sabroso and Adam Wilson to search through, but the conference of criminals was nearing its end and all he had to show for his explorations so far was an inkling— a instinctual *guess*, as the professor might put it—that Smythe and

Wilson were companions in some form of communication beyond Fell's knowledge. Likely, Matthew surmised, of debauchery and garbage-pit mischief. But there was nothing to indicate that either one was a traitor.

So where to go from here?

Minx Cutter would be waiting for him at eight o'clock at the stable. Something to show him, where the whales played. If she could get him a horse, fine. If not, he was certainly not walking that distance. Not in the daylight, at least. But when night came, perhaps that would be the time to go Berry-hunting. If he could get out of this castle without being seen by anyone.

Promptly at eight o'clock, Matthew approached the stable and found Minx standing outside on the road there with two horses— Esmerelda and Athena once more—saddled and ready. She was dressed in her brown breeches, her riding boots and a black waist-coat over a pale blue blouse. He didn't quite know what to say to her—*may I ask if you happened to visit my room last night past midnight?*—so he said nothing. If he expected her to suddenly gush forth about the encounter, he was sadly disappointed. She swung herself up astride Esmeralda and watched him approach with a blank stare as she held Athena's reins.

"Good morning," he told her. Was his voice a shade shaky? Yes, it was. Her stare was formidable, and there was something accusing in it. "How did you get me the horse?"

"I said I needed two horses. One for myself and one for my riding companion. I wasn't asked whom, and I didn't volunteer the information. Are you ready?"

He answered by taking the reins and getting up into Athena's saddle.

"Your nose is better today?" she asked as they started off.

"It's not quite as swollen. I can breathe a little more through it."

"And you had a restful sleep?"

Matthew wasn't sure what he'd heard in that question. "I did sleep, yes," he said.

"Good. I want you to be sharp this morning."

Sharp was not exactly what he was feeling, but he decided not to contest the statement. He followed Minx away from the stable and the castle and out onto the road that led to Templeton, as the sun grew warmer and the sky more blue and brightly-colored birds flew in circles over Fell's paradise.

When they reached the cliffs where Minx had brought him on the first day, the whales were already surfacing amid the waves, spouting white foam into the air and jostling each other with playful but gentle abandon.

Minx dismounted and walked to the edge, where she stood watching the parade of leviathans. Matthew also got off his horse and joined her, and together they stood under the hot glaring sun as the beasts dove and surfaced again, flapping their tails like the banners of huge gray ships.

"Aren't they beautiful?" Minx remarked, with no emotion.

"Yes, they are," Matthew answered, warily.

She turned toward him. Her gold-touched eyes in the strong and beautiful face seemed to be on fire.

"Kiss me," she said.

He did not wait for a second invitation. Truly, then, this was who had visited him last night. He stepped forward and kissed her, and she held his kiss and pushed her body against his, and then he felt the knife under his chin pressing into his throat and when she drew her face away the fire in her eyes had grown into a blaze.

"You're a very good kisser, Matthew," she told him, "but you're no Nathan Spade."

He might have stammered something. For sure he swallowed hard, though the blade was right there ready to carve his Adam's apple. He felt the sweat fairly leap from his pores.

"No Nathan Spade," she repeated. "And exactly why are you here, pretending to be him?"

Did he dare to clear his throat, with that sticker so poised? No, he did not. "I think," he said with a Herculean effort that might have impressed even Hudson Greathouse, "that you're mistaken. I am—"

"Matthew Corbett," Minx interrupted. "You see, I knew Nathan Spade. I was in *love* with Nathan Spade. And, as I say…you are no Nathan Spade."

Somehow, from his deepest recesses, he found the courage to compose himself against the blade. *I want you to be sharp this morning,* she'd told him. Indeed he sharpened himself, in that instant. With a faint smile he said, "Not even a little bit?"

"Not even," she replied, "the littlest bit of your littlest finger."

"Ow," he answered. "That hurts."

"The knife?"

"No. The sentiment." He was aware of the sheer drop to the playground of the whales. "Did you bring me here to show me how efficiently you might kill me and dispose of the body?"

"I brought you here to make sure no one followed or overheard. You *are* Matthew Corbett, are you not?"

"You...put me in a predicament."

"I'll answer for you, then." The pressure of the blade against Matthew's neck did not lessen a fraction. "Of course I knew at once you weren't Nathan. He and I were lovers in London. Against the professor's rules, as you might know. I wasn't sure who you were until I saw how you reacted when Adam Wilson mentioned killing Matthew Corbett at the table that night. You almost spilled your wine. Probably no one noticed but me. Then I knew who you must be. And I knew also why you must *be* here."

"An interesting fiction," Matthew said, clinging to his misguided hope.

"You were brought to this island by Professor Fell to find out who told the authorities that a shipment of Cymbeline was en route for a meeting with a Spanish warship on the high seas." Minx's face was close to Matthew's, her eyes still ablaze and her breath smelling faintly of lemons. The knife was still pressed firmly against his throat. "You are a problem-solver, are you not? In the employ of Katherine Herrald? And you were brought here under the charge of Aria Chillany." The knife prodded. *"Answer."*

Matthew sighed heavily. The game was up. But, strangely, he felt another game was just beginning. "True," he said. "All of it."

"The professor has suspects? Who are they?"

"Three. Cesar Sabroso, Adam Wilson and Edgar Smythe."

Minx smiled grimly. "Oh my God," she said. The knife went away from Matthew's throat. She held it loosely at her side. "What are you looking for? Evidence that one of them is a traitor?"

Matthew decided there was no point in lying. He feared the point of Minx Cutter's knife. "The professor thinks two may be involved. And that there is some evidence to be discovered, yes." From the corner of his eye he caught sight of a whale surfacing.

It spouted from its blowhole spray that seemed to form a question mark in the air before it shimmered away.

"Two traitors?" Her blonde brows lifted. "How astute of him."

"Oh? Meaning what?"

"Meaning," she said, her lips very near his own, "that there *were* two traitors. You are looking at one of them. Can you reason out who the second might have been?"

He didn't have to reason it out. He plainly saw the answer in her face, and he felt as if the uneasy earth of Pendulum Island shook a little bit more under his boots.

"Nathan Spade," he replied.

"Bravo," she said, and her blade came up to give him a congratulatory tap on the chin.

FOUR

THE DEVIL'S BREAKFAST

TWENTY-SEVEN

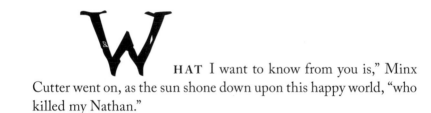HAT I want to know from you is," Minx
Cutter went on, as the sun shone down upon this happy world, "who
killed my Nathan."

Matthew was staring at the ground. He had to do so, to keep
his equilibrium. He was late in answering, therefore the beautiful
knife-thrower gave her own reply.

"Aria Chillany killed him, didn't she? He disappeared one evening, on his way to meet me. I never heard from him again. Madam
Chillany has a reputation for killing her ex-lovers. And yes, I knew
they had been involved with each other. That was the past. He and I
were looking toward the future. So…she killed him, didn't she? For
the reason that Professor Fell learned Nathan was selling diplomatic
secrets to the highest bidder?"

"That," Matthew said.

"I told him not to go there," Minx replied. "I told him…don't
be greedy. I said…the professor will find out. It was enough that
we knew about the Cymbeline and the shipment of it to Spain.
That came from one of the professor's rotten apples in the basket

of Parliament, after a few drinks of wormwood in the whorehouse. Then we knew what was about to happen…and we knew we couldn't *allow* it to happen."

"Couldn't allow it?" Matthew frowned. He was always aware of where the knife was. Currently in her right hand, at her side again. She held it with her thumb caressing the ivory handle, like an object of love. "What do you mean? You two suddenly became patriots?"

"We were always patriots. Well…maybe not so much as most, but…to sell the gunpowder to *Spain*? No." She shook her head. The fire in her eyes had abated a few degrees, and now some darker sadness had crept in. She slid the knife into her waistcoat, where it had come from. "We didn't know where the Cymbeline is stored when it reaches London from here. A warehouse somewhere on the docks. The gunpowder would be disguised as barrels of tar and nautical supplies. But when we found out that the first shipment was going to Spain, with the help of Cesar Sabroso…we had to speak out and stop it." She stared steadily into Matthew's eyes, and he felt the sheer force of her willpower. "No matter who I am, or what Nathan is…or *was*…we could not stand by and let this powder go to an enemy of our country. So…yes, we are patriotic, in our way."

Matthew looked toward the fort and could see the thin tendril of rising smoke where the chemicals were being cooked. "What makes it so powerful? Using sugar instead of charcoal?"

"It's white powder instead of black. It's stronger than the normal composition, and gives off less smoke. On any battlefield or naval battle, it would give the user of it a great advantage. How did you know about the sugar?"

"It's what I do," he explained. And clarified, "Finding out what I'm not supposed to know."

"All right, then. Now that you *do* know…what are you going to do about it?"

Matthew thought about this for a moment, as he watched the tendril drift in the breeze. And then he decided what must be done, and what he had to do.

"I'm going to get in there tonight," he told her, "and I'm going to blow it up."

Her expression did not change, but her voice was strained when she responded. "You," she said, "are insane."

"Insane to go in by the road, maybe. But through the forest? Maybe not. I think I could find something there to make a fuse or two. *If* I can get into the storehouse. But I'll cross that river when I get there." He searched her eyes and found nothing. "The professor can't be allowed to create this gunpowder in quantity. Much may be stored already in London, ready to be shipped...but if it's made here, here is where it must be ended."

"Insane," Minx repeated.

He was thinking furiously. Sweat was on his face, not necessarily from the thinking but from the morning's sullen heat. "If I'm successful, I'll need a way to get off the island quickly. A ship. I believe I know who might be convinced to help me with that. I have three hundred pounds that might help his decision and buy him a crew. And I need something else."

"What are you babbling about?"

"I need a traitor. In fact, I need two traitors, to fulfill the professor's expectations." He ran his fingers across his mouth, his gaze directed toward the rolling sea. He had a plan...or, at least, the bare beginnings of one. Much depended upon much. "Let me ask you... if I brought you a handwriting sample say by around noon...could you forge a message by four?"

"Forge a message? What message?"

"I need what the professor expects. Proof of treason. A message, passed from one traitor to the other and hidden in a...shoe, perhaps. Or wherever I intend to plant it. A short message, and perhaps you can help me with this. Do you have any idea when the next shipment of Cymbeline is planned to leave London?"

"No. It was sheer luck our finding out about the first shipment."

"It'll have to be something else, then. Something revealing. But *what*?" He thought for a silent moment. "Who gave Nathan the first information?"

"The honorable Frederick Nash. A dissolute bastard if there ever was one. He is also on the professor's payroll."

"We can work with that. Drag his name into the fray. I'll come up with something." Matthew was thinking he had to get into Smythe's room when the foul man went down for the mid-day meal. Questions nagged at him, though, and one he specifically had to have answered. "You say the powder is stored in a warehouse in

London, but you don't know exactly where? Why doesn't the professor keep it all here, instead of transporting it?" As soon as he asked the question, he thought he knew the answer. "Ah," he said before Minx could reply. "He wants it in a place where the spies from other countries can see it and report to their masters. And he fears another earthquake, doesn't he?"

"What?" She obviously had no idea what he was talking about.

"The tremors," Matthew explained. "There was an earthquake here when the professor was a boy. He can make the Cymbeline here in relative safety. But he fears if there's an accident at the fort, and enough of the powder ignites...there could be another earthquake. That's why I suspect he moves the powder off the island as soon as there's enough to fill a ship's hold. Which I would think would be enough to make a very impressive blast."

"Insane," Minx said for the third time. "You'll never get in there to blow it up."

"Not alone, no. But with help...possibly I will." He levelled his gaze at her. "Yes, Madam Chillany killed Nathan. I won't tell you how. But I will say that if Nathan Spade was standing here...he might also be thinking of blowing the place up." He gave a quiet grunt. "The bad young man found his boundary of evil, didn't he? The line beyond which he would not pass? So yes, Minx...your Nathan would go in there and blow the place to smithereens, just as I intend to. And he would ask for your help, just as I am asking."

"My help? You mean with the forgery?"

"That, and however I might need you afterward. You're very capable. I have need of your capability and your...shall we say... firmness under pressure." He couldn't help but give her a sly smile. "I have to ask...last night...did you...?" He shrugged and trailed off.

"Did I *what*?"

Her tone spoke volumes. The problem-solver was at a loss.

"Never mind," he told her, not without some disappointment. "I have someplace to go. The house of a certain sea captain. Will you come with me?"

"I will," she answered.

Astride their horses and with the map to Falco's house in Matthew's brain, they continued on their journey. Matthew and

Athena were in the lead, and after a moment Minx urged Esmeralda up beside them.

"He was not all bad," she said.

"No one is all bad." Then he thought about Tyranthus Slaughter. "*Most* aren't, at least."

"He wanted to make amends for things he'd done in his past. He wasn't proud of them. When he saw this chance, and he told me about it...we both knew it was right."

"I should say," said Matthew.

She was silent for a time, perhaps reliving poignant memories. "We were going to have a future," she told him. "Married or not, I don't know. We met by chance, really. At a party for Andrew Halverston, the money changer. Also on the professor's payroll."

"Who isn't?" Matthew asked.

"We didn't know we had the professor in common until later. Then...it didn't matter."

"It matters now," Matthew said, turning Athena toward the road that led to Falco's house. "More than ever."

"You should know about being on the professor's payroll." Minx shot him a dark glance. "His enemy...brought to his island to work for him. How in the name of God did that happen?"

"You'll begin to see when we get where we're going," he told her. "One thing I'd like to know from you...who is Brazio Valeriani and why is Fell searching for him?"

"I don't know...but I've heard things."

"Such as?"

"Such as...that the professor has strange interests and ambitions. Valeriani has something to do with those. Other than that, I have no clue."

"Hm," Matthew said. "I should make it my business to find out." He kicked into Athena's flanks to hasten her progress, for he felt that time was growing short and there was yet much to do before he, Berry, hopefully Zed and...yes, Fancy...could escape this damnable island.

Following his mental map, Matthew led them along the cart trail into the woods and to the ascertained house of white stone that stood amid a few others. They both dismounted. Matthew knocked at the door. He didn't have long to wait before a very lovely young native woman with cream-colored skin opened the door and peered out. "Saffron?" Matthew asked. She nodded; her eyes were wide and frightened. "I'm here to—" Saffron was pushed aside, gently but firmly. The fearsome visage of the white-goateed, amber-eyed and creased ebony face of Captain Jerrell Falco took the place of his wife's loveliness. He looked from Matthew to Minx and back again, with a slight frown of disdain. "I didn't think you'd be damn fool enough to come in the *daylight*," he rumbled, like his own earthquake. "Who is *she*?"

"A friend."

"You say."

"You can trust her."

"Too late now, if I don't. You sure no one followed you?"

"He's sure," Minx spoke up sharply, her own brass showing.

"Damn all of you for getting me into this," Falco said. And then he opened the door and stepped back. "Come in."

As soon as Matthew walked across the threshold, he was hit by the embrace of a red-haired adventuress from New York who, at all of nineteen tender years, had found herself in at least twenty years of trouble. Her hair was wild, her dirty face scratched by island brush, and she wore a dark blue sleeping gown that appeared to have been ripped by the claws of wildcats. Berry clung to Matthew so hard he struggled to draw a breath, and then it was she who drew back with a penetrating question: "Who is *that*?"

That being…

"My name is Minx Cutter. I'm a friend of Matthew's." The gold-hued eyes took in Berry, the room, Falco and Saffron and everything; she was as cool as a September Sabbath. "Who might you be, and why are you hiding here?"

"Berry Grigsby," came the frosted reply. "Also a friend—a very *good* friend—of Matthew's. I am here because…" She faltered, but looked to no one for help.

"Because she escaped from the Templeton Inn night before last and got herself in some difficulty," said Falco. "She and the Ga. Where he is, I don't know. Packs of men were nosing around here all yesterday. Searched my house, but Miss Grigsby was under the floorboards in the back room. Not very much to her liking, but necessary."

"There are *crabs* under there," she said to Matthew, her eyes wide and rimmed with the tears of revulsion. There was nothing like feeling crabs tangling in one's hair while rough boots stomped the boards three inches above one's face.

"She kept silent, though." Falco had his clay pipe in hand, and now he lit it from the stub of a candle and blew out a plume of smoke. "Good thing. They were looking to hang somebody for hiding her."

"You were where? On the road to the fort?" The question was from Minx and directed to Berry.

"I don't know about a fort. But we were on a road not too far from here. There were skulls hanging from the trees on both—"

"Stupid girl," Minx interrupted. "Going in there, after you saw the warning? And who else was with you?"

"Her friend. Used to be a slave," Falco offered. From the back room a baby began to cry, and Saffron went to tend to their child. Falco blew smoke through his nostrils, his comment on the situation regarding these visitors to his home and intruders to the life of his family. "You've got me in some shit," he told Matthew. "All you people. Dragging me into your business. Did you hear me ask to have my throat cut by Fell's men? Or to have to watch my wife and child be sliced up in front of me?" The smoke rolled toward Matthew's nose...and to his surprise and relief, he smelled it. "Answer!" the captain roared.

"I shall," was the calm response. "I regret the inconvenience, but I am not only here to rescue Berry, but to rescue you and your family."

"I see how much rescuing you've been doing, sir. Has a horse kicked you in the face lately?"

"No, but two asses did their best. Now listen to me, please. I know you've told me you were loyal to your employer, as long as he pays well. I understand your love for your ship. But did you know that the professor is brewing a very powerful kind of gunpowder in that fort of his? And that he plans to—"

"I don't want to hear this. It's not my business."

"Your business, I believe you once said, is making the best decisions under the shadow of your sails," said Matthew. He let that sink in for a few seconds before he went on. "You also once said you wished for a cargo concern of your own, and hoped that Fell's money would buy it for you. Very ambitious indeed, captain. But you gave warning too, that night in your cabin, that I should take care the professor's world doesn't get into me, because there's a lot of money in it. Do you recall that?"

"I do." The smoke floated freely, changing shape as it roiled.

"I should give you the same warning, captain, because your sails are luffing in the breeze. You will need to decide in the next few minutes what your ultimate destination—and that of your wife and child—shall be."

"What shit are you throwing?" Falco growled.

"I am throwing you a lifeline," said Matthew, staring with great composure into the fierce amber eyes. This man, he realized, could tear his head off with little regret. Yet Matthew had the floor and he intended to keep it. "I can become your employer, if you allow it. I can pay you this night three hundred pounds in gold coins. That's for you, your ship and a skeleton crew. I want to be taken back to New York, along with Berry, the Ga—if he can be found, because I know he's alive—and Miss Cutter, if she wishes to go. *And* one other," he continued, "who I will bring from Fell's castle. I wish to pay you for what you do…ferrying passengers. When we reach New York, I can vow to you that I will not only secure you a place ferrying cargo, but I will work to make sure you are the master of your own business much sooner than you expected. And, Captain Falco, I can do this for you. I promise it."

"He can do it," said Berry. Falco smoked his pipe in stony silence.

It was the second effort, Matthew thought, that was both the more difficult and the more rewarding. He had no intention of giving up, not he who had sunken down into the depths riding a seahorse and found providence in the kiss of an Indian maiden. Oh no…not he.

"I'm going to destroy the gunpowder tonight," Matthew said, with no expression in his voice; it was a cold fact. "Or…as the statement goes…die trying."

"That would be likely," Falco answered.

"A fool's errand, yes?" Matthew's brows lifted. "And who would expect such a fool to get in there and blow that powder to Hell, sir? So…I will have the element of surprise on my side. Now, I don't know the layout of the land or the fort, so I will truly be in the dark.

But I intend to stay in the dark until I get the job done. I'm telling you this because after that powder blows, my friends and I will very quickly need a way off this island. I am asking you, Captain Falco, to afford us that way."

"I told him he was insane," Minx suddenly offered. Matthew bit his lip; he was grateful for her concern but wished her to keep her opinion to herself. She stared at the floor for a moment, the tides of conflict on her face, and then she sighed heavily. "Insane or not, he has a good reason to want to do this. I'm with him."

"Grand for you," said Falco. "Murder for me and my family."

"Deliverance for you and your family," Matthew corrected. "A nice sentiment, that you wished your own cargo business. But you must know by now that no one leaves this island without the permission of Professor Fell. I would suggest that he will use you as he wishes, and at the end of his use the only item of cargo that need concern you will be yourself in a coffin. Possibly also your fine wife and child. For why would he let you leave here and start a new life? No. Impossible." Matthew shook his head. "You'd best mind the set of your sails, Captain. They do cast a long and very dark shadow over your future."

But for the soft crooning of Falco's wife to the child in the bedroom, a silence settled.

Falco stood before Matthew, his brow knit and his gaze distant. He began to slowly pound the pipe's bowl against the palm of his free hand.

Matthew waited. Nothing more needed to be said. Either the ship found its own way or ran upon the rocks. The captain was thinking; he was an intelligent man, and he was testing the currents of what might be as opposed to those that were.

"Damn," said Falco at last; it was more the bleat of a lamb than the growl of a lion, yet it was also a lamb that refused to be slaughtered and to witness the slaughter of loved ones. He had begun his own hard voyage, which all ships must undertake.

"I will need at least a dozen men," said the *Nightflyer*'s captain. "No one will question me. I know that foodstuffs and supplies are being loaded to take you back to New York in three or four days, as goes the original plan I was presented. But it will take time. And you're saying we have only hours?"

"I'd like to leave here at first light." Matthew decided to add: "If all goes well."

"*Hours,*" said Falco, with a bitter edge. "Not nearly enough time. The harbor master will want to see my orders before he allows me to cast off. What shall I show him?"

"A letter of orders, what else?" Minx asked. "Who usually writes the orders? Sirki? Or someone else? And how is the letter delivered to you?"

"Sometimes him. Other times, other people. But it's always on white paper, rolled with a red ribbon into a scroll, and it always bears the professor's seal. The octopus symbol."

"So it's not always the same handwriting? I can take care of that," said Minx. "I can find the paper and a ribbon, but as for the seal..." She looked to Matthew.

"I have an unbroken seal on the pouch of money I was given," Matthew replied. "Can it be used?"

"Removed unbroken and used to reseal a letter of orders?" Minx smiled grimly. "Piece of puffet."

"I will want," said the captain, "to bring along other passengers. My wife's father and mother. Her older brother and his family. He has a farm, just this side of Templeton. Without all of them, I will not go."

It was a complication, but a necessary one. Matthew realized Falco knew the gravity of the situation. When it was clear the *Nightflyer* had flown early and on forged orders, someone's head would roll. Possibly the harbor master's, Matthew thought...and into the beak of the octopus upon whose symbol the unfortunate had relied. "Understood," said Matthew. "I'll leave it you to gather them together, as quietly as possible. I assure you that caution is justified here. There will be no rehearsal, and no room for error."

"Yes," Falco said, to the master of the room.

"I also have my work cut out for me. Minx, we should get back to the castle. I have to get into Smythe's room for a sample of his handwriting. I'll come up with something interesting for you to scribe." The purpose, Matthew thought, was to skewer two pigeons with one spear and thus afford the octopus a double course of corrupted brains. He turned toward Berry and reached out for her...

...and she was there, his lucky star.

He had been so relieved to see her at first that he hadn't known what to say. Words still seemed so small. She grasped his hand and he pulled her toward him like reeling in the most beautiful and scrappy fish in the sea. He hugged her to himself and she clung to him as if he were the most solid rock on Pendulum Island. His heart gave a few hard beats, but when he drew away and looked into her soft and frightened blue eyes he felt the irritated anger flare up once more.

"Why in the name of dear departed Christ did you and Zed leave that inn?" he demanded. "Do you know what trouble you've caused?"

"Zed wanted to find a boat. I wanted to help him."

"Oh, you can converse freely with him now?"

"I can understand him. *Without* words." She pulled away a greater distance. The shine of anger had surfaced from the depths of her eyes and her cheeks had reddened. "I swear, sometimes I think I can understand him better without words than you with them!"

"As your opinion pleases. We have no time for roundabouts."

"The truest thing that's been said!" Falco announced. "I have to go get a crew together. I suppose you're wanting me to keep *her* here until morning?" The *her* being Berry, who looked alternately bewildered and ready to bite through iron nails.

"I do. She's safest here."

"That's a poor statement, but I'll testify to it. If those men come back again, she goes under the floor."

Berry started to protest to Matthew but caught herself, for even she knew that her jailers this time would not be so gracious, and the crabs were more welcome company than rats in a dungeon cell somewhere.

"The *Nightflyer* will be ready at first light," said Falco, his goateed chin lifted in defiance, perhaps, of Professor Fell. "If you've gotten me in this far, I'll have to cast off without you if you don't show up. My throat and the throats of my loved ones are worth more gold than you can possibly pay."

"Agreed," Matthew said. "At first light, then." He glanced quickly at Berry but didn't wish his gaze to linger upon her. She was going to be hell after this mess was cleaned up; but he was determined to give her back as much hell as he could, too.

"Good luck to you," Falco told them when Matthew opened the door for himself and Minx. "If you're caught tonight, please allow them to cut your guts open without squealing my name, won't you?"

"Fair enough, sir."

"Matthew?" Berry stepped forward. She reached out, tenderly, and touched his arm. The anger in her eyes had given way to a frightened concern. "Be careful," she said. "I mean it. Be *really* careful."

"I'll see you in the morning," he promised, and then he and Minx left the house. He hoped it wasn't an empty promise, and that by first light his own head would not be the devil's breakfast.

They reached the road and turned their horses toward Fell's castle, and under the glaring white sun Matthew busied himself conjuring up a message to trap two traitors. Within a few minutes he was satisfied with himself. Smythe and Wilson would never know what hit them. Couldn't happen to two more despicable characters...unless it happened to the Thacker brothers.

And now what lay ahead was truly treacherous territory. Slipping in and out of rooms unseen. The message itself: would it fool Professor Fell? And how to get to Fancy to let her know she was on the edge of her deliverance? Then tonight...the main show and a display of fireworks to end this conference of criminals.

He made a vow that he would kiss Dippen Nack if he ever got back to New York. He thought he must be truly desperate.

"What are you thinking?" Minx asked, urging Esmerelda up beside him.

"About what must be done," he replied. "And...that I'm not so different from Nathan Spade after all, am I?"

She made a noise that might have been a cruel laugh.

"Only in your dreams," she said, and rode on ahead.

Twenty-Eight

MATTHEW had his hand on the doorknob and was about to venture forth from Adam Wilson's room when he heard the sound of clumping boots, slurred and boisterous curses and drunken laughter. He stayed his hand and stood transfixed, as if the Thackers might see him through the door. He judged the time to be quarter after four. The Thackers were indeed getting an early start on the evening's festivities. He wished he could blow them to Hell along with the gunpowder, but that was not likely to happen.

He waited, hearing the noise of their passage dwindle along the corridor. Fancy would probably have been crushed between them. Either that, or she was swimming again in her world of peace and silence. In Matthew's left hand was a small piece of parchment with ragged edges. Earlier he had slipped into Edgar Smythe's room and gotten a piece of clean parchment and a piece with some of the Bard's lines that Smythe had written in his bored doldrums. While he was in Smythe's room, Matthew had heard footsteps approaching the door and then a key slide into the lock. He thought he might have aged a few years in the seconds it had taken him to get out upon the balcony, press his back against the wall and hope that Smythe did not emerge for a breath of air. Instead, Matthew had been treated to the grunting and farting noise of Smythe relieving himself in the chamberpot. Then there'd been another damnable space of time during which Matthew feared the munitions master would come out, pot in hand, to dump his mess over the railing, but this fortunately did not happen. At last the door had opened and closed once more, the key had been turned, and with sweat on his face and itching the back of his neck Matthew got out of the room, relocked it, and as had been agreed upon slipped under Minx's door both pieces of parchment and the octopus wax stamp cut from the leather pouch with the sharp knife she'd given him to use.

Then there had been the waiting.

At nearly three-thirty the small square of parchment was pushed under his own door. There were the two lines, exactly as Matthew had directed. It looked to be Smythe's handwriting, of course. Minx was obviously very efficient at her craft. And then there was the next step, which Matthew had chosen not to skip: he would get into Wilson's room after four o'clock and actually plant the message in a place he might 'discover' it, thereby having an accurate description of Wilson's room and belongings in case he was further questioned. A neatly-folded stocking in a drawer had served the purpose.

And now...out of this damned room with the forged evidence of communication between traitors, and let the heads roll.

He gritted his teeth, turned the knob, looked out for anyone passing by and entered the silent corridor. He was sweating under his arms and as well as on his face. He longed for a breath of New York winter, and to Hell with this infernal paradise. He slid the key into the lock, turned it and then, message gripped in hand, he took a leftward step toward his own room and therefore saw Mother Deare standing in the hallway not five paces distant, her red-gloved hands folded together in front of her, her mouth pursed with the beginning of a question.

Matthew felt his touch of winter. In fact, he was nearly frozen.

The woman approached him. When she stopped, just short of bowling him over, she peered into his face with her bulbous brown eyes.

"A game of Pall Mall is starting in the garden," she said. "Sabroso is there already. So are Miss Cutter, Pons and his Toy. Might you wish to join them?"

"I'm...not much for games. Except chess,"" Matthew managed to answer, even as he fumbled to enclose the piece of parchment in his fist.

"Oh, I think you're very good at all manner of games, Mr. Corbett." She held out a gloved palm. "I'm presuming you've found something the professor should see?"

It was clear—startlingly clear—that Mother Deare knew everything. Matthew got his brain connected to his mouth again. "I have," he said, and handed it over.

She looked at the two lines. "Interesting." It was spoken as if she were studying a not-particularly-interesting insect. "I'll see he gets this. Are you joining us in the garden?"

"No. Thank you. I think...I'm going to go rest for a bit."

"Of course. You should do so. I can have some lemon water brought to your room, if you like."

"Actually...that would be good. Yes, thank you very much."

"My pleasure." She regarded the message once more. "It seems you've done the professor a valuable service. It won't be forgotten, I assure you."

"Glad to be of help," said Matthew, who thought the words tasted indeed of the most bitter lemons.

"Well, then." Mother Deare's froggish face crinkled into a smile. One hand came up and patted Matthew's cheek. "Good boy," she said. "By all means, take your rest." She turned away and walked toward the staircase. Matthew let her get far along the corridor before he got his legs moving. He went to his room, locked the door, sprawled across the bed and stared up at the canopy as slowly his taut nerves relaxed.

He was still in that position, though drowsing in and out of sleep, when there came a knock at his door perhaps a half-hour later. "Who is it?" he demanded, his voice as slurred as any drunken Thacker.

"Myself," replied the lilting voice of the East Indian killer.

Matthew felt a shudder course through him. His heart began to pound. *Steady*, he told himself. *Be calm.* But easier said than done, with that giant at his door. He drew a few deep breaths to clear his head. Then he got up, thought *now is the moment of reckoning* and he crossed the chessboard floor to the door and opened it.

"Good afternoon," said Sirki, who carried a tray bearing a pewter pitcher and a glass. "I was instructed to bring you lemon water."

Matthew retreated to allow him entry. Sirki put the tray down atop the dresser and actually poured Matthew's first glass. He offered it to Matthew, who took the glass and put his nose to it in an attempt to smell anything more powerful than lemons.

"No drugs, young sir," said Sirki. "I promise that."

"You take the first drink, then." Matthew held the glass toward him.

Sirki took it without hesitation. His drink took nearly half the liquid. "Very refreshing." He handed it back. "You've done a service for the professor. Why should he wish to drug you?"

"Old habits die hard," was the reply. Matthew still didn't trust the drink, and set it aside.

"A few questions for you." Sirki's mouth smiled, but the eyes were stern. "You found this message exactly *where*?"

"In a folded-up stocking. Second drawer of the dresser in Wilson's room."

"Do you have any idea whose handwriting it is?"

"I can guess," Matthew said. He imagined what Professor Fell's thought was upon reading the two lines Minx had forged.

We are being watched. Warn Nash.

In addition to giving Fell a pair of traitors, Matthew had given him a third in the form of Frederick Nash, the corrupt and treasonous member of Parliament.

"I presume that Professor Fell knows whose handwriting it is. I have no idea who 'Nash' might be, but I also presume that the professor knows." Matthew frowned; now was the moment to voice his feigned concern. "What I can't understand, is why the message was written down and not simply passed in speaking? It's a simple enough message, after all. So why risk writing it down?"

"The professor has also wondered this," said Sirki, ominously.

"Yes." Matthew felt the sweat begin to erupt at his temples. But it was a warm day, after all. "The only conclusion I can come to—my educated guess—is that my interaction with Mr. Smythe has caused him to...shall we say...panic. Possibly Wilson intended to burn the message at a later date. Or possibly he intended to show it to this Nash person, as evidence of veracity. You know, it's my experience that desperate men often make desperate mistakes."

"Hm," said Sirki. He waited for more.

"Of course," Matthew continued warily, "there was no reason for Wilson to suspect I'd be entering his room today. But he did have common caution enough to hide the message, which speaks to me of certain guilt."

Sirki said nothing for a while, which did not help Matthew's nerves.

At last the giant spoke. "The professor," he said, "has also come to these conclusions."

Matthew nodded. He was aware how heavy his head felt on the stalk of his neck. "Can I also assume, then, that our business is done?"

"It is done, and successfully so, but there is a complication."

"Oh?" Matthew's stomach had twisted into a knot. "What complication?"

"Your friend Miss Grigsby cannot be found. The search continues, but some of the searchers are beginning to believe she may have stepped off a cliff in the dark and fallen to her death either on the rocks below or in the sea."

"Oh my God!" said Matthew, with an effort.

"If she had stayed where she was placed, she would have been fine. In a few days, you'll be leaving here aboard the *Nightflyer*. The searching will go on, but I fear Miss Grigsby will not be returning with you." Sirki stared solemnly into Matthew's eyes. "To that regard, I am instructed to tell you that another five hundred pounds will be added to your three thousand pound fee. Is that agreeable?"

"For me, yes," Matthew answered with grim determination. "For her grandfather, I'm not so sure."

"The professor regrets your loss. I'm sure you will convey that thought to her grandfather? As for the Ga, he is caged in the lower quarters of this castle. He will be returned to you on the morning of your departure, but not before."

"All right." Matthew was starting to breathe easier again. The forgery had passed its test, and Professor Fell had supplied his own story concerning the message: the frightened scribbling of one traitor to another, implicating a third. "Let me ask…what will be done with Wilson and Smythe?"

"They've already been taken to their own cages. They will be dealt with in a short while. Would you like to serve as a witness?"

"Me? No. I don't care to hear their whimpering lies and denials." Nathan Spade could not have spoken it better, Matthew thought. In truth, he feared that his heart was becoming harder by the moment. "But tell me…what will be done?"

"I will take care of them," said Sirki. "As the professor watches, they will be chained naked to two chairs. Their tongues will be removed first."

"Ah," Matthew said, and then thought he might have sounded too relieved.

"One eye will be scooped from each face and crushed beneath the professor's shoe. Next their sexual organs will be removed and placed into their mouths. Following that, their hands and feet will be sawed off. A slow and delicate operation."

"Tiring for you, I'm sure."

"Very much so," Sirki agreed, without a flicker of expression. "Before they can bleed to death, their arms will be sawed off at the shoulders. Again, it's quite an effort on my part, but the professor appreciates my vigor. If they live very much longer, their legs will be sawed off at the knees."

"By that time," Matthew said, "you should be ready for a long nap."

Sirki allowed himself an evil half-smile. "My blade does most of the work, young sir. I just guide it along. But there *will* be much blood, which makes the grip more challenging. Where was I? Oh… at the end, they will lose their heads and everything will be put into burlap bags and carried down to Agonistes. His pet, I think you've seen. So Mr. Smythe and Mr. Wilson will be consigned to the sea in the form of octopus turds. Are you absolutely certain you don't wish to witness the process?"

"Tempting," said Matthew, "but yes, I am certain."

"Understandable. I am empowered by Professor Fell to tell you that he feels this is a job well-done, and if he is in need of your future problem-solving abilities might he count on you?"

"You mean to find Valeriani for him?"

"The professor made no mention of that," said the giant.

Matthew pondered the moment. He hoped to destroy the gunpowder factory and to be on his way with Berry, Zed, Minx and Fancy to the harbor within twelve hours. He doubted if the professor would feel so grateful to him when all that powder went up. "My place is in New York," Matthew said. "I'd like to be left alone."

Sirki seemed to be deliberating this statement. He went to the door and then paused. "You are aware," he said," that the professor never takes 'no' for an answer."

"I'm aware. But...no."

Sirki bowed his head slightly. "I shall pass that response along. Your payment will be delivered on the morning of your departure, along with the Ga." He offered the faintest of smiles. "I regret not being able to kill him, but sometimes one does not always get what one wishes." With that remark, Sirki opened the door, left the room, and closed the door at his back.

Matthew always felt relief when that huge killer departed his presence, and so he did now. He gave Sirki a few minutes to make some distance, and then he took a cautious sip of the lemon water. Yes...it just seemed to be lemons, after all. He drank the rest of the glass. But now he was in need of food, having missed the mid-day meal, and he went along the corridor and down the stairs in search of a fruitbowl or a basket of muffins and corncakes that were sometimes afforded on the dining room table.

As he was going down the steps to the dining room, he heard a muffled scream from somewhere below.

It went on for a few seconds and then stopped on a strangled note.

Matthew saw that indeed there was a basket of muffins on the table. He was reaching for one when the hollow echo of a second scream rose up seemingly from the floor. It sounded to be from a different throat than the first, but also ended brokenly.

He thought that Nathan Spade had had his revenge, and wherever Spade was he considered Matthew Corbett to be a kindred spirit.

Matthew wasn't certain to be happy or sad about that. But it seemed that in the professor's world one dismembered corpse in a bag begat at least one or two others, and so with the deaths of Smythe and Wilson Fate—and Fell—had been satisfied.

Another scream came up, agonized and pitiful. It died down again, and might have broken the heart of anyone who did not know the history of the screamer.

Matthew decided on the biggest muffin in the basket. He took it and, gratified to find it was studded with chocolate chunks, chewed a big bite from it and then returned to his room to wait for the fall of night. Only behind the locked door did he break out in a cold sweat and suddenly have to lose his few bites of muffin and drink of lemon water in a rush of liquid over the balcony's railing.

TWENTY-NINE

A FTER midnight, when the castle had become tomb-quiet and even the Thackers' bellows silenced, Matthew began to stir.

He left his room with a single stubby taper, walked quietly along the corridor and used the skeleton key to open Smythe's room. Alas, the munitions master was not sleeping in this bed, but rather in the embrace of an octopus's digestive system. He and Adam Wilson now shared the lowest of dwellings. Matthew continued out to the balcony, where he considered the drop of over twenty feet to manicured hedges in the garden. Were there fissures in the stone wall he might get his fingertips into? He shone his light downward. Yes, there appeared to be a few worthy grips, courtesy of years of earth tremors. It was this way or no way because for certain he could not risk the stairs and the front door.

He blew out the candle and put it into his coat pocket along with the tinderbox from his room. Then he eased over the balcony, and with the supple strength of youth and damned determination he began his careful descent along the cracked wall of Fell's castle.

The night's banquet had been another affair of seafood, salacious behavior from the two brothers toward the diminished-looking Fancy, drunken laughter from Sabroso at jokes no one had made, Aria Chillany's body pressing toward Matthew and her breath reeking of fish and wine thanks to his returned ability to smell, Toy feeding Augustus Pons and their whispers and giggles like two schoolgirls sharing secrets, Minx silently eating her food without a glance at anyone in particular, and Mother Deare talking about how good it would be to get started back to England in the next few days. Evidently the group would be travelling on the ship *Fortuna*, another of Fell's fleet of transports. Matthew thought that being cooped up with that bunch for nearly two months would be enough to make him dance down a pirate's plank in a fashion that would win appreciative applause from Gilliam Vincent.

Two chairs had remained vacant at the table. "Where are those fuckers?" Jack Thacker had asked, his eyes bloodshot and whitefish foaming at the corners of his mouth. "Playing with—"

"Their sausages?" Mack finished, after which he tossed back a half-glass of wine so deeply-red it was almost black. Between the brothers, Fancy stared at Matthew for a few seconds, her eyes dark-hollowed and weary, before she looked away. She was like a fine animal that had nearly been broken, Matthew thought. Much more time with the brothers, and she would be used up and withered within. Still he had yet to see her smile or even attempt such. But what was there for her to smile about? If he could only get her alone for a few seconds, to tell her what he was planning...

Mother Deare said, "Mr. Smythe and Mr. Wilson are no longer with us."

"What?" Pons pushed Toy's fork away. "Where are they?"

"The two gentlemen," said Mother Deare, with a passing glance at Matthew, "have been identified as traitors to the professor."

"Them *too*?" Jack's mouth was a ghastly mess. "How many fucking traitors have there been at this party?"

"Too many," Mother Deare replied, with a faint motherly smile. "The situation is now stable."

"I think you should take a look at this one's pockets." Mack jabbed his knife in the direction of Matthew. "Turn 'im upside down and give him a fuckin' good shake."

"Not neccessary." Mother Deare took a dainty sip of wine, her red-gloved hand huge upon the stem. "Mr. Smythe and Mr. Wilson have served their purpose, have been found lacking in loyalty and too prideful in their own powers. They were executed this afternoon. Didn't anyone hear them screaming?"

"I thought it was Pons gettin' his ass jabbed," said Jack, and Mack laughed so hard the wine burst from his nostrils.

"Crude vulgarians," Pons replied, with as much dignity as a fat man with three chins might summon. His eyes were heavy-lidded with disdain. He turned his attention to Mother Deare. "The… removal of Mr. Smythe and Mr. Wilson…quite sudden, it seems. I am to believe that they were both important assets—"

"He said, 'assets,'" Jack chortled, and again his brother guffawed in appreciation of the most simple-minded tavern humor.

"Important elements," Pons went on, "to the professor's operations. For them both to be removed…doesn't that bode ill for future plans?"

"'Bode ill,' he says," was Mack's comment. "Buck can't speak a man's English."

Matthew had reached his fill of this particular meal. "Why don't you two shut up? You look dumber than hell. Quit proving it by speaking."

The expressions on the faces of the Thackers froze. Mack's chin trembled a little bit, as the rage worked on him. Jack sopped a piece of bread in fish sauce and chewed it as if tearing out Matthew's throat with his teeth.

"To answer," said Mother Deare. "Yes, those two men were important. You hear me say 'were.' But there are always other talents in the organization to take their places. You can be sure the professor has planned for that beforehand. I am empowered to be the professor's eyes, voice and hands in London, and to adjust persons into their proper places. To promote, so to speak. And I will perform that task to the best of my ability and for the best of the organization. Thank you for asking."

"Pleasure," said Pons, returning his mouth to Toy's waiting fork.

Matthew continued his crawl down the wall of Fell's castle. His right foot slipped in its search for a crevice, he knew he was in for a tumble so he flung himself off into space and headed for the hedges.

They were fortunately not laden with anything sharp or stickery, and therefore he landed amid them with the most minor of scrapes. Then it was a matter of getting himself unentangled from them, putting his feet on firm ground and heading toward the road. There was a yellow moon just past full, the night held a slight breeze, and Matthew was in his element of silence and stealth.

He was only on his way across the gardens a moment or two when he knew someone was coming toward him from the left: a dark shape though moon-painted, a lithe figure converging upon him with little or no hesitation and a confident stride.

"Are you planning on walking the distance?" Minx asked quietly when she got close enough. She was wearing a hooded cape over her clothes, and again Matthew had to wonder if she had been last night's visitor to his room.

"I suppose that was my plan, yes."

"You need," she said, "a new plan. Starting with a horse. Come with me."

"Going where?"

"Going," she answered, "to break into the stable, saddle our two horses and go do your task of exploding some gunpowder. That *is* the task, correct?"

"It is."

"Then come on, we're wasting time."

"Minx," Matthew said, "you don't have to go with me. I can do this by myself."

"Can you?" Though he couldn't make out her face, he knew her expression would be wry, her blonde brows upraised. "I don't think so. Come along, and you should be grateful I've arrived to save your legs and possibly your neck."

"Two necks can be stretched by a noose the same as one. In fact, I'd imagine we'd *lose* our heads if we're caught."

"I agree. That's why we *shouldn't* be caught." *Dummy*, was her unspoken comment. "Stop wrangling and come along. *Now*."

On the way to the stable, Matthew asked Minx how she'd gotten out of the castle unnoticed, and the reply was: "I walked out the front door and spoke kindly to the servant standing there. I'm sure he thinks I've gone for a solitary stroll. Being unnoticed was not my goal…getting out was. Didn't you leave by the front door?"

"No, I chose a more scenic way."

"Whatever it takes, I suppose. There's the stable ahead. Keep your voice low, we don't want to spook the horses and have them announcing us."

Breaking into the stable was as simple as Minx inserting the business end of a blade into a lock that secured a chain across the doors. The lock was broken, the chain removed, and though the horses within grumbled and stomped their hooves none let out any tell-tale whinnies. Minx and Matthew went to work saddling their mounts of choice, Esmerelda and Athena, and within a few minutes were out of the stable and following their moon-shadows along the road.

"I'm presuming you were smart enough to bring something to light a flame," Minx said.

"A tinderbox and candle, yes."

"I brought the same," she revealed. "Just in case."

"Very kind of you."

Minx was silent for a while, as their horses trotted the road side by side. Then she said, "Perhaps you *are* a bit like Nathan."

"How so?"

"Foolish. Headstrong. A man who dares the Devil, if you want the truth. And who makes others think they can dare the Devil, too." She cast a quick glance at him from under her hood. "I'm not so sure that's a good thing."

"You can always decline the dare," Matthew told her, "and turn back."

"Oh no, there's no turning back. But before I set foot on that ship, I am going to kill Aria Chillany. You can count on that, my friend."

Matthew had no doubt she would at least try. Just as he must try to get Fancy out of the grip of the Thackers, in honor of Walker In Two Worlds. It seemed both he and Minx were daring their own devils today, and what devils they were.

The moon had sunk lower by the time they reached the skull-guarded road. "Not here," said Minx when Matthew started to rein Athena in. He followed Minx perhaps another hundred yards, and then dismounted when she did so. Minx tied Esmerelda's reins to a low shrub and Matthew did the same with Athena's.

"Listen well," Minx whispered as they stood at the edge of the dense thicket that protected Fell's powderworks. "I don't know what's in there. Probably there are men up on watchtowers hidden in the trees. There may be bogs and quicksand. We don't dare show a light. The guards would be on us like blood-hungry ticks. We have to move silently and cautiously, and if one of us gets into trouble there can be no shouting for the sake of both our necks...or heads, as you say. If we are separated and one is captured, there can be no talking even if it means...you know what it would mean."

"I do," said Matthew. His nerves were on edge, but his resolution firm.

"All right. Let's go."

Two words that meant: *this is the point of no return.* Matthew and Minx entered the thicket together, and within sixty seconds were facing a yellow-moonlit wall of leaves and thorns the size of a man's thumbnail, on coiled stalks that snaked out in every direction. They spent some time trying to find a way around this obstruction, and yet had to enter the portion of it that seemed the most penetrable. Even so, it was a torment on the flesh and a hazard on the clothing. Matthew felt that if his coat snagged one more time it would fall in shreds from his shoulders. His stockings were ragged and his legs streaked with blood by the time they reached more hospitable forest, which wasn't saying much. The ground became soggy, held together by massive clumps of tree-roots. Even Minx, for all her sure-footed confidence, tripped and fell into the muck several times, and as the bog deepened Matthew's boots were almost sucked from his feet.

They had to stop and rest, for the exertion of travelling through this sticky slop was extreme. "Ready?" Minx whispered after a few minutes, and Matthew answered that he was. On her next step Minx sank into brackish water nearly waist-deep. She continued on, and Matthew followed with one hand guarding the cotton in his tinderbox from being soaked.

The moon descended. From the trees of this ungodly, fetid swamp there croaked, trilled, shrieked and buzzed the insects of the night. As Minx and Matthew progressed, great bubbles of noxious swamp gas bloomed up beneath them like hideous flowers and made such explosive sounds they feared it would be heard by any listening ear. But no torches showed in the darkness nor were there voices, and the two determined travellers slogged onward.

"Careful," Minx whispered, "there's a snake in the water to your right."

Matthew caught the movement of something over there, but it veered away. One snake seen, probably dozens lurking around their legs underwater. What use was there to think of that? Matthew looked up and could see a few stars through the thick treetops. New York seemed as far away as those. But here he was, waistdeep in muddy filth with snakes aslither around his ankles, likely tasting the blood on his shins. Delightful. What he must concentrate upon was not falling into the water, and keeping the tinderbox dry.

The ground began to rise and the water shallowed. Minx and Matthew got out of the muck onto sandy earth wild again with vegetation, and as Matthew brushed a low tree branch something made a noise like the clicking back of a pistol's hammer and—whether exotic bird or treefrog—the thing jumped for its life into the thicket.

"Stop," Minx whispered, and Matthew instantly obeyed.

She reached out into what appeared to be another wall of vines and thorns. She pulled some of the foliage aside and pressed her hand inward.

"Stones," she said. "We've arrived."

Matthew felt for himself. It was, indeed, the fort's outermost wall. Looking up, nothing could be seen of how high the wall was in the overhang of trees. But all was silent save the croak and hum of frogs and night-sprites, and in the distance the note of a bird making a sound like the fall of an executioner's axe.

Now came the problem of finding a way in, and the problem-solver was in the dark. He followed Minx to the left, her hands entering the vines to search the stones. There were no windows, barred or otherwise, and no gate to be found. At last Minx stopped, pulled on a sturdy-looking vine that snaked down along the wall, and said, "This will have to do."

"I'll go first," Matthew volunteered, and Minx let him. He started up along the vine, which swayed precariously but did not give way. Matthew's boots afforded him traction on the stones, and after a climb of some thirty feet he reached the top and hauled himself over onto a parapet. Minx followed with admirable agility, and together they took stock of where they were.

The parapet was deserted, but a single torch burned in a wooden socket on the left about fifty feet away. Beyond that another fifty feet, a second torch flamed. And on and on, around the fort's huge perimeter. Below them stood several buildings of white stone with roofs of gray slate. Far away, toward the center of the dirt-floored enclosure, was a larger building with a chimney, where the gunpowder's chemicals must be cooked and combined. So far there was no sign of any human occupancy though an occasional torch was set out and burning. Matthew looked for what he thought might be the powder magazine. Over on the right there was a long white building with wooden shutters closed over the windows and, telltale enough, banks of dirt built up about six feet high on both sides to act as blast walls. That would be where the powder was kept until it could be shipped out. But where might the fuses be found? Matthew reasoned there had to be fuses here, as the bombs that had destroyed the buildings in New York were fashioned here and if not directly fitted with fuses in this location, then fuses ought to be on the premises somewhere. Unless they'd been made aboard the *Nightflyer*, but Matthew thought the raw materials must be stored here in a safe place. The question being: exactly where? It had taken him and Minx over two hours to cross the thicket and swamp to reach the fort. They were quite simply pressed for time, as the *Nightflyer* would fly at first light with or without them.

Minx said, "I want you to wait here."

"Wait *here*? Why?"

"In this case," she answered, "one is better than two. I can move faster than you. Trust me when I say...you will do better to let me be your..." She frowned under her hood, searching for the words.

"Providence rider?" Matthew supplied.

"Whatever that means. You stay *here*. I'm going to find out where the guards are."

"You can do that and I can't?"

"I can do that," she said, "without getting us both killed. *Stay,*" she said, and then she turned away and strode purposefully off along the parapet.

Matthew eased down on his haunches alongside the wall. This was a damnable thing to let her take such a risk, he thought; yet he had the feeling Minx Cutter was perfectly capable of getting in and out of places he could not, and it might be the ungentlemanly act to let her go alone but it was probably the most sensible.

He waited, listening to the night and watching the torches flicker in the same breeze that stirred the forest's treetops.

He waited longer, and sat down on the stones.

After what seemed like twenty minutes he decided he could wait no more. He was keenly aware of the passing time and the lowering moon, and if Minx had been caught he was going to have to do something about that. He stood up and started along the parapet in the direction she'd gone, and in another moment he came to a stone staircase leading down. He descended to the dirt floor, passed two empty wagons, and continued on beneath a stone archway into an area not quite fully revealed by any torchlight. He moved through a territory of shadows with his back against a wall. It seemed to him his back had been against a wall now for many months. His heart was beating hard and the air felt oppressive. He could smell the bitter tang of chemicals and cooking vats. He came to a corner and paused, peered around and found the way forward clear and so he started off again. He passed under another archway and on between two stone walls leading him somewhere though he had no idea where.

And just that fast, a figure turned the corner before him, took two strides in his direction before he realized Matthew was there and then stopped.

"Who are you?" the man asked.

"I'm new here," was all Matthew could think to say, stupidly.

"The hell you are." A wooden whistle was lifted to the man's mouth.

Before Matthew could kick the man either in the stomach or the groin, which he was considering, there came a solid-sounding *thunk* and the man shivered like a leaf in a high wind. The whistle dropped from his hand, to hang about his neck on a leather cord. The man took another step toward Matthew and then his knees crumpled. As the body toppled forward, Matthew saw the hatchet buried in the back of the man's head.

Minx Cutter was standing behind the now-fallen guard. She put a foot on the man's back and pulled the hatchet loose. The man thrashed on the ground as if trying to swim through the dirt, and Minx hit him again in the right temple just behind the ear.

This time he was still.

"I *told* you," Minx said as she pulled the weapon free, "not to leave there, didn't I?"

"Yes, but I was concerned about you."

"Hm," she said, and she put the blood-wet hatchet's blade up under Matthew's nose. "I entered the professor's employ as an assassin. I killed three men before I decided the job wasn't to my liking. Lyra Sutch trained me for that role. She was as near a mother to me as I could find after my family threw me out." The blade dripped blood upon Matthew's shirt. "I understand you killed Lyra, who helped me grow from a confused girl into a confident woman."

Matthew said nothing; he could not say that at the end of Lyra Sutch's life she was a wretched, demented sack of broken bones and axe-torn flesh.

"But," said Minx, as she lowered the hatchet, "I'm all grown up now. And you are an impatient and foolish milksop." Her left arm emerged from the folds of her cape. Wrapped around the wrist were several gray cotton cords. "I found a storehouse unguarded and unlocked. The hatchet came from there. Also these three fuses, from a crate. The longest should give us fifteen minutes, the shortest about six. Or they can be knotted together as one."

"Excellent," said Matthew, who still had the coppery smell of blood up his nostrils.

"I doubt the magazine will be so easy to get into. I've seen four other guards making their rounds, but they're in no hurry and they've gotten lazy. There's a barracks building where the workers must be sleeping. The professor has done us the great favor of not making his men work all night long like slaves."

"Christian of him," said Matthew.

"Sharpen your blade," she said, correctly judging that Matthew's senses were reeling due to her cold-blooded killing of the guard and her revelation of past mutual acquaintances. She knelt down and went through the dead man's pockets, presumably searching for keys to the magazine. She came up empty, and stood up. Her gaze was both fierce and frigid. Looking upon her frightened Matthew to his core. "You should follow me," she said, and she set off to the left without waiting for him to exit his trance.

The first step was difficult. The second a little easier. Then he was following her, and Minx continued on looking right and left but never glancing back.

They came to the magazine, the long building of white stone with the gray slate roof. A distant torch gave enough light to fall upon two locks on the door. Minx broke one with her knife's blade, but the second resisted her. She told him, "Keep watch!" as she struggled with the more intricate mechanism. *"Damn,"* she said through gritted teeth, when it still defied her. "Hold this," she commanded, and she gave him the bloody hatchet the better to concentrate on her lock-breaking.

Matthew heard the voices of two men raised in conversation. It was coming from somewhere off to the left. There was a bray of laughter; something obviously had hit one's funny bone. Minx continued her task as Matthew turned himself in the direction of the voices. He could see no one, but the men seemed to be coming closer. Minx's blade worked at the lock, the sharp tip digging at the stubborn innards. *Hurry,* he wished to say, but she knew what she was doing. The knife jabbed, the voices came closer still, and Matthew thought he might have to kill someone with this hatchet, to burden his soul further with death.

But then the men took a turn away from the magazine, for the voices began to diminish, and a moment afterward there came a metallic *click* and Minx whispered, "Ah. Got the bastard." The lock fell to the ground. Minx pulled a latch and pushed the door open.

It was utterly dark within. She took the hatchet from him and said, "Light your tinderbox."

Matthew took a moment fumbling with the thing. He got a spark in the wads of cotton and from that touched the wick of his candle. He looked to her with apprehension, wondering if the merest flame in that enclosure would set off the powder, but she motioned him in and he gathered his balls from where they'd shrivelled up into his groin and crossed the magazine's threshold.

She closed the door behind them. "Impressive," she said, as Matthew's candlelight showed barrel upon barrel of—presumably—Professor Fell's Cymbeline. Matthew counted fifteen just in the realm of the light, and beyond it were dozens more. A shipment must be imminent, he thought. The place looked to be nearly full.

He hadn't realized he was holding his breath. He had the same feeling of dangerous pressure as he'd experienced upon the stone seahorse. If two small Cymbeline bombs could have blown that house on Nassau Street to splinters, what would dozens of barrels of the powder do?

"I'm counting sixty-two," Minx said. "I hope you're ready for a brilliant bang."

He let his breath out, thinking that he'd already had one of those last night.

Minx strode toward the first barrel. She lifted her hatchet and quite readily bashed in the top of it with three blows. Matthew winced at the noise; surely that was going to bring someone running. Then Minx put her shoulder into it, overturned the barrel, and light grayish-white grains began to stream out upon the dirt. She repeated this action with a second barrel, and again the gunpowder poured out of it onto the earth. "I think," she said, "that will be enough." She uncoiled two of the cotton cords from her wrist and placed them in the grains of destruction, stretching them out toward the door.

"Light them," she suggested, sweat sparkling on her cheeks.

Matthew bent down, picked up the end of one fuse and touched the candle to it. His hand was trembling, but at once the red eye opened and the fuse began to sizzle. He did the same to the second. The nitrate-saturated cord began to burn steadily toward its target. There would not be time nor opportunity to destroy the actual chemical works, but no doubt this would be a monstrous explosion and might serve to blast everything in the fort to pieces.

"Now," said Minx, with just a trace of nerves in her voice, "we get out."

They closed the door and latched it behind them, just for the sake of tidiness. Then Matthew was following Minx as she ran the way they'd come, seeking the stairway to the parapet. There were no guards in view, but no time for undue caution. They were both aware that very soon a little part of Hell would open on Pendulum Island.

Once up the steps, they sought the vine that had brought them here. It was like searching for a peg in a haystack. Everything from this height looked flimsy, unable to support either of them. In a few minutes they would have to learn how to fly.

"Hey!" someone shouted, from ahead. "You there!" For the want of anything else, the guard began to blow his whistle and then he came at a run toward them with a drawn sword.

His run was stopped by a knife that entered the pit of his throat, thrown from a distance of nearly twenty feet. He gagged and grasped at the knife's handle to pull it out, but then he was staggering off the edge of the parapet like a clumsy drunk and he toppled into the darkness below.

Another voice, further away, began shouting for someone named—it sounded like—Curland. Minx leaned over the parapet, seeking a way down. Matthew looked back toward the magazine. If the guards got in there, they might yet stomp out the fuses. "I'm here!" he shouted toward the other shouter, just to confuse the issue. "This way!"

"We've got to go over," Minx said, and now her voice did quaver for even her tough spirit quailed at the thought of those fuses burning down to their merry damnation. "Right here," she told him, and motioned toward thick vines and leafy vegetation that had melded to the stones. Without hesitation she swung herself over the wall, gripped hold of whatever her fingers could find, and started down.

Matthew caught a movement to his left. A heavy-set man carrying a torch was coming up the steps. The gent looked big enough to be a match for Sirki. Minx was almost to the ground. Matthew couldn't wait. He climbed over, grasped vines and leaves and found places to put his boot-toes into. Halfway down there was a cracking sound and Matthew felt the vines start to pull away from the stones. At the same time the man with the torch leaned over the wall and thrust the flame at him to get a better look.

"The magazine!" the man suddenly shouted over his shoulder. Matthew saw that horror had rippled across the craggy face. "My God! Check the magazine!"

Matthew reached the ground with help from the vines pulling away from the stones. Minx was already slogging into the swamp. Matthew followed her, thinking that if the guards put those fuses out all this had been for nothing. The water rose up past his knees, then over his thighs to his waist, and snakes be damned. He heard shouting from the fort, which filled him with fresh alarm. *Damn it!* he thought. *The fuses should have burned down by now! Where was the—*

His thought was never finished. It was knocked from his head by the roar of a thousand lions mixed with the shriek of five-hundred harpies and carried along by the burning breath of sixty dragons on the wing, and he was thrown insensible into the muddy drink, sinking down into the realm where the reptiles coiled and twisted safe from the evils that men did.

THIRTY

A HAND gripped the back of Matthew's coat and jerked him up from the water. He sputtered and coughed, spewing liquid from mouth and nostrils. Night had turned to day, and he had to squint against its glare. Hot winds rushed through the swamp, bending trees and tearing leaves loose in green flurries.

"Keep moving!" Minx shouted, for shouting was the only way to be heard above this symphony of the cataclysm. She, too, had taken a spill into the soup. Her face and the curls of her hair were darkened by muddy slime. She started off and pulled Matthew along as he fought to find his balance.

He looked back and saw nothing but white flashes and red centers of flame. It appeared as if the main wall of the fort had been blasted down. The Cymbeline's thunder was deafening; Matthew's ears rang like seventeen Sabbath bells and he could feel the continuing detonations in the pit of his stomach. He saw something on fire fly up into the air, and then it too exploded with a bone-jarring report and a flash that nearly burned the eyes blind. Another object rose up, burning, and also exploded in the ash-swirled sky. The barrels, he thought. Some were being blown out of the magazine and detonating overhead. A rain of pieces of flaming wood and chunks of scorched stone was falling around them, splashing heavily into the swamp. "Move! Move!" Minx shouted, up against his ear so he could hear her above the din.

He did not have to be told a third time.

He staggered on, as birds flew for their lives from burning branches. Minx slipped and fell and he pulled her up as she had saved him. A flaming barrel came down on the left and blew trees up from their roots and a geyser of water when it exploded. Part of the thicket over on that side was already burning, and still the barrels were coming down to blast their Cymbeline across the tortured landscape. The heated winds blew back and forth and the shockwaves knocked Matthew and Minx hither and yon as if they were made of flimsy paper. Gray smoke whipped across this battlefield. Perhaps twenty yards ahead of the struggling pair they caught sight of something hanging in the upper branches of a burning tree that might have been a human torso, black as a fistful of coal.

More explosions ravaged the night. The barrel bombs were flying, some to blast their flaming innards overhead and others to crash into the swamp and forest before they detonated. The noise was like the collision of three armies using triple-mouthed cannons, firing in confusion to the north, south, east and west. Another massive blast and belch of red fireballs rose up from the wrecked fort, and suddenly part of a burning wagon came crashing down in front of Minx and Matthew so close their eyebrows were singed.

"This way!" Minx shouted, and grasping his arm she guided him at an angle to the left. He realized she was looking for the road to get them out of this fiery morass, and he followed her gladly and yet still a bit woozy in the head.

They sloshed through the muck with flaming comets whirling overhead and the thunder of explosions making the earth shiver. Matthew looked toward the fort and saw nothing but a pall of smoke with red fires burning within. *Good*, he thought. If the chemical works was not totally destroyed, the next shipment of Cymbeline surely was. And there had to be enough damage in there to make rebuilding a costly and time-consuming task. *Good,* he thought again, and narrowly missed getting tangled in thornbranches that had a snake coiled amid the stickers.

They came out upon the road after what seemed a trek of fifteen or twenty minutes. Was the first shade of light showing to the east? It was hard to tell, for Matthew's eyes were still dazzled. Fires growled and crackled here and there amid the thicket, burning underbrush and trees.

"Can you hear me?" Minx shouted at him, and he nodded. Her face was both stained with mud and ruddy with heat. She stared back for a few seconds at the smoke-covered fort, her eyes glittering with wild emotion between terror and exhilaration.

It was Matthew, then, who first saw the two men with torches stagger onto the road before them. One held a cutlass with a chopping blade about fourteen inches in length. Both men were bloodied by scrapes and cuts, their clothes dirty and dishevelled. Matthew's first thought was that they had been atop a watchtower that the blast's winds had knocked to the ground; they looked more fearful than fearsome, yet the sword meant business.

"What happened?" the man in the lead demanded. It was a foolish question, so he asked another: "What are you doing here?"

Minx regarded the men with a tight smile. "What do you think, you idiot? We blew the place to pieces."

"What?"

"You don't get anymore questions," she said, as she reached into her waistcoat for the second knife that was hidden there.

The swordsman took a step forward to strike at Minx, who brought the blade out and started to throw it, but in the next instant all thoughts of edged combat were ended.

The ground shook under their feet.

It was not just a tremor. It was a side-to-side motion that made true the name of Pendulum Island. It was so severe both the two men and Matthew and Minx were knocked to their knees, and in the eerie stillness of its aftermath there was a shrill keening of wind whipping through the trees and in the distance the urgent howling of dogs.

With the second agony of the earth, a crack winnowed along the road and engulfed a shower of gravel and crushed oyster shells.

The man with the sword gave a bleat of terror. He struggled up, dropping his cutlass and torch, and ran along the road in the direction of Templeton, perhaps to see to a wife and child. The second man sat on his knees for a moment more, stunned and blinking, and then he too stood up and, following his torchlight, began to shakily walk away from Matthew and Minx as if strolling through a dreamscape. Or rather, a nightmare, for he hadn't gotten very far where there was a ghastly low rumble of stones grinding together in the troubled guts of the island and he was whipsawed down again as the ground shifted under his boots. This time the shaking went on for perhaps six seconds, an eternity, and when it was over the man stood up again and continued determinedly walking away until his torchlight was only a faint glow.

Minx got to her feet, and so did Matthew. Her voice was choked with tension when she said, "We've got to—"

"Yes," he answered, for the devil's breakfast was being served early this day. He picked up the swordsman's fallen torch and cutlass, thinking that both might be useful in the hours ahead.

They reached the end of the road, where the skulls had hung before the earth's shaking had dislodged them, and they spent some time retracing their path and searching for the horses that had obviously torn loose from their moorings and were no longer there. They had no opportunity to go to Falco's house; either the captain was already getting the *Nightflyer* in order, or he was not. Matthew was betting his life, and the lives of others, on Falco being true to his word. They therefore began walking toward Templeton as quickly as they could manage, and both noted the fissures—some the width of a hand—that had opened in the road. From time to time small tremors shook the earth, and it was clear to Matthew that the blast of Cymbeline had awakened the foul spirits of Pendulum's past.

In Templeton, the town was illuminated by the blaze of torches and the street was crowded with citizens if not fully terrified then well on the way. Here and there a brave soul tried to calm the throng, but there was the sense of entrapment on an island doomed by its own history. Wagons were pulling out, loaded with family belongings, on the way to the local harbor wherever that might be. Minx motioned Matthew over to a wagon that was for the moment abandoned by its owner, and within another thirty seconds she was cracking a whip over the team's heads and the horses were carrying herself and the providence rider away from Templeton toward the castle of Professor Fell.

The moon sat on the horizon. Early light stained the eastern sky. Minx's whip was urgent. The castle came into view, also torch-lit. Matthew clutched his own torch and the sword, and he was thinking furiously that he might have to slash some Thacker flesh to get Fancy loose from their grip.

They pulled up in front to find the entry unguarded. The tremors obviously had sent the servants off to tend to their own families. Matthew saw fresh cracks in the white columns of the porte-cochere. Minx dropped the reins and drew her remaining knife, for she had business this morning with Aria Chillany.

Augustus Pons, Toy and Cesar Sabroso were in the candle-lit foyer, wearing their night clothes and expressions of terrified bewilderment. "What's happening out there?" Pons asked the two arrivals as they went past to the staircase. He had seen the sword and the knife and their swamp-dirtied clothes, and he added to this question another query in the voice of a frightened child: "Is it safe?"

"No," Minx said. "It is definitely *not* safe. Where is Madam Chillany?"

"Upstairs. All the way to the third floor. She and the Thackers."

"And Fancy?" Matthew asked.

"With them. They were going to the library's balcony for a view. Something exploded. Didn't you hear it?"

"Yes," Matthew said, his hearing still an issue of bells ringing. "We did hear it."

"The whole place *shook*," said Toy. His eyes were huge. "It was like the end of the world."

"For some," Minx said, like a grim promise. With candlelight glinting from the blade of her knife, she started up the stairs two at a time with Matthew at her heels. Matthew saw that a number of fissures had appeared in the staircase wall, and the stained-glass window depicting Temple with his bloody and haunted eyes had collapsed upon the risers as so much meaningless debris. Before they reached the top, another tremor made the castle groan like a sick old man in an uneasy sleep, and somewhere in the walls there was a pistolshot *crack* of stones breaking under God's own pressure.

Matthew figured only the Thackers would be stupid enough to get to the highest balcony of Fell's castle while an earthquake was in progress. Madam Chillany was obviously still addled in the head from the doctor's loss of head. As Minx pushed open the pair of polished oakwood doors, Matthew found exactly what he knew must be happening: the Thackers in rumpled clothing, drinking from the bottles of wine and spirits that had been replenished on the table, and Fancy in a dark green gown standing between them, staring through the open balcony doors at the somber gray light that advanced upon the sea.

"Oh ho!" said Jack, wavering on his feet with a bottle tipped to his lips.

"Boyo," Mack added, sitting sprawled upon one of the black leather chairs with a bottle in one hand and another on the floor beside him. Obviously neither brother turned away the opportunity to drink, even at the end of the world.

Matthew noted that the shaking of Castle Fell had dislodged a few dozen volumes from their shelves. The treasures lay underfoot. They had been trampled on by Thacker boots, for ripped pages and torn bindings were in evidence like so many wounded soldiers.

"Where is Aria Chillany?" Minx demanded.

"Was here," said Mack.

"Ain't now," said Jack.

"I have to find her," she told Matthew. "I have to finish it for *him*. Do you understand?"

Matthew nodded. "I can handle this. Go. But for God's sake be—"

"I am always careful," she interrupted. "For my own sake." Then she turned and left the library, and he was in company with the two animals and the young woman he must set free from their grasp. "Didn't you hear that blowup?" Jack asked. "Place shook like a whore with the crabs." His bleary eyes aimed toward the cutlass. "What the fuck are you up to? No good?"

"Actually," Matthew replied, "I am up to *good*. I am leaving this island within the hour, and I'm taking *her* with me." He motioned with the torch at the Indian girl, who had turned toward him. She was expressionless, her beautiful face perfectly composed. Her raven's-black hair moved slightly with the breeze that came through the balcony's entrance. She was waiting, and she knew he was not leaving without her.

"Damn," said Jack. He shook his head. His smile was bitter. "You are one piece of work, Spadey."

"My name is not Nathan Spade. I am Matthew Corbett, and I want you to remember who bested you."

That statement caused a shock of silence. Then, slowly, Mack stood up one of the bottles in his hand. The flesh seemed to have drawn more tightly over his facial bones and his eyes glittered. "Corbett, ya little shit...I say...you ain't takin' Fancy nowhere..."

"...boyo," Jack finished, with a gritting of his teeth.

"Will you come over here, please?" Matthew asked the girl.

With that, Mack Thacker broke the bottle on the table's edge. Gripping the back of Fancy's neck he put the jagged edges to the side of her face. She winced, but otherwise did not move.

"Come take her," he said. "'Cause in another minute, she ain't gonna be good for nobody."

And so saying, the younger Thacker began to draw the broken glass across the beautiful girl's cheek and the blood welled up bright and red.

Jack snorted a laugh. The girl shivered, her sad gaze on Matthew; one hand pushed weakly against Mack's arm, but she had seemingly come to the end of her rope and was all played out.

Matthew gripped torch and cutlass and stepped forward to the fight.

❖

Minx Cutter knew which door belonged to Madam Chillany's room. She knocked on it, waited for the knob to turn, and then she kicked it as hard as she could kick.

The door flew open and Aria Chillany fell backward into the room, toppling over a white-upholstered chair. Minx walked in, taking note that the other woman was fully dressed in a gray gown and upon the bed was a bag she'd been packing. It appeared Madam Chillany had been about to leave the castle, possibly to find any safer place she could. By the eight tapers of the overhead chandelier cracks had appeared in the walls and chunks of plaster had fallen from the ceiling.

"What's wrong with you?" Aria sat up, rubbing a bloodied lip bitten by a tooth. "Are you *insane?*" Then she caught sight of the knife.

"No, not insane. Just determined. Madam Chillany," Minx said, "I'm going to kill you."

"*What?*"

"Kill you," Minx repeated. "For murdering my Nathan."

There was a harsh inrush of breath.

"Yes," came the reply to that statement. "Nathan was my lover. My *love*," she clarified. "You killed him. Matthew told me so."

"*Matthew?* What..."

"No more time for lies. Stand up and take this in your black heart."

Aria Chillany came up off the floor. Her eyes were wild. With a sweeping motion she grasped the leather handle of the bag on the bed and swung it at Minx, who stepped back out of its way. Then Aria's hand went into the bag and came out with a short but deadly blade of her own, and flinging the bag at Minx she followed it with her body and the knife flailing at the other woman's face.

≫•≪

"Come on, boyo," Mack Thacker taunted, as the broken glass sliced Fancy's cheek. Matthew strode toward him with the sword upraised, and suddenly Jack Thacker threw his bottle at Matthew's head and instead hit his left shoulder as Matthew dodged aside. Then Jack gave a strangled cry of rage and, his face swollen with blood, rushed across the room at Matthew.

Fancy—the pretty girl who had sat alone for so very long—came to life. She grasped Mack's arm and sank her teeth into his hand, and he shouted in pain and grabbed a handful of her hair. The broken glass lodged against her throat. She kicked into his shin and tore loose from him, as brother Jack collided with Matthew and fought him for both the sword and the torch. A knee rose to smash into Matthew's groin and the orange-haired head thrust forward to bust against Matthew's skull, but Matthew avoided the blows he'd known were coming and swung Jack away from him with the strength of desperation.

"Kill him! Kill him!" Mack hollered, as the Indian girl leaped upon his back and locked an arm around his throat from behind. He flung her off and came at Matthew with the broken bottle.

But before Mack could reach him Pendulum Island, in its agonized throes, shifted once more. This time the library's planked floor shook beneath their feet like—as Toy had said—the end of the world. There was a cracking noise like the bones of a behemoth being broken to pieces. Something deep in the guts of the castle made a hollow ringing noise like an exotic gong. The balcony windows shattered. The faces of the cherubs in the ceiling's clouds fell away, exposing ugly gray plaster. Matthew was knocked to his knees and both brothers skittered to the floor. The torch rolled away from his fingers, setting fire to the scattered volumes.

And then the truly horrific happened, for in this quaking of tormented earth the very foundation of Fell's castle was loosened, the seams of broken stone could not hold, and suddenly the entire library room pitched at a twenty-degree angle toward the cliff's edge and the sea below and the books flew off the shelves like the flapping of paper bats.

Matthew, the Thacker brothers and the fallen Fancy slid along the crooked floor through the battlefield of burning books. The balcony itself began to split away from its stone bindings with the noise of small cannon fire and plummet piece by piece into the ocean. The window curtains were whirled away and downward as if into a vortex, but they snagged in the hanging balustrade. Fell's castle had become a construction of torn parchment and forgeries, for all its strength against the earthquake. The gray morning became an open mouth ready to swallow Matthew, the Thackers and Fancy. Matthew saw the remaining stone seahorse topple down on its last ride. The library's furniture and burning books tumbled around the sliding figures, and the problem-solver from New York reached for the bloodied Fancy as she scrabbled for a grip on the splintered planks. He caught her right arm with his left hand, but together they were going over the edge.

➤·◄

When the worst of the earthquake hit, Minx Cutter and Aria Chillany were locked in combat. They staggered around the room, grasping at each other's knife hands and trying to get their own blades free. As the floor heaved and the walls cracked, their battle did not falter for death had entered the room and must be satisfied.

Madam Chillany spat into Minx's eyes and tried to trip her but Minx was too nimble for that. They kicked at each other as the deadly blades were checked in stalemate. Then Minx drove her enemy backward against the dresser so hard the breath burst from Aria's lungs and pain stitched her face. Aria pushed back with frantic strength and tried to wrench her knife hand free, but Minx had it gripped. With a scream of rage Madam Chillany took the risk of releasing Minx's wrist to scratch at the gold-hued eyes and drew blood across the cheekbone. The knife came at her, a wild and unaimed blow, and grazed Aria's shoulder.

Then the two women separated and, as Fell's castle groaned and shrieked in its agonies, they searched for an opening the better to stab the other to death.

✦•✦

Matthew used the cutlass.

He got his boots turned to give himself some friction on the floor, and with the strength of the damned he chopped the sharp edge into one of the floor planks. With the other hand he held onto Fancy, stopping their slide toward the hanging ruins of the balcony and the sea below.

Then a weight grasped his ankles and nearly broke his arm from its socket as he held onto the sword's leather grip. Matthew looked backward to see the sweating red visage of Jack Thacker as the thug crawled up over his legs. Mack had caught himself on an edge of broken plank and had hold of one of Jack's ankles. For a moment Matthew thought his spine would break as the weight pulled on him, and he was near losing his grip on the cutlass. The sweat had burst out like a mist around his face. He was close to letting go... he feared he couldn't take the weight an instant more, his shoulder was about to be pulled from its socket and the cutlass was starting to work free.

Fancy kicked Mack in the face with a sturdy shoe. She did it a second time and then a third and a fourth, into the nose and mouth. Mack's features became rearranged. He spat out a mouthful of blood and a couple of broken teeth and reached with one arm for Fancy's legs to pin them. She squirmed away from him and kicked him once more, in the throat, as he flailed at her. He made a garbled, hideous noise that sounded like *Brother* spoken from the depths of despair, and then he blinked heavily and wearily as he lost his grip on Jack's legs and slid away, through the fiery pages of torn books, through the glitter of broken glass from the windows, and out upon the tilted balcony.

"*Brother!*" Jack screamed in response, the voice of human agony.

Mack Thacker gripped hold of one of the curtains that hung from the balustrade. He swung back and forth for a moment, as much a pendulum as Fell's island. Then he was betrayed by the bitch called Fate, perhaps a female he had alternately wooed and scorned during the course of his dissolute life. She had the last laugh, for the curtain tore and with his fingers still locked in the fabric Mack fell toward the sea trailing a piercing cry. Upon his head followed several pieces of stone balusters, a nasty conking to be had while broken-toothed, bloody-mouthed and throat-mangled.

"*Brother!*" Jack called again, and Matthew saw tears burst from the dazed green eyes.

But then the elder Thacker righted his senses and refound his rage, and he began to crawl up Matthew's back as the cutlass quivered on the edge of breaking loose.

⇥⇤

Aria Chillany grasped a handful of Minx's hair and flung her back against a fissured wall. This time the breath burst from Minx's lungs, and then Aria came at her with the knife. Minx had forgotten that Aria's usefulness to Professor Fell also involved murder, and perhaps she too had been trained in the bloody arts by Lyra Sutch. The knife flashed out and caught Minx's waistcoat as she twisted aside, but she could feel the blade kiss her ribs. Then Minx struck out but Aria had already retreated. When the women came together again it was a blurred and confused battle of life and death, all artistry of knives forgotten and nothing in its place but the savagery of survival.

Aria's blade rose up and slashed. A cut streaked across Minx's forehead. She countered with a strike into Madam Chillany's left shoulder that brought forth a shrill cry of pain. Then they were flailing and staggering, striking at each other as best they could. Aria's teeth snapped at Minx's left ear and then sought the flesh of her cheek. Minx hit the other woman in the jaw with her free hand and as Aria fell back she stepped forward into another swing of Madam Chillany's blade that missed opening her throat by a half-inch.

The chill madam's eyes flashed with murder, as blood stained her mouth. She feinted once, twice and then drove in again when Minx tried to counter the second move. Instead of retreating, Minx measured Aria's stride and also stepped forward, bringing her knife up for the blow. They crashed together, Aria's blade seeking an eye but instead slicing a cut across Minx's left cheek and into the hairline, and they spun around in a mad circle for a few seconds like dancers at a bedlam ball.

Minx knew.

She felt her adversary falter. Felt her legs start to give way. And then the circle of the death dance ceased, and Aria stared at Minx with a yellowed face, her mouth opening in a gasp of shock. The sapphire eyes moved to look down upon the knife that had found her heart, and the blood that was streaming out upon the gray gown.

Minx twisted it.

Just because she could.

Aria's knife rose up in a trembling hand, to thrust itself into the hollow of Minx's throat.

Before it could find its target Minx reached up and grasped the wrist, and she said in a rasping voice, "You are done."

Aria smiled thinly. She spat bloody foam into Minx's face.

And then Madam Chillany's eyes began to recede into their sockets, and in another few seconds she was just a dead woman who had not yet given up her soul to that which waited on the other side of the partition. Minx let her wrist go. The knife fell free to the floor. Minx placed her hand underneath Madam Chillany's chin and pushed her backward off the cliff of life. But she left the blade in her heart for good measure.

⇻⭰

Jack was a nimble climber. He came up over Matthew's back and hooked an arm around the throat, at the same time clawing at Matthew's eyes.

"You bastard," said Fancy, and some certainty in her voice made Jack look at her. In time to see the torch she had stretched for and retrieved from the floor smash itself into his face. "Lick this," she told him.

Sparks flew around Matthew's head and bit his scalp. He heard some of his own hair crisp. Heard also Jack Thacker's scream as the torch flamed his eyes out and seared his lips like pieces of grilled beef. Then Jack's arm was off Matthew's neck and his fingers were tending to his own blinded orbs, and with a shrug of his shoulders Matthew pushed the remaining Thacker brother off his body and away. Matthew looked back as the Irish rowdy slid down onto the sagging balcony, Jack's face scorched red under the orange hair with the sprig of gray in it and the swollen eyes sealed shut. With a cry that might have been both pain and defiance Jack went over the edge, and as he went the rest of the balcony crumbled after him with a similar noise. As a last comment upon the life and death of Jack Thacker, Pretty Girl Who Sits Alone flung the torch toward his watery grave.

THIRTY-ONE

OLD on," Matthew said. He could smell his own sweat and burned hair. He felt a hundred years old, but now was not the time to give in nor give up. He had said this because he felt, also, the hand of Pretty Girl Who Sits Alone trying to open the fingers that had seized her arm.

"Matthew," she said quietly, tasting the name for the first time.

He tightened his grip both on her and the cutlass. Above them the ceiling of clouds and cherubs had begun to resemble a ravaged Hell rather than the repose of Heaven. Around them the burning books flamed and at any other moment Matthew might have wept for them.

"I can't go home," she said, quieter still.

"We can get up there." Matthew saw places in the splintered planks that might serve as hand and foot-holds to climb up to the door. The ceiling was beginning to fall in. The clouds were heavier than they looked. Time was quickly running out, for tremors still disturbed the cracked walls and tilted floor. "Come on," he said. "We have to go."

"No," she said. "That way is for you, not for me."

He peered into her face. The blood crawled along her cheek, but she seemed neither to notice nor care; her soul had already turned away from the flesh that contained it.

"We're both going up," he vowed, aware that it was only a matter of seconds before either the ceiling collapsed upon them or the cutlass's blade pulled loose.

"I came to your room," said the girl, "to give you the only gift I could. Now I need you to give me a gift. Let me go, Matthew."

"I won't. No."

"You must. I want to go dreaming now. I want to wash myself clean. Don't you understand?"

"You're *alive!*" he said.

But she shook her head, sadly still.

"No," she answered, "I am not."

And he did understand. He hated the understanding of it, but he did. She was part of nature, had been defiled and debased, and she wished to return to what she had been. Perhaps her feeling about death was completely contrary to his...or perhaps she just believed in a better afterlife than he. Whatever, he knew she wanted this gift...and yet...how could he open his fingers and give it to her?

"There's a ship waiting." He prayed to God it was still waiting, for the gray light was strengthening and the first ruddy glow had appeared to paint the waves. The sweat was on his face, his shoulders and back were cramping, and he couldn't hold this position much longer. To emphasize the danger and lack of time, a piece of the ceiling as big as a kettle crashed down upon the tilted floor a few feet beyond the girl.

"It waits for you," she answered, her face calm, her eyes soft and yearning for peace.

"No," he said. "No, we're both going."

"Matthew...whoever you are, and whatever you are...you must know that being free means...I make my own choice."

"The wrong choice."

"*Mine,*" she said.

Her fingers began to work again, at his. Hers were strong. She stared into his face as she worked, and he resisted. Yet as his fingers were pushed away, he began not to try so very hard.

"I will find him," she said. "I will tell him about you. He will be very glad to hear."

"Who?" Matthew asked.

"You know," she told him, and then Pretty Girl Who Sits Alone smiled.

And slid away.

As she went toward the edge she turned her body, and Matthew saw her go into the air as if diving into a new life, one he could not possibly understand. She went silently and beautifully, even as he cried out as if struck to the heart. Which he was.

She disappeared in a billow of dark green, like an arrow returning to a forest unknown. And perhaps her forest did lie beyond the blue silence of the deep, and in that awesome place beyond the comprehension of Matthew Corbett she would return to who she had been, proud and innocent and clean.

He did weep. Not for the burning books and the ideas of men that flew away on their wings of ash, but for the Indian girl who had just taken flight from this world to the next.

"Climb up! *Hurry!*"

Matthew looked up toward the door. Minx Cutter stood there, with a bloodied piece of bedsheet pressed to her forehead. Another cut on her left cheek leaked red. She wavered on her feet, her strength nearly gone. Matthew reasoned that Aria Chillany had gone to a reunion with Jonathan Gentry, which would be her small and nasty room in the diseased mansion of Hell. It appeared to him that Minx was holding herself up with willpower alone, and on that account she was a formidable figure.

"Climb *up!*" she repeated, urgency in her voice, as various sounds of cracking stone came from the walls and ceiling. Another large chunk fell, to Matthew's right. White dust powdered the air. It was time to get out of here, and quickly.

The first reach was the most dangerous. He had to let go of the cutlass and grip the edge of a splintered plank. Then he started up using similar hand-and-foot holds that were precarious at best. When he got near enough to Minx she leaned down and grasped his outstretched hand, and pulled him up into the warped corridor.

"The bag of gold," Matthew told her. She already had gone to her room to get the forged orders for the release of the *Nightflyer*, complete with the professor's octopus stamp, but it was doubtful such a paper would be needed today. The staircase was still intact, though the ceiling was falling to pieces, and on the second floor Matthew took a moment to enter his room—its floor crooked and the left wall partially collapsed—and retrieve the moneybag, which he shoved into his shirt. He realized then that the room to the left of his, though it had a balcony the same as his own, was not really a room and had been empty, according to the map he'd been given. The collapsed wall revealed another staircase curving down. It had to be, he realized, the stairway to Professor Fell's domain. Not by happenstance had Matthew been given the quarters next to it.

He entered the corridor again, where Minx waited. Without hesitation he kicked the next door in. It swung open easily, for the quake had already sprung its lock.

"What is this?" she asked.

"You should go out to the wagon," he told her. "Keep anyone else from taking it. I'm going down this way."

"Why? What's down there?"

"Him," he said, and she understood.

"I'll wait only for a short while. Falco might have taken the ship out already."

"If he has, he has. We'll find another way off."

She nodded and peered into the dark staircase. "Good fortune," she said, and then she turned and went her own path.

Matthew couldn't blame her. He didn't want to go down those steps either, into that darkness, but it had to be done.

He descended. A few torches had been set into the walls, but they were all extinguished. The staircase shook beneath his feet and stone dust rained from above. The castle was dying, perhaps to join the rest of Somers Town in its underwater sleep. Fate, it seemed, had caught up with Fell's uneasy paradise. Still Matthew descended, past the first floor and into the castle's guts. Or bowels, as might be more proper. The staircase curved to the left, the risers cut from rough stone. He came upon two torches still burning, and he paused to take one of them from its socket. Then, his confidence made more solid by the light, he continued on his downward trek.

A gate of black iron was set at the bottom of the stairs, but it was unlocked. Matthew pushed through and winced as the hinges squealed. Another torch burned from a wall in the narrow corridor ahead, and Matthew followed its illumination. Above his head there were nearly human groans as stone shifted against stone; even here, at this depth, the castle had been mortally wounded. Deep cracks grooved the walls and floor. Matthew walked on, pace after careful pace. He came to a branch in the corridor and decided to follow the straighter route. It led him to the wooden slab of a door that hung crooked on its hinges. He pulled it open and found a spacious white-walled sitting room and a candelabra with three tapers still burning atop a writing desk. The ceiling, riddled with cracks, was painted pale blue in emulation of the island's sky. The furniture was tasteful, expensive, and also painted white with gold trim. Matthew went through another doorway and found a bedroom with a large, canopied white bed. His attention was drawn to what hung on a number of pegs on the wall next to that bed: the tricorn hats Professor Fell had worn on his visits to Matthew's room, a white wig the same as worn by the castle's servants, and a battered straw hat that might have been the topper for any of the island's farmers.

He felt time was short, but he had to open and search a chest of drawers in the bedroom. He discovered in the drawers not only the elegant suits Fell had worn as well as the opaque cowl and the flesh-colored cloth gloves, but the sea-blue uniform of a servant. Also there were regular breeches with patched knees and white shirts that appeared worn and in need of stitching. All would have fit a slender man a few inches taller than Matthew. In addition, there were the shoes: two pair polished and gentlemanly, one pair scuffed and dirt-crusted.

He began to believe that Professor Fell at times dressed as a servant to move about the house and as a regular native to move about the island. Which begged the question...was Fell a native himself? A man of color? And perhaps Templeton...his son...had been harrassed and beaten to death on a London street partly because his skin was cream-colored, and darker than that of the average English boy? There was a reason, Matthew realized, why Temple's portrait had been done in colored glass.

But the real question was...where was Professor Fell *now?*

The deep noise of grinding stones told Matthew he had to find a way out of here, or retrace his path to the staircase. He went through the doorway out into the corridor again, his torch held before him, and started back the way he'd come. He was not very far along when he caught sight of another torch coming toward him, and a giant figure in white robes and a white turban illuminated in the yellow light.

Sirki stopped. They faced each other at a distance of about thirty feet.

"Hello, young sir," said the East Indian giant, and the light he held made the diamonds in his front teeth sparkle.

"Hello," Matthew said, his voice echoing back and forth between the walls.

"We have suffered quite a mishap here. Quite an explosion, up at the far point of the island. Do you know anything about that?"

"I felt it, of course."

"Of course. I see your stockings are very dirty. Muddy, perhaps? Did you get through that swamp all by yourself, Matthew?" Sirki waved a hand in his direction. "No, I don't believe you did. Who helped you? It's not only me asking. The professor would like to know. When that blast happened, his first thought was of you. And of course you were not in your room. Neither was Miss Cutter in hers. Now...why would *she* have helped you?"

"She likes me," Matthew said.

"Oh. Yes. Well, then." Sirki withdrew the sawtoothed blade from its sheath in his robes and walked forward a few steps. Matthew retreated the same number. "The professor," said Sirki, "has left this place. He instructed me to find you, and when I went to your room I found that the stairway was revealed. You *had* to come down here, didn't you? I am also instructed to tell you...that your services are no longer needed, and unfortunately Professor Fell will be unable to pay you your three thousand pounds."

"I *thought* he might wind up withdrawing that offer."

"Hm. He asked me to tell you that he will not be very much damaged by this little incident. Certainly he would not have wished this, but he has many irons in the fire." Sirki inspected the brutal edge of his blade. "He is sorrowful for you, though. That you chose to hurt him out of your...how did he put it?...your blind stupidity. Ah, Matthew!" He advanced a few steps nearer, and again Matthew retreated. The hideous weapon gleamed with reflected torchlight. "To have come so far and be on the verge of such *greatness*...and then to fall back again, as dirty as the swamp."

"The swamp," Matthew said, "is cleaner than the professor's soul."

"He wishes me to cut off some part of you and bring it to him to demonstrate that you are dead," said the giant. "What would you suggest, young sir?" To the silence that followed, Sirki smiled and said, "Let me decide."

He strode forward, demonic in the torchlight. The sawtoothed blade was upraised, capable of horrendous injury with one swing. Matthew backed away, his heart hammering. He thrust the torch forward to keep the beast at bay.

"No use in that," Sirki said almost gently. "I shall put that down your throat if I please."

And Matthew knew he could. Therefore Matthew chose the better part of valor. He turned and ran for his life.

Sirki came after him, taking tremendous strides. The branch in the corridor was ahead. Matthew took the untrodden way, running as fast as he could. Sirki was right behind him, the white robes billowing like the wings of a deadly angel.

The corridor suddenly widened into a space where there sat two simple chairs with dark stains of what might have been blood upon and beneath them. Gory chains still lay about the chairs, but there were no bodies. Smythe and Wilson had already gone to the tearing beak and eight arms of Agonistes. Matthew's light displayed three cells. He was in the dungeon under the dining hall, probably used to confine pirates and other criminals of note. In the center cell stood Zed, bald and bearded and wearing his ragged clothing. Zed had his hands gripped around the bars, and when he saw Matthew the mouth in the tribal-tattooed face gave a mangled roar of recognition.

Matthew heard Sirki coming. He saw a ring bearing three keys hanging on the wall. Sirki was almost into the chamber. Matthew dropped the torch to the floor and picked up one of the chairs. He threw it at Sirki's legs as the giant came through the corridor, and Sirki crashed down upon the stones.

Matthew plucked the keys off the wall and ran to Zed's cell. The first key did not fit. He looked back and saw Sirki up on his feet, lumbering toward him. The wicked blade flashed at Matthew's head, but he had already ducked. Sparks flew up from the meeting of sawteeth and iron bars. Matthew threw the ring of keys between the bars into Zed's cage, and then he got hold of the fallen torch and backed warily away as Sirki advanced upon him.

"This can go more easily for you," Sirki promised. "I've grown to respect you. I can make your death very quick."

"I'd rather stretch my life out a bit longer."

"I'm sorry, but that will be im—"

Sirki was interrupted by the noise of the cell door banging open. When the giant looked in that direction to see Zed emerging from the cage Matthew stepped in and struck the torch at the side of his head, but Sirki had already recovered and deflected the torch with his own. Then he whirled to meet Zed with his blade...an instant too late, for Zed's fist met Sirki's mouth in a jarring *smack* of flesh and bone and though the knife swung viciously at Zed's chest the Ga had darted away with admirable agility.

Sirki was caught between Matthew with his torch and Zed with his fists. He slashed first at one and then the other, and both kept their distance. Then Zed plucked up one of the lengths of chain from a chair. Sirki grinned in the flaring light. Blood was on his mouth, and he was minus a diamond as well as a front tooth.

"Ah!" he said. "I do get to kill you, after all."

Matthew lunged at him with the torch from the right side, aiming at the knife hand. Zed swung the chain and struck Sirki a blow across the left shoulder. Sirki spun toward Matthew and rushed him in an attempt to cancel the weaker threat, but Matthew swept the torch past Sirki's face to keep him away. Then the chain whipped out again across Sirki's back, and now the giant in an instant of what might have been panic threw his torch at Zed and followed it with his own huge body and the deadly blade upraised.

Matthew had already seen, in the Cock'a'tail tavern in New York the October before, what Zed could do with a chain. Now Zed stood his ground and lashed the chain out; it curled around the forearm of Sirki's knife hand, and just that fast Zed used the momentum to swing the giant crashing against the bars of the nearest cage. Sirki did not give up the knife, and grasping the chain with his free hand he hauled Zed toward himself like reeling in a hooked fish.

Zed's feet slid along the stones. He tried to right himself but the giant's pull was too strong. The knife waited with what seemed to be eager anticipation.

Then Matthew struck Sirki across the left side of the head with a second chain he'd picked up. The killer's turban unravelled from the blow. Sirki's eyes glazed for perhaps two seconds, his knife wavered and in this space of time Zed was upon him.

They grappled for the blade. It was the battle of the giants, brute against brute. Zed smashed Sirki in the face again with a heavy fist. Sirki grasped hold of Zed's throat with his free hand, an enormous implement of murder, and squeezed hard enough to make the cords stand out. They whirled toward Matthew in their fight and hit him with their shoulders, picking him up off his feet, throwing him to the floor and leaving him breathless in the winds of violence. He was amazed to see Sirki actually lift Zed off the floor with the hand at his throat. Zed hammered at Sirki's face and head while grasping the knife hand to keep those sawteeth from flesh. They slammed against the opposite wall so hard Matthew thought it would complete the destruction of the castle that the earthquake had begun. From above pieces of stone fell, and drifts of dust. Still the two fought on, Sirki's fingers digging into Zed's throat and Zed reshaping the giant's features with the mallet of his fist.

Zed began to make a gasping, gagging sound, and Matthew saw his blows weakening. Sirki was about to defeat the Ga, an unthinkable proposition. Matthew's torch had spun away in the collision and lay beyond the fighters. He had to decide what to do, and quickly. Though he was afraid out of his wits he took a running start and leaped upon the giant's back, at the same time looping the chain around Sirki's neck and squeezing as if his life depended upon it.

Sirki thrashed wildly but Matthew hung on. He was a rider of a different nature this time, and damned if he'd be thrown. The giant's hand left Zed's throat to reach back for Matthew's hair, but suddenly there was a crunching noise and Zed had attacked the knife hand with ten fingers. He succeeded here where he had failed in their battle on Oyster Island, for Sirki's knuckles sounded like walnuts being stomped under rough boots. The knife clattered to the stones, but just as quickly Sirki kicked it out of Zed's reach. Matthew still hung on, as the wounded giant pitched and bucked. Zed hit Sirki so hard in the jaw that the man careened back and nearly broke Matthew's spine against the wall. Then Matthew slithered off, his breath and strength gone, and through a red haze he saw Zed take his place by leaping upon Sirki's back. The Ga grasped the chain and began to strangle the giant, the muscles in his forearms strained and quivering. Sirki fought back by slamming Zed continually against the wall with blows that Matthew thought must be near breaking bones, yet Zed would not be thrown off nor denied his moment of revenge.

The chain sunk into the flesh of Sirki's throat. The giant's eyes bulged and blood streamed from his nostrils. His mouth opened in a hideous gasp, and Matthew saw that the second diamond-studded tooth had been knocked out.

Still Sirki fought. Still Zed clung to his back and choked him with the chain, which had now nearly disappeared. Matthew thought with horror that in another moment Sirki's head was going to be cleaved off by the chain. Sweat stood out in beads on the faces of both men, and then Sirki's eyes began to bleed.

Still Sirki crashed Zed against the wall, though the fury was weaker. Still the muscles of the Ga's arms worked. Sirki began to emit a high keening sound, an eerie gasping for departing life itself. His eyes were wide and wild and as red as the sun going down.

Then Sirki's legs buckled and he fell to his knees. Suddenly he was not so gigantic. Zed stayed astride him. The Ga's teeth were gritted, his huge shoulders thrust forward, his body trembling with the effort of delivering death to one who would not accept it. Sirki made an effort to stand. He got one foot planted and, incredibly, began to lift himself and Zed off the floor. But the pressure from Zed's hands and the chain never faltered, and suddenly Sirki's face took on a waxen appearance, the eyes pools of blood, and from his gasping mouth a dark and swollen tongue emerged. It quivered rapidly, like the tail of a rattlesnake.

Something crunched inside Sirki's neck. The head hung at an angle, as Gentry's had upon being sawed off at the dinner table. The giant's body shivered, as if feeling the chill of the grave. Matthew saw that the hideous eyes were sightless. At last Sirki's spirit seemed to flee the body, for the keening gasp ceased on a broken note to go along with the broken neck.

Zed let go of the chain, which was buried somewhere in there. He climbed off Sirki's back. For a moment the giant remained on his knees, obstinant far beyond the end. Then the corpse pitched forward and the stone floor added a cruel smashing to the twisted face.

Zed crumpled to his own knees and released a shuddered moan. He was all used up.

But the stone dust was falling now in greater volume. Matthew heard a dozen cracking noises from above. Suddenly a piece of stone the size of Sirki's dead body crashed down on the other side of the dungeon, followed by smaller bits of rubble.

"We have to get out!" Matthew shouted, and standing up he grasped hold of one of the Ga's arms to pull him to his feet, a task he could accomplish only in his most boastful dreams.

Language barrier or not, Zed fully understood. He nodded. Something on the floor nearby caught his attention and he scooped it up before Matthew could see what it was. Then, getting up on his own power, he took Matthew by the back of his collar and pulled him into another corridor at the far right of the room. It was dark in here and Matthew could see nothing. In a few seconds Zed stopped. There was the noise of a bolt slamming back. Zed pushed forward. A heavy door opened into gray morning light. The garden lay before them, and a pathway toward the front of the castle. Now Matthew took the lead, urging Zed to follow.

Matthew fully expected Minx to be gone, but she was still waiting at the wagon and tending her wounds with the bloody cloth. "Did you enjoy your wanderings?" she snapped at him, though there was some relief in her voice. "You damned fool!" she added, and then she took stock of the Ga. "Who is *this*?"

"My new bodyguard," said Matthew.

Minx used the whip to spur the team into motion. As they took off at a gallop along the road to the harbor, there came a noise like the discordant shrieking of a chorus of demons. Matthew and Zed looked back to see a shimmer of dust rising up around Castle Fell. Suddenly part of the cliff itself broke away, and the entire castle tilted toward the sea. The cobra head of one turret toppled, then a second and a third. Pieces of red slate flew like gulls. Every arched window that had not already broken shattered in an instant. With a tremendous, ungodly grinding of catastrophic forces fully half the castle tore away from its own tortured stones and pitched downward into the waves, leaving furniture hanging from rooms and splintered stairways leading to no destination but the somber sky.

"My God," Matthew whispered.

Zed gave a rough grunt that might have been accord.

Minx Cutter had never looked back. "To Hell with all of 'em," she said, and she lashed the team for greater speed.

THIRTY-TWO

MATTHEW realized that miracles did happen. The *Nightflyer*, as beautiful a ship as he had ever seen, was still docked. Minx drove the wagon nearly up to the gangplank. Any harbormaster either had not arrived here today or had left to see to his family.

"Damn if you people aren't *prompt*," Falco sneered from the deck, his voice as booming as any cannon and his twisted cane propped against his right shoulder. "Did you stop to eat your corncakes?"

Minx went up the plank first, followed by the Ga and then Matthew. There were a few men hauling lines and working on deck, but not nearly the crew that had brought them over. "I rounded up twenty-six men," Falco told Matthew, as he lit his clay pipe with a small taper. "Four of those haven't arrived, and three others decided they weren't going to leave their wives and children after that damn tremble started. I said to bring them all along, but they couldn't get their belongings together fast enough to suit me. They may show up yet, but so far we've got a crew of nineteen men on a ship that operates with forty. That means you, the Ga, and the bleeding lady will have to *work*." He frowned at Minx through a pall of smoke. "What the hell did you get into? A knife fight?"

Minx just laughed as if this were the funniest thing she'd ever heard, and her laughter rang out across the ship like church bells. Then she winced and gave a very unladylike curse, because her face hurt like hell.

"I do have someone on board who can sew stitches," said the captain. "Myself."

"Matthew!"

He recognized that voice, all right.

Berry had emerged from the doorway that led below. She was wearing a gray cloak over the crab-stained sleeping gown. Her feet were bare and dirty. Her hair was tangled, her eyes swollen from sleepless worry. She looked a mess. She crossed the deck toward the new arrivals, and she looked hopefully and expectantly at Matthew. She started to reach for him, but something about his posture and attitude stopped the gesture.

"You can thank Miss Grigsby," said Falco, "for our still being docked. She said you would come, no matter what. She believes in you, Mr. Corbett. More than I *do*, it seems, because as you can see we have two longboats tied up ready to row us out of the harbor. Lucky for you, she's very persuasive."

"Yes," Matthew said. "Lucky for me."

He smiled at her then, for he felt his heart open and the sunlight pour into it, and Berry poured herself into his arms.

He felt her heart beating, hard and fast. He crushed her to himself. Their shadows became one on the deck's plankings. They had shared so much already, for better *and* for worse. Even though Berry was dirty and wretched in her current state, Matthew couldn't help but think she was so very beautiful, and that she always to him smelled of the grass of summer, of cinnamon and the perfume of a wildflower meadow, and...

Life.

Then he caught himself, short of falling.

"Listen to me," he said, and he saw his tone of voice make her blue eyes blaze. "You've caused me no end of trouble! Why you left that inn, I have no idea! And traipsing about at night? Do you know what might've happened to you? My God, girl! I ought to put you over my knee like the child you are and give you a good—"

A hand with fearsome strength closed upon the back of his neck, and suddenly he was looking into a pair of deepset black eyes in a solemn, bearded African face decorated with tribal scars that appeared to spell out a Z, an E and a D.

"Mr. Corbett," Berry said frostily, "I think you should mind your manner of speech while on this voyage. And please correct your lack of respect, starting this instant."

He might have answered, if his throat had been in working order. It seemed his new bodyguard had his own ideas about who commanded his loyalty.

"Quarrels must wait for the open sea," the captain said, with a puff of smoke that drifted into Matthew's face. "Right now we've got to get this ship out of here. I don't want to think what might be coming down that road at any moment. So…my new additions to the crew…you will join the men already in those longboats. You will take orders from Mr. Spedder, my first mate. I expect you to pull hard and steady. With just the two boats, we'll be lucky to get out of this cove in another hour." He spoke to Zed in their common tongue. At once Zed released Matthew and was first down the gangplank.

"Ladies," said Falco, "I mean you as well. Get to it!"

As Matthew walked between Berry and Minx on their way to the longboats tied up at the bow, he realized that before they reached New York—if, pray to God, they ever did—they were going to know every inch of the *Nightflyer*, have worked their fingers to the bone and have an affair of both love and hate with every sail and every mast. Their affairs of love and hate were about to begin, commencing with the longboat's oars and the first mate's roar of "Row! Row! Row!" amplified through a tin voice-horn.

The captain was correct in his judgement of how much time the two longboats and their crews would need to row the *Nightflyer* out of the cove into tide and wind. It took a little over one hour, after which Matthew thought his shoulders were near falling off and Berry would have cried if that might have done any good, but tears would not move sailing ships. They returned to the *Nightflyer* by means of rope ladders lowered over the side, and the longboats were cast off to drift. Matthew, Berry, Minx and Zed were instantly put to work on tasks involving the hoisting of sails and the tying down of ropes, of which there seemed to be hundreds aboard ship and all excess to be coiled neatly and out of the way.

It was going to be pure hell, Matthew realized, and no one this trip would be a passenger save perhaps Saffron, her child, two other women of middle age, an elderly woman and three more children who were aboard.

Falco aimed the *Nightflyer* to the northwest. The sails filled and swept them along. The sun had broken through the gray morning clouds and painted the blue sea with gilded caps. There were over a dozen other smaller boats—native craft—in the water around Pendulum Island, embarked from the local harbor that was somewhere in the vicinity of Templeton. They were circling about, their masters and passengers waiting to see if they would have an island to return to. When Matthew stood at the railing and looked back at the island he could see the haze of dust rising in the area where Castle Fell had stood, and fires still burning in the wreckage of the fort and the ravaged woods. For the most part, though, the quake seemed to have ended.

He thought of what Sirki had said, in his last moments of life. *He asked me to tell you that he will not be very much damaged by this little incident.*

It seemed to Matthew that that was the professor's pride talking. Great damage had been done to the professor's schemes and enterprises. His refuge half-destroyed, the gunpowder works likely fully destroyed, the storehouse of Cymbeline gone up, his trusted Sirki gone down, the brothers Thacker finished off, the remains of Fell's weapons man and finances expert consumed by an octopus, and…of Aria Chillany? Matthew hadn't asked Minx about that yet, but it was obvious who had survived that bitter confrontation.

But what of Augustus Pons, Toy, Cesar Sabroso and Mother Deare? The problem-solver had no clue. Either they had survived, or they had not. He expected they had. Especially Mother Deare, who seemed to know a great deal about survival.

And Pretty Girl Who Sits Alone. Gone dreaming in her blue silence, which hurt Matthew's heart but made him realize he could not be the champion for everyone, and he could not make life-or-death decisions for them either.

The sun lay heavy upon him. He was tired, near exhaustion. Finding a hammock below deck and falling into a peaceful sleep would be his idea of paradise right now, but until Captain Falco said he could leave the deck here he stayed.

The *Nightflyer* had been out of harbor for nearly an hour, and Matthew staggering around doing whatever task he was ordered to do by the first mate, when the very same short, thickly-set bulldog of a man hollered to him over the noise of wind and spray, "You there! Deadwood! Captain wants you! *Now!*" He hooked a dirty thumb toward the upper deck where the helmsman steered the ship. Falco stood at the stern viewing something behind them through a spyglass.

On climbing up the set of steps to reach that exalted poop deck, Matthew saw immediately what was the captain's object of attention. A three-masted ship, sails spread, was at their back maybe a mile or so distant.

"That's Grayson Hardwick's command," said Falco, with the pipe gripped between his teeth. "Mr. Hardwick is one of the professor's best...shall we say...providers. His sloop carries twelve guns. Mr. Landsing!" He was addressing the helmsman, a fair-haired native lad. "Course change twelve degrees port."

"Twelve degrees port! Aye, sir!"

"They're after us?" Matthew asked.

"You," said Falco, "win the prize." He turned toward the first mate, who had followed Matthew up. He said quietly, with the tone of full and calm authority. "Full sails, Mr. Spedder. Everything we've got and more. And when you deliver the orders, do remember that our lives may depend on three extra knots."

Spedder hollered at the crew in a voice hard enough to shred the bark off a tree, and at once the experienced crew went to work raising whatever sails were not already catching wind.

"Shall I help?" Matthew asked.

"Stay put. I don't want green hands tangling ropes right now." Falco put the spyglass to his eye again. "That little bitch is coming on," he said. "Going to be close enough for an aimed shot in a couple of hours. But my *Nightflyer's* fast too, when she needs to be. We'll just wait and see." He turned to watch the progress of his men aloft in the shrouds, and spotting some hesitation he did not like he leaned forward on his cane and shouted, "To the task, ladies! Get that royal up!"

The morning moved on. Water was provided to the crew, and bits of limes to chew on. Falco allowed Berry to join Matthew at the poop deck's railing, watching Hardwick's armed ship close the gap. Every so often Falco ordered the helmsman to change course a few degrees, and he monitored the wind by watching the smoke of his pipe. The sails held full and steady, and as the *Nightflyer* hissed through the dark blue waves flying fish leaped before the bow.

Berry voiced the question that had been poised like a sword-point in Matthew's mind. "Is *he* on that ship?"

"I don't know."

"If he's not dead...he won't let you go that easily."

"He's *not* dead," Matthew said. "And yes, you're perfectly correct." His eyes narrowed against the glare, he watched the vessel coming on with a mixture of dread and fascination. Dread that he should be the cause of the *Nightflyer* being blown out of the water, and fascination that of all the people in this world he alone might now be the prime object of Professor Fell's cold and calculating wrath.

"He knows you must be here, doesn't he?"

"Oh, yes." Matthew was sure of it. When Sirki had not returned with some bleeding part of Matthew, the professor had to realize his giant had been vanquished. "He knows."

Captain Falco watched the sails, his amber eyes taking in every detail. Then he turned to Matthew and Berry. "I assume you two are very tired."

"Very," Matthew answered.

Falco nodded. "You can sleep when you're dead. Which I don't intend to be, this day. Mr. Spedder!" The first mate came over. "Send a man aloft to tighten the lower right edge of the topgallant. I don't want any luff in that sail. Then pick five men, and make sure the Ga is among them. Pass out every axe, saw and cutting tool we have. I want the cabins cleared of all heavy furniture. The beds, the dressers, the chairs and washstands...everything over the side. The doors too. Start with my cabin."

"Aye, sir."

"Oh...Miss Grigsby and Mr. Corbett will be joining that work detail. Go along with you, children!"

Thus began a hideous afternoon, but one with no uncertain purpose. Axes fell, saws worked and hammers knocked things to pieces small enough to be carted up to the deck and thrown over. Minx Cutter joined the workers, as did Saffron who had given her baby to the elderly woman to watch over. Saffron had tended to Minx's wounds as best she could, washing them and wrapping a cloth bandage around the deeper of the two, the forehead cut. But Minx was sullen and silent, and Matthew made sure to stay out of her way. It appeared to him that killing a woman was not to her liking either, and possibly the spirit of Nathan Spade still did not rest easily in her memory.

Starting with the captain's cabin, one cabin after another was cleared of its furniture. Whether they had much of an impact on the ship's speed was hard to say, but Matthew noted in the late afternoon as he helped pitch another bedframe over that Hardwick's craft had not gained anymore between them but was holding steady.

As the sun was sliding down and deep violet began to paint the eastern sky, the job had been finished. Everything possible had been broken apart and cast off, even the doors. The *Nightflyer* was now a creature of sails and hull with fewer innards. Would it be enough? Even Captain Falco seemed not to know.

But as the darkness descended, there came a flash of fire and a concussion from the direction of Hardwick's cannons. A volley had been sent flying. Without waiting for an invitation, Matthew, Berry and Minx climbed up to the poop deck and there stood the captain at the stern railing peering again through his spyglass.

"The balls troubled fish, nothing else," said Falco, who himself sounded weary onto collapse. It was possible only the cane was holding him up. "But they're reloading."

A second volley was fired. Thunder rolled across the sea. Six geysers of water shot up two hundred yards from the *Nightflyer*'s wake.

"Wasting their balls and powder," was the captain's comment. "Dark falling. They wanted to get their shot off while they could still see. We'll have no lights on this ship tonight." He paused, watching the other vessel, and then he said, "But I speak too quickly."

"What is it?" Berry asked.

"Hardwick is changing course. Going to...north by northeast, it appears. Crossing our stern." He grunted. "Giving up the chase, or *pretending* to. But I think Hardwick knows he can't catch us in the dark, or *find* us for that matter."

"Thank God," said Minx.

"Thank the axes, saws and hammers. Thank your strength. Thank those sails above your heads. I think we've seen the last of the revenge."

"The *what*?" Matthew asked.

"*Temple's Revenge*. The name of Hardwick's ship."

"May I?" Matthew held his hand out for the spyglass, and Falco gave it to him. Through the lens, Matthew could see the dim shape of the vessel moving away to their starboard side. As he watched, he saw first one oil lamp and then another flare to life aboard *Temple's Revenge*. Several lamps were lit. Matthew wondered which one spread its glow upon Professor Fell and what guise he maintained on that ship.

Indeed, the professor had called halt to the chase, probably on the advice of the ship's master. They were heading north by northeast? To England?

I think we've seen the last of the revenge, Falco had said.

The ship...yes, Matthew thought. But the revenge...no.

Never, if he knew Professor Fell.

"We should run without lamps for a few hours longer," Falco decided. "In the meantime, we have candles below in the galley. To illuminate your mutton stew, biscuits, shelled peas and cups of lemon water."

"That at least *sounds* good," said Berry, who was so tired she could hardly stand but also so famished she couldn't sleep without eating.

"Oh, the first five nights, it *is* good. You will not be as coddled on this trip back as you were on the trip here. You will eat with the crew, and what the crew eats...because you *are* part of the crew."

"Fair enough." Minx lifted her chin and gave Falco a haughty stare that might have withered any other man to cinders. "Just don't let anyone get between my food and my knife."

"I'm sure that won't happen, miss," the good captain said, with the nod and slight bow of a gentleman. "After you put your knife away, you might consider letting me look at those wounds. I'm not sure a needle and catgut are needed, but scars would not be to your liking."

Minx didn't reply. Matthew was thinking that she bore her scars within, and any on the outside paled in comparison.

After the meal in the galley, the ship settled down for the night. Watches were set, and much to his chagrin Matthew was given an order by Mr. Spedder to report to the poop deck at eight strikes of the ship's bell. Four o'clock in the morning, by his knowledge of that damn bell ringing on the way over. He was assigned a hammock in the cramped and—it must be said—smelly quarters amid the other men who were not on duty, the women and children being quartered elsewhere, and within a very few minutes of taking his boots off and stretching out into the netting he was gone to the world.

However weary he was, he awakened before the eight bells. He lay in the hammock, assaulted by the snoring, rumblings and fartings of the men around him. He was greatly bothered by something he could not rid from his mind.

The Lesser Key Of Solomon, the book was titled. The compendium of demons and spells to raise them. What were the odds that he would have found a second copy of that tome in Professor Fell's library? Like the stealing of sugar, it boded ill. And it boded evil, to be perfectly honest about it. Also…another thorn in his mind…the matter of Brazio Valeriani.

I shall pay five thousand pounds to the person who locates Brazio Valeriani, the professor had said. *I shall pay ten thousand pounds to the person who brings him to me. Force may be necessary. You are my eyes and my hands. Seek and ye shall find.*

Ten thousand pounds. A fortune. For one man?

Why?

The professor's words: *If you found him I would pay you enough to own that little town of yours.*

Again: *why?*

Matthew knew himself. This was going to eat at him, day and night. Yes, Professor Fell's castle and refuge and gunpowder plant and much of his criminal Parliament might be destroyed—for today—but there was always tomorrow, and the professor was nothing if not industrious. And ambitious.

But what exactly was his ambition?

He knew his own mind. He could not let this rest, and neither could *he* fully rest.

The ship's bell sounded eight. Matthew got up at once, pulled on his boots and rid himself of the palace of snores.

His instructions had been to report to the poop deck and make the rounds of the deck, every thirty minutes turning an hour-glass mounted on a gimbel next to the ship's wheel and tending to the the bell until he was relieved in four hours. A lovely proposition, for one so weary as he. Yet when he went on deck and the fresh breeze hit his face and he saw the huge sky full of stars and a silver moon still just past full shining upon the sea he thought he was so lucky to be alive in this month of March in this year of 1703. He had survived so much. He was so much stronger than before. Before when? Before yesterday.

He greeted the man on watch who awaited him for relief and also greeted the helmsman. His responsibility, Mr. Spedder had told him, was to keep accurate time by the bell: one bell in thirty minutes, two in one hour, three in ninety minutes and so on. The hour-glass's sand was already running for the first half-hour of the morning watch, and thus Matthew began his initial round of the deck.

The *Nightflyer* was flying smoothly this night. The waves were kind to the girl's hull, and kind also to a landlubber's stomach. The sea all around was dark, not a light showing. *Temple's Revenge* had gone its own way, carrying Professor Fell to his next crime against humanity.

Matthew was on his second round when he was joined by a figure wearing a gray cloak. Her red hair was still tangled and matted, and her feet were still dirty. She was still a mess, but she was a welcome sight on this silent voyage.

"May I walk with you?" Berry asked.

"Of course."

They walked without speaking. They were comfortable in their quiet. Then Berry said, "I'm sorry I caused you trouble."

"It's all right."

"No, really. I stuck my nose in where it didn't belong. I regret putting you in the position of looking after me."

"I managed," he said. "I just thank God you weren't hurt."

She nodded. They reached the bow and started again toward the stern, as the *Nightflyer* spoke softly around them and the sails stretched wide before the currents of night.

"You are changed," she told him. "Forgive me for saying this. But Matthew...you never came back when you went after that man."

"Yes," he had to say. "I know."

"You can tell me. What happened, I mean. I'll bear it for you."

Something in her voice broke him. It happened just like that. A voice, offering to listen. Just like that. He resisted, because it was so awful. Because the Gray Kingdom still had him, and it was so very strong. Because this world was not the world he'd imagined it to be, and because he was lost in its harshness.

"Oh," Matthew said, and it was nearly a tormented moan. He stumbled in his progress, and just like that he knew the moment had arrived to unburden himself because Berry Grigsby had offered to listen.

"Tell me," she said. She took his hand. "I can bear it for you."

He clasped her hand. Tightly, and more tightly still. She was holding him, it seemed, to the earth. Without her grasp, he might be swept away. He stopped, and they stood together amidships on the *Nightflyer*, and he looked at her in the moonlight and starshine and saw her blue eyes gleaming. When he opened his mouth he didn't know how he would begin; he just trusted that it would all make sense.

He told her. About everything. About Tyranthus Slaughter and his crimes and horrors, about Lyra Sutch, about the sausages made from human flesh, about the hideous cellar where the bodies were hacked to pieces, about the moment when he knew he would have to kill the woman or be killed himself, about what it felt like to drive an axe into the flesh of another human being.

And, in so telling, Matthew opened up his box of pain and began to weep.

He wept not only because of that experience, but because he was changed. Because he could never go back to a place of innocence, and because this world had tainted him. Because he had not asked for this, but because this had been thrust upon him. And his weeping became crying and his crying became sobbing for the lost boy who had been Matthew Corbett, who now had to become a man whether he liked it or not. And not only any man, but a man who knew what dark things hid underneath the stones. Professor Fell was in him, and how could he get that disease out? There was only one way...to destroy the professor, and the evil that he did. Only one way...to continue the course he had been set upon.

As Matthew sobbed, Berry put her arms around him. She did not tell him to be calm or to be quiet, for she knew he needed to sob, to clear his eyes and his mind and his heart, for she knew also he had so much ahead of him.

She kissed his cheek, and held him, and when he had finished his recounting of this tale of terror and tribulation she whispered into his ear, "You did what you had to do."

It was the truth, plainly spoken. Matthew said with an effort, "Yes. I did."

And though it was the dark of night, a little sunlight broke through.

"Never," she said, "doubt yourself. Yes, it was terrible. But *never* doubt, Matthew...that you are where you are, for a reason."

He nodded, but he could not speak.

"As God said to Job," Berry said. *"I will demand of thee."*

"Yes," Matthew answered, as he stared out at the unfathomable sea. "I understand."

She kissed his cheeks and took the tears. She held his hand and walked with him a distance further, and he realized he was late in turning the hour-glass and ringing the bell. But he didn't hurry for he felt as if he had all the time in the world, that the gray kingdom was a passing country of the soul, and that it might take a while longer...but day by day, if he concentrated on getting there, he would get closer by small steps once again to the realm of joy.

Berry left him to return to her own hammock and a few more hours of much-needed sleep. Matthew was on his way to the poop deck when a shadow moved at the mainmast. A tinderbox sparked, a flame stirred, and a clay pipe was lighted.

"Matthew," said the captain, "do you not know that I am always aware what time it is, whether the crewman on watch rings the bell or not?"

"I'm sorry. I was—"

"Talking with your friend, yes. I wandered over that way, and heard a bit. I hope you don't mind. After all, this is *my* ship."

"I don't mind," Matthew said.

"Nice night for a talk, isn't it? All those stars. All those mysteries. Yes?"

"Yes," was Matthew's reply.

"You're a terrible watchman and a worse time-keeper," said Falco. "Those errors should get you whipped."

I've been whipped before, Matthew thought, but he said nothing.

"Getting me off my floor where my bed used to be." A spout of smoke drifted up and was blown away by the breeze. "I should whip you myself."

"It *is* your ship," Matthew said.

"For certain, she is." Falco leaned against the mainmast, a slim shadow in the dark. "As I say, I heard a bit. A little bit, but enough. I will say this, and mark it: every captain must realize, sooner or later, that to progress his ship sometimes means casting things overboard that are no longer needed. Do I make myself clear?"

"Aye, sir," replied Matthew.

"Now you're mocking me. But I will give you that, Matthew. I will also give you one minute to get to that bell, ring it twice for five o'clock—though you will be nearly twenty minutes late—and turn the glass. Then you will continue your rounds and you will pay attention to your duties. Clear again?"

"Clear," was the only possible answer.

"Go," said the captain. As Matthew started to hurry away, Falco gave out a voluminous puff of smoke and said, "And thank you for ruining my taste for sausages for the rest of my life."

Matthew couldn't help but smile.

It was a very good feeling.

Thirty-Three

O N the warm and sunny afternoon of the seventeenth day of April, a trumpet sounded from the crow's-nest of the *Nightflyer*.

Matthew Corbett, bearded and sun-darkened, stood up from his task of swabbing the never-ending deck. He peered forward, one hand visoring his eyes.

"We're home," said Berry, who had come to his side from her own job of stowing away ropes into neat coils. She was wearing a blue floral-print dress from Saffron's wardrobe. She had learned she was a natural at nautical crafts, and had become proficient at such things as reading a sextant, tying knots of twenty different kinds for different tasks, and actually keeping wind in the sails on the few times Captain Falco had allowed her to take the wheel. In fact, the captain had told her she had an easy touch with the *Nightflyer*, and he wished some of the men aboard could read the wind as well as she.

"*Home,*" she repeated, and she felt the leaping of joy within her heart but also a little sinking of sadness, for her adventure—a dirty and dispiriting spell in the brig, fearsome men with torches and swords, crabs in the dark under a wooden floor, violent earthquake and all—was almost ended. And almost ended were the days—the little more than three weeks—she had spent with Matthew, for aboard this ship he seemed to have all the time in the world and never shunned her... whereas, in the town that lay on the island before them...

Ever the same.

Matthew saw Oyster Island ahead on the port side of the ship. And beyond it, New York. The forest of masts at the Great Dock, and beyond them the buildings. The shops and homes, the taverns and the warehouses. The lives of people he cared about. His own life, renewed. He was the captain of his own ship now, and he had done as Falco directed. Over the course of this voyage he had made a great effort to throw overboard from the ship of his soul those things that caused him pain, grief and regret, and that he could not change no matter what. Revealing those personal agonies to Berry on deck, in the quiet under the moon and stars, had been a revelation to himself. How much he trusted her, and how much he also cared about her. Yet...

The shark was still in the water, out there somewhere.

The shark would not rest. It never rested. It would think, and plan, and wait...and then, sooner or later, it would stop its circling and attack. Would it come after Berry? Would it come after anyone to whom Matthew held an attachment?

He didn't know. But he did know that Professor Fell never forgot, and so he was not done with the professor and he was certain that the professor was not done with him.

A small fleet of longboats was rowing out to meet the new arrival. The harbormaster or one of his representatives would be aboard one of them, to find out where the ship was coming from and what it was carrying. In just a little while, then, the word would begin to spread that Matthew Corbett and Berry Grigsby had returned from their nearly two months absence. Lillehorne and Lord Cornbury would want to know the whole story. And Hudson Greathouse also. Matthew decided it was time to be honest with everyone and get things out in the open. But to go so far as to allow Marmaduke to write a story for *The Earwig*? Matthew wasn't so sure about that.

Minx Cutter joined Matthew and Berry at the railing. She was in good health and had scrubbed herself from a washbasin this morning. Aria Chillany's knife would leave only a thin scar across Minx's forehead, but it was hardly anything. She had come into her own on the voyage also, and had been quite admired by the crew when she showed them her knife-throwing abilities. Particularly when Captain Falco had volunteered to stand on deck and have Minx outline him against a bulkhead with blades. That had gone over greatly with everyone except Saffron, who didn't intend to raise their child alone.

The three hundred pounds in gold coins had been paid to the captain and the account settled. In fact, Falco had told them that as members of the crew Matthew, Minx, Berry and Zed were entitled to a share, to be divided up when they reached New York. And so they were almost there, as the longboats came alongside to get their towropes tied up. Then there would be a short while for the rowers to guide them to a harbor berth. A rope ladder was lowered, and who should come aboard but the new assistant to the harbormaster, a man who knew ships and their cargoes and who prided himself on being watchful that no enemy of New York was trying to slip past his guard.

"Lord God! Am I lookin' at a a phantom, what'cha might say?" asked old wild-haired Hooper Gillespie, made more presentable in a new suit. He took in Berry and his eyes got wider. "*Two* phantoms, then? Am I dreamin' in daylight?"

"Not dreaming," Matthew replied. It occurred to him that the phantom of Oyster Island was standing only a few feet away. Zed had shaved for the occasion of returning to New York, and since he'd done the work of three men and on this voyage eaten the meals that three men might have consumed he was as big and formidable as ever before. "Miss Grigsby and I are glad to be home," said Matthew.

"Where ya been, then? Everybody's gone near crazy tryin' to figger it out!"

"Yes." Matthew smiled at him, and squinted in the sun. He scratched his beard, which would soon be coming off with the strokes of a new razor. "Let's just say for now that we were in someone's idea of paradise."

"Huh? That don't make a hog's lick a' sense! Think you're tryin' to rib old Hooper, is what I think! Yessir! Rib 'im!"

"Is this a typical New Yorker?" Falco asked with his pipe in his mouth, drawing nearer to Matthew.

"No," Matthew confided. "He makes more sense than most."

The *Nightflyer*, a sturdy gal, was towed into harbor. Matthew smelled the earthy aroma of springtime. The air was warm and fresh, and the hills of New Jersey and north of the town were painted in the white, violet, pink and green of new buds and new foliage. By the time the Nightflyer had been guided in, docked and tied up, Hooper Gillespie had seemingly told everyone in New York that Matthew and Berry were arrived, for a sizeable crowd had gathered and still more people were converging upon the wharf. Of course anytime a ship of large size drew in to port a throng of merrymakers, musicians and food peddlers appeared to hawk their talents and wares, but it was as clear as the weather that today the names of Corbett and Grigsby had true worth.

The gangplank was lowered. Matthew decided he would take his ease going down it, as he only had the one much-worn outfit left.

"Oh my Jesus!" shouted someone from the crowd. A familiar voice, usually directed toward Matthew in the form of irritating questions concerning the activities of a problem-solver. "Berry! My girl! Berry! Let me *through*, please!"

Thus the moon-faced, rotund, squat and bespectacled figure of Marmaduke Grigsby either shoved his way forward or was allowed to pass, and seeing his granddaughter navigate the gangplank broke him to tears that streamed down his cheeks and caused him to look the most miserable man on earth on perhaps the most joyous day of his life.

When Marmaduke flung himself at her in a bone-crushing embrace the energy of his delight staggered Berry and nearly took them both swimming, but for Matthew's catching them from careening across the wharf.

"Oh dear God!" said Marmaduke, his eyes still flooding. He had to take off his spectacles to see. "Where *were* you? Both you and Matthew gone...no word for days and then weeks...I'm a puddle, just look at me!" He crushed Berry close again, and Matthew saw Berry's eyes widen from the pressure. Then Marmaduke looked at Matthew and the round face with its massive red-veined nose and slab of a forehead that walnuts could be cracked upon flamed like a warlock's rum toddy. "*You!*" The blue eyes nearly burst from their sockets and the heavy white eyebrows danced their jigs. "What did you drag this poor child into?"

"I didn't exactly—"

"I should make you pay for this! I should throw you out of that abode of yours and see you in court, sir, for—"

A finger was pressed firmly against Marmy's lips. "Hush that *nonsense*," said Berry. "He didn't drag me into anything. I went where we were taken. Neither of us wanted to go. I'll tell you all about that later, but right now all I want to do is get home."

"Oh, my bones are shaking." Marmy put a hand to his forehead. He looked near passing out. "I've been chewed to pieces over this. Dear Lord, I've prayed and prayed for your return." He fired a quick glance at Matthew. "The return of *both* of you, I'm saying. Granddaughter...will you help me walk?"

"I will," she said, and took his arm.

"Please," said Matthew before Marmaduke could be helped away in his state of disrepair, "don't walk straight to a pen when you reach home, and begin to pepper your girl with ink and questions. Berry? Would you please allow a few days to pass before you give any information to anyone?"

"I want to sleep for a few days, is what I want," she replied, and though Marmaduke scowled at the thought of a broadsheet to be filled with a delicious story that he was yet unable to bite into, he allowed himself to be guided through the crowd.

Others came up to greet Matthew. There was Felix Sudbury and Robert Deverick, John Five and his wife Constance, the widow Sherwyn she of the all-seeing eye and sometimes flowing fountain of a mouth, Phillip Covey, Ashton McCaggers, the Munthunk brothers, Dr. Polliver, Hiram and Patience Stokely, Israel Brandier, Tobias Winekoop, Sally Almond, Peter Conradt and...

...the owner of a black cane topped with the silver head of a lion, which now was placed underneath Matthew's nose so as to steer his attention to the waspy wisp of a man dressed in pale yellow from breeches to tricorn, topped with a white feather plucked from the dove of peace.

"Mr. *Corbett*," said Gardner Lillehorne, making it sound like the nastiest curse ever to leave a man's lips. "Where the *devil* have you been?"

Matthew regarded the long, pallid face with the small black eyes that seemed to be either perpetually angry or eternally arrogant. The precisely-trimmed black goatee and mustache might have been painted on by a nerveless artist. "Yes," he answered. "That's where."

"Where what?"

"Where I've been."

"What the devil are you talking about?"

"That's right," said Matthew, with a slight smile.

"My God," Lillehorne said to his cur Dippen Nack, who stood glowering beside his master. "The man's lost his bird."

"I've been with the devil," Matthew clarified. "And I'll be glad to tell you about him. You and Lord Cornbury, whenever you please. Just not this afternoon. *Oh.*" He remembered his promise to himself, the one he'd made when he'd fully realized the enormity of his dangerous situation on Pendulum Island. He stepped forward and kissed Dippen Nack on the forehead, proving to himself that a promise made was a promise kept.

Nack in stupefied horror fell back. Nack nearly fell over a wharf-board crack.

And then through the crowd came a man who, it appeared, no longer needed a cane. He walked tall and steady, he looked strong and wolfish and ready for any battle ahead. Perhaps it was also due to the very comely—strapping, it might be said—blonde widow Donovan holding his hand and all but cleaved to his side.

"The wanderer has returned," said Hudson Greathouse. "I believe you have some tales to tell."

"I do. And as I have said to the High Constable, I am more than willing to tell everything to him, to Lord Cornbury, and to you. And *you*, first."

"Over a bottle of wine at the Trot, I presume?"

"Two at least."

"You are buying?"

"I am currently without funds, though tomorrow I will be paid for being part of the crew of that fine—"

He was unable to finish, because Hudson had picked him up and hugged him, and when Hudson put his strength into it the back was pressed to the test. Fortunately, Matthew's back passed that test, and he was returned to the ground unbroken.

"Seven o'clock tonight, then," said Hudson, who suddenly had something in his eye and was trying to get it clear with a finger. "Don't be a minute late or I'll hunt you down." His eyes examined Matthew's face. "You look older."

"Yes, I know."

"It's the beard."

"I love the beard!" said the beauteous widow. Her hands roamed Hudson's chest and shoulders. "Something about that… makes me tingly."

"Really?" Hudson's brows went up. "I shall lose my razor this evening," he decided.

Others came up and either shook Matthew's hand or whacked him so hard on the back he thought he might yet be crippled. Hudson and his lovely departed, and so did Lillehorne and his ugly. Matthew had caught sight of Minx Cutter moving through the throng, speaking to no one, putting distance between herself and him. And also, possibly, distance between herself and the memory of Nathan Spade. He would find her later. Right now he looked around for someone in particular, a person who would be easy to spot if indeed he had left the ship.

It seemed, however, that Zed had never come down the gangplank.

Matthew went back up, to where Falco was still giving some orders to tidy the deck before any of the others might leave. "Where's Zed?" Matthew asked.

"Forward," Falco answered, and indeed there stood Zed at the bow, staring out across the town that had known him as a slave and then never known him as the phantom of Oyster Island.

"Isn't he departing?"

"Oh yes, he's departing. As soon as I find a full complement of crew, and I am able to restock my ship, we'll be departing. That would be a week or so, I'm thinking. Until then, Zed is a guest on my ship and he prefers to remain here until we leave."

"Until you leave? Going *where*?"

Falco relit his pipe with a small taper, and blew smoke into the world. "I am taking Zed home to Africa. Back to his tribe's land, where he has asked me to take him by drawing me a very persuasive picture. And paid me, also."

"*Paid* you? With what?"

Falco reached into a pocket. He opened his hand. "These. They're very fine diamonds."

Matthew realized what Zed had picked up from the dungeon floor as the castle was crashing down. Not a single object, but two. Sirki's front teeth were larger in Falco's palm than they'd appeared in the giant's mouth, and so too were the sparkling diamonds larger.

"I'll be damned," Matthew had to say.

"Damned by *one*, at least," Falco corrected. He returned the teeth to his pocket and clenched his own teeth around the pipe's stem. "You'll be foremost in his mind. Mark that."

"I do mark it."

"I intend to find a house and leave Saffron and Isaac here. I hope you'll look in on them from time to time."

Matthew nodded. He'd only learned that Isaac was the child's name when they were several days at sea. "I don't believe I told you, but I knew a great man named Isaac," he said.

"Let us hope my Isaac grows up to be great. Well…I trust you will make good on your promise to held me find a position carrying cargo when I return?"

"I'll make good."

"I somehow knew you would say that." Falco reached his hand out, and Matthew took it. "I also know, Matthew, that you and I are tied together by the bonds of Fate. Don't ask me how I know this. Call it…knowing which way the wind blows." And so saying, he blew a small white spout of Virginia's finest that was caught by the soft April breeze and carried out over the sea.

Matthew walked forward to where Zed was standing motionless, as he must have sometimes stood watching the life of New York pass by from the rooftop of City Hall. When Zed realized Matthew was there, he instantly turned himself toward his visitor. Matthew thought that, whether at war or at peace, the Ga was a fearsome sight. But there was nothing to fear now. At least for a while, the war was over. And…perhaps…Zed's long life of peace was soon to begin.

"You've saved my life more than once," Matthew told him. "You probably can't understand me, but I thank you for your…um…*presence*. I'm sure Berry won't let you leave without speaking, and neither will McCaggers. I wish you good fortune, Zed." Matthew thought it was peculiar, that he would never know this man's real name. And also, in a way, terribly sad. He held out his hand.

Zed took a step forward. His mouth opened. He tried to speak. He tried very hard. He squeezed his eyes shut to try to make the stub of his tongue form a word. His face contorted. But for all his strength, he had not the power to utter a single syllable. His eyes opened. He took Matthew's hand in a grip that tightened just to the point of breakage. Then he put a finger beside his left eye and drew that finger out along a line until it pointed at Matthew.

I'll be watching you, he said.

And somehow Matthew was sure of that. Even at a distance from here to Africa. If anyone could cast their eye across a sea, to view a world left behind and those left in it, Zed could.

"Goodbye," Matthew said, and when he left the *Nightflyer* Zed was still standing at the bow, silently regarding what he was leaving and ready perhaps to take the daring flight into his future.

Matthew was on his way home along Queen Street, thankful to have gotten through the throng and all the well-wishers, when a voice called, "Matthew! My God, there you are!"

He paused to look behind. Of course Matthew had instantly recognized the voice. Effrem Owles, tall and gangly, with his large round eyes behind his spectacles and though only at twenty years of age the premature gray streaking his brown hair. As befitted the tailor's son, he wore a very nice tan-colored suit. But here was the rub: Matthew felt a pang of guilt as Effrem approached. Though Effrem smiled as if the entire world was his thread and needle, Matthew knew he must still be in great pain. After all, the family business had been destroyed by Professor Fell's Cymbeline bombs. And, truth be told, Matthew felt responsible for that catastrophe because he had resisted the professor's will.

"I heard you and Berry had arrived! I thought I'd get there to see you, but..."

"But here you are now," said Matthew, and he clapped his friend on the shoulder. "You look fine, Effrem. How's your father?"

"He's very good, Matthew. But where have you been for so long? I understood you were in the hospital that night, and then you just vanished?"

"A long story. One I'll keep for some other time. All right?"

"Of course. I won't press you." They began walking together, side by side and north along Queen Street. After a moment Effrem said, "I suppose you haven't heard, then?"

"Heard what?"

"The news, Matthew! Oh, how *could* you have heard? Come with me, won't you?"

"Come with you where?"

"To the shop! I want to show you!"

Effrem started striding away, and Matthew followed. They were heading toward the corner of Crown and Smith streets. A fateful corner, Matthew thought. It was where the Owles' tailor shop had stood, before it had been blown into burning bits. The pang of guilt became stronger. Matthew faltered. He wasn't sure he could go on.

"Keep walking, Matthew!" Effrem urged. He stopped to wait for his friend and for a haywagon to trundle past. "I know you must be tired, but I want to show you—"

"Effrem," said Matthew. "I do remember. All right? I know what happened to your father's shop. I'm so very sorry, and I hope you don't hold it against me. Now…there's no need for you to take me to the ruins. I will do whatever I can to—"

"The *ruins?*" Effrem's eyes had widened. "Oh no, Matthew! Not ruins! Come on, it's not much further! Please!" He grabbed at Matthew's sleeve to pull him along.

They came in sight of the corner, and there Matthew stopped as if he'd run into a stone wall.

Not ruins.

A new tailor shop, built with sturdy red bricks and a coppered roof. Matthew got himself moving again, and as he neared the beautiful place he saw painted along the bottom of the glass window in front: *Effrem Owles, Master Tailor.* And below that, *Benjamin Owles, Consulting Tailor.*

"I have the shop now," said Effrem proudly, and he did puff his chest out a little. Then he waved at someone and called, "Here he is! I found him!"

Matthew saw a slim young woman approaching. She was dressed simply and elegantly, in a dark blue gown and a hat the same. She had jet-black hair, and she was quite the lovely. She walked with a purpose, and her purpose was to reach Effrem Owles by the fastest possible route. Thus she gave Effrem a smile that shamed the April sun, and he returned that smile, and by those obvious clues it did not take a problem-solver to deduce that love bloomed eternal and between the least likely couples.

"Hello, Opal," said Matthew.

"'lo, Matthew," she said, but she was all eyes for her owl. "We heard you got back. Effrem went runnin'."

"Missed him at the dock, though. Had to catch up."

"I'd like to be *caught* up." Matthew regarded the new tailor shop. "Built so strongly, and so quickly! It must have cost a pretty penny!" He had to ask the next question: "Your father had enough money to rebuild?"

"No, he didn't," Effrem answered. "But…that was before."

"Before what?"

Effrem looked at Opal. "Go ahead, tell him."

She scruffed the street with a shoe. She shrugged. "Just a *thing*, it was. I mean, it didn't mean *nothin'* to me. So I thought…y'know… somebody could get some good from it."

"Will you speak sense, please?" Matthew urged.

She lifted her face and peered up at him with her very bright blue eyes. "The ring you gave me. With the red stone. Turned out it was the nicest ruby the jewel buyer ever seen."

Matthew made the sound of a man being punched in the stomach by a baby's fist: *"Oh."*

The ring from Tyranthus Slaughter's treasure box. Presented to Opal for her good deed in helping Matthew uncover Lyra Sutch's plot, back in October. Matthew thought that knowing he had been responsible for such a kindness as this would have made Slaughter's bones writhe in the grave.

"That is wonderful," said Matthew.

"*She* is wonderful," Effrem corrected. He put his arm around her shoulders, she put her arm around his waist, and suddenly Matthew felt like he needed to put his arm around a crate of wine bottles and drink to good deeds, good luck, good fortune, and the goodness of love.

Effrem excused himself from Opal for a moment while he walked with Matthew back to Queen Street. "Listen," Effrem said quietly, though the street was certainly not crowded. "About *Berry*."

"What about her?"

"I am out of her picture. Yes, I do believe she fancied me. But Matthew, I can't be courting *two* ladies!"

"No, it would be unseemly," Matthew agreed.

"Correct! So…if she asks about me, or says anything…would you be the one to tell her that I am walking the serious road with Opal?"

"The serious road?" Matthew didn't wait for an explanation, nor did he need it. "I certainly will be the one to tell her, if she asks."

"Thank you!" Now it was Effrem's turn to clap Matthew on the shoulder. "My God, isn't it splendid?"

"Isn't what splendid?"

Effrem looked at Matthew as if he had just arrived from another world. "To be alive!" he said, with a broad and giddy grin. "She's waiting for me, and we're going to Deverick's place for coffee. See you soon at the Trot?" He had already started walking in the opposite direction.

"Soon," Matthew promised, with a smile that was neither so broad nor so giddy but quite as meaningful, and then the two friends who thought it was so very splendid to be alive continued on their separate paths.

THIRTY-FOUR

s they waited at the table in Sally Almond's tavern for the person who was coming, Matthew scanned the blackboard upon which was chalked the evening's specialities. Two fish dishes, one chicken, one beef and one pork. One of the fish dishes interested him, but he decided to drink his glass of red wine and think about it before ordering.

"To all present," said Hudson, lifting his own glass.

He was answered by Matthew raising his glass, and by Minx Cutter raising hers. They drank, and then they listened to the strolling musician play her mandore and sing "Go No More A-Rushing" in a sultry alto voice.

There was no rushing to be done this night. It was the last week of May, which had prompted someone to request the song, its first line being "Go no more a-rushing, maids in May." A rain shower had passed through this morning, but the earth needed its blessing. Everything was normal in New York, which meant anything could be expected at any time, from a group of Indians stalking along the Broad Way to a hog wagon breaking down and the hogs leading a merry chase along the length of Wall Street. Matthew had shaved. He had purchased a new suit from Effrem. It was cream-colored with a dark brown waistcoat. He had on new brown boots and a new, crisp white shirt. He was dressed his best in honor of the person who would be joining them, she'd said in her letter, at half past seven. According to the tavern's clock, she would arrive in eight minutes.

"Another toast?" asked Hudson, this time with a glint of mischief in his eyes. He waited for the glasses to be raised. "To those who have tasted the grapes of crime, and found them bitter."

Minx drank. "But sometimes," she said as she put her glass down, "the most bitter grapes make the sweetest wine."

"Ah ha! But yet…sweet wine can poison, the same as bitter."

"True, but what may be sweet to me may be bitter to you."

"Yes, and what you may drink of poison may be pleasure to me."

"Gentleman and lady?" Matthew said. "Shut up." They ceased their verbal joustings as if suddenly remembering he was sitting between them. Minx shifted in her chair. Her face was placid. She showed no emotion but surely she was nervous, Matthew thought. This was a momentous night for Lady Cutter. This was the night she had bought with her aid to Matthew on Pendulum Island. This was, truly, the first night of the rest of her life. The clock ticked on, and Matthew noted that Minx glanced at the progress of its hands and drank without waiting for a toast. "Very well, Mr. Corbett," Lord Cornbury had said that morning in April, two days after Matthew had arrived home. "Begin, please." And thus Matthew *had* begun, telling the green-gowned governor, the purple-suited High Constable, and the regular-clothed Chief Prosecutor everything there was to tell, from start to finish. He of course had to mention Mrs. Sutch's sausages as background, and Prosecutor Bynes had had to excuse himself and rush from the office for it seemed he and his wife had been great partakers of that particular meat product. Matthew had told his listeners about the false Mallorys, Sirki, the bombs being set off in his name, the abduction of Berry, the voyage to Pendulum Island, the Cymbeline works…all of it.

And everything also that he knew of Professor Fell, and the fact that the professor had escaped on a vessel called *Temple's Revenge* and a letter might be sent to the authorities in London to begin a search for that ship.

When he was finished Matthew asked for a glass of water, and to his credit Lillehorne went out and returned a short time later with a glass and a pitcher full of water freshly-drawn from the nearest well. Then Lillehorne had sat down in the corner seat he'd occupied and he and Lord Cornbury had stared at each other seemingly for a minute, neither one moving, as if to ask each other if they believed what they'd heard.

"Thank you, Mr. Corbett," the ladyish Lord had said at last. He didn't seem to want to lift his green-shaded gaze from his desk. "You may go now."

Matthew had stood up. "You might at least send a letter requesting that Frederick Nash be investigated. Also the money changer Andrew Halverston."

"Yes. Noted, thank you."

"I would think this is of vital importance, gentlemen." He used that word lightly. "There is a warehouse somewhere in London that may still be stocked with the Cymbeline. The professor may yet intend to sell that powder to a foreign army...or, it might just be sparked into an explosion that would level the buildings around it and kill many—"

"Noted," Cornbury had interrupted. "Thank you for your presence and your time, and you are free to go."

Matthew had looked to Lillehorne for some kind of support. The High Constable had repeated it: "Free to go."

Berry had been waiting for him outside the governor's mansion, beneath a shady oak, in case they had also needed her testimony. "Didn't they believe you?" she asked as they walked toward the Broad Way. Today she was a festival of colors, a veritable walking bouquet of April flowers from her pink stockings to her darker violet gown to her red throat ribbon to her white straw hat to the puff of yellow buds that adorned it.

"I think they believed me, all right. I just think they're overwhelmed. They don't know what to do with the information." He gave her a wry glance. "I don't think they want to get themselves *involved*."

Berry frowned. "But...that seems against the spirit of the town!"

"I agree. They have the facts. What they do with them now is their business." He stepped back for a passing team of oxen pulling a lumber wagon, also bound for the Broad Way. The carriages and wagons were thick up there, in the area of Trinity Church. So much traffic, some kind of regulation was soon to be needed. Just yesterday there had been an afternoon squabble between a man hauling a wagon full of tar barrels and a street hawker pushing a variety of wigs in a cart. In the ensuing collision, it was determined that tar and wigs did not mix. And neither did tar clean up very easily from the street.

"Where are you off to?" Matthew asked her as they strolled.

"I'm with you."

"Yes. Well…I'm on my way to see Minx Cutter. I've gotten her settled into a room at Anna Hilton's boarding house. You know, over on Garden Street."

"Oh, yes."

"I'm watching over her," Matthew said, and instantly knew this was the wrong thing to say. "Tending to her, I mean." Wrong again. "Making sure she stays in town."

"Where would she go?"

"I don't know, but I want to make certain she doesn't go anywhere."

"Why?"

"Someone is coming," Matthew said, "who I think would like to meet her. In fact, it is *essential* that they meet."

"Who are you talking about?"

In Sally Almond's tavern on this May evening, the clock was two minutes away from seven-thirty. Matthew turned himself to watch the door.

"She'll be here, don't fret," said Hudson. "I'm going to order another bottle. That suit everyone?"

"It suits me fine," said Lady Cutter, with an intimation in her voice that she could drink the great one under the table ten times and again.

As they had walked along the Broad Way that morning in April, Berry had been silent for a few moments, contemplating this interest in Minx Cutter. Then had come the question that Matthew had been expecting: "Do you care for her?"

"Who?"

"You *know* who. Minx Cutter. Do you care for her?"

"I care *about* her."

Berry had stopped suddenly, positioning herself in front of him. Her eyes were keen. Her chin was slightly uplifted. She wore her universe of freckles proudly. "You delight in playing with me, don't you? Your word games and your...your mismeanings. I am asking you this question, Matthew. Do you care—in a romantic way—for Minx Cutter?"

He thought about this. He looked at the ground. He looked at the sky. He looked at his own hands, and polished with a sleeve the buttons on his coat. Then he looked into the face that he considered so very beautiful, and he knew the mind behind it was beautiful and so was the heart, and he said as coldly as he could on such a warm day, "Maybe I do. What of it?"

She wore a stricken expression. But only for a few seconds. If she had come to pieces in that short span of time, so she reassembled herself just as quickly.

"I see," she said.

But Matthew knew she did not see. Matthew knew that very easily Berry's head could have been parted from her body at the neck by Sirki's blade, and that her beauty might have curdled in the guts of an octopus. Or that she might indeed have walked off a cliff in the dark and fallen to her death. Or been found by the searchers and wound up...what?...beaten and ravished in a cell? He couldn't bear to think of any of those possibilities, and how close some of them might have been to coming true. So last night he had made up his mind what to do, and now—this moment—was his opportunity.

He had decided to make her hate him.

"Minx Cutter is...fascinating to me," he said. "So different."

"I'll say different, too. She wears a man's clothes."

"She is *unique*," Matthew plowed on. "A woman, not a girl."

"Hardly a woman," was the retort.

"*All* woman," said Matthew. "And very exciting to me in that way. You know, one gets tired of the ordinary." He thought that might be the shot that knocked her down.

But Berry was still on her feet, and still on his side. "I think you'll find out for yourself that some *ordinary* people, as you say, are *extraordinary*. If you cared to look closely enough."

"I live an exciting life," said Matthew, and he nearly cringed at his own self. "Why would I want less in my romantic life?"

"Why are you so cold today? This isn't like you!"

"It's the new me," he told her. And possibly there was some truth in that, for he wasn't exactly sure he'd left all of Nathan Spade behind.

"I don't like the new you very much, Matthew," she said. "In fact, I don't like the new you at all."

"I am who I am. And who I will ever be." He frowned, impatient at his own heartless lies. "I have to get along to see Minx now. Would you excuse me? I'd rather walk alone than be entangled in a ridiculous discussion like this."

"Oh, would you?" She nodded. Her cheeks were very red and the freckles looked like bits of pepper. But deep in her eyes—and this wounded his soul to see—was a hurt that he thought he would rather tear his own orbs out than have to gaze upon. "All right then, Matthew. All right. I thought we were friends. I thought...we were something, I don't know what."

"I don't know what either," he answered, like the bastard of the world.

"I can't...I don't understand...why..."

"Oh," he said, "stop your prattling."

"I came to help you, if you needed me. That's all I ever wanted, Matthew! To help you! Can't you see that?"

"That's the point I'm trying to make." He drew a breath, for this next thing might be the killer. "I was wrong to have confided in you on the ship that night. It was weak, and I regret it. Because the fact is, I have never needed you. I didn't yesterday, I don't today and I will not tomorrow."

And this time, he saw the little death in her eyes. It killed him, most of all.

"Fine," Berry said. And again, as the ice closed in: "Fine. Good day to you, then." She sounded a bit choked, and she quickly cleared her throat. Then she turned and began walking quickly away, and six strides in her departure she turned again toward him and there were tears on her face and she said in a voice near collapse, *"We are done."*

It was good that she got quickly away, for Matthew got himself going in the opposite direction, not toward Garden Street at all, and he staggered like a drunk though he had only put down the water, and everything seemed blurred and terribly wrong, and his heart ached and his eyes felt as if they were bleeding. A few steps and he broke the heel off his right boot, which made him limp even more drunkenly. And also like a drunk he found himself sitting under a tree in the Trinity cemetery, surrounded by those who had already known their share of life, love and loss, and he sat there for a time wishing some ghost would whisper to him about strength and fortitude and the will to keep going and similar such bullshit but no ghost spoke and so therefore he wiped his eyes, roused himself and went on his way and he thought that somewhere in Heaven or Hell one spirit applauded him and that spirit's name had been Nathan. Who now was long deceased, for all the good love had done him.

Before he left that village of the dead he had the overwhelming urge to call out for her, as if she could hear him. To call out and say he was sorry, that he was a liar and hadn't meant any of it but that he was frightened for her and frightened of Professor Fell for her. So it all came down to fear. But he didn't call out, for it would have been for nothing and anyway the dice had been thrown. *We are done.* Three words he would take with him when they rolled him over into his own bed in this very same village of silent sleepers.

"Yes," said Matthew, as he watched the door of Sally Almond's tavern at seven-twenty-nine by the clock. "By all means, another bottle."

"You've been drinking a lot lately, I notice." Greathouse poured the last of the red wine into Matthew's glass and held up the empty soldier for the waitress. "Why is that?"

"Thirsty," Matthew answered.

There was a small *tick* of metal from the clock as the minute hand moved. And just that soon, the door opened and in walked Katherine Herrald.

She was now, as she had been in October, a trim figure who drew attention and admiration. She was about fifty years old, with sharp features and penetrating blue eyes. She was straight-backed and elegant and there was nothing aged or infirm about her. Her dark gray hair, under a fashionable cocked riding-hat a rich brown hue, was streaked with pure white at the temples and at a pronounced widow's peak. She wore a dark brown dress ornamented with leather buttons and cinched with a wide leather belt. Around her throat was a scarf nearly the same color as the Stokelys' Indian-blood-colored pottery. She wore brown leather gloves. She came across the tavern directly to their table, as Matthew and Hudson stood up to greet her. She was their employer, her dead husband the originator of the Herrald Agency and himself murdered by Tyranthus Slaughter on orders of Professor Fell. Back in October she'd told Matthew she was going to England and then would be returning in May. So here she was, and when she'd arrived yesterday morning she'd sent a letter to them from the Dock House Inn, announcing her presence. Matthew had written back: *I have someone you need to meet. Her name is Minx Cutter, and she was once an associate of Professor Fell.*

"Hello, Miss Cutter," said Mrs. Herrald, offering her hand. Minx took it. "I'm interested in hearing about you. Interested as well in hearing your story, Matthew. Your letter skimped on details. After I have a glass of wine and determine what I'd like to eat, I want to know everything." She sat across from him, the better to read his expressions.

Matthew nodded. He was thinking that in two hours or so, after his story and Minx's had been told, Mrs. Herrald was going to aim her eyes at the princess of blades and say, "You seem to have taken a few wrong steps in your progress through life, Miss Cutter. Yet here you are now, on a straighter path. It took great courage for you to know I was coming, and to know my history with the professor, and to sit at the table with me. I have a feeling you are never lacking for courage. I must ask: are you at all interested, Miss Cutter, in the process of *discovery*? For if you are—and if you are interested in continuing along your current path and possibly righting other wrongs—then…you and I should talk a little further."

Before that, though, there was food to be ordered. Sally Almond herself came over to take their requests.

Matthew had been thinking. About predators, in particular. About the sea of life, and the creatures that roamed it. About the dangerous currents his business—now his calling—put him into. It was, really, sink or swim. He still had so much hurt in his heart for Berry. Yet he felt he had to leave her to protect her, to move forward, to prepare for his next meeting with Professor Fell. It would be upon him, likely sooner than he thought.

The next thing on his ticket, however, was to respond to the latest letter from a certain Mr. Sedgeworth Prisskitt of Charles Town who was asking for a courier to escort his daughter Pandora to the annual Sword of Damocles Ball, held in Charles Town in late June. He wondered why a father would have to pay for an escort for his daughter. Was she that ugly? He wondered also what sort of events the trip might offer, for with a name like Pandora...surely there was a box somewhere that once opened, out escaped...

...what?

It remained to be seen.

But the matter of predators was still on his mind. The matter of terrible and evil things gliding in the dark, perhaps circling him even now.

He was famished. Such thoughts would hold until after dinner and wine.

Matthew studied the blackboard for a moment and then told Sally what he would like.

She replied that it was freshly-caught, was excellent, and that forthwith she would bring him the platter of roasted shark.